D0805251

THE DEMETER CODE

RUSSELL BROOKS

THE DEMETER CODE

By Russell Brooks

Copyright © 2014 by Russell Brooks

This is a work of fiction. Names, characters, places, and incidents are products of the author's imagination or are used fictitiously. Any resemblance to actual events, locales, or persons living or dead is entirely coincidental.

13-Digit ISBN (print version):

978-0-9867513-7-0

13-Digit ISBN (ebook version):

978-0-9867513-6-3

Chapter 1

The Hooper-Adams Hotel, 16th Street, Washington, DC. 1:36 PM, Friday.

"Watch where you're going, dammit," snapped the woman.

Doctor Nita Parris had bumped the woman's shoulder as she passed through the revolving door, rushing from the street into the hotel lobby.

Parris turned halfway around, raising an open palm. "Sorry." But she wasn't. The woman had the audacity to blame her. *She* was the one texting on her mobile while walking, and in a crowded room on top of that. Her teenage self would've cussed her out rudely, or even slapped the phone out of her hand. Not the typical behavior of a woman with a PhD in biochemistry. She could hear her aunt being vexed and breaking out the Barbadian accent. *"Why yuh gunnah stoop to she level for? You better than dat."*

Those were the days when Parris was quick-tempered and got into a lot of fights—and won them. Even some of the boys didn't dare trouble her. She'd proven repeatedly that she could stand her ground with them, and even out-sprint them. When she'd wound up in the headmaster's office—which had been frequently—he'd always ranted on about how bright a future she had, considering that she was one of the school's top students. He'd pointed out that with her aptitudes she ought to be setting an example.

But that was the past. She wouldn't stoop to the level of some self-absorbed socialite. Especially when her asset was eight floors above, fearing for his life.

Despite having spent the last five years living in the DC area, she had never been inside any of its hotels—even for an op. To anyone else in the lobby who happened to notice her, she was probably just another twenty-something black woman.

She wore a navy blue pantsuit with a cool belt that looped through silver-toned grommets, a pair of low-healed Blahniks, and a bumblebee-shaped brooch, pinned below the mandarin-style collar, on the left side. Her black, shiny hair—not too long, just enough to reach the base of her neck—was tied back in a ponytail. Observers would likely think that she was either a guest, there on business, or a lawyer meeting a client. Either one was fine by her.

Parris scanned the lobby on her way to the elevators. Aside from catching the occasional whiff of perfume or aftershave, she spotted two Wall-Street types, laughing over a beer, through the doorway of the hotel restaurant. On the opposite side, two children were chasing each other around their suitcases while their parents addressed the receptionist. She then passed an Asian family, speaking Mandarin, followed by an elderly Italian couple. She couldn't speak the languages, but she recognized a few words.

One man stood out from the others. He was to her left, leaning sideways against the adjacent wall. His profile screamed *gym-nut*, wearing jeans and an unzipped windbreaker to show off his pectorals. All he appeared to care about was what was on his iPhone. Either that, or, seeing that he had a clear view of the elevators, he was keeping an eye on who went in and out.

She didn't stare at him, or anyone else, because of the potential that any given person in the lobby could be part of a surveillance team. She spotted a decorative mirror on a support beam, a few feet away. She walked past it, turning her head toward the mirror as though she happened to spot it by chance. She stepped back to look at herself. To the casual observer, it would appear as though she was fixing her hair, but she was buying time. She straightened the brooch while she watched Gym Boy.

One mistake she'd seen from fellow agents in the past, while doing counter-surveillance training, was that once they lost a tail, they settled into their comfort zone—a position ripe with a false sense of security, never thinking there might be a second, or even third, pair of eyes on them.

Parris knew a lot about being in a non-surveillance comfort zone. While she had done her tradecraft training, she'd wound up with two stinging paint-gun blasts—one to the chest and one to the side, above her hip. Not a mistake she'd made again. After all, her doctorate was in biochemistry and microbiology—she was used to being a perfectionist. It's also what got her recruited into the CIA as a weapons analyst before becoming a field agent.

Parris licked her fingertip and ran it across both eyebrows. "Dewan, you see me yet?"

"I got you." Dewan Douglas—her newest tech support—answered through her earpiece. He would've hacked into the hotel's closed-circuit television long before she arrived—playing big brother from his safe haven at Langley, Virginia. It helped, but it wasn't perfect. There were always spots the CCTV was blind to, and a professional would've been smart enough to hang out in those areas to avoid being seen.

Parris brushed a strand of hair from her jacket sleeve. "Gym fanatic at seven o'clock."

"I saw him," Dewan replied. "He arrived there with some chick, who's now on her way down from their suite. They've been guests for the past four days, so I wouldn't worry about him."

She trusted that Dewan would've used face-recognition software, to locate and identify Gym Boy through the hotel's CCTV archives, and cross-referenced it with the hotel's guest list.

She headed for the elevator, grabbing her cell phone from her belt clip to call her asset, Tim Weyland. "Timothy?"

"Who...who's this?"

"You know who it is. I'm on my way up."

"Are you armed? Because I know they're going to be coming for me with some very big guns."

He spoke fast, so he must be scared shitless. "You're going to have to calm down and let us worry about who may be coming after you." Parris pressed the elevator button. One of the six doors opened but it was already going down. She did a quick once-over of the three people who walked out. Nothing suspicious.

"How can you tell me to calm down?" Weyland still spoke at warp-speed. "You're not the one they're trying to kill."

Parris sighed as she hit the elevator button two more times, as though that would make it arrive faster. "Stay in your room. I'm coming to get you. Got it?"

There was a brief pause on the other end. "Y-y-yeah."

An elevator's door opened with a *ping*, and Parris got in, then hit the eighth-floor button, followed by the close-doors button—hoping that they would shut before anyone else could enter. Yes, it was easier for her to say what she'd said to Weyland than it was for him to live it, but what was she supposed to tell him? All she cared about at the moment was getting him away from this hotel and handing him over to the FBI, who'd take him to one of their safe-houses.

The elevator came to a stop and the doors opened. Parris checked both directions as she stepped out. "You still there?"

"I'm here," Weyland answered.

"Good, I'm almost there."

She headed to her right, where the hall connected with another in a *T*. Footsteps echoed toward her, followed by Weyland popping out from around the corner. He wore horn-rimmed glasses, a knapsack, and a Green Lantern shirt under his unzipped windbreaker.

Oh for the love of...

There were so many curse words that she wanted to shout out right now. She'd told him to stay in his room—for several good reasons. The main one being that the floor had not yet been cleared of potential hostiles.

Weyland had inadvertently made himself an easy target. He was supposed to have met her at Union Station two hours before, only to stand her up.

She'd had a team search his apartment and monitor the police bandwidths. Nothing. When Parris had called him on his cell all she got were messages telling her that the number was no longer in service—which only worried her more. Fortunately, Weyland had made contact with her, letting her know his whereabouts.

He pointed behind Parris as he approached. "Are we taking the elevator or the—"

An electrical surge shot through Parris's nerves as she grabbed him by the front of his jacket and threw him against the wall—putting her weight behind her forearm to pin him. "Listen to me, because I won't repeat myself. When I tell you to wait—whether it's at Union Station or in your hotel suite—it's not a request. You got that?"

His lower lip trembled as the blood rushed from his cheeks. Weyland rapidly nodded.

That was too easy for her tastes. Parris pushed harder against him, watching his face go paler. "Are you sure?"

He nodded with his mouth agape. "Yes, I understand. It won't happen again. I swear."

"Good." She released him. "I hope you didn't shit your drawers." Parris checked their flanks before she looked back at Weyland, who took a deep breath and straightened his glasses.

She grabbed his arm. "Come."

He nearly dropped his knapsack after being yanked so ruggedly. He was five feet nine, had unkempt, sand-colored hair, and weighed roughly a hundred sixty pounds when Parris first met him. But right now, he appeared to have lost ten to fifteen pounds. It was as though he hadn't eaten well for the past several days. She wouldn't be surprised if *that's* what set off his employer's radar. It was his employer whom she had recruited him to spy on—thus putting a hit on him.

There was a *ping* from the elevator and the chambermaid exited with her laundry cart. She was around the same age as Parris, standing about at five feet eight. Although her movements weren't suspicious, Parris still had every reason to be paranoid. In situations such as this, hyper-vigilance was often a life saver. For instance, the laundry cart was the ideal place to hide a firearm with a suppressor.

The maid knocked on the first door. "Housekeeping."

"Dewan," whispered Parris as she kept walking. She slid her

hand behind her and under her jacket to the Springfield EMP in her hip holster.

"Go ahead," Dewan answered.

"Is there anyone registered in room ten fifteen?"

"Timothy's the only person on that floor."

They were less than forty yards away as the maid reached inside the laundry cart, then swung a firearm in Parris's direction.

She drew first, sidestepped in front of Weyland, then disengaged the thumb safety, took aim, and squeezed the trigger. The bullet caught the would-be assassin in between her eye and left ear—throwing her into the wall before she slumped to the floor.

Parris turned to see Weyland ducking, with both hands covering his ears.

"You okay?" Parris asked.

The shock was all over his face as he breathed rapidly, nodding a few seconds later.

She scanned both ends of the hall. "Stay close."

She ran to the woman, keeping her sidearm pointed toward her target. She noticed her weapon. It was an HK USP Tactical with suppressor—not a bad choice for this situation. It was both small and light.

Parris kicked it away, out of habit, even though the threat had been eliminated. She turned at the sound of running and saw her asset bolting in the opposite direction.

"Weyland," Parris yelled, holstering her weapon and taking off after him. Being a former NCAA champion sprinter, she closed the gap quickly.

He skidded as he made his way around the corner at the T-junction, heading to the emergency stairs.

"Weyland, stop," Parris yelled again after she rounded the corner. But he didn't listen. Poor guy, probably never saw someone get shot before, and right in front of him too. And now he was in a state of *fight or flight.*

"Parris, you've got to stop him now," Dewan cried out as Weyland was less than twenty yards from the emergency exit. Her heart skipped a beat when a tall, bulky man wearing a waist-length jacket exited the staircase and collided with Weyland. She saw an object fall from the man's hand. It was a sidearm.

"Weyland, move." She quickly drew her EMP and took aim. But Weyland tried to beat the would-be assassin to the gun. He was successful, but the bigger and stronger hitman grabbed Weyland's hands and aimed the gun upward, the two men struggling as they fought for control of the weapon.

Shit, I told you to move.

The gun swung in Parris's direction and a shot fired. She ducked into a roll as plaster and dust rained down on her. She shook it off and aimed at the man, who easily outmatched Weyland in size—being at least six feet one and likely weighing in around two hundred and twenty pounds.

The man kept Weyland between them, making it next to impossible for her to take a clean shot. The two of them were on their knees as a second bullet struck the wall to the left, between them and Parris. For a split moment, the sidearm was pointed away and she had her opening, she had to take it—situations such as these rarely gave second chances.

Parris holstered her sidearm and charged, her goal, to knock both of them over. But as she was closing in, the assassin elbowed Weyland in his jaw and knocked him to the floor. Parris watched for a moment, when the hitman got up and then turned to her, but she already dove and tackled him. She hoped she had caused him to tear his anterior cruciate ligament. Once that was torn, not only would the assassin have a lot of difficulty walking, but he'd be in a shitload of pain. The man went down with her, but she didn't hear him scream in agony as she'd hoped. However, he lost the gun.

Good enough for her.

She made a quick draw of her EMP and went to aim it, only to have it slapped out of her hand, sending it sliding across the carpet in front of Timothy. That's when Parris saw her asset on all fours, crawling for it.

The assassin leaped forward and caught Weyland's legs, holding him down. Although he kicked and thrashed, it was useless, as the hitman had him pinned down too well.

Looking behind her, Parris saw the assassin's gun. She reached over, grabbed it, then spun around and pointed it at him. "Hey!"

The assassin turned to her, his eyes widening when he noticed his own gun aiming at him.

Parris squeezed the trigger—which to her surprise and horror— jammed. She tried forcing it, but it wouldn't fire. She slapped the magazine, racked the slide, then got back on her target, squeezing again. Still nothing.

Shit!

The killer turned away and crawled over Weyland to reach for Parris's weapon—no time to think, only react. She dropped the sidearm and charged the assailant, leaping over Weyland into a jump side-kick, just as their attacker swung the EMP around. The kick knocked his arm to the side—making his shot go wide and, subsequently, knocking the gun out of his hand. She landed in front of him and followed through with a knuckle blow to his throat.

He gagged and his head dropped as he stumbled back.

Parris seized the moment to put her full weight behind the side- kick, executing it right into his chest, sending him flying through the emergency exit door.

Unfortunately it also resulted in him kicking her EMP into the stairwell with him. Parris charged through the doorway while it was still open. She couldn't leave to chance that he'd get her gun. If luck was on her side her attacker would've fallen down the stairs, but it wasn't. He had caught himself with the aid of the wall that separated the upper and lower side of the staircase, and he was eyeing something on the floor.

The EMP.

She raced toward it, but he surprised her with a foot-sweep— catching her by the side of her ankles and sending her crashing to the floor. She heard the gun scrape across the concrete as he snatched it from the floor beside her. When she flipped herself over, she was looking into the barrel of her own gun, a sinister grin not far behind it.

There was a crash as the emergency exit door flew open, banging against the concrete wall. Weyland was hollering through it as he threw himself onto the hitman.

Holy shit. The nerd was having an adrenalin rush.

The collision sent them both into the dividing wall between the staircases, causing the sidearm to go flying, and in the midst of the melee, it was kicked down the steps. Weyland's attempt lasted less than three seconds, as he was thrown face-first into the wall, then dropped to the floor, landing on his back.

That was more than enough time for Parris to get up, but not before a large set of hands grabbed her by the collar, pulling her downward, where she was then kneed in her stomach. The blow forced the air out of her, sending her into a daze as she fell backward. After she landed, the attacker put the full force of his substantial weight on her chest, pressing down as his hands wrapped around her neck.

Instinctively, she grabbed at the monstrous grip, fighting for even one ounce of air, but with no luck. Most of the air in her lungs had been expelled from the knee to her gut and she felt an increasing burning in her lungs. Having landed on her back, she was fighting in the worst position she could be—rather than landing her own punches, she was expending her energy trying to get up while defending herself. It didn't help that this guy was both larger and physically stronger than her.

She did the only thing she could, lashing out, aiming for his eyes, but only connecting with his chin. She went back to trying to pry his hands from around her neck, but he was too strong, and she was losing her strength.

She kicked out hard, trying to plant the soles of her feet against the wall in order to push herself back. If she could do it, it may just be enough to make him lose his balance and grip, at least temporarily. But it didn't work, as she sputtered, not even with enough force to get a drop of spittle out.

Her brooch.

She released one of his wrists and felt around the left lapel of her jacket until she touched the brooch. She yanked it out, exposing the jagged tip, bringing it up underneath one of his hands, slashing at his wrist, hoping to sever an artery. In her clumsy haste she couldn't determine how deep the cut was, but he yelped like a wounded pig, and that was assurance enough.

As he shifted backward, Parris used those critical seconds to drive the sharp edge of the brooch into his other hand—the only area within reach that was exposed. This cut wasn't as careless. This time the needle went deep and she felt it connect with resistance—maybe a bone or tendon—causing him to grunt and roll off her, grabbing his wrist.

Air.

She needed lots of it, more than what was in this unventilated stairwell. Her stomach, lower chest, and neck were on fire, but she could take the pain. What mattered now was sucking in as much oxygen as she could, while forcing herself to get up. Parris needed to be on her feet, even if she was still weak, she had to have both feet on the floor. She was in no shape to continue fighting this behemoth in hand-to-hand combat while lying prone. Even with his injured wrists, she wasn't sure she could win that fight.

But she could beat him to the EMP. She stumbled forward, to head down the stairs, when she felt something catch her ankle—causing her to fall toward the edge.

The EMP was right in front of her, on the landing below. She could still do this. She still had a chance.

Grabbing the edge of the railing, she heaved herself forward on her stomach and slid down the steps—each edge cutting into her chest and stomach, sending more jolts of pain. She couldn't give a shit about that. The gun was the priority.

Just as she was nearing the landing she heard footsteps running behind her, but gravity and momentum were on her side. The steps became louder, and she could swear she felt the killer on her heels, but Parris crashed onto the landing, grabbing the EMP as she rolled over onto her back. Throwing both arms upward, she squeezed the trigger in rapid succession.

Four bullets tore into the man's chest, leaving a bloody mess in their wake. Parris rolled to the side as the killer's body went limp, slumped sideways into the wall, then tumbled headfirst, crashing beside her.

She looked at his hand and saw that the brooch still protruded from it, while blood poured out from under both wrists. He lay on his stomach with his head facing her, his glass-like eyes reflecting a dead stare—absolute emptiness.

As she regained her composure, Parris was still gasping for air. A buzz coursed through her arms and legs—the good old adrenaline surge from being in a near-death situation.

Rolling onto her knees, she huffed and puffed a few times, then got to her feet, bending at the waist, grasping her knees for support—still holding the EMP. She gave the bastard one last look before she stood upright, walked over, and bent down to remove the brooch from his bloody wrist. As she did, she felt a draft in the seat and crotch area of her pants, then reached behind to feel the spot.

Shit. Another pantsuit ruined. Another she may have to throw away.

It wouldn't be so bad if there were more black people designing pantsuits, or, at least, a fashion designer who knew how to compliment a black woman's physique.

A loud coughing from up the stairs caused Parris to swing and aim her EMP in that direction. "You okay, Weyland?"

"Nita?" he wheezed.

Parris stepped around the assailant and saw Weyland at the top of the stairs. At first, he leaned against the wall, holding the metal banister, then he made his way down—one step at a time.

She holstered the EMP as she went up to help him. He had a black eye, some facial bruises, and looked as though he was about to collapse.

"Hang on there, Geronimo," she said as she caught him. Parris then turned around, draping Weyland's arm around her to help support his weight. She felt for her earpiece. Luckily, she didn't lose it during the fight. She spoke into it. "Dewan?"

"Yeah, Doc."

"Are the stairs clear?"

"Yes, an extraction team's on its way. ETA is three minutes, but you'll have to hurry. The DC police are on their way."

Dewan was right. She did have to hurry—the last thing she needed was to be arrested. That type of exposure would jeopardize the op, exposing both her and Weyland.

"How's the asset?" asked Dewan.

She and Weyland rounded the corner of the next landing. "He's hanging in there, but he'll need medical attention."

"Can both of you make it to the delivery entrance in the basement?"

Parris coughed. "I don't think we have a choice."

Fortunately, Weyland was close to Parris's height, which helped her support him as they made their way downstairs.

As they neared the basement floor, she could still feel the ghost-like grip of the attacker's hands around her neck. She wanted to reach up and rub her throat, but her hands were full—she shook it off instead.

Moments later they exited into the alley and into the crisp autumn air, where two intelligence officers, dressed as EMTs, waited behind an ambulance. They helped Parris and Weyland into the back of it. The engine was still running, so once the doors were closed, the driver sped off with the sirens blaring.

Weyland whimpered as he was helped onto a gurney. "They tried to kill me. Why did I ever do this?" He continued with his rant until one of the agents injected him with, what Parris assumed, was a sedative. He soon fell asleep.

The other agent grabbed a first-aid kit and knelt down in front of her, examining her face before he tended to the cut above her left eye. "Jesus. He got you good."

Parris looked him in the eye. "So what. I got him better."

Chapter 2

Sentinel Road, Rockford, Illinois. 6:17 PM, Friday.

Aubrey Lee Collins had serious doubts whether he'd get away with what he had done. For the past week he'd been popping Kaopectate pills, but his stomach problems persisted. He had cleared all of his debts with the money he'd made from selling company secrets, and still had a lot left over. The idea of seeing a shrink came to mind, only for him to second-guess that thought a moment later.

Quit beating yourself up. You did what you had to do, for Tina and your future child. Anyone would've done the same thing had they been in your shoes.

Standing outside the front door to his cottage, Collins glanced up and down his street—focusing on his neighbors' homes. Surely, some of them had to be keeping up appearances too. He wasn't the only person to have made a bad investment here and there, although, his had nearly bankrupted him and his wife, Tina. For the past eight months he'd managed to keep their financial problems hidden from her. It was better off that she didn't know, considering that she was almost eight months pregnant.

Besides, banks and other financial firms were known to be careless with their clients' money. When *they* made mistakes, it was always the little guy who suffered and the ones who screwed up rarely even got a slap on the wrist. He thought of AIG, back in 2008. Those fuckers should've gone under. But no, the government bailed them out instead. Who was there to bail him out? What the fuck?

Then there was his employer, Sementem, and its executives. They weren't saints either. They'd been involved in illegal practices for years, pissing off three-quarters of the planet. Yet the company was never held accountable for any of their crimes. Collins couldn't recall any top execs spending a day in jail. In the end, it all came down to who had the deepest pockets. So, when Collins stole company secrets—ones that sent the company's profits through the stratosphere—and sold them to some European guy, who was willing to pay him two hundred thousand dollars for them, he didn't hesitate.

Come to think of it, he should've asked for more—like half a million. Then again, he wasn't in a position to bargain. These guys were pros. They did their research and knew about his problems. That's how they knew that he'd be their best target. But it didn't matter anymore. This was *his* bail-out, one that would cover the balance he owed on the house and then some.

So why did he feel like shit? He sighed and let himself in his house. What's done was done. It was time to move on.

He flicked on the switch, but the lights didn't turn on.

Why's it so dark in here? Maybe Tina is asleep.

Collins walked to the next light switch down the hall. He flicked it on, then off, then on again. This one didn't work either.

"Tina?" A few seconds went by and still no answer. *Where are you?*

He put down his briefcase, took off his shoes, hung his coat, then walked to the kitchen. He'd walked through there in the dark hundreds of times, enough to know where to step without a second thought. He and Tina had purchased this single-family cottage nearly two years before, and he'd never tripped over anything.

He grabbed a beer from the refrigerator and just as he was about to close the door, he realized that the inner light didn't turn on either.

Oh come on. Not a freaking blackout.

Collins pushed the door as he walked away from the fridge. It slapped shut as he opened the beer can, then took a swig. Tina would have a hissy-fit if she caught him drinking before dinner. He was about to head back the way he came, when he caught of glimpse of light from behind the curtains by the back window.

Oh come on. He walked to the back porch door and parted the curtains slightly to see his neighbors' houses. On the other side of the fence, he could clearly see Pete and Janet Morrison moving back and forth between the stove and the kitchen table, while their son—what was his name again?—played on his Sony PlayStation in the other room.

Son-of-a-bitch!

They had power. He glanced up and down the street. So did all the other houses.

Something wasn't right.

He didn't drive through a blackened street on his way home, he was sure of that. Collins returned to the front and went outside, feeling the cool evening breeze. He looked up and down his street. Lights were on everywhere, so why not in his home? He'd paid that with all the other bills he'd caught up on, so it couldn't be a disconnection.

He closed the door and turned around, smiling. Of course. It was a prank. He looked around him, as if he thought someone might pop up from behind a wall or the sofa and shout *surprise*.

"All right, joke's over. You got me." What was the occasion, though? It wasn't his birthday. Not their wedding anniversary.

No one answered him.

He could go check the circuit breaker in the garage, but decided to call Tina first. She was rarely a foot away from her mobile. Collins grabbed his phone from his belt clip, scrolled through the list of contacts and tapped the screen on Tina's name. There was a ringing on the other end, followed by a musical ringtone upstairs a second later.

Killing Me Softly? The Fugees? That wasn't the ringtone she'd programmed for his number.

The thought of her lying on the floor, unconscious, popped into mind. His heart pounded as he ran up the stairs—two steps at a time—following the music to the master bedroom. He came to an abrupt stop at the bedroom doorway as he grabbed onto both sides of the threshold.

Collins swallowed hard. He could see now why Tina hadn't answered him.

The room was lit with a few candles and, near the foot of the bed, Tina sat, bound to one of two dining room chairs—gagged, eyes wide and overflowing with tears.

A dark-suited, bald man, with a very distinct mole on his left cheek, stood beside her, pressing the barrel of a firearm against her head. "Mister Collins."

Collins switched his eyes from his wife to the window. The sound of the man's voice was rich and full of British swagger, with a texture that could likely charm the panties off a woman, but it burned in Collins' chest as though he'd downed a glass of over-proof whiskey.

Collins leaned away slightly, his foot sliding backward across the carpet.

Away from the candlelight, another man had been shrouded in the darkness, his appearance obscured. This was likely intentional, at least judging by the suit he wore, which was as dark as midnight, with the exception of the moon-colored tie. As the man approached him slowly, his Gucci belt buckle glistened in the candlelight. The same light now brightened one side of his head, exposing a strong, solid face with flawless ebony skin, sturdy cheekbones, and full lips. His hair was in locks—not long and wild, but short and static, yet still infused with a reggae flair. But it was the one eye that wasn't obscured by the shadows that got to him the most. Its penetrating nature made him feel that his mind was being probed. *Shit.* This man—whoever he was—knew of his vices.

"Don't leave so soon," said Short-Locks.

It was then that Collins noticed that he had backed almost two feet away from where he'd stood. He stopped, and, as Short-Locks slowly closed the distance between them, Collins felt himself shrinking.

This guy was built. He wasn't bulky, but more of a Jamie Foxx type—only much younger. Then again, when it came to African-Americans, Collins was never good at guessing their age.

"Black Don't Crack" was a joke he often heard from his African-American friends—and for good reason.

"Your wife was wondering when you'd arrive."

Short-Locks then placed a hand on Tina's shoulder. She closed her eyes tightly, crying louder from behind the gag.

"I hope you don't mind that we kept her company."

Collins looked back at Tina, then at Baldy, and then to the man with the short locks—who he assumed was Baldy's superior. His breath shortened as he fought for the words. "Who...who are you? What do you want with us?"

Collins saw the whiteness of Short-Locks' teeth as he smiled while cupping his hands. "Don't be coy. You know why we're here."

Shit. He knew.

Short-Locks then turned to Tina. "On the other hand, I can accept that maybe she might not know about your mounting debts, the late payments on your home, the bank threatening to repossess, over and over again. You have a stable job with a stable income, but it wasn't enough, was it? You needed more." He ran his fingers through Tina's black hair. "Especially since Tina will give birth within the next few weeks."

Collins' mouth hung open as Tina closed her eyes and cried louder. Short-Locks placed one hand on the back of her neck while putting an index finger to his lips as he looked down at her. *"Shhh."*

Collins' back tightened, hearing the man draw out the *Shhh* very slowly. Silent at first, but then gradually louder, with a silent finish.

Short-Locks turned to him. "Did you honestly think that you could steal from a restricted network of files and no one would notice?"

Oh God. They do know. Collins swallowed hard. "Listen, my wife doesn't have anything to do with this. It's me. I'll do anything. Just don't hurt her."

"Will you? I'm curious. Is it the love that you have for your wife of three years that's motivating you?" He put a hand on Collins' shoulder as he gestured toward Tina's stomach. "Or is it for your unborn child?"

He didn't know how to answer. He was afraid to say that it was both. The man's grip on his shoulder tightened as he forced Collins to walk with him to the empty chair beside Tina.

"Have a seat."

He had no alternative. He obeyed the command.

"We're going to play a simple game, with simple rules. All you need to do is answer truthfully and you'll be fine. Any questions?"

Collins looked up at him and shook his head.

"Excellent. Two hundred thousand dollars was deposited into your HSBC bank account in Bermuda, in exchange for an item you stole from Sementem. Who paid you?"

Collins saw how Tina looked at him with big eyes. She had stopped crying.

Short-Locks turned to her too. "Oh yes, you heard right. Your husband was paid to steal from his employer." He then turned to Collins. "The lengths one will go when one's broke."

Short-Locks leaned over to his ear. "So, let's have it. Who's your buyer?"

The heat of the man's breath on the side of his face made his lower back tighten, to the point it conjured pain from a pre-existing back injury. Collins looked at Tina, pleading his apology with his eyes, hoping she understood. He had a suspicion that any answer he gave this man wouldn't be the right one. "I...I...I don't know his real name," he stuttered. "I only know him as France."

"France?" said Short-Locks. "Your buyer's a woman?"

"N-n-no, it's a man," Collins stuttered. "H-h-he spoke with some funny European accent."

Short-Locks scrunched up his face. "Funny accent? I'm insulted. We could bloody well say the same about you Americans."

A tear ran down Collins' cheek. "I'm sorry. I don't want to insult you. I mean, I didn't mean to insult you."

"Shhh!" Again, he dragged it out.

Collins hushed, save for the loud breathing through his nostrils that he couldn't help.

Short-Locks walked away from him appearing to be deep in thought. He then spun around as though a light bulb had appeared over his head.

"Ah." Short-Locks took out an Android smartphone, tapped it a few times, then approached Collins with it, holding it up in front of his face. "You mean, Franz Müller, correct?"

Collins glanced at the picture and nodded quickly with wide eyes. "That's him."

Short-Locks patted Collins once on the shoulder. "Good. Now I'm going to ask you the same question again, and you're going to tell me who was your buyer. And you're going to pronounce his name properly."

Collins made a face as he looked at Short-Locks. *Is this guy kidding? He already knows who the buyer is. I just confirmed who he was for Christ's sake.*

"Say his name!" Short-Locks yelled, causing Collins' heart rate to skip a beat.

"It's Franz. His name is Franz Müller. I swear I don't know anything more about him." Collins closed his eyes tight to stop the tears from flowing as he heard Tina's muffled sobs again.

Short-Locks smiled. "There, there. Don't you see how easy this game is? It's much better when you don't murder your pronunciations of foreign words. It's so barbaric."

Collins didn't wait for him to ask the same question twice. He just nodded. "Is that all?"

"You dare break the rules of the game by asking *me* a question?"

"I'm sorry," sobbed Collins.

"Shhh." Short-Locks tapped his lips, thinking. He then turned to Baldy, seeming to have just noticed something. "I doubt she's going anywhere, so you can lower your weapon. By the way, go turn on the power."

The henchman lowered his sidearm from Tina's face and left the room.

Short-Locks grabbed the television remote off the chest of drawers when he heard Baldy coming back up the stairs. He then turned on the wall-mounted high-definition television in front of the bed. He flipped through the channels, stopping on a station which played orchestral music. He raised the volume to the point that the rumbling timpani drums vibrated the windowpanes and rattled the furniture. He then tossed the remote on the bed, grabbed Tina's arm, and pulled her out of the chair.

"Shall we?" He began to dance a waltz with Tina. She seemed to resist, but he appeared to be hurting her in order to make her dance with him.

What the hell? This man's a lunatic. I gave him what he wanted, why couldn't he and his partner just leave?

He didn't dare say this out loud, but decided to raise his hand to catch his attention. Short-Locks noticed it, pulled Tina closer to him and spun her around to make her face Collins.

"Yes?" Short-Locks said loudly.

"I played your game. I gave you what you asked. What more do you want from me?"

"Nothing more," Short-Locks yelled. "You played well."

Collins' eyes widened. He couldn't believe what he just heard. "Does that mean you'll let us go?"

Short-Locks turned Tina back around to face him, then shook his head. "I'm afraid not."

"What? But you said I won."

"No, I didn't." Short-Locks resumed dancing with Tina. "I said that you played well. You see, the loser of this game was already predetermined. That's why I'll always win."

He shoved Tina onto the bed. She landed on her back and he pulled out a sidearm from a concealed holster, and fired a round into her head and another into her stomach.

Collins screamed as he saw the blood-stained feathers of the pillow fly above his wife's body. His screams left him ignorant to Short-Locks jerking him out of his chair. Before he realized it, he was lying next to his wife, soaked in her blood as the assassin forced the gun into his hand with his finger on the trigger, forcing it into his mouth, gagging his scream. Collins fought back but couldn't match Short-Locks' strength—who didn't show any sign of strain or effort in his eyes.

"Shhh."

It was the last thing he heard before the trigger was squeezed.

Chapter 3

Bar Le Griffon, Place du Maréchal-Foch, Montauban, France. 10:05 AM, Saturday.

Ridley Fox took a swig from his bottle of Heineken as he watched Manchester United score another goal against FC Barcelona. There weren't any loud cheers or cantankerous groans around him from rowdy, boisterous European football fans. After all, Eurosport was only showing the plays of the week.

It was a slow, early part of the afternoon, and the only company Fox had were two men shooting pool, a waitress, a man sitting four barstools away, and the owner, who was presumably in his office in the back. Although they all looked harmless, at the right price they could be a threat. Fox knew the game all too well, which was why he wouldn't allow himself to get too inebriated.

He had taken on several different identities and many different faces in the past. This evening he was David Conlon, the mercenary whose last hit ended with a drug lord and a handful of his associates' body parts floating off the shores of Cartagena.

Originally, the CIA's goal was for Fox to recruit Conlon. That plan fell through, leaving Fox with no other option but to take him out. He not only got his ass chewed up by his superior, General Paul Downing, but also from the new Director of Central Intelligence, DCI Sue Ellen Merrick.

For the CIA, a killer was an asset. For Fox, and anyone else who'd been a SEAL, or in his case a former Joint Task Force 2 Warrant

Officer—JTF2, Canada's SEALs—it was hard to negotiate when you were about to be killed. Actually, the general understood, considering his military history. As for Merrick, forget it.

Replacing Conlon wouldn't be difficult. After all, Fox was fluent in twelve languages and was also a skilled impersonator. And the fact that very few people saw his real face only helped. His natural hair color was dark auburn and he was normally clean shaven. But for the past several weeks he'd let a full beard grow an inch, dyed it black with specks of gray—which was close to Conlon's last known appearance. Presently, he wore slightly used cross-trainers, an old pair of loose-fitting jeans, a thick black windbreaker, and a concealed Glock 19. It was pretty cool for this day, near the end of November—only 44 Fahrenheit.

Taking on someone else's identity was so common for Fox that it had become second nature. Ever since the CIA had recruited him, after the JTF2 no longer had any use for him, he'd lived the life of a ghost. He'd lost count of the number of people he had been over the years. Whenever he needed fake travel documents, cash, a sidearm, access to a local safe-house, it would all be provided for him. Items he'd need while in the field would come to him in the form of a dead drop.

Now, as Conlon, he'd get among the inner circle of Monzer Alghafari—a notorious Syrian-born arms dealer and a royal pain in the ass to the US, and to most European authorities. Like others, such as Alghafari, they always did business with bigger fish. One of his clients was known to be a former CIA informer-turned-terrorist, Faouzi al-Umari. This guy had earned his spot as America's most wanted terrorist for the bombings of two American Embassies—in Egypt and Morocco, respectively. He'd also claimed responsibility for the bombing of a cruise line. His supplier, Alghafari, was such a thorn in America's side that he was even wanted by the DEA's Special Operations Division since the late 1980s.

Back then, they once had what they thought was a solid case against him for smuggling drugs into New York. The case was thrown out when some key witnesses suddenly *disappeared*. It wasn't until Congress passed the Patriot Act after 9/11—a bill that would give law enforcement agencies more power to arrest anyone suspected to be related to terrorist activities—that the DEA thought of performing a sting operation against him that would land his ass in jail.

But where men like Alghafari attracted powerful friends who hated the west, he also attracted enemies, such as the CIA. Fox's superiors managed to convince the DEA to hold off on going after Alghafari, at least until Umari was either captured or killed. Once that was done, Fox would pass any additional intel on Alghafari to the DEA to help them nail him.

Gaining Alghafari's trust was another complicated matter. His inner circle was tight, including friends within the Centro Nacional de Inteligencia—Spain's national intelligence service—who provided him with protection in exchange for intel. Becoming friends with him wasn't going to be easy.

To America's advantage, a Greek national by the name of Costas Viglakis was already in their custody, and he was well acquainted with Alghafari. For the past several months a DEA agent cozied up to Viglakis and eventually became friends with him. When Viglakis was comfortable with him, the DEA agent began bringing him traditional Greek meals. Viglakis couldn't resist the Keftethes, the Pork Souvlaki, or even Youvetsi. He even brought him Melomakaronas—the honey walnut cookies—that were a favorite around Christmas.

Eventually they struck a deal that his prison sentence would be commuted in exchange for him meeting with Alghafari, and then recommending Conlon to him. The whole operation took a year to set up. To their delight, Alghafari eventually took the bait. From what Viglakis told the DEA, Alghafari was interested in having Conlon do *little things* for him.

Fox took another sip of his Heineken, and after he put it down, he couldn't help but stare at it while wondering when he'd be contacted. He doubted that Alghafari would leave his palace-like mansion in Marbella to meet him here. One of his associates would most likely do so instead. And even though it came with the job, he hated waiting on others.

To those around him, Fox was simply focusing on the Heineken bottle, but from where he sat he had a partial view of the front door—watching who came and left—and the rest of the bar. If anyone thought that they could jump him, they'd be limping away—assuming he afforded them the chance to do so.

The man who sat four barstools away began to be of concern. He had checked his cell phone three times in the past two minutes. After the last time, he'd texted something. Fox also noticed that he had two beers, while barely watching the television, and he wasn't speaking to anyone. He doubted that the man—if he was involved in some form of ambush—would be directly participating, with two beers in his system. He'd be too busy taking a piss that he'd end up messing up the timing of a planned hit. However, he may be a watchman for a hit.

Although Fox never once stared in his direction, he caught the man stealing glances at him at least five times. Whatever he was up to, Fox would let him make the first move.

There was a jingling at the doorway, and another man entered. The other guy looked over his shoulder, and a smile came to his face. He slid off his barstool and went to the man with outstretched arms. "Jacques."

They exchanged hugs and then left together. Old friends? A gay couple? Who knew? Who cared? One less person for Fox to be concerned about. There were now three people left in the bar, plus the owner in the back.

Just as the door was about to click shut, it was pushed back open by another man. The two men at the pool table simultaneously looked at him. The way that he walked was the first thing Fox noticed—he appeared to be favoring his right leg. However subtle, it was enough for Fox to guess that it may have resulted from a previous injury.

When the man called Jacques had entered, the two men at the pool table didn't pay him any attention. It wasn't the same for this guy, though. Within moments of him entering, Fox caught them both glancing at him, and then briefly at each other, before returning to their game.

That was a bright flapping red flag.

These three men were acquainted. But how?

Fox didn't care. All he knew was that the men at the pool table hadn't come to this establishment play a game of billiards.

The new arrival sat down adjacent to Fox, where he rudely called out to the waitress to bring him a beer. He wore a thin wool coat, had a small crop of brown hair on his head, and a thick moustache.

Again, Fox kept facing the TV while surreptitiously watching the patron, who Fox knew was watching him too.

The waitress came by and placed a beer in front of the man. *"Aimeriez-vous d'autres choses?"* she asked him.

He answered her with a shake of the head and a back-handed wave.

Fox saw the corner of her lips curl into a sneer before she walked away. He felt like telling the jerk to at least thank her. He would've done so a long time ago. Back in his early high school days, when he was a scrawny, one-hundred-and-twenty-pound weakling, he would often be taunted and bullied by the older kids. They picked on him because he could never fight back. Actually, he had tried, only to get his ass kicked for it.

His best friend at the time, Mark, could only be there for moral support, being that he suffered from cerebral palsy and relied on crutches. Mark was actually better in all of his classes than Fox had been, and he would often help him with his homework. In return, Fox would take the hits for him whenever the smart-ass kids came around. He couldn't fight them, and Fox knew that it was dangerous what he did, but Mark was the only real friend he had.

The jerk who sat adjacent to Fox reminded him of those older kids. He just wasn't dressed as well—with probably more ego than common sense.

The man nodded once at Fox. *"T'es nouveau ici?"*

He'd asked if Fox was new there, but he ignored the question. He'd expected the man to start off that way—by calling out to him. And he'd persist in doing so until Fox acknowledged his presence.

The man slapped the counter twice with an open palm. *"Toi-là. Je te parles."*

Fox took out his Android and pretended to check it, then put it away to watch the television, which was showing a dish soap commercial.

The man slid off his barstool, took his beer, and made his way toward Fox as the waitress disappeared through a door behind the counter. He already knew that there was a baseball bat hidden beside the cash register. If a fight was about to happen, she must have known that the bat wouldn't be much use. Unless she left to go warn her boss, so that he could return with a sawed-off shotgun. Then again, keeping a firearm hidden beside the cash register would've been more ideal. Which could mean that the owner probably anticipated that bullets would be flying.

Fox had underestimated Alghafari's connections. Someone must have tipped him off as to Fox not being the real David Conlon, and this was how the favor was being returned. An entire twelve-month op gone to waste. He could escape through the back, but who knew what, or who, may be waiting for him. Getting out through the front was the simplest and smartest route. Moustache Man and the pool players might attempt to block him. Aside from their billiard cues, they most likely had their sidearms duct taped underneath the table.

Moustache Man now stood so close to Fox that he could smell the onion on his breath.

"T'es sourd?" asked the man. Again he was ignored. But he decided to push his luck, and reached for Fox's beer bottle.

The former JTF2 operative snatched his wrist, jamming his thumb deep into the space between the radius and the ulna. Fox stood, looking at Moustache Man, watching the pain spilling from the man's eyes as he grunted.

A beer bottle, if mishandled, was a weapon. To Fox, this was enough indication that this asshole had just initiated a confrontation.

The man's body twisted as Fox wrenched his arm behind his back and bent him over the counter. Then he grabbed his beer bottle with his free hand and clocked it over the back of the man's head before releasing him. He slid off the counter to the floor, like a badly placed tablecloth.

Fox quickly drew his G19 while swinging around to face the two billiard players, just as one of them was moving to reach under the table. Their eyes met for a split second before Fox squeezed the trigger—striking him in the shoulder. The guy went down, knocking over a table. Fox then aimed the G19 at the other, who, on seeing he was bested, had the smarts to back away from the table with his hands held up high.

Fox stepped away from the counter as he kept his eyes on the pool player. *"Reculez, les mains derrière la tête."*

The man did as he was told and placed his hands behind his head as Fox approached. When his legs were no longer hidden by the billiard table, Fox shot him in the left kneecap. The man hit the floor, screaming, while clutching his knee, unleashing a series French curse words.

Sure, he was unarmed, but if he had backup on the way, neutralizing him now was the smartest option.

Fox checked his flanks as he rushed over to the two men he had shot. The first one was attempting to pull himself across the floor with his good arm. Fox grabbed a chair on his way over and slammed it down, impaling the back of his good hand with the splintered edge of one of the chair's legs. The guy released a garbled wail that went on, even after Fox lifted the chair and threw it to the side. Blood geysered out of his hand as he rolled over onto his back, gritting his teeth while tears poured from both eyes.

"Go present yourselves, in person, to Alghafari so that he can see how he's fucked up royally," yelled Fox with a Welsh accent. "Tell him that I'm coming for him."

A loud ringing came from behind the counter. Fox didn't look in that direction, but checked his flanks instead. A ringing phone was a perfect distraction. Most people in Fox's shoes would've turned to look for it, inadvertently opening themselves up to a surprise attack. Instead, he stepped to the side where it would be impossible for anyone to get a clear shot of him through the bar's front windows. He did so while checking the doorway behind the bar.

The phone stopped after the third ring. Fox anticipated

someone coming out from the doorway behind the bar, most likely the owner, with a shotgun. He glimpsed toward where he'd been sitting before. The jerk with the moustache was still on the floor. He shot a glance to the doorway. The adrenaline coursed through his body, and he stiffened both arms to steady the Glock. The owner would have to jump out to get a clear shot, and that's when Fox would nail him.

The two men he'd subdued were still wailing. He mentally blocked out the sounds as his attention was split between the door behind the counter and anyone that might attempt to come running through the front door with guns blazing.

An object slowly emerged in the doorway as Fox gradually squeezed the trigger. More of the object emerged—it was a phone, being held out for him to see. Next someone held out a stained, white bar rag, waving it—the universal signal for surrender.

But Fox didn't lower his gun as a short, plump man emerged, unhurriedly. It was the owner, and he held the rag at face level in one hand, with the phone in the other.

He placed the phone on the bar counter. *"C'est pour toi."*

Seriously? The call was for him? Fox walked over to the bar, checking his flanks before he grabbed the phone. "What?"

"Señor Conlon, this is Monzer Alghafari. How are you?"

The man had a very slight Arabic accent, and Fox could barely hear him above the cries coming from next to the pool table.

"Better than the goons you sent to kill me," Fox answered, maintaining the Welsh accent.

"Yes, about that, I must apologize. I had to make sure that you're the man I want to work with. The fact that you're speaking to me now confirms."

"You have—hold on." Fox turned to the crying men. "Shut up, for fuck's sake."

The cries stopped immediately. Fox held the phone to his ear. "As I was about to say, you have ten seconds to convince me why I should still work for you."

"The going rate for your services is one-point-five million pounds, but I'll gladly double it."

"What kind of job are we talking about?"

"Ask François, the owner, for the envelope he received in the mail earlier today. For your inconvenience, there's five thousand euros in it. The remaining fifty thousand is waiting for you in a safe at the De L'Europe Amsterdam Hotel, where you're registered under the alias Samuel Ashdown. The rest of your money will be wired to you once the job is done. I suggest you get yourself cleaned up, buy yourself some new clothes, relax, and I'll see you at five PM tomorrow evening. Oh, by the way, don't worry about the police. At this moment, they're conveniently breaking up a dog-fighting tournament."

Fox heard a click on the other end. He put the phone on the counter, turned to the barkeep and stuck out his hand. *"L'envelope. Tout suite!"*

The man reached beside his cash register and handed it to Fox, then backed away.

Fox took the envelope, while keeping his Glock aimed. *"Appelle la serveuse et viens devant, tous vous deux."*

The owner called the waitress, who came from the back, shaking, with her hands up. She then joined him in front of the counter.

Fox gestured toward the wall with the gun. *"Au mur. Assis sur les mains."*

They both scurried over to the wall and sat down on their hands, with their backs to it.

Fox heard groaning close to his feet and saw the moustache man getting up onto his knees. He kicked him in the head, sending him back to dreamland. Minding his surroundings, he tore open the envelope and glanced inside, where he saw a thick wad of cash. He didn't have time to count it, but was confident that the five grand was there. He stuffed the envelope inside his jacket, then made his way over to the entrance and left.

Chapter 4

Liberty Hills Golf Club, Beach Park, Illinois. 12:20 PM, CST, Saturday.

Mitchell Stayner didn't know whether to choose the Ribeye Steak Sandwich or the Buffalo Wing Sandwich. His friends had already given their choices to the college-freshman waiter. Steve Haas and Brigadier General Bryan Jeansonne were, respectively, the CEO and CFO of the private military contracting company, Skilling Lay & Rigas— better known as SLR.

He felt their eyes on him as they sat adjacent to him, around the circular table, covered in a white tablecloth with swan-shaped napkins. Stayner had made much more complicated decisions while being CEO of Sementem—the world's largest chemical and agriculture biotechnology corporation—such as his involvement in his company's decision to purchase SLR. He'd known Haas since they'd both attended the London School of Business, whereas Jeansonne was recently hired, straight out of the army, as the company's CFO.

"Jesus, Mitch. This ain't a twenty-four-hour eatery," Jeansonne said.

Stayner looked over his options again, not wanting to choose one and then regret his decision when the meal was served. Oh screw it. He'd held up everyone long enough. "I'll have the Black and Blue Steak Salad." Something new, how bad could it be?

Sometimes decisions involved risk taking.

The waiter nodded, complimented him on his choice, and took their menus. Haas then undid the buttons of his cardigan and turned to Jeansonne. "How's Janet and the kid?"

Jeansonne took a sip of his water and looked at him. "She's fine. All teary-eyed at seeing Bud heading to college. I thought that she'd be happy getting him out of the house. He's always blasting that damn trumpet."

"So, he's pursuing a degree in music," Stayner said. "Good for him." The truth was, he couldn't care less what Jeansonne's son got his degree in. He had lost his last-born son several years ago to bacterial meningitis. Some anti-GMO activists were saying that it was karma for all the years of his company's so-called unethical business practices and their destruction of *natural* agricultural foods.

Fuck them.

His company had helped provide solutions where there were none. The price of vegetables and other food products would be too costly for those idiots to afford had Sementem not been around. The GMOs his companies designed helped stave off the destruction of crops worldwide, by pests and weeds—the main culprits behind low crop yields. Poor yields equaled higher-priced goods, it was simple math. Not that any of them had any business sense.

"The *music*?" Jeansonne looked disgusted. "Are you kidding me? If I had my way with him, he'd have enlisted and would be serving our country. He'd have a much better chance at getting a decent job with an army background than blowing some damn horn. What's he going to do with a music degree anyway?"

"There's plenty," Stayner said. "He could be a teacher, or, who knows, he may wind up in the Chicago Philharmonic."

"Whatever." Jeansonne rolled his eyes and sighed, his lips flapping like a horse's. "At least he got a full ride. There was no way in hell I was going to pay for that shit."

Stayner rapped his index and middle finger simultaneously on the table. "Language, Bryan. You don't want to lose your club membership, do you?"

Jeansonne laughed. "Please. They ain't kicking us out. Besides, we tip too well."

"*We*," Haas nodded his head once at Stayner, while eying Jeansonne, "as in us two. *You* always find something wrong with your food and blame the waiter."

"Whatever I tip is my business," Jeansonne said, just as the waiter was returning with their beers. He waited for the kid to leave before he continued. "Besides, these chumps are lucky they get anything. They charge so much for meals here you'd think they were mixing cocaine in the mayonnaise."

Jeansonne looked over both shoulders before leaning in closer to Stayner. "Speaking of mayonnaise, what's become of your situation? I read about Collins being involved in a murder-suicide. What's that all about?"

Jesus, why did he have to bring this up here?

"You really want to discuss that now?" Stayner answered as he pointed to everyone with his eyes.

Jeansonne narrowed his own gaze. "I need to know."

"All you need to know is that everything's being handled as we speak," whispered Stayner.

"Handled how?" Jeansonne lowered his voice too. "Your guy has quite a way of doing things."

"He's right." Haas wiped his mouth with the napkin. "Collins' passing may look suspicious to some people. We don't need this kind of attention."

Stayner poured himself a cold one. "Collins was suffering from the extreme stress of being thousands of dollars in debt, while trying to come to terms with his wife expecting."

Jeansonne nearly spat out his beer. "His wife was pregnant?"

"Jesus Christ," said Haas, throwing his napkin down. He rested an elbow on the table and held his head.

Stayner smiled as he watched the two of them show their disgust. He was surprised that the pregnancy was not mentioned in the press. Maybe the story was still developing.

"Yes." Stayner took a sip. "She was expecting."

"And this doesn't bother you?" asked Jeansonne.

"Why should it? Collins was a danger to the company."

"Not his wife," said Haas.

"What do you know about this guy of yours?" asked Jeansonne.

"I know him well enough to trust him to contain this situation. After all, he's the one who discovered the theft," said Stayner.

Jeansonne leaned over the table, closer to Stayner. "Some advice...the next time you see him, tell him to tone it down."

Stayner grinned. Not because he was happy, but it was his way of covering up any anger building up inside him. No one tells him who to hire. And no one dares tell him how to handle a situation. SLR was a subsidiary of Sementem, not the other way around. He was the alpha-male sitting at this table.

Stayner leaned toward Jeansonne too. "I have a better idea. Why don't *you* tell him?" He did his best to stop himself from laughing as he saw the lines crinkle on Jeansonne's forehead. Then he sat back and straightened himself in his chair.

Jeansonne's lips moved as he muttered something blasphemous under his breath, then, with a scowl, he grabbed the bottle and took a huge swig.

"By the way." Stayner took a drink of his own beer. "How's the situation with that Sparks girl?"

"Settled out of court," said Haas. "She had a change of heart. I guess she knew that she couldn't win."

Stayner crossed his legs, setting his beer down. "Or maybe she couldn't afford the fees associated with a lengthy court trial. Of course, the costs related to her parents being in that long-term care facility would already be too much for her to handle."

He paused as he watched Haas and Jeansonne glance at each other. "That must've been a nasty car accident," he said. "It's a miracle they survived."

Jeansonne shook his head. "We never told you about her parents. How'd you...? You didn't."

"We're in this together, gentlemen. If anything goes south for one of us, we all go down. It's just business." Stayner held up his beer in a gesture of toast. "You're welcome, by the way."

Chapter 5

Huntsville, Alabama. 1:54 PM, CST, Saturday.

"What do you think you're doing?" Katy Sparks yelled into her cell. "You can't just go into my bank account and withdraw money without telling me." It then occurred to her that everyone, in every checkout line, was staring at her. Great. Now half the supermarket knew she was broke.

"We won a money judgment against you, Ms. Sparks," said the customer care agent. "That's what happens when you don't pay your debts."

"My parents are in a nursing home trying to recover from a car accident. I need that money to help pay the mortgage or else we're going to lose our house." A tear rolled down her cheek as she held her forehead. "Please, I really need that money. I promise I'll pay you back."

"Nice try, Ms. Sparks. Yesterday someone was telling me that they needed the money to euthanize their dog. But I'll give you credit for your creativity, even though it's not original."

The heartless bastard. Sparks pressed the off button on her mobile and stopped short of smashing in on the floor. What the hell was she supposed to do for dinner?

She let her head drop as she took a deep breath, then looked up at the sixty-something African-American cashier she knew as Lydia. "This is so embarrassing. I'm sorry, but I won't be able to…"

"That's all right, Katy," said Lydia. "Lord knows those credit card people are even bigger crooks than the ones in Congress."

She glanced at the grocery bag Lydia's helper just filled. "What do I do with all of these?"

"Don't worry yourself," said Lydia. "We'll take care of it."

"Thanks." Katy wiped away a tear. "Again, I'm sorry."

"No need to apologize." Lydia closed the cash register drawer. "We've all been there."

Katy left the store, struggling to hold back more tears. Never had she been so humiliated. Almost a year prior to today, she'd been on her way to making a difference. Not just for herself, but for her country. She was the quality control technician for Elemental Food Services, or EFS, which was the food services division of the army contractor, SLR. She'd been earning around twenty-five hundred monthly, including room and board, while working overseas in Afghanistan at Camp Iron Eagle.

It was a dream job, which quickly spiraled into a nightmare. She'd just wanted to do her job, but instead she had to deal with a bunch of incompetent dining room managers and army personnel who couldn't appreciate her work ethic. What did she get in return? Personal threats and then blamed for the deaths of thirteen army officers. Never mind that this was after she had warned the kitchen staff and EFS of the unsanitary conditions that were putting people's health at risk in the dining halls.

Complaining to SLR was useless. They never even bothered to take her seriously, as was shown with unreturned phone calls and emails. With no income and mounting interest on her student loans—which at this rate would take her over thirty years to pay off—there was no way that she could afford a half-decent lawyer who would at least help her to negotiate a reasonable settlement. And then the car accident that nearly killed her parents.

More expenses.

So much for killing herself to get her microbiology degree. Four years of college with the goal of making a better life for herself, all gone to pot. She couldn't even afford to get an oil change, blowing the car's engine on the I-20 two weeks ago. Now she was stuck taking the bus. What was even worse was that all the friends she'd thought that she had were suddenly too busy to help her out.

These thoughts just made her grit her teeth and fume as she walked through the parking lot, while ahead of her and to the left, she saw her bus fast approaching.

Shit.

She ran, passing between four parked cars, as the bus slowed down at the stop. She waved her hand as she ran. "Wait."

A Dodge Ram pickup truck screeched to a stop in front of her, blocking her path. She took one look at the driver and knew that this was going to be trouble.

"What you doing here, Katy? I thought I'd never find you." Seeing her scruffy-faced ex-boyfriend, Tony—or Butch, as his lowlife friends called him—made her nearly choke on her own saliva.

"Get away from me," Katy answered as she went to circle the truck from the back, not taking her eyes off the bus.

He reversed, blocking her. "Whoa, not so fast," said Butch with an elbow hanging out the window frame. "We've got some talking to do."

"No we don't." Katy went to circle the truck from in front. Shit, the bus was at the stop, collecting passengers. She'd never let Butch control her. That wouldn't happen. Besides, he wouldn't be stupid enough to hit her here in public. But that thought faded quickly as Butch surprised her by grabbing her arm, pulling her closer to him.

"Let go of me," Katy yelled as Butch's fingers cut into her right forearm. "I swear I'll scream."

"Will you just listen to me, for crying out loud?"

If she had any reason to scream, it would be for that stupid tattoo of the semi-nude woman on his upper arm. She hated it almost as much as she hated Butch. "We're through, just get over it." She began beating his arm with her free hand.

"Cut it out." Butch didn't appear to be too bothered by the slaps she gave his arm. "I just want to talk to you, like two civilized adults."

She didn't know what came over her, but she suddenly punched him, landing a blow to his right cheek. His head snapped back so far that he lost his baseball cap.

"Motherfuck!" Butch stammered as he lost his grip.

Katy flew back, tripping in the process, and fell in a spin—grazing the side of her head on the side-mirror of the car to her right. Vortexes clouded her vision as she reached back to the spot where the pain radiated from. All she saw in front of her was the missing hubcap of a '96 Chevy Malibu.

Through the throbbing, she faintly heard Butch cussing at a hundred words per minute, then she heard the truck door open and slam. There was Butch, standing over her, silhouetted in front of the sun. It was inevitable now and she immediately curled up in a fetal position as she waited for the first kick to strike her.

Just get it over with and spit on me. That's what you always do.

"You never learn, do you? You little cun—"

That's when Katy heard a loud buzzing noise, which was accompanied by Butch's grunting. She took a quick peek, just in time to see him convulsing erratically for a few seconds before falling backward with a loud thud. Another silhouette took Butch's place, as Katy was blinded by the sun behind them. Moments later the same person put their hands on her.

"No, don't touch me. Get away," Katy screamed as she slapped and kicked at her aggressor, until she heard her name being called.

"Katy, listen. I'm here to help."

It was a woman's voice, thin, yet commanding. Katy opened her eyes, and the first thing she saw was the woman's light, three-quarter-length jacket. She then looked at her face, which was framed by shoulder-length blond hair, her eyes hidden behind a pair of sunglasses. Katy determined she was likely in her early- to mid-twenties. Maybe slightly younger than Katy was. She looked at Butch who was on his back. "Did you…"

"He's fine, just out for a while. Listen…"

"Who are you? And how'd you know my name?"

"My name's Jill St. John," the woman answered. "I've been checking up on you for the past several months. Ever since your involvement at Camp Iron Eagle."

Her mouth hung open. "You've been spying on me?" She

shoved both hands into Jill's chest, knocking her back so that she fell on her hands. "Get away from me, whoever you are."

Katy used the Chevy for support as she got onto her feet. She still felt pain where she'd bumped her head, but that would have to wait. For now she needed to get away from this strange woman. But when she got up, Jill was already standing, holding both palms out as though she were surrendering.

"Look," Jill said, "I know that this is a lot to absorb, but I can tell you that you weren't at fault for the deaths of those thirteen men and women."

Katy felt a cool breeze that made her hold her breath. "What did you just say?"

Jill checked her flanks, then approached Katy. "The so-called insurgents who took out the military transport—that was all staged."

Katy narrowed her eyes as she took a hard look at this woman. "What…what are you saying? How do you know all this?"

Jill took a step closer to Katy and held her forearm. "You were a patsy to a cover-up that goes a lot deeper than a simple case of food poisoning."

All of a sudden, Katy forgot about the pain in her head. She saw Jill look to the side as a car slowly approached Butch's truck from behind. Jill then walked past Katy, pulling her ten cars away, where they both stopped. Jill did another scan as though to be sure that no one could overhear them. Whoever drove past Butch's pickup didn't seem to notice that no one was inside, and kept driving.

Katy stood so close to Jill that she could tell that her blond hair may be a wig. "What do you know about what happened at Camp Iron Eagle?"

"Not everything," Jill answered. "But a lot more than you, apparently."

The back of Katy's throat was dry and she swallowed hard. *What the hell am I hearing?*

Jill took Katy's wrist gently. "I know you want answers, and I can get them for you. But I can't tell you much right now." Jill did a quick scan of the parking lot. "At least not here."

"What do you want from me?" asked Katy.

"Your assistance," Jill answered, letting go of Katy's hand. "You're ruined. You don't have any money, your parents are recovering in a nursing home, and you're about to lose the family home. You have a choice. You can stay here, pretend that we never met, and struggle on your own. Or, you can come with me and help me bring down the bastards who murdered those men and women, and ruined your life."

Katy looked away from Jill, briefly, unable to comprehend what she just heard. This was too good to be true. A complete stranger just happened to show up when Butch was about to hurt her, offering her a chance at fixing her damaged life. "But what about my parents? They need me."

"Don't worry about them. I'll see to it that they're taken care of. I'll even get the bank off your back."

Katy looked into Jill's eyes. She appeared to be genuine in what she said. "How?"

"As I said earlier, let me worry about that." She shot a glance over her shoulder. "Besides, Butch isn't going to do much for you, is he?"

She had a point there. "What did you do to him?"

Jill opened one side of her jacket to reveal a stun gun in a hip holster. "He'll be out for a while."

Katy crossed her arms, rubbing them with both hands. "I...I don't..."

Jill narrowed her eyes. "I can help you get your life back for God's sake. Let me help you."

Katy stared at her. Something wasn't right. "What are you getting out of this?"

"I lost someone dear to me in that attack you were blamed for," Jill answered. "You saw things over there, things which could help me expose those people for what they did. You're my best chance at helping me set things right—for both of us. So what's it going to be?"

Katy pondered what she said. Whoever Jill was, if that was her real name, she must have gone through a lot of trouble tracking her down. She wouldn't have come this far unless she had a plan.

Jill sighed as she shook her head, took out her smartphone, and began typing something on it. About twenty seconds later, Jill turned to Katy. "Call your credit card company and check the balance."

What?

Jill shoved the phone at her. "Go on. Call them."

Katy stared at the phone hesitantly before she took it. She called her bank and asked to be forwarded to the credit card department. It took a few moments before she was transferred to a friendly-sounding Latina. She asked how much she owed, and when she got the answer she felt the blood drain from her face.

No, this can't be real. She looked at Jill, who appeared to be more frustrated by the minute. Katy thanked the representative, switched off the call, and handed Jill back her phone.

"As I said, I have the means." Jill put away her phone. "Your parents *will* be taken care of and you won't lose the house. So what's it going to be?"

Why not? It can't get any worse than this, can it? "I'll do it." *There, that felt better.* "What do I have to do? I mean, where are we going?"

"Overseas." Jill began to walk away, and Katy ran to catch up to her. "But we're going to make a quick stop in Atlanta first."

"What for?"

"You're going to need a new passport and a new identity," Jill answered. "Welcome to the big leagues."

Chapter 6

Amsterdam, The Netherlands. Saturday night.

F ox stared at the other parked trains through the window as the Thalys pulled into Centraal Station. When he left Montauban, he took the forty-minute bus ride to Toulouse. From there he caught a flight to Paris where he switched to the train—riding the Thalys to Amsterdam and arriving at 10:28 PM. Sure, it would've been quicker to fly directly to Amsterdam, but Fox wanted to use the crowds at Charles-de-Gaulle airport to lose anyone who may have been tailing him.

When he got to his hotel, the receptionist handed him the envelope containing the rest of the money Alghafari had promised him. He thanked her and requested to put both envelopes he had in the hotel safe for the time being. Not having any luggage to worry about, Fox left the hotel and walked to the city's famous Red-Light district. This hour was ideal for *window shopping*. After all, that's what the real Conlon would be doing.

The temperature was slightly above freezing as Fox walked with his hands in his jacket pockets. Where he was going would've normally taken him approximately twenty minutes, but he took the most indirect route to help him spot anyone who may have been following him. Although tedious, it was an effective anti-surveillance technique. And although using a combination of main streets and narrow pedestrian-only footpaths added another forty minutes to his trip, he saved himself the trouble of having to send another two, or more, people to the ER.

The evening chill wasn't going to stop anyone from coming to this area of town. The allure of sexual gratification was stronger than the hunger for a basic meal. And the Red-Light district was flooded with individuals looking to get their next quick sexual fix. Fox was surrounded by all sorts of people. He heard people speaking Dutch, picked out a few Brits and Germans, and even overheard a bit of Swedish and French.

There were very few parked cars next to the canal as most of the area was taken over by pedestrians. Fox turned onto a cobbled street with the canal to his right, where the strong whiff of marijuana stung him. Ah, the Coffee Shop—not to be confused with Starbucks, but instead a place that would be heaven for many American college students.

The male punk, whose hand brushed too closely to Fox's ass, learned the hard way why it was wrong to assume that he could pick anyone's pocket. Fox grabbed his fingers and squeezed them to the point he heard a satisfying crack, then twisted his hand to force him down on his knees.

"Je hebt de verkeerde persoon, vind je niet?" He told him that he'd picked the wrong person.

"Ja," he squealed. *"Het spijt me."*

It was pathetic how these guys only apologized when they were under pressure. Fox knew that the thief didn't get his wallet, so he shoved him to the ground. The punk scrambled away, pulling his hood over his head to obscure his face. Being a pro, Fox knew how to surreptitiously lift one's wallet off them by bumping into them. Shit, this guy may be a pro to the unsuspecting person, but to Fox he was an amateur.

He continued walking, catching a few more whiffs of weed while being dazzled by the flashing neon lights of one of several peep shows. He turned into an alley that was tightly boxed-in by the same two- or three-story gable-style buildings that lined the canal. To his right he glanced at the seemingly never-ending stretch of bikini-clad women in windows. All different shapes, ages, heights, and nationalities. He had passed six windows, but the seventh, with a small Asian girl, caught his eye. Fox paused with his hands in his pockets as he watched her. She had short, shiny, jet-black hair, cut in a chin-length bob. Her curves and movements nearly took his attention away from her ribs, which were visible when she turned sideways—bending over backward to form a bridge. She hadn't been eating well lately. Probably on purpose, in order to keep her body the way it was. The girl couldn't have been a day over eighteen. He then noticed the blue stacked heels she wore. This was definitely the place.

She winked at him twice, then turned around and wiggled her tiny ass, before lifting her left leg straight up over her head. Damn, she was flexible. And she loved to show it.

Fox also saw it as the signal.

He moved in front of the glass door to the right of the window display and waited. The dancer left her booth and let him in. Fox entered and heard the girl locking the door. He turned around to see her smiling as she approached him, not wasting any time putting her hands on him.

The hooker was so short—at about four feet seven—she was forced to reach as she walked her fingers up both of his arms, then across and under his shoulders, stopping once they came to the middle of his jacket. Without a word, she slowly pulled down the zipper, fully exposing the shirt underneath.

As Fox stared into those dark brown eyes of hers, she began to rub her palms on his chest. She exhaled long and audibly as her small hands groped the solid muscle underneath.

He felt a warmness grow from inside as his hands found their way down her back, which was far as he could reach. "How much?"

She continued caressing his chest, finding both nipples to play with before working her way down to his abs. The girl slowly licked her lips. "Eighty euros."

Despite her very youthful appearance, her voice was very sensual. Maybe she was older than she appeared. If she wasn't, then she'd had some damn good training.

He gestured down the hallway. "After you."

She knew how to put on a good show, right down to the way

she wiggled her hips as she walked, leading Fox to a bedroom near the end of the hall. Inside, it was dimly lit by a lamp that sat on a small stand next to a double bed. In the corner stood an empty coat rack that was on the verge of falling apart.

Fox heard the door close behind him, followed by the sound of heels walking away. No sooner had the hooker left, when another door, adjacent to the first one, opened. A brighter light partially illuminated the area around him as Fox turned to see a familiar face. As usual, she was dressed in one her trademark dark-colored pantsuits, along with a pair of stacked Blahniks. He knew that she had a tight body underneath the no-nonsense business attire—remnants of her years as a track athlete. Nonetheless, Doctor Nita Parris was way too humble to show it off. Fox recalled telling her to loosen up a little, but that never appeared to be in the cards for her.

"I hope you weren't getting too comfortable." Parris looked at Fox, briefly, before turning and walking around a small table that was propped against the wall. He didn't hear her Barbadian accent, then again, that usually only came out when she was around other West Indians. He remembered once answering her in Bajan Creole a few years back. The deadpan expression she'd given him was priceless. But she'd gotten her point across. Some dialects were strictly off limits—especially to white people.

Fox followed her in, closing the door behind him. "I don't do little girls."

Parris snickered. "That's news to me. Word has it that you'll jump on anything in a tight skirt, or less."

"Now *that* wouldn't be too scientific of you, would it? Aren't you the one who keeps telling me that you'd rather see proof than rely on rumors? Even the ones you start."

Parris winced. "Ouch."

Fox noticed the slight bruises to her face—her makeup couldn't cover it all. "You've been in a fight. How's the other guy?"

"He won't be pressing charges, in case you were wondering. Unfortunately, Weyland was compromised."

"And?"

"He's safe now. A bit in shock when I last saw him, but the

medics think it'll be a few days before we get anything out of him."

Fox noticed that she didn't look at him as she answered. "One could hope."

Parris glanced up at him. "He better. The FBI's taken over at this point. The manhunt for Umari's been going on for almost five years. Weyland was our best chance for locating him. And now he's under medical care."

"You kept him alive," Fox said. "That's what counts."

If there was one thing Fox admired about Parris, it was her tenacity. Like a pit-bull, once she sunk her teeth into her target she never let go.

But he accepted her frustration, keeping in mind that Umari was originally a CIA informant who had turned. Using the skills he'd gained from his training, he had masterminded the bombings of two American Embassies and a cruise ship. While searching for him, the Agency discovered that a local security firm that Weyland worked for—Bismarck Securities—was bankrolling Umari's activities. Weyland's job was to hack into networks of Bismarck's clients in order to test the strengths and weaknesses of their systems. Parris not only recruited him but was also his handler. For the past three months, he'd fed them intel every two weeks.

Parris picked up a briefcase from the corner and placed it on the table. He came beside her as she opened it. It was then that he noticed the scratches on her knuckles as she handed him his new tablet and smartphone. Fox remembered how she had kicked him in the shins when they'd met on their last mission, something he'd probably deserved for a prior incident.

"Your new tablet has a special feature. The techs over in OST installed an electron microscope into it."

Fox understood that OST was the acronym for the agency branch of the Office of Science and Technology. He faked his surprise with a mock gasp. "No way."

Parris gave him a deadpan stare, as though to tell him to grow up. In return he smirked, as though to tell her to lighten up.

"If ever you need to use it, just activate the app, take your super magnified picture, then send it as an email attachment, straight to Langley for analysis."

"That's all?"

"Yes," she answered. "You'll be happy to know that next year there'll be an app that will allow you to control an army of Fembots too, if that's what you were wondering."

Fox grinned while tilting his head and she imitated him, even cocking her head at an angle.

"Riiight," Fox answered in a jaw-dropping Doctor Evil impersonation. Apparently she *did* have a sense of humor after all.

"I expect you'll be recording your conversation with Alghafari?"

"Are you kidding? Alghafari will have me checked for any transmitting devices the moment he and his bodyguards enter my suite. Besides, I wouldn't be surprised that he'd be walking with a jamming device."

"The DEA won't be too happy about that."

"Fuck the DEA," said Fox. "If they want to send someone on a suicide mission, let them use one of their own. We need Alghafari to track down Umari, so we can't screw this up."

"Duly noted," said Parris. "Our intel indicates that Alghafari has a USB flash drive in his possession. We don't know what's on it, but we think that he's going to ask you to deliver it to a buyer."

"I hope that's not all he plans to have me do."

Parris rolled her eyes. "Quit bitching. He's obviously testing your loyalty and your competence."

"He also doesn't want to set foot in the country where this transaction is taking place. That way he'll avoid any criminal charges in case the deal goes sideways."

"Whatever his reasons are, we need to find out what's on the flash drive before you deliver it to the buyer. That's when Dewan and I will assist you."

"I doubt it'll be that simple. Alghafari'll have the flash drive sealed in a way to make it tamper-proof."

"Or he won't," said Parris. "Lately he's been getting sloppy. Using his home phone and bragging that it's the most secure phone in the world. He's also been throwing his money away at casinos in full view of any potential would-be snipers, claiming that he has the best bodyguards money can buy."

"Good, he thinks he's invincible," said Fox. "Any idea who the buyer is?"

"None. Despite his sloppiness, he's still been able to keep some things under a tight wrap." Parris handed Fox an earpiece. "You're going to need this too. I'll always be close by."

Fox placed the earpiece inside his right ear as he left the room. "Close enough to be in my arms or the other way around?"

"Close as I need to be."

Fox paused as he turned back toward Parris. "I have an idea. If I don't wind up in your arms by the end of next week, I'll treat you to dinner."

Parris shook her head slowly. "Ain't happening."

Fox smirked. "Why so defensive?"

Parris cocked her head to the side and raised an eyebrow. "Stay focused."

Fox chuckled and turned around to leave. "I'm just messing with you."

"Sure you were," she answered. "Oh, another thing."

Fox looked over his shoulder. "What?"

"Get a haircut and a shave," she answered. "You look like you've just walked out of the bush."

Chapter 7

De L'Europe Hotel, Amsterdam, Netherlands. Sunday morning.

A new video featuring Umari was currently the focus of this morning's news. Even though Fox had the television on, at most, he paid attention for five minutes before his mind began to wander. It was the usual threat-laden rant where Umari claimed that his organization would continue targeting Americans everywhere in Africa. Nothing new.

Fox switched the channels with the remote as he felt movement beside him under the sheets. A hand slid up his chest, pinching his left nipple. It was a bit too hard for his liking, so he slapped the hand away.

"Hey," the brunette groaned as she stuck her head out from under the sheets. "Why so grumpy?"

Fox ignored her. She had already served her purpose. Now if only she'd take a hint and get lost.

"Not too talkative this morning, are you?" She brushed a few strands of tousled hair from over her eye before resting her head on his lap. "You know, we can go for another round."

"No thanks," Fox said as he continued switching the channels. She still wouldn't take a hint.

She then tried a new tactic and put her hand on his abs. "I never had a chance to really count how many you have. I'm guessing you have more than a six-pack." She giggled as she drew with her finger between each one, but then began to slide her hand lower.

Enough of this. Fox grabbed the side of her head with his right hand and shoved her hard, sending her flying off the bed, pulling the sheets with her. "Do I have to spell it out for you? I'm not in the mood." Fox looked back at the television. "You'll find your money on the bathroom counter when you freshen up."

She grabbed the edge of the bed to help herself up and then pulled off the sheets she was tangled in. She stood there naked as she stared at Fox for a moment, as though she hoped that he would acknowledge her. When he didn't, she stormed off—grabbing her one-piece that hung on the front bedpost.

Fox glanced at her as she stomped away, fuming as she slipped her dress over her head. The he heard running water for about fifteen to twenty seconds before she came back out. Through the bedroom doorway, he saw her standing with her purse in one hand and her fur coat hanging over her other arm—staring back at him.

"Fuck you!" she yelled.

Fox didn't even respond, instead, raised the volume on the television until he heard the front door slam. It had been nearly two months since he'd fucked a total stranger. Although she had a nice body and face, he still felt an emptiness, and this hollow feeling was something he got more frequently as time went by. When he'd been in his late teens to early twenties, his hormones were more rampant than an entire junior varsity football team combined. He'd never felt at a loss after having sex with a woman, even if it was just a blowjob. Now that he was in his early thirties the fuck-and-go didn't do much for him anymore. The urge was still there, but there was nothing to savor. If he had to think about it, he'd felt more this way after he'd lost Jessica—his fiancée, who was murdered a few years back. *Aw, dammit.* There he went again, thinking about her.

He couldn't let that happen. It was part of the package deal with the choice he'd made a few years ago: move on and start fresh with a new life. It was that, or hunt down the people who'd killed her. There wasn't room for both. And even though the weapons consortium and Jessica's killers—The Arms of Ares— had not been very active since he and Parris last confronted them in Tokyo, tracking down a wanted terrorist was the priority now.

The only reason men like Faouzi al-Umari killed so many people was because of men like Alghafari.

He scratched his chin and felt his beard, then got up, not bothering to put on his boxer briefs, and went to the bathroom and stood in front of the mirror, naked. He had to admit that the beard looked a bit odd on his face. He ran his fingers through it and then through his long hair. It was all part of the original cover.

Parris was right. I do look, and feel, as though I just came out of the bush. Fox went to the phone in the living room and dialed 0. The receptionist answered after the first ring.

"Good morning, Mister Ashdown," said a young male voice. "How may I assist you?"

"Good morning. I'd like to order room service and a stylist." Fox carried the cordless phone back to the bedroom.

"Both can be arranged. What would you like for breakfast?"

"Crepes. Bring me the dish with the most meat on the side, with no beans. And make sure that there's a pitcher of freshly squeezed orange juice."

"Right away, sir."

Fox was about to switch off when he remembered something. "You still there?"

"Yes, Mister Ashdown."

"Get room service to bring it up in an hour, not before. And the stylist thirty minutes later."

"Very well. Is there anything else you'd like?"

"That'll be all, thanks." Fox then switched off the phone and rested it beside the television. From where he stood, he let himself fall forward to the floor where he caught himself in a push-up position, and spent the next fifty minutes doing calisthenics.

After that he got in the shower, and room service arrived just as he was drying himself off. Never being too sure, he put on the bathrobe and answered the door with his G19, instructing the service man to leave the breakfast cart outside and to expect a generous tip waiting for him when he came to collect the cart in an hour.

He was done eating in about fifteen minutes and the stylist arrived another fifteen minutes later. He was expecting it to be a woman, but it turned out to be some guy in his early twenties named David. Fox didn't care that he was super flamboyant, or that he wouldn't stop complementing him on how the ladies would be constantly after him once he was done *cleaning him up*. He just wanted someone who could transform him.

Fox was never bored for a moment during the time that David took. All he thought about was Alghafari. This guy saved face by owning a legitimate import/export business, but dealt with the illegal arms trade since the 1990s. There was so much fighting in the Middle East that selling weapons was a sure way to earn a living. Alghafari's older brother, Nasif, was the better trafficker, having taught Alghafari everything he knew. The relationship was cut short several years before, the day a rocket-propelled grenade was sent through the window of an office building in Beirut where Nasif had been meeting a buyer.

Many speculated that it was the Mossad, considering how Nasif was getting too close to Yasser Arafat. It later turned out to be a rival arms trafficker. Alghafari gladly returned the favor by having a rocket launched through his rival's living room window while he, his wife, and four-year-old kid were enjoying dinner. Of course, Alghafari had never been convicted of blowing away what was left of the man's bloodline. Even though the prosecution had an airtight case against him, there just happened to be a witness who went missing, while another developed a case of amnesia.

At the age of thirty-five, Alghafari married a seventeen-year-old Lebanese woman with whom he had four daughters with. He often joked that he married his eldest daughter when he entertained guests at his sprawling mansion in Marbella, Spain. Although he'd inherited his brother's contacts, he'd built on it and developed that list with many powerful people—even those who worked in Spanish Intelligence. With that sort of cover, it was next to impossible to send Alghafari to jail.

While studying Conlon, Fox had met with a colleague who'd been stationed in Italy twenty years before. He had compiled a huge file on Alghafari and his activities. But the most important thing he took away from that meeting was that Alghafari had reached such a status in the arms trade business that money wasn't his biggest priority. Men in his position were mostly concerned about cover, or protection for themselves and their families. There was a time that Alghafari had even approached the United States to act as an independent smuggler. His brother, Nasif, was more successful back in the 1970s and the early 1980s. The US gladly worked with Nasif, but they refused to have anything to do with the younger brother.

But if there was anything to say about Alghafari, he definitely wasn't an idiot. Alghafari knew that international laws with regards to weapons trafficking were so weak that a weapons shipment could represent a violation of international law but still be perfectly legal in many nations. As for Interpol, they didn't have any arresting powers and were nothing more than a clearinghouse for warrants that individual nations might elect not to enforce. That's how Alghafari knew how to play the game and play it well. He'd structure his deals so that he didn't violate national law. How? By acting as a third-party broker. From his home in Marbella, he would negotiate between the supplier in a second country and a buyer in a third. The weapons could then be shipped directly from one country to the other, while his commission was wired to a bank in a fourth. Alghafari wouldn't have set foot in any country where the crime transpired—and as long as he remained in Spain, he hadn't committed any crime.

Alghafari was a Syrian and had done business primarily with Islamic Fundamentalists and other radicals, but he wasn't religious. And although he hated the United States, he embraced the western lifestyle. He'd dine with radicals one day—preferring to cook for them himself rather than have the kitchen staff do it—but still celebrate Easter and Christmas. In fact, it took a crew of fifty to decorate his villa with Christmas lights and he'd fly in a few pine trees from Finland. His daughters attended Oxford University and had all studied law, except for one, who studied medicine.

The phone rang close to 5:50 PM and the receptionist informed Fox that Alghafari was on his way up. He thanked her before hanging up. There was a knock on the door a few minutes later.

Fox brought his G19 with him and stopped five feet away from the door. "Who is it?"

"The same person the receptionist told you was coming up." It was clearly Alghafari's voice.

Conlon was this precocious. Had Fox not acted this way, Alghafari probably would've known Fox was an imposter. He holstered his Glock and answered the door.

"Buenas tardes," greeted Alghafari. He was a handsome man in his early sixties, with a strong nose, hooded eyes, and close-cropped gray hair. Years of being in the business, along with heavy smoking and drinking, had taken its toll on him. He was dressed in a tailored navy suit, and wore a Hermès belt with a buckle in the shape of an *H*. Alghafari was flanked by two men, who appeared more to be retired linebackers than military men. They both wore tailored navy suits and had goatees.

"Come in," gestured Fox. As his hand was extended, one of Alghafari's bodyguards jumped at him, grabbing Fox's arms and spinning him toward the wall.

"Hands against the wall and spread your legs."

"Let him go," yelled Alghafari as he hurried to close the door.

The guard turned to Alghafari, surprised, and then released Fox and backed away.

Alghafari walked in with a scowl. "What's wrong with you?"

The guard bowed his head to Alghafari. "My apologies, señor. I thought—"

"Baahh." Alghafari waved him off. "Señor Conlon's here on my behalf." Alghafari then turned to Fox. "Please accept my most sincere—"

Fox raised a palm. "Please." He walked past the guard, giving him a look of disgust as though to say, "Try that again, you dumb fuck."

He looked over his shoulder at Alghafari as he headed to the bar. "May I offer you a drink?"

"Why not?" Alghafari said. "We haven't officially celebrated our new business relationship. I see that you've gotten yourself groomed. It suits you, I like it."

Shit, Alghafari must've had eyes on him somehow. Maybe one of his goons had snapped a picture of him with a smartphone before they got themselves shot. "Thanks."

Fox grabbed two glasses. "What would you like?"

Alghafari took a seat on the middle stool as his men remained standing, one near the entrance and the other near the door to the bedroom. He gave the drink rack a onceover and leaned on the bar surface while he rubbed his chin. "I'm in the mood for something Irish. How about a glass of Bailey's straight, with ice."

Fox dropped three ice cubes into Alghafari's glass with the tongs, then poured the Irish Cream over them, then he did the same for himself and raised his glass to the Syrian.

"To our new partnership," said Alghafari.

"Likewise." Fox took a gulp and leaned on the bar with his drink in hand. "So, what am I going to be doing?"

Alghafari swallowed fast, as though he was caught off guard. "Straight to business, I see. You're anxious."

"It's been eight months that I've been out of the game."

He nodded and smiled. "Understandable." He adjusted himself on the barstool, as though to make himself more comfortable. "The job's simple. I want you to deliver a hard drive for me. The purchaser will meet you in Düsseldorf tonight at precisely ten PM. I'm sure that you know the importance of not being late, as the purchaser will not be there if you're as much as a minute past ten."

Shit. Fox realized he'd have less than four hours. The drive alone would take two and a half. Dewan may just have enough time to decrypt the hard drive, but it would be cutting it pretty damn close. Come to think of it, wasn't he supposed to deliver a *flash* drive? That would have been more manageable.

"Your car is already in the hotel garage," Alghafari continued. "The address is in the glove compartment and the parcel is in the trunk."

Fox raised his glass to his lips and finished off his drink. "That's it?"

"Were you expecting something else?"

"A bit more than just running an errand."

Alghafari smiled and nodded. "This is not a job for just anyone. I'm hiring you because I need someone with excellent anti-surveillance skills. That's why those thugs weren't able to get the best of you back in the bar."

"Gotcha."

Alghafari slid his empty glass toward Fox and got up. "For identification purposes, you'll introduce yourself as *Thor's Hammer*. Once the delivery is made your fee will be wired to your account."

In other words, Alghafari would pay him once he'd paid himself.

They shook hands and Alghafari and his goons left.

Chapter 8

Sunday Night.

Fox stood at the curb outside the hotel's entrance while he waited for the valet to bring him his car. It didn't take long. Soon he saw the BMW M3 Coupe driving down Nieuwe Doelenstraat then pulling over into the valet parking. Fox tipped the driver fifty euros, got in, and drove off down the one-lane street.

He pulled over a few streets later to check the car's built-in GPS. Fox went to deactivate it only to discover that it had already been done. Kudos to Alghafari for being smart, and, not to mention, considerate. Nowadays, anyone with a laptop and a Wi-Fi connection could hack into a car's GPS system to track its location.

Fox then did a thorough sweep of the car with his smartphone. Unlike conventional ones, Fox's phone had an app which detected any listening devices up to a range of twenty feet. That was ideal if he were in a meeting and had to worry about someone listening in on him, or if he were in a city with CCTVs on the streets. But since he was checking a car, he reduced the app's settings to a two-foot range. If a bug was detected, the phone wouldn't only vibrate, but an arrow would blink on the monitor to point out its location. In fact, the phone was so sensitive that Fox had to turn off his earpiece while he scanned.

Once he was done with the inside, he popped the trunk and got out of the car to scan the exterior. He opened the trunk and saw the knapsack Alghafari had told him about. He gave both the bag and the trunk a onceover with the phone. The car was clean of any bugging devices.

He turned off the app and set the mobile in the trunk. He then unzipped the knapsack to find the hard drive. So much for accurate intel, telling him that there'd be a flash drive. Oh well, nothing Dewan shouldn't be able to handle. He zipped the bag shut, grabbed his phone, and took them both with him before closing the trunk. Fox got back in, plopped the bag on the passenger seat and pressed the engine-starter button. He then took the shortest route to the highway.

Fox's smartphone had another app that would cause it to emit a subsonic signal scrambler, or SUSSER, which would block out transmissions given off by any surveillance devices that may have been hidden in the car. The only problem with relying solely on a scrambler while driving was that the moment Fox stepped away from the vehicle, any hidden devices would continue transmitting—revealing the car's location. Although more tedious, scanning for the devices made more sense.

An hour had passed since he'd left Amsterdam, traveling mostly on the E35. For most of the ride he'd noticed that someone was following him, remaining three cars behind as he passed the road sign that announced he was entering the city of Duiven. He saw that the Gulf service station was fast approaching, so he took the exit ramp toward it. A few hundred yards in, the road split in two, with one side leading to the actual service station while the other ran behind it, leading to a stretch that made up the truck stop. Fox took the latter road and drove into the parking lot. He counted eight trucks and two other cars there, all parallel parked, and drove to the end. Finding an isolated spot in front of the other vehicles wasn't difficult, and once he was parked, he turned off the engine and waited.

Fox watched through the rearview mirror as another set of headlights was heading his way. It was the same car that had followed him from Amsterdam and it came to a stop behind him.

The headlights turned off and Fox could see that it was a blue Audi. As expected, Parris was at the wheel and Dewan sat beside her. When Dewan got out, Fox lifted the bag from the passenger seat.

Dewan sat down beside Fox and closed the door. "What's up?" He was only nineteen when he'd been recruited by the agency, not too long after Parris and Fox had rescued him from a doomsday cult on a prior mission. He was a skinny, six-feet-tall, African-American with a bald-fade. There were very few computers or security systems that Dewan couldn't hack into and wreak havoc if he wanted to.

Fox took out the hard drive and handed it to him. "Here you go."

Rather than take it, Dewan stared at it as though it were contaminated. "What's that?"

"What the hell does it look like?"

"I know *what* it is. Where's the *flash* drive?"

Fox held it closer to Dewan. "This is all I have, so take it."

"You were supposed to get a *flash* drive, not a hard drive."

"Flash drive, hard drive, soft drive. What's the difference?"

Dewan sucked his teeth as his head dropped in his hand. "Oh, Jesus, take the wheel!"

"Are you telling me that you can't decrypt this?"

Dewan scrunched up his face. "Boy, who you think you're talking to? Of course I can decrypt it. But I'm going to need more time."

"How long?"

"A few hours, perhaps a day, depending how complex the encryption is. And *you* don't have that time to spare."

Fox went to toss the hard drive into the back seat but stopped mid-throw. "Shit."

"What's going on over there?" came Parris's voice through their earpieces.

"Fox brought the wrong drive," snapped Dewan.

"And you brought me a cantankerous computer nerd," quipped Fox.

"Shut up, both of you!" That was all it took for Parris to silence them. "Alghafari must've made a last-minute change. We won't have enough time to find out what's on the drive before Fox meets the buyer, so we'll just have to find a way to get the data after the buyer has it."

"You'll have to follow him," said Fox.

"And switch his hard drive with a duplicate," Parris replied.

"That sucks ass," Dewan grumbled as he got out.

Fox shook his head and dropped the hard drive in the passenger seat. He then started the car, and was back on the highway with Parris and Dewan a few cars behind. He didn't worry about losing them because Dewan would've already paired his tablet with Fox's smartphone in order to know where he was heading. The pairing was secure, only giving Dewan access to Fox's whereabouts, unless Fox manually changed the settings on his phone to block him. As he drove he glanced at the hard drive.

What the hell's on that thing?

Chapter 9

Nördlich Henkelstraße, 40589, Düsseldorf, Germany. 9:37 PM, Sunday.

The area Fox drove through was southeast of the city The area Fox drove through was southeast of the city center— an area which was currently going through a major restructuring. What was once a pre-Second-World-War detergent factory, which had closed down in 2006 to relocate, had since been purchased by a Berlin-based developer. With the assistance of a Belgian architect, the old factory was being converted into lofts, for both housing and office space. Some of them were already inhabited.

Fox parked the M3 adjacently, across the street from the address he'd been given, which was a three-story low-rise building with underground parking.

He grabbed the bag and got out of the car. "Going in solo, guys."

"Gotcha," Parris replied through his earpiece. She would've been nearby, while Dewan would be in an Internet café, a safer distance away.

Fox crossed the street to the building, whose entrance from the sidewalk led down a small stairway onto a concrete path to the door. On either side were concrete borders that were a little over three feet high, as well as some grass and a few bushes. Beyond the door was a staircase that was visible from outside via a glass enclosure.

He removed the earpiece and tucked it in the corner behind the concrete border, within the bushes below the glass enclosure. He then turned to the intercom and pressed the top button.

"Wer ist es?"

He remembered his code name—Thor's Hammer—and replied. *"Es ist der Hammer des Thor."*

There was a buzz, and Fox pulled open the door, then entered. He walked up the staircase to the third floor and opened the metal door before entering. The room had nothing but a set of cylindrical concrete support beams. It was slightly illuminated, not too bright, but just enough for Fox to see two men in suits about twenty to thirty yards ahead, standing beside a foldout table with an open laptop. The larger of the two men stepped ahead of the other, a shorter, bald man who was no taller than five feet four. Even with his powerful gait and broad shoulders to match, Fox still wasn't impressed. These were the types that were hired more for their menacing looks than their abilities to actually physically fend off an aggressor. Unlike Alghafari's men, this one was casually dressed.

The guard gestured with one hand as he blocked Fox's path. *"Hände über dem Kopf."*

Fox sighed and obliged, putting down the bag and raising his hands above his head as he was told. The guard patted him down.

"You're early," his boss said in German-accented English.

"Is that a problem?" Fox asked. "Because if you're not happy, I can drive around the block a few times and come back in eight minutes."

"No, no, no. That's fine," he answered as his guard checked Fox's ears, then removed his Glock and his cell phone, taking out the battery and the SIM card, and placing them on the table next to the laptop. He then grabbed the bag off the floor and handed it to his boss. The laptop had already been placed at an angle so that Fox couldn't see what was on the screen.

The buyer sat down in front of the laptop, removed the hard drive from the bag, connected it with a flat set of cables, and then began typing on the keyboard, making sure that Fox couldn't see the password he typed in order to access the contents on the drive. No surprise there. He'd even taken the precaution that there weren't any windows behind him in the event someone was watching from outside.

Fox watched the man as he studied the contents of the drive. These guys were usually the types that never took care of themselves physically—relying more on their own personal wealth to attract members of the opposite sex, and paying goons to protect them when they went out. Fox questioned the man's taste, though, surprised that he hadn't had his suit tailor-made. His stomach protruded so far over his belt that the buckle wasn't even visible, plus, the jacket was so tight that it couldn't even be buttoned. Fox guessed his priorities weren't with fashion.

It took close to fifteen boring minutes of waiting before the fat man nodded his approval. *"Exzellent."*

The buyer looked at Fox, taking out his cell phone and calling someone, telling them that everything checked out. He then pressed a button, dropped the phone back inside his blazer, and stood while closing his laptop. "Your employer should receive his payment shortly."

The man disconnected the hard drive and put it back into his bag when Fox raised a palm. "Hold on. No one leaves until I get confirmation that my employer was paid." He then stared at the bodyguard, narrowing his eyes. "No one. And I'm going to need my phone and my gun."

The fat man shrugged his shoulders. "Of course." He nodded to his bodyguard, who handed Fox his gun.

He holstered it, and was then given the parts of his phone—which he put back together himself. Fox turned on the phone, entered the password, and waited, keeping his eyes on the guard, who eyed him back. The testosterone building between the two of them was obvious, but Fox knew that the man wouldn't dare fight him if it came to that.

The fat man sat back down during the wait, checking his watch once and sighing. A few minutes passed, and Fox felt his phone vibrate. It was an IM from Alghafari, confirming that he received the payment. The phone buzzed again a few seconds later, this time from the bank confirming the deposit.

The fat man gave Fox an open gesture. "Are you satisfied?"

Fox nodded and offered a two-finger salute. *"Auf Wiedersehen."* He then left.

*** *** ***

The Air Iberia flight touched down at Málaga-Costa del Sol Airport slightly behind schedule due to a departure delay. Even though Alghafari's contacts in Spanish Intelligence had advised him to use another private jet, since his was under repairs, he had brushed them off as being overly paranoid. He wasn't going to spend his life living in a constant security bubble. Besides, if someone wanted to get to him at the airport or on this plane, they'd have to bomb one or the other, or both, in order to get to him—something that was highly unlikely. It wasn't as though he was flying to China or to South America. He was only going to be in the air for three hours, and once he touched down in his adopted Spain, Alghafari would be in his stronghold.

There wasn't much conversation between him and his bodyguards during the forty-minute drive from Málaga, but his iPhone buzzed just as he was twelve minutes from home. It was an instant message indicating that he'd just been paid for Conlon's delivery.

Alghafari laughed a raspy smoker's laugh as he turned to the guards. "Conlon delivered. Am I great at picking them or what?" He opened the app for his offshore bank, transferred Conlon's share to his account, closed the app, then texted him the message: *Will have another job for you soon. Enjoy your evening.*

The Benz drove past the front gate and onto the uphill driveway that led to the white marble mansion at the top. Schwarzwald Industries was a new client, and hopefully they'd require his services again in the near future.

Alghafari's stomach growled, loud enough that he was certain the driver heard it up front. He'd held off from eating the airline food and settled for a scotch before taking a nap on the flight. He got out now, leaving the guards behind, as his driver would take them away since they were both off duty.

He walked inside, past the curving marble staircase, and headed straight for the kitchen. A juicy filet mignon sounded about right, or he could warm over the shish kebabs he'd made yesterday. Then again, he could just keep it simple and prepare a good old-fashioned American-style cheeseburger. Alghafari couldn't get over the fact that the nation he'd love to see wiped off the earth—next to Israel—could be home to such great food. High in calories and fat, but mouth-watering nonetheless.

"Joumana," Alghafari called. His wife usually greeted him unless she was in the home movie theater.

He opened the fridge door and reached inside the freezer to grab some hamburger meat that he had prepared before freezing a few days before. That's when he heard the loud cries. Alghafari stepped back from the fridge, looking in the direction where the sound came.

"Joumana? Is that you?"

The cries didn't cease. His heart raced and his face heated, making him drop the meat onto the counter and run to the foyer, not even bothering to close the fridge door. The first person he saw was a man in a black suit, standing in front of the entrance. Alghafari studied the man's face, he wasn't one of his guards. He turned to the sounds of movement behind him and saw another stranger who was dressed the same way. This one blocked his path to the kitchen. That's when he heard his wife's sniffling coming from the top of the staircase.

Alghafari looked up and saw a black man with very short dreadlocks, dressed in a dark suit and a silver tie. The man towered over his wife, squeezing her arm as they walked down the marble steps. What made Alghafari gasp was when Joumana held her head at an angle, her face was discolored with hues of red and purple.

His jaw dropped. He spent hundreds of thousands of euros per year on security. The grounds were patrolled by three mastiffs, along with armed guards. These men shouldn't have been able to walk in there, let alone get past the front gate.

"Hello, Monzer." The man's accent was unmistakably British. "How was Amsterdam?"

He knew where I was? How?

"How dare you? Breaking into my house and hurting my wife." Alghafari started beating his chest with his finger. "Don't you know who I am?"

The man with the small dreads didn't answer him as he continued to descend with Joumana. He showed a half-smile as he maintained eye contact with Alghafari, totally unfazed by his tone.

"I don't know who you are, or what you want," Alghafari started calmly before he blew up, "but no one lays a hand on my wife."

"My, my, my. The seemingly untouchable Monzer Alghafari, rendered impotent," the Brit said as he let go of Joumana. She sobbed as she ran into her husband's arms. "Just in case you were wondering, I didn't rape your wife. As you can see, she can still walk."

Alghafari held his wife's head in his chest as he quieted her down, then balled up a fist and gritted his teeth.

The Brit appeared to have noticed Alghafari's action and pointed to his hand. "Don't bother."

After several seconds of hard staring and flaring nostrils, Alghafari unclenched his fist.

"Oh, about your staff," said the man as he briefly looked over his shoulder, "those who were here have taken an early retirement. I take it you haven't ventured into the back yard yet."

Alghafari gasped. "You, you murdered them—"

"Shhhh."

He didn't know what it was, but that shush made his nerves go numb.

The Brit lifted the chair that was next to the entry table and carried it over, then brought it down hard on the tiles, the noise echoing throughout the room. "Let's play a game. The rules are simple," he said. "I'll ask you a series of questions and you'll answer them, truthfully. There won't be any questions from you, only answers. Do I make myself clear?"

Alghafari glanced at the other men before looking back at the Brit.

"I'll take that as a yes," he replied as one of his henchmen came over and pulled Joumana away from Alghafari. She screamed, trying to cling onto her husband, but it was useless.

"Don't hurt her," begged Alghafari, turning to the smiling Brit.

"She'll be fine for now," he said. "In the meantime, let's play."

Chapter 10

Nördlich Henkelstraße, 40589, Düsseldorf, Germany. 10:27 PM, Sunday.

That was an easy three million, deducted from the twenty million euros Alghafari most likely collected. But alas, it wasn't his to keep.

Fox went outside and grabbed his earpiece from where he'd left it, fitting it back into his ear on his way to his car. He tapped it once to turn it on.

"How did it go?" asked Parris.

"Boring," Fox answered.

"It can't be worse than what we've been doing," said Dewan.

"You want to trade places?" asked Fox. "Oh right, you're not field trained."

"Sure we can," answered Dewan. Then, imitating Fox, "Oh right, your abilities on a computer are limited to jacking off to porn."

"Where's the buyer now?" Parris interrupted, obviously attempting to diffuse any bickering between Fox and Dewan before it escalated.

"He hasn't left the building yet, but he should be right behind me." Fox looked back, but saw no one on the staircase. Then, laughter on the sidewalk across the street caught his attention. Fox looked toward the chuckles, seeing a young couple across the street, walking toward his car. The man appeared to be heavily inebriated as he clung to his girlfriend for support, singing something in German. She was no better, as she also looked to be a bit plastered, but not as much as he.

"You're quiet," said Parris. "What's going on?"

There was a car close to him on the opposite side of the road, several yards in front of his. Fox walked toward it, but when he got to the middle of the street he dropped down to one knee as though to tie his shoe.

"I'll get back to you," Fox answered as he lowered his head, still staring at the young couple. If this was a trap, then he'd still be able to reach his Glock.

The man suddenly grabbed the woman and sloppily started kissing her, forcing her back against the wall of the building beside them. She yielded a bit too easily, wrapping her arms and a leg around him.

Really? Those two were obviously looking to time their attack to coincide with him being on the sidewalk.

Fox stood and continued walking to his car, reaching into his outer jacket pocket.

"Hey, *kumpel.*" Fox was now less than three feet away from them. *"Sie werden diese benötigen."*

The guy came up for air to see what Fox had said he was going to need. Fox was holding out a condom wrapper—one he had from the night before. The gold-colored wrapper shone under the nearby streetlamp, which also helped Fox to see their faces.

The man and woman appeared to be surprised at Fox's gesture. The guy looked back at the woman briefly before turning back with a smile.

"Danke."

There was a slight hesitation before he reached out to take the condom, but Fox surprised him by holding on to it. When the guy realized that Fox wasn't letting it go, there was another eye-to-eye contact. The look Fox saw wasn't surprise, but various mixed emotions. In addition to seeing apprehension, his face flushed as though he was thinking, *Oh shit, he knows.* Screw the woman, the *boyfriend* just outed them both.

Fox released the condom, and with the same hand, he grabbed

the man's wrist. He then twisted it in front of his chest while sidestepping him in such a rush, that when Fox swung his opposite arm around, grabbing the boyfriend by the chin, the man was already off balance and on his way down, arm still extended, crashing onto the sidewalk. Within the few split seconds that had passed, Fox locked the boyfriend's arm in such a way so that he couldn't move.

He noticed the girlfriend reaching for something, so he threw a hundred and sixty pounds of pressure into a forward kick to her stomach—crushing her against the wall of the building behind her. The impact was so powerful that he'd nearly deflected himself. There was no telling how badly he'd hurt her. A blow such as that one, combined with the impact against the wall, would've surely left her bleeding internally.

Fox briefly watched as the girlfriend fell forward onto the sidewalk. His focus switched back to the man, who he still had his arm locked around, as he growled under the pain Fox put him through. He shifted his bodyweight and forced the man to turn slightly onto his side, exposing his lower back where Fox caught a glimpse of an object tucked away in the seat of his jeans.

Fox snatched the gun—a P226 Sig Sauer—then released him so that he'd fall onto his back. He then placed the barrel over his left eye, demanding to know who'd sent him. *"Wer hat dich geschickt?"*

The man didn't answer.

"Sag mir, wer Sie geschickt und Sie erhalten mit nur einem gebrochenen arm entfernt." Now Fox had promised that if the man told him who'd sent him, he would at least get to walk, with only a broken arm.

Still no answer, so Fox fired one round that burst his eyeball.

Then he turned to the woman, who was trying to stand, and kicked her in the chest to put her onto her back. She had both hands raised as she stared at him, fright in her eyes.

"Können Sie es besser?" He asked if she could do better, but the answer appeared to be no. Fox put a round right in the center of her forehead, which slammed the back of her head into the blood-stained concrete.

Fox's radar went off again, making him look toward the loft's staircase. He was just in time to see the fat man and his bodyguard staring at him through the glass wall of the second-floor landing. The gunshots must've caught their attention. The metal door behind them swung outward, striking the bodyguard and knocking him forward, into the fat man. Out from the darkness, a person of average height and build, dressed in black and wearing a ski mask, lunged at the bodyguard with a handheld black object, pressing it into his neck. The guard convulsed for a few seconds before falling over onto the fat man, causing them both to tumble down the stairs with their attacker close behind.

"The target's been jumped. Hostile going for the package," yelled Fox as he ran back across the street to the building's front door, which would've still been locked from the outside. When he looked beyond the glass on the side, he watched as the assailant ran by on their way to the basement.

"Is there another way out of the garage?" asked Fox.

"There's a second exit at the back," answered Dewan. "It leads to a pathway between two other buildings onto the adjacent street."

"That's where the guy's heading," said Fox.

"I'll cut him off," answered Parris.

His first instinct was to shoot off the lock, but that would be useless, considering these doors were built to withstand such forms of abuse. If anything, he'd end up catching a ricocheting bullet.

Fox took out a lock pick from his jacket pocket—one which could open over 95% of the world's common locks, one which he always kept on him. He unlocked the door and yanked it open, pointing his sidearm down the stairs. Seeing that it was clear, he proceeded.

Once at the bottom Fox came to another door, which he pushed open slowly. The assailant had used what appeared to be a Taser on the guard, meaning that there was less of a chance that he carried anything else. Fox pushed the door open all the way and quietly proceeded with the gun aimed low.

The fat man had chosen this location, at this time of the evening, not for the stylish decor, but obviously because they expected it to be secure. Which would explain why there was only one car in the six-spot lot—obviously his. There was a loud click of a closing door that caught Fox's attention. He saw it and sprinted. Just as he was about to charge through the door, he looked over his shoulder to the sound of two gunshots, which appeared to have come from the staircase. That's when he heard another gunshot through his earpiece.

"Parris." A few moments went by and there wasn't a response. "Parris, answer me." Still nothing.

***

On another street, behind the building Fox was in, Parris had parked near the walkway that led up to it from the back. She got out and had headed down the path with her EMP in hand, ready to intercept the thief. She had already been party to one blown mission with Timothy Weyland. She wasn't going to have a second one happen on her watch. Mishaps such as this occurred every once in a while, which was why a backup strategy was always in the cards. Parris *was* that backup.

Someone was fast approaching from around the corner, so she stepped to the side, behind the wall of another building, right at the corner where the walkway curved. Timing the speed of the footsteps, she jumped out into the path with her gun drawn— surprising the thief just as he rounded the corner.

"That's far enough," she yelled.

The assailant nearly tripped after stopping so suddenly, both of his hands raised, one holding the hard drive.

She hoped that she wouldn't have to use her sidearm. From his physique, she could tell that it was a man, and whoever this guy was, he'd be an important asset. Lord knew how he found out about this meeting, but if he was working alone, then he'd know what was on the hard drive, and from where it was stolen. Maybe he'd be able to divulge why Alghafari was interested in its contents. Better yet, she might find out if there was a connection to Umari.

Parris aimed for his pelvis. "Toss the drive to the grass and take five steps back."

She saw the look in his eyes when she took aim. Like any man having a gun pointed below the belt, he gave her the universal don't-shoot-me-there reaction. The thief nodded twice in surrender as he gently tossed the drive to the grass beside the path.

Maintaining eye contact with him, while keeping the EMP pointed at his pelvis, she knelt down to where he threw it. With her free hand she felt around the grass until she touched metal. She grabbed the drive and then stood.

That's when Parris heard the click of bullet being chambered behind her.

"Drop the gun." It was a woman's voice.

Parris sighed. *Stupid, why didn't I think that he'd have backup?*

"The grass will do," the woman continued.

Parris saw no other alternative and did as she was told.

"Good. Now give him back the hard drive."

Parris looked the man in the eyes. His grin annoyed her as he reached over to take the hard drive from her.

Bad move.

The moment that his fingers touched it, Parris snatched his wrist with the opposite arm and pulled him forward—putting him off balance. She then spun around behind him, keeping his arm locked. The movement was swift, making it impossible for the woman to take a clear shot. Parris would now use the man as a shield while she threatened to break his arm if it came to that. It was a huge mistake for the woman to make her hand the drive to him rather than make Parris toss it to the ground along with her weapon. Someone with a proper training wouldn't have made that error. This meant that these two may just be ordinary crooks. The lack of light made it difficult for Parris to see the woman's features. All she saw was someone who was about five feet six and weighed no more than a hundred and twenty pounds, with her hair possibly tied into a ponytail.

Two gunshots in the distance caught all three of them off guard, but Parris heard them even louder because of her earpiece—which wasn't a good thing for her at the moment. She felt the man push back against her, causing her to accidentally drop the hard drive.

The man hollered, maybe because he'd jerked while Parris had his arm locked, causing him pain.

"Parris," came Fox's voice.

Not now, Parris thought as she rushed to grab the hard drive, but the woman fired a bullet that struck the ground near the tips of her shoes.

"Parris, answer me."

Parris didn't answer as she kept both eyes on the woman in front of her.

"Step away and hold your hands up high," the woman said.

Parris did as she was told as the man grabbed the hard drive and tossed it to the woman, who caught it with her free hand. He then took the EMP and ran with it, while the woman walked backward slowly, keeping Parris at bay with her sidearm. After she put enough distance between them she turned around and ran.

"Wherever you are, Parris, start the car. Hostiles in pursuit," yelled Fox.

Just then, Parris heard a bullet ricochet off a lamp post a few yards away. She turned to see Fox running toward her. He then stopped, spun around, and dropped to one knee, firing off four more rounds before he got up to run.

"Come on," Parris yelled as she sprinted away. She glimpsed over her shoulder to see that Fox wasn't too far behind. She got to the end of the pathway just as a car zoomed by. She got to the street just in time to see a set of taillights speeding away before the car vanished around the corner at the next block. She couldn't get a make of the vehicle or the license plate, as it had shot by too fast.

Parris ran to her car, taking out the automatic starter on her keychain and pressing the button as she neared it. She got into the driver's seat just as Fox slid across the hood to the other side and hopped in. Within seconds Parris floored the accelerator. They didn't get far before three shots were fired, and the rear window exploded into shards of flying glass, the bullet lodging itself into the side, right next to where Fox's seatbelt was attached.

"I thought these windows were bulletproof," yelled Fox.

"You wish," screamed Parris as she swerved the car around the corner.

"Do you have the hard drive?"

"Lost it."

"What?"

"Dammit. I said I lost it!"

"How the hell did you lose the drive? I chased the guy right to you."

"It's kind of hard holding onto something when you have a gun pointed at you from one side and people are shooting at you from the other."

Fox punched the dashboard. "Shit, man! Did you at least get a look at him?"

"There were two—one was a woman—and their faces were hidden," she answered as she ran a red light.

"Great. It's all gone to hell."

"Actually, guys," came Dewan's voice through their earpieces. "The entire conversation between Parris and our mystery woman was recorded. I'm running a voice analysis right now. We may get something. I'm fine, thanks, by the way."

Parris ignored the last sarcastic remark he made. She knew that at the first sign the operation was in jeopardy, Dewan would've made his way over to the train station and caught the next ride out. Other than that, he gave her some hope that not all was lost. She didn't know how Fox felt at the moment, but he still appeared to be pissed off.

"What happened back there?" asked Parris calmly.

"Someone took out the buyer and his bodyguard. I chased him into the garage when I heard two shots behind me. I'm going to guess the guys who were chasing me are the ones that shot them."

"Did you get a look at them?"

Fox shook his head. "Just the two I took out on the street."

"It would be good if we knew who they were working for."

"Maybe someone the buyer outbid for the hard drive," said Fox.

"Now that the three of you are safely away," came the voice of their superior, General Paul Downing, through their earpieces. "Dewan, get on the next flight home. As for both of you, Parris and Fox, get over to The Hague. I'll be waiting for you at *precisely* eight hundred hours."

Whenever the general accentuated the word precisely, he really meant it. He was one to kick up a fuss if the person he waited on was a minute late.

"Sir," said Fox, "I'd like to get in touch with Alghafari. My cover with him hasn't been blown yet."

"You'll get your ass over here, pronto," the general spat. "Alghafari's dead."

Chapter 11

Düsseldorf, Germany. 11:20 PM, Sunday.

Parris and Fox drove, spending a short while zipping from one end of the neighborhood to the next until they were certain that they weren't being followed. They then ditched the Benz and stole a Volkswagen Passat, switching the license plates with a spare that Parris had in the trunk of the Benz. Its broken rear window would've surely attracted unwanted attention from a fellow motorist, or even worse, a highway patrol officer, who would've been on the lookout. It could also be assumed that whoever killed the buyer and his bodyguard were most likely monitoring the police radio frequencies. They were probably members of the same group who took out Alghafari, who'd been found with his wife, tied to a rock at the bottom of one of their swimming pools. Their three daughters had been contacted by the authorities and were expected to leave school under their protection.

As usual, Parris took the longer, indirect route, getting on and off the major highways at some of the towns and taking smaller, less-traveled roads before getting back onto a major highway. So far they weren't being tailed.

Parris heard the seat beside hers sliding back before hearing it recline. She glanced at Fox and rolled her eyes before changing lanes to overtake a semi. "Getting comfy?"

"Yeah."

Parris didn't say anything else but turned on the right-hand indicator as she switched lanes to get in front of the truck.

"What's the matter?" asked Fox.

"Nothing."

"Then why'd you roll your eyes?"

"I didn't roll them."

"Yes you did."

"No I didn't."

"Sure you did. I saw you roll them right after I laid down and before you overtook the semi."

Parris sucked her teeth and rolled her eyes. Why'd he have to choose this moment to get on her nerves?

Fox pointed at her. "There, you see? You did it again."

"So what if I did?"

"For starters," Fox scratched above his left eyebrow, "something's clearly bothering you."

"I'm...I'm fine."

Fox shrugged his shoulders. "Okay, if you say so."

Parris shook her head. "Now *you* don't sound convinced."

"I'm not."

"What is it with you?"

"What is it with *you*?"

"Don't try to flip this back on me."

Fox sat up, raising the back of the seat at the same time. "Pull over, it's time for me to drive."

Parris shot him a glance. "What?"

"You heard me." He undid his seatbelt. "Pull over."

"Why?"

"Because you're pissed. Or should I say, vexed, as they do in Barbados," Fox answered. "This is a DWM-related accident waiting to happen."

"A DWM?"

"Yeah, a DWM—Driving While Mad. My dad always used that term to describe my mom whenever she got behind the wheel when he felt that she shouldn't be."

Parris gently pressed down on the accelerator. "Sure. Fine. Whatever."

"I'm serious." Fox tapped Parris's elbow. "Let me take the wheel."

She pulled her arm away from him. "Go to sleep. I got this."

"Fine, then let's talk."

"About what?"

"About what happened tonight."

Parris eyed a set of taillights up ahead. She then shrugged her shoulders and sighed. "Then talk."

"Okay." Fox put his seatbelt back on. He watched as Parris flew by two cars without turning on the indicator lights while she changed lanes. She didn't even bother to switch back into the right-hand lane, but continued accelerating in the fast lane.

"I'm waiting," said Parris.

"Right," said Fox shaking his head as if he'd been lost in thought. "How are we going to explain this screw-up to Downing? Technically this is your second."

"*My* second?" Parris shot back. "This was *your* op. I was merely assisting you."

"Who lost the hard drive?"

"Oh, for the love of God."

"Thank you."

"So this is what it's about?" said Parris. "You want to play the blame game?"

"I'm not trying to blame you for anything."

"Really? I recall a few moments after the rear window was shot out, you blamed me for losing the hard drive."

"No I didn't."

"You're denying it."

"I never blamed you for anything."

"Actually," came Dewan's voice through their earpieces. "Nita's right, Ridley. You *did* blame her. I can play back the recording if you want."

"What the fuck?" yelled Fox. "How long have you been eavesdropping?"

Parris looked at Fox briefly and gave him an I-told-you-so smile.

"For the whole ride," Dewan answered. "You don't think I'm

bored sitting here waiting for the next train. Besides, a *brotha* can use some entertainment."

Parris watched Fox tap his earpiece to turn it off. She decided to keep hers on. They were silent for the next two miles as Parris slowed down from one hundred and twelve miles per hour to seventy-seven.

Parris sighed as she decided to break the ice. "So *how* are we going to explain this latest screw-up to Downing?"

"I don't know," said Fox. "I'm open to suggestions."

"Our intel wasn't accurate, for starters," she said.

Fox nodded once. "I believe that's something we can both agree on."

"Can we agree that there were two parties that were after the hard drive?" asked Parris. "There were thieves and there were some contract killers. And the latter party most likely didn't anticipate the thieves intercepting the hard drive."

"That sounds right so far," Fox answered. "Meaning that whatever was on that hard drive must be very valuable."

"Someone's planning to get rich from selling whatever's on it," said Parris.

Fox shook his head. "When I said *valuable*, I didn't mean it in that sense. Here's the thing about Alghafari, he's not motivated by money. He's motivated by power and vengeance. He hates America because our country worked with his brother but rejected him. That's why he's aided terrorist groups in any capacity that he could, including Umari's. Trust me, had he been offered a chance, he would've contributed to causing nine-eleven."

"And you're absolutely sure that he didn't divulge any clues to what may have been on the hard drive?" asked Parris.

Fox shook his head. "I mean, he'd been getting sloppy lately. He just couldn't be sloppy enough for our benefit."

Parris saw Fox grab her tablet from the back seat. She took a quick peek at what he was doing. He would've been using his own, except he would've left it behind in the BMW. Dewan would've sent a self-destruct command to it—frying the motherboard. "What are you looking up?"

Fox tapped away at the screen. "Using the face-recognition

app to find out who the buyer is." The app wasn't complicated. All Fox had to do was enter as many physical characteristics on the buyer as he could remember—from eye color to cranial shape, size of nose and lips, and the color of his skin. When he was done, he'd hit ENTER on the virtual keypad and wait as the program flipped through hundreds of photographs from the CIA's database.

About three minutes later, she heard Fox sigh. "And?" Parris asked.

Fox held the tablet at an angle for her to see. "Our buyer. His name's Helmut Brunner. He is, or I should say, *was* an executive for a German bio-agricultural firm."

"You sound disappointed," said Parris.

He dropped the tablet on his lap. "Are we supposed to believe that this is nothing else but a case of corporate espionage?"

Parris took the exit from the A-73 and drove around the loop onto the A-67, where she went westbound toward Antwerp. "It's not too farfetched. I mean, corporate espionage occurs all the time."

Fox turned to her. "Or maybe this guy, Helmut Brunner, was working for someone else. Someone with terrorist connections."

"I'm not saying that you're wrong," she said, "but perhaps Alghafari was simply trying to expand his client base. After all, he *has* lost a few over the years. So it's normal that he'd try to recuperate. Besides, corporations influence governments."

"That's assuming that whatever was on the hard drive, Alghafari stole it from one of Brunner's competitors. But how often do corporations hire hitmen to protect their secrets? And for them to take out Alghafari, that was a pretty bold move. Someone would have to have some pretty powerful connections to even get close to him. Look how long it took us to do that?"

"We weren't looking to assassinate him," said Parris.

Fox took another look at Brunner. "You've got a point."

Parris checked her rearview mirror to see if she spotted any familiar vehicles from the past twenty miles. So far they were in the clear. "Then again, whoever killed Alghafari was someone he already knew."

"That would be my guess."

"Now, what about the thieves?" She glanced at the tablet in Fox's hands. "Any news on them yet?"

Fox checked his instant messages. "Nothing yet." He rested his elbow against the window. "You said they were a man and woman team?"

"I'm positive."

"Jesus," sighed Fox. "How could our intel not have picked up on them?"

"They were good enough to slip under the radar of Alghafari and Brunner's killers. Probably some underground group."

"Then we need to contact someone who works in the underworld in order to find them."

"Yeah, like who?" asked Parris as she overtook another car.

"I have someone in mind."

Parris pondered on who it might be as she passed another car before moving back over into the right-hand lane. When the thought came to her, she shot Fox a look. "Not him."

"If he doesn't know, then he ought to know someone who does."

She looked back to the road. "We need to be in The Hague in a few hours. You can't just go gallivanting off like that."

"Then cover for me. Just tell Downing that I'm following up on a lead."

Parris sucked her teeth as she shook her head.

"Come on. Saint Petersburg's less than three hours away."

"I don't care about how far you have to go. You're going to walk up to Maksim Antanov, of the Saint Petersburg Mafia, and expect him to help you?"

"You betcha!" Fox answered doing his best Jim Carrey impersonation. "Besides, it's worth a shot. He owes me one, considering that I didn't kill him when I could've."

"He's not stupid." Parris shook her head. "He knows that you won't kill him because he's an asset. Besides, what makes you think he's going to help you? His father passed away, so it's safe to say that your leverage against him has expired."

Parris referred to the fact that Antanov junior was a cross-dresser. Something that would've been a huge embarrassment had the knowledge been made public.

"I've got new leverage."

"Oh yeah, what kind?"

"The kind that could send his ass to jail for a long time unless I help him."

"Oh really?"

Fox looked at Parris. "What would you rather do? The longer we wait, the less chance we have at recovering the hard drive's contents. Or would you prefer that Alghafari's killers beat us to it?"

Parris didn't answer him. She knew that he was right, and that it may be their one chance at recovery. Lord knew when Weyland would start talking again. And even if he did, there wasn't a guarantee that he'd be able to give up any more information about Umari. That's unless his employers were to crack under the pressure.

She took the exit for the city center of Eindhoven. "The general's going to tear me another one for this."

"You ought to be used to it by now," said Fox. "Besides, he's torn me several and I'm still walking." He then held up her tablet. "I'm going to have to borrow this."

"You mean *permanently* borrow."

Fox smiled. "Yeah, pretty much."

Chapter 12

American Embassy, The Hague, The Netherlands. Monday morning.

Doctor Parris felt a knot in her stomach, which kept getting tighter the closer she got to the fortified building. She remembered getting the same queasy feeling on the mornings before she'd have a track meet. Even though she was an experienced sprinter, who was favored to win most of the time, it was a nervous feeling she could never shake. Leave it to Fox to abandon her so that she could face the music on her own. Boy would she give him shit if he didn't locate the hard drive—and fast.

It still frustrated her that Weyland's cover had been blown. Not that these things couldn't happen, but she'd been so certain that everything was perfect. That was her op—*hers*. And the intel he was giving them was the most useful they'd had in years.

Despite what Weyland had put her through—with his disappearing and reappearing act—Parris could relate. The CIA often used the Non-Official Cover, or NOC, program, where individuals would gain access to places of interest, either as students or professionals. They would then pass on secrets to the agency. Parris had worked under NOC in the past. A previous mission had her working at a Tokyo-based pharmaceutical company. The only thing about NOC was that if ever you were caught, the CIA would leave you out in the cold. The current mission, however, required someone with network security expertise. The Agency could've slipped in one of their own. Instead, they chose to recruit an employee of Bismarck Securities. Parris eventually became his handler.

Never mind that the CIA was breaking the law by spying on Americans. This was about getting the bigger fish. Besides, they weren't trying to access the phone numbers or emails of random citizens. They were spying on individuals they had every reason to believe were traitors to their own country. However, in this instance, they collaborated with the FBI, Homeland Security, and the NSA in a special joint task force. Everyone working for Bismarck Securities, as well as their clients, were put on a watch list. All of their daily activities and habits were compiled, everything ranging from whom they went to lunch with, right down to their favorite toothpaste. A team of analysts would then eliminate individuals who were irrelevant. Truth be known, the CIA could, and usually would, investigate anyone they damn well felt like investigating. These agencies were all beasts who were competing for funding in an intelligence community that spanned around thirteen institutions at present. Sometimes, they all played well together by sharing info, but at other times, it was every man for himself—sadly, at the country's detriment. Parris already knew this, but it wasn't her call to make as to what was shared with whom, and when.

She mentally pushed any thoughts of Weyland or Bismarck Securities out of her mind when she walked into the embassy and arrived at the security checkpoint. She knew the drill. She removed her purse, belt, and stacked heels. Parris then placed them on the conveyer belt before walking through the metal detector. Once she was cleared, she retrieved her belongings.

The reception area outside of the ambassador's office was quaint, with the president's picture on one side and the vice president's on the other. Below was a dark blue rug with a bit of red and white thrown in, bordered with stars. Sitting behind the desk was the ambassador's secretary.

"Good morning," the secretary said with a smile. "You must be Doctor Parris."

Parris nodded as she returned the smile. "That's correct."

The secretary picked up the phone, said a few words, and then hung up. "You can go in."

She wouldn't have minded waiting a few more minutes. Parris didn't even get a chance to let herself really sink into the comfort of the couch, which she could've easily dozed off in. She got up, walked past the secretary, and entered the office. If there was a reason for her to have a knot in her stomach before arriving, it just got tighter at the sight of who was present. Her superior, General Paul Downing, and Ambassador William Brown were there as expected, however, when she saw that DCI Sue Merrick was sitting in the ambassador's chair, behind his desk, her chest also tightened.

Merrick was the Arctic Vortex in a dress. A smile was foreign to her, but even when she did, it was like a glass of dry wine with burnt toast—the two just didn't mix. She cut her teeth in the intelligence community when she was on the Senate Select Committee for Intelligence. Seeing her sitting in the ambassador's chair didn't surprise Parris. Merrick was always the *I-don't-give-a-fuck-I'm-in-charge* type. There were even rumors floating around the intelligence community—as well as Capitol Hill—that Merrick would be running for the presidency next year. Her capturing Umari would certainly boost her chances at winning over voters.

Merrick only wished that she could've taken credit for stopping the bioweapons attack—otherwise known as *Pandora's Succession* within the intelligence community—three years before. The impending attack, had it been successful, would've surely wiped out most, if not all, human life on the planet. All with the exception of the doomsday cult that had perpetrated the attack. Of course, those events were, and could never be, made public. And even though Parris and Fox were responsible for stopping Pandora's Succession, Merrick still treated both of them like dirt. As far back as she could remember, she never referred to Nita as *Doctor* Parris. At least Downing treated her with respect. After all, he was the one who'd recruited her. Dewan Douglas also owed a lot to her and Fox, considering that they rescued him from the same doomsday cult responsible for the attack.

"Hello, Nita," said Merrick.

Parris swallowed. "Director Merrick. I didn't expect—"

Merrick raised a hand. "That's your problem, Nita. You never expect anything fast enough. Which explains why you and Ridley fucked up last night." With the same hand, Merrick aggressively pointed to the chair facing her. "Sit down."

Parris took the seat while Downing and the ambassador watched from an adjacent couch. She felt as though she was in detention, or facing some disciplinary committee. But she couldn't allow herself to be intimidated, even if this was Merrick's idea of an ambush. She crossed her legs and kept a poker face.

"Jesus fucking Christ!" Merrick threw a file folder on the desk. "Two opportunities to locate Umari and you and Ridley blow it. By the way, where is he?"

"We got separated," Parris answered.

"Bullshit." Merrick narrowed her eyes. "Both of you escaped in the same vehicle."

"We did," said Parris calmly, "but he thought we'd have a better chance at losing whoever followed us by splitting up."

Merrick rolled her eyes to the ceiling. "Oh, I see. Next thing you're going to tell me is that you lost contact with him, right?"

"I never said that."

Merrick wagged a finger. "Don't be sassy with me."

Although it would be so easy for her to roll her eyes, and the temptation was high to tell this woman to *fuck off*, she'd never be able to get away with it. She continued to play it cool. "Is there a reason why we were called here?"

"What the hell do you think? Of course there is. And as much as I feel that neither of you have an excuse for your epic screw-ups, I thought that I'd grant you a chance to explain yourselves and preserve any dignity that you still have." Merrick leaned back in her leather seat, crossing her legs. "So let's have it. I'll hear Ridley's side of the story soon enough."

Parris, in her calmest manner, described everything that happened from the time she met Fox with Dewan in Duiven, up until the point that she was jumped by the thief, before being shot at.

"And you both suddenly decided to split up," said Merrick.

"That's what I said."

Downing cleared his throat. "I believe that Fox, if he's not on his way here, must be pursuing a lead from a different angle. Even though we lost Alghafari, Fox's cover as Conlon is still pretty much intact."

"And he couldn't check in to let us know this?" asked Merrick. "We don't even know where the hell he is."

"With all due respect, Director," said Parris. "Fox and I believe that whoever assassinated Alghafari and Brunner, they're most likely enemies of Umari. Maybe they could lead us to Umari's whereabouts." As ironic as it was, the bull Parris just spewed could actually fly.

Merrick turned to Parris. "Fox wouldn't be trying to locate that hard drive, would he?"

"We never had time to discuss what we were going to do next," Parris answered.

"I should hope he's not looking for it," said Merrick. "Because that's not the priority."

"Then we ought to make it a priority." *What the hell am I saying?* "The more we know about it, the more we'll know about Alghafari's killers—"

"Yes, and they'll lead us to Umari," interrupted Merrick. "Nice theory, but there's no intel indicating that Umari's linked to the hard drive, or even to Brunner. So we're not wasting time pursuing the hard drive."

"Alghafari wouldn't have just hired anyone to deliver the drive," continued Parris. "He wanted the best because he knew of the sensitivity of the drive."

"No shit!" said Merrick. "Alghafari's made dozens of these transactions in the past fifteen months. That's how he makes a living, in case you didn't know."

There she goes again, being condescending.

"None of his transactions lately had anything to do with Umari," spat Merrick. "Snakes like Alghafari thrive on money and power. If the DEA thinks that there's something of value on the hard drive, let them go after it. I want Umari."

Merrick took a deep breath and put a hand to her forehead. She then exhaled as she leaned over the desk, her eyes slanted as though they were probing Parris's mind. "There's something else I'd like to discuss, and this pertains to Ridley."

What does this have to do with the current situation? "I beg your pardon?"

Merrick picked up a pen and began tapping it on the desk surface. "You've been working with Ridley for the past two to three years. What's it been like?"

"There's nothing much to say," said Parris. She had a feeling that Merrick didn't buy it.

"How would you personally rate his performance?"

Why the hell would she be asking this? All field operatives undergo all types of evaluations all the time. Parris looked over at Downing, who nodded. She then looked back at Merrick. "I think the results speak for themselves. And I'd say considering how Fox managed to get in on Alghafari's inner circle says a lot."

"Yes," said Merrick. "He also killed the real David Conlon when he was supposed to help us capture him. But, go on."

Parris closed her eyes and took a deep breath. "If you don't mind me asking, where is this going?"

Merrick stopped tapping the pen, much to Parris's satisfaction, as it was beginning to annoy her. "Ridley lost a loved one a few years back, and the perpetrators of this person's death were operatives working for the group we know as Ares."

Oh Lord. The woman couldn't even bring herself to say that it was Fox's fiancée.

"Throughout the time that you were with him, was there any sign that," Merrick hesitated for a bit as her eyes wandered in a semi-circle, "thoughts of this person appeared to surface?"

"If you're referring to his fiancée," said Parris, "then the answer is no." She was beginning to see what this meeting was about. She didn't know what Merrick's beef was with Fox, but it was obvious that she was after him.

"You don't sound too sure of that."

"Why would you say that?"

"We've run psychological assessments on Ridley for over a

year. The results were rather interesting."

"How so?"

"The assessment revealed that he still suffers from the trauma of having lost his fiancée."

There, she finally acknowledged her as Fox's fiancée.

"Some of his test scores were below what we would expect from a field operative." She then looked at Downing. "I still wonder how it is that he was allowed out in the field in his state."

"Despite the results, Director," said Downing, "had it not been for the unavoidable mishap, Fox still accomplished what he set out to do. And speaking from experience, test results don't always accurately predict performance in the field."

Thank you. For a moment Parris had been starting to wonder whose side he was on.

Merrick appeared to stifle a chuckle as she turned to Downing. "Are you implying that these assessments are a waste of time?"

"That's not what I implied," Downing answered when he was interrupted by the office phone ringing.

Merrick raised a palm, silencing him, as she took it.

Parris watched her as she uttered another curse word under her breath before answering.

"Hello…yes I'll hold for him." She sat back in her chair and crossed her legs. The only person who Merrick would hold for was the president. A few moments went by and she began speaking. She mentioned a few things about making developments, changing her tone with her fake smile on top of it. About half a minute later she hung up, the frown quickly replacing the smile as she shook her head and sighed.

She then stood while looking at Parris. "Leave it to our president to save your ass, Nita. He's called a meeting, so I have to head back to Washington." Merrick sighed as though she'd lost an opportunity at scoring a victory. "We're going to continue this chat another time."

"Director, if I may," said Parris, "I'd like to have the chance at debriefing Weyland when he's ready to speak. I've already built strong a rapport with him, he trusts—"

"Out of the question." Merrick headed for the door without

even looking back. "The FBI's babysitting Weyland in one of their safe-houses. Don't bother trying to contact him. It's out of our hands."

Parris uncrossed her legs. "I thought we were in joint task force."

"We are," said Merrick. "We have people, *qualified* people I should add, who're capable of assisting the FBI in their debriefing of the geek you recruited." She then turned to Downing and the ambassador. "Good day, gentlemen."

"Director," they answered simultaneously.

That's it? She wasn't good enough for the DCI to say good-bye to. This was after being shot at and…oh…what was the point. This woman always played hardball. She had the nerve to openly castigate both her and Fox, who, despite his flaws, was still one of her closest friends and confidants.

Once the door closed, Downing gave a sigh of relief and turned to Parris and Brown. "I thought that damned dragon lady would never leave."

Parris turned to Downing. "Sir, is it true what she said about Fox?"

"I'm afraid so." Downing stood with the help of his cane, then walked over to Parris and leaned against the desk, resting his cane beside him. She couldn't help but be impressed at the fact that the Gulf War injury, which had cost him his leg, didn't slow him down. "You should've seen her before you arrived, barging in here as though she owned the place, slamming the door. She was really pissed off at what happened last night, and I have to say that I don't blame her." He then looked her in the eye. "What the hell went on last night?"

"We failed to anticipate other parties," answered Parris. "They got the jump on us and got away with the hard drive."

"At ease, Doctor Parris. You're not a kid in the principal's office." Downing didn't smile, but she knew him well enough that he was showing his sense of humor. He was obviously reminding her of where she had come from, as the principal's, or rather, the headmaster's office, as it was called in her native Barbados, was a place that she was well-acquainted with.

Downing then turned to the ambassador. "Would you mind giving us a moment?"

"Sure," Brown answered as he got up. "Would you like me to bring you something? Tea? Coffee?"

"Bring Doctor Parris a cup of jasmine tea." Downing then looked at her and winked. "No sugar."

How about that? He remembered.

"Sure thing," the ambassador said before he left.

Downing then leaned slightly forward on his cane. "Tell me the truth. Why isn't Fox here? You and I both know that you didn't split up."

There was no way of hiding anything from Downing. He knew her well enough to know that she and Fox always had each other's backs. "Fox believed that the hard drive's contents may hold some important information with respect to national security. I didn't agree with him at first, but after further consideration, I believe in the possibility."

"So you know where he went?"

"He's hoping to get answers from Antanov."

Downing closed his eyes while he nodded. "I see. Always the maverick."

"Should I assist him?"

Downing shook his head. "No, I think Fox has that covered well enough on his own. I have another assignment for you." He reached inside his blazer and took out a rolled up manila envelope and handed it to her. Obviously he hadn't wanted Merrick to know about it. "As it turns out, things weren't a total loss last night. Dewan was able to make use of what he recorded through your earpiece. He used the voice signature of your woman thief and cross-referenced it with her known contacts."

Parris opened the envelope. "Who is she?"

Downing shook his head. "Her true identity is still a mystery. But we know that she's a professional identity thief with numerous aliases. As for the man she was with last night, we've had better luck."

Finally.

"His name's Bram Kamphuis, thirty-three years old. He

was arrested for hacking into Scotland Yard five years ago. Unfortunately he managed to get off because there wasn't enough evidence to hold him. He lives in Amsterdam, but our intel revealed that he may be hiding out in the city of Nijmegen, which is also in the Netherlands. The address where we believe he's staying is inside the folder."

Downing then leaned on his cane. "I want you to find him and bring him in for questioning. Agents Demeere and Gessner will assist you. If we're lucky, he may help us find out more about Alghafari to help put us back on the path to finding Umari."

Parris looked at the picture and then back at Downing. "Does Merrick have any idea of this?"

"Don't you concern yourself with her," Downing answered. "One thing you learn from being in the army is that results are obtained from being out in the field, not from behind a desk. Merrick's an old-school bureaucrat, and I'll be damned if I'll let her tell me how to run an op."

Parris smiled. "Understood."

Chapter 13

Roman Club, 23 Zagordny Prospekt, St Petersburg, Russia. Monday afternoon.

The afternoon had brought a brisk chill that blew from the Neva River, swaying the signs that hung in front of some of the businesses as Fox walked past them. After his plane had touched down, he replaced his fall jacket from the night before with a warmer three-quarter-length leather he purchased from a boutique. Under it he wore a Gucci suit with black dress shoes—all purchased from the same store. He paid the taxi driver extra to take the most indirect route and then drop him off four blocks away from the Roman Club. From there, he walked the rest of the way. Again, Fox made several turns at each intersection rather than take the direct route. No one appeared to be following him. Several minutes later he stood across the street from the restaurant, where he scanned the entrance and its surroundings surreptitiously.

The restaurant was closed at this hour, which was normal as it opened from eleven-thirty in the morning to two in the afternoon. It would then reopen at four-thirty for dinner, then, around eight o'clock, a live jazz band would perform and patrons could dance until the restaurant closed at ten o'clock at night. On weekends, the restaurant had longer operating hours, serving traditional European and Russian cuisine at fifty to one hundred American dollars a plate. If you were among the majority of people who didn't want to look cheap, you'd throw in an eighty dollar bottle of wine. To the average person, it was five-star dining. To Fox, it was all that and the perfect money-laundering operation.

Previous intel indicated that Maksim Antanov—the son of the late Yuri Antanov, a ruthless mob boss who loved to use his cement trucks for purposes other than their intended function—would be inside. With his father gone, Maksim Antanov inherited his old man's construction company, which he merged with his own. Fox's previous encounter with Maksim was when he'd led a team to his restaurant, posing as food inspectors. It was believed that the international arms consortium, The Arms of Ares, or Ares for short, had contracted Antanov Junior's company for reasons unknown. The mission went sideways with his team being temporarily imprisoned in the restaurant's cold storage. The op took an interesting twist when Fox uncovered some compromising photographs of Antanov and his top bodyguard, Efim Volski. Although the mission was a success, Fox was never able to look at a Victoria Secret catalogue the same way again. Considering Russia's anti-gay climate, Antanov couldn't afford losing his reputation, or being cut out of his inheritance. Whereas Antanov Senior was all bark with the ferocious bite of a pit-bull, Antanov junior was all bark with the nibble of a chihuahua—at least to Fox. Fox knew that he didn't scare Antanov, but at least he got his respect ever since he had recruited him as one of his informants.

The intel Fox had gotten from Antanov Junior led him to Chechnya. It was there that his construction company had "fixed up" an old, abandoned bunker that dated back to the Chechnyan war—one of several that were scattered throughout Russia and other former Soviet nations. The bunker had been converted into an underground laboratory that was used by Ares for weaponizing a hyper-deadly microbe called Pandora. It was a close call for Fox, as he was captured, beaten, and nearly killed. Some of the errors were made on his behalf—ones he'd never repeat. As they say, one learns from their near death experiences. To the best of Fox's knowledge, Antanov junior never dealt with Ares since their last encounter. Nor was it likely that he'd ever do business with them, considering that Ares had seemingly disappeared. At least, that's what the analysts were saying.

When Fox was convinced that he wasn't tailed and that nothing was out of place in front of the Roman Club—he doubled back and crossed the street. Picking the front door lock wasn't a problem, and once he had the door open, he walked in. The place was dimly lit and spartanly furnished, with chestnut-colored hardwood floors, round Formica tables and hard-backed wooden chairs. The place was quiet, with the exception of five rowdy men who were sitting around one of the tables near the back. They had not yet noticed Fox, as they were focused on their card game.

Fox went over to them and managed to get within ten feet of their table before one of them noticed him, gave him a *what-the-fuck* expression, then signaled the others. Like rabbits scrambling from their holes, they leapt up from their chairs and surrounded him. Antanov's top henchman, Efim Volski, was among them, and he and the others made sure their sidearms were visible.

"I love your security," said Fox in Russian. "Anyone can simply walk in. I guess Antanov must've eliminated all of the competition."

Volski—a bald, heavyset man with a goatee, weighing close to three hundred pounds, and slightly taller than Fox—stepped up to him. Fox couldn't hold back the smile as he saw that his nose was scarred and slightly crooked—remnants of their previous encounter.

"Hello, Volski," said Fox.

"You've got nerve showing up here, yes?" Volski growled in Russian.

"Come on," Fox chuckled. "Don't tell me that you're still mad at me for what happened last time."

"The restaurant's closed and you're not welcome here," Volski kept his threatening tone as he then pointed to the door. "So get the fuck out."

Fox took a step closer to him, maintaining eye contact with Volski while watching for any movement among the other three men. "I didn't come here to eat. I came to see your boss."

"He's not available."

"Then make him available. By the way, how are your balls?"

Volski growled as he formed a fist.

"Enough!" came a yell from the back. They all turned to see Antanov quickly approaching. He was slightly more built since the last time they had met, with his dark hair combed back, blue eyes set into a narrow face with a pointed chin. He was straightening one of his black suspenders as he pushed his way past his men.

Fox turned to Antanov. "Call off your dogs."

Volski narrowed his eyes.

"Why?" asked Antanov, turning both palms outward for effect. "Why should I call off my men?" He took a few more steps forward until he was close to Volski.

Antanov glanced around the restaurant, gesturing with one arm. "You think you can just walk in here, uninvited," he yelled while pointing to himself, "and have the audacity to give me orders?"

"If these men are supposed to be securing your establishment," said Fox, "then why is it that I've been able to just walk in here and get within a few feet of them before they noticed me? Had my inclinations been on the sour side of things, they'd be dead. And so would you."

Antanov gave a stern look to his men before turning back to Fox.

"I see you still haven't lost the tough-guy routine." Fox then looked at Volski. "And neither has your human cement truck."

"Human cement truck?" Volski looked as though he was about to throw himself on Fox, but Fox already had a counterattack planned that would've left Volski's neck in a brace.

"Stoy!" Antanov yelled.

Volski stopped as he looked at his boss, then back at Fox, with a reddened face.

"You have three seconds to state your business," said Antanov.

"Sure," said Fox. "Your father's kickback scheme with local government officials…investigators are closing in, soon enough they're going to link it to you and shut you down permanently. Need I say more?"

Antanov remained silent for a bit. Long enough for his henchmen to stare back at him as though they wondered what they were to do. He then sighed and held his head down, shaking it, as he pinched the bridge of his nose before turning to one his henchmen. "Bring us a drink."

Fox joined Antanov in a booth where he took out his tablet and showed him the picture of the woman who had stolen the hard drive. "Do you recognize her?"

"Nyet. Sorry I can't help you," Antanov answered and slid the tablet back over to Fox.

He would've preferred that he had a name to go along with the picture. According to Dewan, she had several aliases. Fox slid the tablet back to Antanov. "You didn't even look at it."

"I'm telling you I've never seen her." The tablet was pushed back to Fox.

"You know people who know people. If you wanted to find out who she was, and where she would be within the week, you'd be able to."

"Tell me about this so-called kickback scheme my father—God rest his soul—was involved in."

"The Investigative Committee of Russia is about to investigate collusion between construction companies and city hall, right here in Saint Petersburg. You've inherited your father's construction company, which means that once the investigation is complete, you'll be implicated in a series of deals which involve paying kickbacks in excess of four-point-four million euros to elected city officials, in exchange for contracts. And that was only within the last year prior to his passing."

Antanov clenched his fists and closed his eyes at the mention of the money.

Fox brushed a lock of hair from his forehead. "How much will you be willing to bet that six days from now, give or take a day or two, the police will raid your businesses, seize all your bank accounts, and your three houses?"

Antanov sighed and looked away as Fox slid the tablet back over to him.

The Mafia boss picked it up, looked at the picture and ground his teeth. "Email me this picture. I'll find out what I can."

One of the henchmen arrived with the drinks, left them for Fox and Antanov, and then he departed.

Fox raised his glass to Antanov. "You get me what I want, and I'll get the police off your ass."

Chapter 14

Nijmegen, The Netherlands. 2:28 PM, Monday.

Hours had passed and Nita Parris still hadn't heard from Fox. *Why did he have to be so stubborn?* For a moment, Parris had thought that Merrick was going to have her spy on him. She probably would have done so had it not been for the well-timed interruption. Downing sending Parris after this punk hacker/thief was a bit of a relief. She had the suspicion that he had done so purposely, in order to keep her away from Fox for the time being.

Dressed casually, wearing a baseball cap and carrying a grocery bag, the average onlooker wouldn't give her a second glance. Kamphuis, given what was already known about him, would most likely have hidden video surveillance set up around the entrance to the building, as well as the doorway to his apartment.

The two men Downing had assigned Parris had already done reconnaissance and were able to confirm that the mark was inside, with another man, in an apartment on the third floor. It was likely that the second man was a fellow hacker.

Parris switched the shopping bag from her right to her left hand. "Anything special happen in the last ten minutes?"

"Nothing," replied her team member, Wim Demeere. "Just an electrician entering the building about five minutes ago."

"And?" Parris rounded the street corner.

"Still working on it," came Dewan's voice. "The company's

legit, well known across the region."

Parris saw the blue-and-white trademark colors of the electrician's van parked five vehicles ahead. She didn't look to the opposite side of the street where Demeere and Gessner were sitting inside a red van with tinted windows. It was parked a few buildings away, out of sight of anyone in the building they were keeping watch over. She was now close enough to the company van where she could see the license plate. The obvious jumped out at her when she noticed that the number designation did not begin with the letter B, causing her heart rate to kick up a notch.

"Guys," Parris quickened her pace, "the van's got stolen plates. Demeere, Gessner, cover the exits, I'm going in." *How could they not notice that?*

She let herself in with her lock pick and strolled inside, while keeping her head low, letting the peak of her baseball cap obscure her face from the cameras overhead. Once inside, she dropped the grocery bag and ran to the stairs, which were a few feet from the entrance, sprinting to the third floor.

Parris had her EMP in her hand the moment she rounded the banister. The run would've left the average person out of breath, but this was nothing more than a warm-up for her.

She ran slower, toward Kamphuis's apartment, keeping as quiet as possible in order to maintain the element of surprise. With the exception of hearing two people arguing in one of the apartments she passed, it was relatively quiet. Based on the intel she had been provided, each apartment had a bolt lock, along with a chain lock. Nothing that Parris couldn't get around with a well-placed kick, unless Kamphuis had reinforced the door. The same intel had also provided Parris knowledge of the floor plan. The first place that anyone might be would be the living room, which would be immediately to her right as she entered.

She stood in front of Kamphuis's door, backed up with her sidearm in hand, and lashed out her leg, placing all the impact close to the door handle. The door flew open, along with broken pieces of the threshold, and Parris stormed in sideways, keeping her back to the wall and a two-handed grip on the EMP as she pointed it into the living room. Kamphuis and his roommate were slouched upright on the one couch, both of their heads hanging back, blank stares, each with a single red dot on their foreheads.

Crouched on the ground beside a toolkit was a bald man with a mole on his left cheek, dressed in uniform and in the process of removing the suppressor from his sidearm.

"Drop the weapon. Hands over your head," Parris yelled. Keeping aim with one hand, she sidestepped to the door and pushed it shut. "Lock your elbows and turn around, away from me."

The electrician obviously realized that he had been bested. He took the suppressed weapon by its barrel and tossed it on the floor toward her. He then did as instructed.

"Kneel and put your left hand out in front of you, then lower yourself to the ground." Parris watched him as he obeyed. "Now, lay down flat, arms straight out to the sides, palms up. Turn your head away from me and cross your ankles. If you move, I'll assume you're going for your weapon, and I *will* shoot you."

She then took out a pair of flex-cuffs and approached him. The man was around five feet eleven. She also wagered that he was definitely physically stronger than she was, like the hitman who'd been sent after Weyland.

The man remained still as Parris knelt and twisted his body at an angle, grabbing one arm, pulling it lower so that she could twist his fingers. That way it would be impossible for him to grab her EMP and use it against her. She then tucked her sidearm in its concealed holster in the back of her jeans. Now that he was in a locked arm position, she cuffed that hand.

The electrician tugged his arm, twisted, and threw his weight around. Parris squeezed the open end of the plastic handcuff while she went to grab the same arm in an attempt to pin him to the floor. But he did another maneuver that was too quick for her to respond, which didn't allow her to grab him. He was trying to break free from her, and once he accomplished that, Parris would be in a hand-to-hand combat with him, something she really couldn't afford to get into at this moment.

If there was a good time for one of her partners to assist her, it would be now. And they should both be hearing her grunts through their earpieces.

"Heading up to assist," she heard Gessner say.

The assassin began to gain control as he pulled Parris to the floor, knocking over a tower of what appeared to be DVDs or CDs, but she still hung onto him.

The electrician broke free and got to his feet, but Parris was still on him. He threw a punch to her face, a blow which she deflected by using an inside block. But she wasn't successful, and he landed a punch to her right shoulder, knocking her back into the flat-screen television set. There was a large crash as it fell off its stand. Parris grabbed on to it in order to block her fall—as being on the floor would put her at a fatal disadvantage. She then saw the electrician produce something shiny.

A knife.

From that proximity, he'd stab her before she had a chance at a quick draw of her EMP.

The DVDs.

Parris grabbed one and tossed it, striking the electrician in the left eye.

Got him.

The electrician cried out as he turned his head to the side, covering his eye with his free hand. This gave Parris the half second that she needed as she threw herself into him, wrapping one arm around his waist, while the other went for the knife, seizing his forearm. The killer went down, dropping the knife and hitting the back of his head against the floor as the momentum sent them both sliding into the wall. Parris clenched her fists and furiously unleashed a series of blows to his face—eventually breaking his nose as his blood covered her knuckles.

Parris then flipped him over onto his stomach, grabbed the cuffed hand by his fingers and twisted them as she pulled his arm behind his back. She quickly seized the other hand and pulled it behind, having his hands cuffed moments later. She then slid back onto his ankles and brushed a few strands of hair off her forehead, breathing heavily. It was then that she noticed that her cap had fallen off.

Gessner crashed through the door with his sidearm drawn,

startling Parris.

She sighed as she shook her head. "Nice of you to show up."

Gessner closed the door while holstering his weapon. "I got here as fast as I could."

Parris turned her captive over. His face was a bloody mess. "Who sent you?"

Rather than answer, Parris saw his jaw move—he had just bitten down on something.

Oh shit, don't let it be that.

He began frothing at the mouth as his body spasmed underneath her. It was too late. The potassium cyanide pill he had somehow snuck into his mouth would kill him in a matter of seconds. She slammed her palms into his chest and got off him, sitting on the floor, with her back to the wall. She then looked at Gessner, who peered into the living room at the two corpses on the couch.

He sighed and turned to Parris. "How'd you know the plates were stolen?"

Parris looked away from him. "The van's plates had the wrong first letter for a commercial vehicle."

Gessner's head dropped as he held his hip with one hand while holding his forehead with the other. He turned around and paced toward the door and then came back. She could tell that he knew he'd fucked up, and would soon blame himself for Kamphuis's death.

Parris caught her breath. It was over, there wasn't any sense yelling at him. She could hear Merrick's teeth gnashing already as she would've been soon touching down at Dulles. Parris knelt over the assailant and she searched him, hoping that he'd have something of value. She pulled a set of keys from his pants pocket.

"Heads up." Gessner looked her way just as she tossed him the keys. "Take his van someplace else, where it can be searched."

Parris then removed the electrician's baseball-type company hat and tossed it to Gessner. "Put this on." They could never risk a nosy neighbor, passing pedestrian, or driver watching them search the van on the street. They'd most likely get suspicious and call the police.

Parris turned to Gessner just as he was leaving. "Hey."

He stopped to look back. "Yes?"

"I'm not covering for you again. Is that understood?"

Gessner nodded. "I understand. And thanks." He then left, closing the door behind him.

Parris heard his footsteps walking down the hall as she removed the electrician's wallet from his other pants pocket and searched it. There was his fake driver's license, and four hundred euros in the form of four one-hundred-euro bills. Inside the back sleeve of his wallet was a folded receipt, which she took out and opened. The writing was a bit faded, but it appeared to have come from a service station called Turbo, located on State Route 37 in Bloomington, Indiana.

She took out her Android smartphone and tapped on the app for fingerprint storage and ID. The screen changed to white with a black square outlined in the middle. Parris then took the electrician's hand, then pressed his thumb to the screen in the center of the square. The screen flashed, and she repeated this with his other fingers. She most likely didn't need to take prints from every finger. But the more samples she provided the better. Parris then sent the fingerprint images to Langley as an email attachment.

A few moments later Parris was exiting the building with the grocery bag she had left at the bottom of the staircase. Demeere pulled up to the curb, where she hopped inside.

As they drove away, Dewan called. "I got a match on the first set of prints. And you caught yourself a big one."

"Go on," Parris answered through her earpiece.

"His name's Radovan Babić, former Bosnian intelligence."

This was the problem with dealing with intelligence operatives. Some of them retire from the field, get bored, and do private— sometimes *illegal*—work for someone else.

Parris then remembered the receipt and took it out. "Do me a favor. Try to find out as much as you can about the area surrounding the Turbo Gas Station on State Route thirty-seven in Bloomington, Indiana."

"Let me guess," said Dewan. "You killed the guy who could've given you that info, right?"

Parris sucked her teeth. "Just find it."

"Okay, I'm on it. *Dayum.*"

Just as Dewan hung up, and Demeere turned onto the ramp leading to the highway, she heard a ringing through her earpiece, having turned her ringer off before the op. She tapped it once. "Hello."

"Parris." It was Fox. "Meet in Bangkok, ASAP. I've just located our mystery woman."

Chapter 15

Sukhumvit, Bangkok, Thailand. Tuesday night.

The northeast monsoon blew a cool, dry air over the city, one that was a welcome respite from the heat that had draped over Bangkok in the prior months. The previous month of October had seen severe flooding, ravaging various parts of the country. For Fox, who was playing a game on his smartphone while surreptitiously surveilling the massage parlor across the street, it was one of the more comfortable times of the year to be here. He was sure the hundreds of people around him, who were either shopping or eating at one of the several outdoor restaurants or street vendors, agreed with him. Had Fox been here in April, he would've been standing in forty-degree Celsius temperatures.

The massage parlor was on the second floor of one of several attached four-story buildings with their protruding, brightly-lit signs that hung over the sidewalks on both sides of the street—seemingly going on for miles. According to Antanov, the woman Fox was pursuing moved around constantly but spent most of her time in Bangkok. It wasn't much, but enough for Fox to go on.

Thanks to the woman's original voice recording that was captured from Parris's earpiece, the CIA now had a voice signature. All that had remained was to upload it to one of their Keyhole satellites in orbit and have it zero in over Bangkok to listen to every phone call—either over a landline or a cell phone. It had taken a few hours, but the asset's voice was eventually intercepted twice, with her phone calls being recorded.

The call that was intercepted was actually one with the massage parlor receptionist as she spoke to the asset—who was currently out of town, calling to book an appointment. Fortunately, Fox was able to catch the shortest flight to Bangkok from Saint Petersburg—which was a little over twelve hours.

The target woman went by many aliases. Even Antanov couldn't provide Fox with a real name. The only one he gave was LJ Kentowski—a professional cyberthief who traded in secrets, both government and corporate.

By the time he'd arrived in Bangkok, an IM from Dewan provided him with all the details he needed. The first person Kentowski had spoken to was someone from the massage parlor. The second person was someone who worked at an art gallery. By the time he had finished reading the IM, Fox had learned the names and addresses of the places Kentowski had contacted.

It had been less than forty-eight hours since Kentowski and Kamphuis had intercepted him and Parris, but it still gave Kentowski more than enough time to sell the hard drive. To whom was anyone's guess, at least for the moment. China and Russia were the usual suspects. But then again, Syria and Iran could be added to the list too.

Fox had already drunk two bottles of water and a Gatorade. With it being almost twenty-five degrees Celsius, even though it was evening, it was important to keep enough fluids in his body to compensate for loss due to perspiration. A lack of fluids could lead to him feeling lax and sleepy—not ideal for surveillance, where lack of being alert could mean the difference between apprehending a person of interest and letting them slip away. However, it was also important not to go overboard with the hydration. He didn't want to spend his time in front of the urinal and let the target slip away.

It took roughly twenty minutes until he saw Kentowski squeezing her way through the crowds of merchants and pedestrians. She had long, flowing black hair and appeared to be of mixed race. It was hard to tell from where he stood, but she definitely had an exotic skin tone. She wore a simple strapless one-piece dress with a tropical floral design and carried a shoulder bag that was large enough to hold a tablet.

Fox stood close to a flower stand, which was a few yards to his right. Keeping his eye on Kentowski, who had just entered the massage parlor, Fox went to the flower merchant and pointed to a bouquet. She took her time to wrap the flowers in a thin decorative tissue paper. He handed her a few bills and took the flowers, telling her to keep the change, and then crossed the street.

Impatient, Fox ran up the stairs, two at a time, to the second floor where he heard the relaxing nature sounds with a soft music score playing through the speakers. There wasn't anything fancy about the place—it wasn't a high-end massage parlor, only large enough to hold six or seven rooms at most. For someone who most likely earned at least a quarter of a million dollars per transaction, the average person would've been surprised that Kentowski didn't go to one of the more luxurious massage parlors, or have a personal masseuse come to her place. On the other hand, though, she may simply be acting out the identity which she had stolen.

The reception area was temperature regulated and carpeted, with three wooden chairs for guests, and guest slippers. On the counter were incense candles, which gave off an ocean-like fragrance.

The receptionist was absent from behind the counter at the moment, so Fox walked to it and leaned over to take a peek. He saw the appointment book open and displaying the evening's appointments. A quick scan and he noticed LJ Kentowski's name listed.

Fox heard footsteps approaching and he backed away from the counter just as a short, plump Thai woman walked through the beaded curtain behind it. She smiled, showing him a perfect set of white teeth.

"Hello, are you a walk-in or do you have an appointment?" the lady asked.

Fox showed her the flowers. "Actually, my girlfriend just arrived. She doesn't know that I'm in town, so I want to surprise her."

The receptionist smiled. "Oh, you must mean Laura Jean."

"That's her," Fox replied with a nod.

"No problem," she giggled as she gestured down the hall. "Her masseuse hasn't started on her yet. Just walk down the hall. She's in the fourth room on your left."

Fox nodded once, with a wink. "Thanks." He walked away, but soon stopped and turned back to her as though remembering something. "Oh, tell the masseuse to give us a few minutes."

"No problem," she answered, smiling as she sat down

Fox returned the smile, seeing how gullible she was, and then found the room easily. Although his Glock was well concealed in his IWB hip holster—perfect for someone wearing a t-shirt, as he was at this moment—he doubted that he'd need it. At least not to shoot anyone. Each room had a sliding door and he slowly slid hers open and peeked inside. LJ lay face down on the massage table, looking away from him. She was naked, with only a towel covering a short area of her buttocks. She didn't once look up, so Fox let himself in, closing the door behind him.

Damn, why do the best-looking ones always have to show up naked in the middle of an op? But Fox couldn't let that fine figure of hers distract him. He approached her from the side, stopping near her waist. She was still face down in the hole that was carved out of the headrest, with her arms cradled in the armrest below, making it impossible for her to see him.

He set the flowers down on the floor at the foot of the table and then placed a hand on her lower back, sliding it up slowly to her neck. She wasn't tense at all, which is all he needed. He then positioned his hands on her neck and massaged it gently. Her neck and shoulders moved as she inhaled deeply, then exhaled. She must have thought that she was in a safe place, because the fact that Fox didn't rub oil on his hands before he massaged her should've been a dead giveaway that something was amiss. Nonetheless, he kept massaging as she had clearly yielded to him. After having gotten her in her comfort zone for nearly half a minute, he leaned close to her ear and spoke in his most seductive voice, maintaining the Welsh accent.

"How much were you paid for the hard drive?"

As he expected, she reacted by trying to lift her head, but Fox grabbed a fistful of her hair and yanked her head up, quickly cupping her mouth with the other.

"You really pissed me off," Fox hissed. "So don't give me an excuse to hurt you."

He felt her muffled screams in his hand and gave a hard tug of her hair to silence her. "Where's the hard drive? And don't you dare scream, unless you want me to accidentally snap your neck."

Fox uncupped her mouth slowly. She puffed loudly as she caught her breath. Kentowski didn't answer—either she was scared of having her neck broken, or she was holding out.

"You know what?" Fox grabbed his G19 and held it in front for Kentowski to see. "I know a better place where we can talk." He then backed away to where she had hung her dress, snatched it off the hook along with her panties, and tossed them to her. "Get dressed."

Keeping the G19 pointed at her, Fox used his other hand to grab Kentowski's handbag from the floor, where it lay beside her heels. He unzipped it and peeked inside. Sure enough, he saw her tablet. He also saw what appeared to be passports. He took them out and found Australian, Finish, Canadian, British, and Italian passports.

"Look, I don't know who you are," Kentowski pleaded as she sat on the edge of the table. "But if it's money you want, then I can pay you."

Fox was down on one knee facing her as he put his G19 on the floor so that he could check each passport. "I don't want your money. I want the hard drive."

Whoever Kentowski really was, she certainly didn't play around. These were some of the best forged passports he'd ever seen.

He looked up at her as she turned away from him to slip on her dress. "Who did these for you?" Fox looked back inside each one. "Loni Flowers, Pam Goodliffe, Jill Delbridge, Lori Giovanetti, Sylvia Massara? Christ, how many other identities have you stolen?" Fox dropped them back in the bag.

She put her panties on before turning around. "Enough to get by."

"Really?" He picked up the G19 and got up, then walked over to her, grabbing her by the crook of her arm. "We're going to walk casually out of here. And when we pass the receptionist you're going to smile for her as though you're looking forward to getting the best fucking you've had in weeks."

"She'll never fall for it," said Kentowski. "She'll call the police."

Fox squeezed her arm. "And if she does, I'll have to get away as quickly as possible. That means *permanently* getting rid of any excess baggage. Besides, if I shoot you now, it would take several minutes for the police to get here, which is more than enough time for me to get lost in the crowds. I'll be out of the country in less than an hour, with your tablet. Even if I don't get the hard drive, I'm sure it'll give me what I want. You still want to test me?"

No answer.

"Didn't think so." Fox poked the barrel of the G19 into her side. "Now let's see that Joe Biden smile."

By the time they passed the receptionist she managed to force a smile. They were soon back outside where Fox brought her to his car—a hatchback—and made her get in the driver's seat while he sat beside her.

Once he got in, Fox handed her the keys, which she snatched from him. "Where are we going?"

He lowered his sidearm, but still made sure it was visible for her to see. "Oh, I don't know. How about we go to your day job? I'd like to take a look at some art."

Kentowski's chest rose. He had struck a nerve.

"Yeah, I know about the art gallery you anonymously own," Fox said. "Every thief needs a place to launder, right?"

She looked away as she started the car, then drove off.

A half hour later they were in the Wattana district, which was a mash-up of high-rise apartment buildings, residential houses hidden behind stone walls, and small shops. Fox felt boxed in as they drove down the narrow two-lane street, where a moped was parked on the sidewalk on every second to third street block.

LJ turned into a cul-de-sac that also served as a side entrance to the gallery. Fox twisted the key in the ignition to turn off the engine and then palmed the keys. Holding her bag with one hand and the G19 with the other, he kept an eye on her as they got out simultaneously. She didn't seem to be the type who'd risk screaming for help—not that her cries wouldn't be drowned out by the combination of traffic and loud music that surrounded them.

Fox felt his foot bump a glass object, which rolled away. It was a beer bottle, reminding him that the area wasn't short of its share of winos. He picked it up, then circled the front of the car to LJ's side. He handed her the keys from inside her bag and she used them to unlock the side door. Fox followed her inside, pulling the door shut behind him, then locking it. He heard the beep of an alarm system, obviously the preliminary sounds it made before the cavalry arrived, unless the code was entered to disarm it.

"Wait," Fox said as she was about to enter a code. "Allow me." He then whispered to Dewan through his earpiece, asking for the code. Fox entered it and the beeping stopped. Many high-end security systems had two disarm codes. The first one was the regular activation/deactivation code and the other was a distress code. Kentowski would've surely entered that, had he allowed her to disarm the system. It would have alerted the alarm company that their client was in danger, and they, in turn, would have alerted the police. But hacking into the building's security was child's play for Dewan, and he had already figured out the regular code not long after the CIA intercepted the call Kentowski had made to the gallery earlier.

Fox turned to LJ. "After you."

He followed her down a short hall that was partially illuminated by the streetlights from outside. She went to turn on the light switch, but Fox intervened.

"Keep your hands down. There's enough light for us to see our way to your office." The last thing he needed was a curious person wondering why the art gallery was still open after closing hours.

"This isn't something you see every day," said LJ.

Fox followed her through the main showroom to a set of stairs. "What's that?"

"A hitman who's environmentally conscious."

He stopped and held up the bottle. "You mean this?" He then smashed it against the wall beside him. Pieces fell on the steps, which he then swept with his foot so that they covered the entire lengths of the two stairs.

LJ spun around, startled, grabbing the banister to catch herself from falling.

Fox responded by raising his gun. "Keep walking."

Holding up both palms as though she were surrendering, she turned around and proceeded to the top of the steps. Even though Kentowski's name didn't appear as the owner of the gallery, it wasn't a guarantee that someone else wouldn't be determined enough to track her there too. And if there were any unexpected visitors, the sound of crushed glass under their feet would be Fox's improvised alarm system.

When they got to the second floor, they walked through another showroom before they came to LJ's office, which was tucked away in the front corner of the building. Glancing to the end of the hall, Fox saw a door. The only place it could lead to was the balcony that wrapped around the side of the building, above the cul-de-sac where they had parked, to the front of the building above the street.

As they entered, the streetlight outside the window shed enough light through the blinds for them to see their way around. The office was furnished with a double-pedestal dark wooden desk, with an executive chair, in front of the window. The surface was clear, with the exception of a desk lamp, what appeared to be a fountain pen in its stand, and a small stack of *Post It* papers. Adjacent to it, in the corner against the wall, was a three-feet-high file cabinet. Two contemporary Eastern paintings, similar to the ones found in the showrooms, were hanging on the walls.

Fox gestured to the side. "Over there."

While Kentowski obeyed and stood against the wall, Fox closed the office door and then went to the window behind her desk, peeking through the blinds to scan the street below. Given that the road wasn't wide enough for anyone to park on either side, had he and Kentowski been under surveillance, their trackers would be forced to be out in the open. Anyone who was hanging around while talking on their cell phone or listening to an iPod was fair game. It was less likely that someone would be spying on them in one of the buildings across the street, unless they knew in advance that Kentowski would be there at this very moment.

Fox moved away from the window when he was satisfied that they were in the clear, and searched the drawers of the desk. It wasn't unusual for someone in Kentowski's line of work to have a gun hidden away in the desk. Sure enough, he found a Smith & Wesson M&P 9mm. Easy to purchase down here, considering that American guns were more popular in Thailand than the less-coveted Chinese weapons. He took it out, disassembled it, dropped the parts back in the drawer, then closed it.

He then gestured to the guest chair in front of the desk. "Sit."

Kentowski shrugged her shoulders, walked over to the chair, and sat.

Fox then sat down in the executive chair and placed his own gun on the desk, far enough out of Kentowski's reach. "Let's start this one more time. Where's the hard drive?"

A few moments went by where she sighed, then looked down at the table. "I don't have it."

"I didn't ask you if you had it or not. I want to know where it is."

"With someone else." She looked up at Fox. "And they're long gone."

She wasn't going to give up the information he needed. At least, not this way. He could alert Downing and have him send over a team who would detain her in a safe-house way outside of town. She'd be put under harsh interrogation until she gave up. However, the entire procedure of waiting for a team to get there, then transportation, and then the actual interrogation could take several hours—even days, depending on how long she could hold out. The overzealous terrorists could sometimes take several days before they cracked. But this woman wasn't a soldier, or an intelligence operative who would've gone through serious anti-interrogation training. She was a cyberthief, who spent most of her criminal career hiding behind a laptop. There was no doubt that she'd crack under the agency's advanced interrogation, but Fox wasn't the most patient man when it came to certain things. He could try negotiating with her, let her know the consequences of not cooperating.

He reached into her bag, took out her tablet, and turned it on. "I've been told that you have an extensive client list. You've hacked into the networks of multinational companies and law firms who are negotiating settlements. You trade in secrets, traces of which may, no doubt, be on your tablet."

Fox then tapped on the screen at a few of the icons, searching the folders. "And if they're not here, then I may be able to find something which could lead me to them. To make a long story short, I can, and will, eventually find out who you've worked for and what you stole for them. With that info, I'll gladly contact their victims and expose you. You'll be out of business in no time, that's if someone doesn't put a hit on you beforehand."

But all of the folders were empty. She'd obviously deleted her files, or had them stored elsewhere. She was smart, and had obviously been in the game long enough not to carry her client list on her, where someone could steal it. Dewan would be able to do a thorough search and find the client list, but Fox had another idea.

He took out his Android, tapped its screen a few times, then placed it on the table in front of Kentowski—showing her the picture of her deceased colleague. "I almost forgot. Someone got to your partner. So it's safe to assume that the same people also put a hit on you. Oh yeah, Alghafari and Brunner were also taken out. I'm sure you would've heard this on the news. Maybe not Brunner because he's not as infamous."

Fox paused, allowing her to absorb what he'd just shared with her.

Kentowski glanced at the picture of her partner, blinked a few times as she swallowed, and then looked away. "A lot of people want me dead. It comes with the job. You ought to know."

"It didn't take me long to find you. Do you think the people who murdered Alghafari, Brunner, and your partner are far behind?"

"You got lucky."

"No, *you're* lucky that I found you first." Fox leaned closer to her, maintaining eye contact. Even though she looked away, she had to know his eyes were still on her. "These people managed to take out one of the most well-protected arms dealers in the world. I'm sure you did your research on Alghafari when you infiltrated his network to learn of the meeting in Düsseldorf. Whatever's on that hard drive, the people Alghafari stole it from aren't interested in negotiating its return. They want to eliminate all knowledge of what's on it. That includes everyone who came in contact with it—including us."

"You look just like them." LJ gazed at Fox. The way the shadow from the blinds landed on her face, her eyes and lips were in the light, her nose and forehead in the dark. "You don't give a shit about me. So I sure as hell ain't helping you."

"You're right," said Fox. "I *don't* give a shit about you. I've got contracts to fulfill and I don't need the distraction of having another person trying to kill me. I stood to gain a lot of money working for Alghafari. Now he's dead. I don't know when or where my next paycheck's coming from, but almost two nights ago I had half a dozen people try to gun me down. And I want to know why."

Fox sat back in the chair as he let her think about what he'd just told her.

"So, you can either tell me what's on the hard drive or where you hid it, and hopefully I can use that knowledge in order to get our would-be killers off both our asses." He grabbed his G19 and crossed his legs. "Otherwise I'll just take your tablet and earn whatever I can with it. You decide."

Kentowski looked away from him again, as though she was considering Fox's offer. He figured that by now she'd realize that she didn't have too many places to hide, now that he had her tablet.

"I don't have the hard drive on me," she said.

Fox sat forward and leaned over the table. "Who'd you sell it to and what's their interest in it?"

She smiled as she shook her head. "It's not for sale."

"Bullshit."

She looked at him, narrowing her eyes. "I didn't and won't sell it."

"Then why'd you steal it?" asked Fox. "I came all this way for you to tell me that the hard drive's worthless? What are you trying to pull?"

"I'm not trying to pull anything," she yelled. She bent over and held her head for a few moments, then exhaled heavily before she looked up at him. "The hard drive contains evidence that could send several people to jail. Unfortunately, it was damaged as my partner and I were making our getaway—courtesy of it being struck by a bullet. Everything was fine until some woman got in our way. A friend of yours, no doubt."

"Why would Alghafari sell incriminating evidence when he could simply use the hard drive to blackmail whoever it belonged to?"

The woman shook her head. "It wasn't just about him making a quick buck off the contents. It goes a lot deeper than that."

"Then what's on it that's so precious?"

She paused as though in thought. "I can't tell you everything. All I was able to get off it was a chemical formula."

"For what?"

"I don't know. As I told you before, the disk was damaged, or else I'd be able to tell you more."

"Could you draw this formula?"

She shook her head.

"Who did Alghafari steal it from?"

She remained silent.

"There's no sense in keeping things from me. I can always walk away from here, call my contact who led me to you and let him know where you are. This will be a lucky day for those who want you de—"

"Alghafari stole it from Sementem. You ever heard of them?"

"Sementem?" Fox thought back to where he'd heard the name. "They're the world's largest bio-agricultural conglomerate."

"Bingo," said Kentowski. "And if the stuff on that hard drive was as dangerous as I think, they'd go to extreme lengths to suppress its contents from becoming public." She then closed her eyes, inhaled, and then opened her eyes, looking at Fox as she breathed out. "God. The hard drive was supposed to have everything about the chemical formula—how it works, not to mention where and how to use it. With what's left on the disk I don't have too much to work with."

"What's your beef with Sementem that you'd go to these lengths to steal this from them? You don't seem to fit the character of someone who gives a damn about GMOs and such."

"It's personal," she said, looking away with a smirk. "Not that you'd care."

"Try me."

The sound of crushed glass that echoed across the showroom made Fox snatch his sidearm and raise his other hand, palm out, in order to silence Kentowski. He then put his index to his lips, glancing at LJ as he did so, then went to the door. He peeked out in the hall. It was mostly dark, but there was still some reflected light. Whoever was there didn't bother turning on the lights. And aside from Parris, no one else should've known that he and LJ were there. Even if it was Parris, she would've called in advance. This was an ambush.

He rushed back to the desk and grabbed his smartphone then shoved it in his leather belt clip. He then grabbed the tablet and ran back to the door.

"You look tense," said Kentowski. "What's wrong?"

Fox couldn't believe that she'd ask that. "Remember those nice people I was talking about earlier? They just found us."

Chapter 16

"Now would be a great time for me to have my gun," said Kentowski.

Fox shot her a glance and shushed her. Give her a gun? Yeah right. She'd shoot him the first chance she got and then bolt. Fox stuck his head out, looking toward the showroom. The shove he got from behind was hard enough that he stumbled into the hall.

Jesus Christ! That goddamn bitch is going to get us both killed. He turned to the sound of running as he saw LJ dashing to the balcony door. He couldn't bother with her now. The real threat was in the showroom. When he looked back, Fox saw the first, of probably many, darkly dressed figures lurking near the end of the hallway. The blood rushed straight through his left arm as he aimed and fired a shot. The man went down, only for Fox to see a bright muzzle flash and hear loud gunshots.

He jumped back in the office for cover as he heard the bullets strike the walls. He then leaned out through the doorway, took aim, and fired three more shots. As long as he kept shooting, they wouldn't dare enter the hall from the showroom.

Fox ran for the exit, bursting through the door, catching himself on the balcony railing outside. He looked to the right and saw Kentowski, without her shoes, hanging onto the lower rung of the rail, her legs dangling above his car. Before he could say anything, she let go, fell, and landed on the roof. It was a clean drop, where she slid off the roof and onto the ground.

Something wasn't right. These guys were pros. They would've cased the building and sealed all exits before entering. That's when Fox looked to the entrance of the cul-de-sac and saw a sentry walking toward Kentowski with his gun raised.

"Get down," Fox yelled, catching the attention of the sentry. That moment of hesitation was all Fox needed to nail him with a single shot to the right hip. The sentry spun around before he hit the asphalt, screaming. Fox then climbed over the rail and let himself drop. His maneuver was rushed and clumsy, all one hundred and ninety-two pounds of him landing with such force that all the windows exploded outward and he dented the roof. In addition, he lost the tablet before he rolled off, just as the first few bullets tore into the car from above.

The tablet. It was still on the roof of the car. Shit.

These guys didn't seem to have a care in the world who they'd attract. Any moment now the police would be on their way.

Fox's hand touched something on the ground. It was one of Kentowski's shoes. Where was she? Fox looked to where he'd last seen her and spotted the asset running barefoot down the street. The gunmen must have noticed her too, as they began shooting at her instead of him. Fox stood up from behind the car and fired three quick shots. He saw two of the three gunmen drop down onto the balcony as the third ran back inside.

Fox then spotted the tablet—or what was left of it—on the windshield, being held up by one of the wipers. He snatched it and broke out in a sprint. He couldn't afford to lose Kentowski. God forbid that should that happen because he probably wouldn't be as lucky finding her a second time. She was roughly thirty yards ahead, just exiting the cul-de-sac onto the street. Fox's heart almost stopped as he saw her wildly run out into the street without looking either way.

"Kentowski. Wait," Fox screamed. There was a loud screeching of tires, seconds before he saw her get plowed by a city bus.

Fuck.

The shock made Fox stop where he was. Why the fuck did she run from him? She had to have known that doing so was suicide. So close. Fuck, he was so goddamned close to making progress.

All of it gone to shit.

He had to get out of there, since crowds would soon gather. Fox jogged to the street, and by the time he got there, he saw the bus was stopped, along with other motorists coming from both directions. He looked at the tablet—it was destroyed beyond the point of recovery. He tossed it to the side and walked down the road, away from the melee. It wasn't as though he could stick around and search through Kentowski's office at this point. He knew he was close to uncovering what was on the hard drive, or at least where it could be found.

Fox rounded a corner onto a busier street. This was what he needed—crowd cover—and as he contemplated another major loss, he disappeared within the masses.

Chapter 17

Sathorn Unique Tower, Soi Charoen Krung 51, Bangkok. 12:12 AM, Wednesday.

Parris parked her Hyundai Tucson rental outside one of many Parris parked her Hyundai Tucson rental outside one of many buildings that had once symbolized Thailand's economic boom—and bust—of the 1990s. She took out a pocket flashlight from her purse and then shoved the bag under the car seat. She then climbed out of the SUV and checked her flanks. Satisfied that she wasn't being watched, she closed the door.

Dressed in a matching Dolce & Gabbana sleeveless top and trousers with a pair a Blahniks, she walked up to the twelve-feet-high wire fencing, which enclosed the forty-seven-story skyscraper. Thailand had ancient ruins, which were a symbol of the nation's past glory. The Sathorn Unique Tower was an example of a modern-day ruin. It wasn't one that was destroyed by invading armies, but rather one of many that were left to decay as a result of the economic downturn. Its cold, lifeless structure, which was to be a luxury skyscraper, did nothing more than haunt the city skyline.

Parris turned on her flashlight and pointed it at the gated doorway, noticing that it wasn't completely secure. When she pushed one, it opened wide enough to let her through. Only one person who could've gotten around the locks came to mind. And he was somewhere inside the ruins ahead of her. Once she got past the gate, she looked up at one of several eerie three-story-high arches that were ahead.

Parris gazed at the structure. "Where are you?"

She didn't hear an answer through her earpiece. Instead, she saw a red dot appear on the gravel and concrete at her feet. The dot moved forward toward the building.

Okay. So he wants me to follow a laser penlight. She looked up to see where it came from. From what she gathered, it came from the fourth floor, right above the arch. Shining the flashlight on the ground in front of her, she followed the red dot toward the arch before it vanished. When she passed under the arch, Parris looked around until she saw the red dot drawing a circle on the wall, about twenty yards away. Every step she took echoed around her and she wished Fox had chosen a better location to meet. For him to want to be in such a dreary place only meant that he was in a bad mood. She trusted that he had cased the building beforehand—if there were anyone else in there, a homeless person seeking shelter perhaps, she wouldn't be impressed. Still, she had to work to suppress the feeling she might run into an unexpected occupant.

For some reason it reminded her of her last year in elementary school. She and two of her friends would, every once in a while, break into homes while its occupants were away. It was never more than a quick break in, grab anything small and valuable in under two minutes, then get out. They knew the risk of not heading straight home from school. Forget about the police. The real threat came from their parents. Either the mother or the father would be waiting at the front door with a belt or a wooden spoon. That was the case for her friends' parents, but not Aunt Bev. Parris never recalled her raising a hand to her, even though she sometimes felt as though she'd deserved a lash or two.

Back in those days, Parris and her friends knew nothing about casing a place properly. One afternoon they'd made the mistake of entering a home that was still occupied. Parris had felt something was odd when she'd heard a sound, coming from either the television or the radio. It only took a few moments before they walked in and found the elderly woman, dressed in her nighty, sitting on her couch—dead. Her only company had been the flies and *Days of our Lives*—which had been playing on an old tube TV.

Her friends had screamed and bolted on seeing her, but not Parris. Up to this day, she still didn't know why she didn't run. It was the first time she had seen a dead body. The woman's head hung over, her hands on her lap, with a pile of old newspapers by her feet. Flies swarmed around the room—crawling in and out of the glass of ginger beer on the small wooden table beside the couch. Her friends didn't even call out to her to get her to follow them. Maybe they did, but she was too engrossed in her surroundings to hear them. Too fascinated by what she saw. Who was this woman? Did she ever have any children? Did she have any friends? How long had she been dead? These were all questions that had swarmed her mind.

There was a fluttering of wings above her now, and she jumped to the side as she shone the beam in the same direction.

Bats. At least a dozen.

When she got to the wall she saw that she was in front of an unfinished escalator. The stairs and the entire structure of the escalator was already installed, but without power it remained lifeless. The laser light shone down from above, onto the bottom of the escalator, and up the stairs. Parris followed it for the next three floors until it vanished.

"You're late," came Fox's voice from the side of the building that overlooked the entrance.

Parris turned and saw him standing at the edge, gazing at the illuminated skyline. She walked toward him. "I wasn't aware that I had an appointment."

"You can never be too early," Fox answered as Parris joined him at the edge.

"Tell that to the airlines." She looked up to the sky and, ironically, a plane flew above the city in the distance. "I get the impression that you're not in a talkative mood."

"What gave you that idea?"

Parris looked at him. "For starters, you're standing alone in a condemned building. Not the safest place to be, which you'd know had you bothered to read the warning signs outside."

Fox kicked a pebble off the edge. "Sometimes it's good to be alone. Since the library's closed, this was the next best place where I could find some peace and quiet."

Parris stared at him, trying to penetrate his emotional armor. Although Fox was stubborn, arrogant, and a bit rebellious, she had seen him at his weakest. She remembered that moment in Tokyo, when he broke down and inadvertently called her Jessica—his fiancée. Fox never liked to talk about her much. Especially about the night she had been murdered in what was made to appear to be a traffic accident. That moment was the catalyst which eventually got him dismissed from the JTF2, and recruited by Downing. But she refused to believe that Fox had always been the man who stood before her. She knew that he didn't get along too well with his father and wound up leaving school to join the army, but she had the feeling that there was something more than that.

"You want to ask me something?" Fox said.

Jesus. He's still in his anti-surveillance mode. "No. Why'd you ask?"

He looked at her and cocked his head at an angle, curving an eyebrow. "Seriously?"

Okay. He's on to me. "Forget about it."

Fox then looked back toward the skyline and rubbed his temple.

Parris gazed there with him and crossed her arms. "We're no closer to finding the hard drive, right? And the asset?"

Fox didn't answer.

Parris nodded. "I see."

She heard a set of screeching tires, followed by a blasting horn, and looked down toward the intersecting street. She didn't hear a crash. "Merrick says hello, by the way."

Fox smirked. "Sure she does. What does she want?"

"She's looking for a reason to hang you. Me too, for that matter."

Fox turned to her. "She was in The Hague?"

"Yup, an impromptu visit." Parris uncrossed her arms and turned to Fox. "She came to rattle our cages for the blown mission from the night before. Now we'll have to explain the fact that our mystery woman's dead."

"Mystery woman, LJ Kentowski, whatever the fuck she wants to call herself." Fox then stared back out at the rooftops. "I got an update that you found her partner."

"He was already dead by the time we arrived. And just as I captured his killer, he swallowed a cyanide pill."

"Swell."

"But he left behind a clue to his previous whereabouts."

Fox raised an eyebrow as he turned to Parris. "Do tell."

She looked back at him. "I found a gas station receipt on him."

"Whoopee!" Fox chuckled and looked back toward the rooftops. "He probably filled up his getaway vehicle before his hit."

"I thought of that too," Parris answered. "So I got Dewan to check for any current homicide or deaths in that area, around the time he would've been there. Didn't find anything."

"Where was it, by the way?"

"Bloomington, Indiana."

Fox smirked. "So, what we've got is a hitman who was probably catching a Hoosier's game."

Parris paused, trying to make sense of what Fox meant.

He closed his eyes and shook his head with a wave. "Forget I said that."

"Anyhow," said Parris, "were you able to find out anything?"

"Not much," Fox answered just as they were interrupted by both their cell phones ringing. They tapped their earpieces.

"Guys." It was Dewan.

"What is it?" answered Parris.

"OST has analyzed the recording of the telephone call LJ made earlier. They filtered out the background noise and determined that she was probably in a post office. We found one in Sukhumvit. I hacked into their CCTV archives and spotted her earlier today, emptying out her post office box."

"That means that she has an apartment in Bangkok," said Fox. "Were you able to see what she received?"

Parris was thinking the same thing he was—a letter addressed to her would be a huge clue as to locating where Kentowski lived.

"She was very careful and is obviously aware of Big Brother," said Dewan. "I got some help reviewing the archives and we got lucky. Several days ago, when she was collecting her mail, she happened to drop one of her letters in full view of the CCTV."

"Another alias?" asked Fox.

"Yeah, man. She's also known as Paula Lane. So I did some more digging and found out that a Paula Lane owns property in Sukhumvit—a condo in a high-rise. This sista's living large."

Parris looked up at Fox and smiled. "Send us the address now."

Chapter 18

Sukhumvit, Bangkok, Thailand. 1:10 AM, Wednesday.

The drive from Sathorn Tower to LJ/Paula Lane's condo was roughly twenty minutes as it was only about twenty-two miles away. LJ/Paula Lane lived in a two-bedroom, one-bathroom unit on the seventh floor of a twelve-floor condominium high-rise, in one of the most sought-after residential areas in all of Sukhumvit. The neighborhood was well-developed as the high-rise was surrounded by single houses, up-market retail shops, and restaurants.

Dewan had warned them that there was an alarm system within LJ's unit. When he went to hack it he learned that, for some reason, it wasn't activated. Fox used his lock pick to let him and Parris inside the building, as though they were residents. They took the elevator to the seventh floor, where LJ's unit was one door to their left. Once he got past the lock, Fox entered first, leaving Parris to close the door behind them. Surprisingly, the lights were still on. The unit was decorated with contemporary furniture and the hardwood floors had a glow to them.

"Don't you find it odd that someone who's so security conscious would leave her home without activating the alarm?" asked Parris.

"I was thinking the same thing," answered Fox. "But, if there's one thing I can say about Kentowski is that she can keep a clean house." Fox walked down the hall toward the master bedroom ahead, taking a look inside the powder room on the way.

"I'll say," Parris said from the kitchen area. "There's nothing mistakable about the fresh scent of pine."

Rather than walk into the master bedroom, Fox rounded the corner to the right and went into the dining room, where he saw Parris to his right. He looked through the living room, where there was a great nighttime view of the city.

Their eyes met briefly. *Fresh pine scent?*

That's when he understood that they were thinking the same thing. Not another second passed before they both drew their sidearms.

Fox walked back to the master bedroom, his Glock pointed toward the floor. He slid his free hand against the wall until he felt the light switch and flicked it on. The queen-sized bed adjacent to the door was low to the floor—impossible for anyone to fit underneath. There was another door that connected to the bathroom. He pushed it open and did a quick scan—a Jacuzzi, a shower with a stained-glass door, and double sinks. No one there. That's when his attention switched to the walk-in closet. The door was closed and he reached for the handle, then nudged the door open with the tip of his foot, quickly raising the Glock. There was nothing but dresses and a shoe rack full of Choos and Blahniks.

"Get on the floor, now!" Parris yelled from the guest bedroom. It was followed by cries from another woman. Fox hurried to join Parris in the other room. When he got there he saw her pointing her EMP at a young woman who screamed even more when she saw Fox. He realized that his gun must have frightened her again, so he kept it low—having one weapon pointed at you was enough.

"Who are you and what are you doing here?" Parris yelled.

"I...I...my name's Katy Sparks. I'm just a guest, I swear," she cried. She was definitely a southerner, reminding Fox of Jodie Foster's accent in the movie, *Silence of The Lambs.*

"And mopping floors after one in the morning?" said Parris.

"I...I...was bored, and..." Sparks stuttered.

"In the dining room. Now," ordered Parris as she took a step back, giving Sparks some space. She did as she was ordered, trembling as she kept her hands held high.

Fox walked ahead of Sparks into the dining room, with Parris following behind her. He stopped short of the four-seat square table, where he pulled out one of the chairs and turned to her. "Sit."

She looked up at Fox and Parris as they surrounded her. "You're them, aren't you?"

She thinks that we're hitmen. Time to have some fun. Fox held back a grin as he looked at Parris, who had secured her weapon in the hip holster. He then flanked Sparks on one side while Parris went to the other. "*Who* do you think we are?"

"You came here to kill me and Jill. I swear this wasn't my idea. I didn't really want to go along with this."

Jill, as in Jill St. John, another alias.

Parris leaned her face close to Spark's ear. "Do we look like killers to you?"

"With the way you handled that gun and threatened me with it," she trembled as she gave both of them once-overs before nodding, "yeah, you do."

"You'll have to pardon my associate" Fox took a seat adjacent to her. "She tends to be a bit rough at times. You're lucky. Sometimes her trigger finger squeezes out of habit."

"And *bang*." Parris leaned back, waving her arm in an arch. "Brains all over the floor."

"Who are you people?"

"We're Rob and Fab," said Fox.

"That's short for Fabiola," quipped Parris.

Beads of sweat materialized on Sparks's forehead as she looked at Parris. She then turned to Fox. "I don't want any trouble. I swear. I'll do whatever you want."

"Good. You can start off by telling us where Jill's hidden the hard drive," said Fox.

Sparks looked at him. "Huh?"

Parris slammed her hand on the table, startling the girl. "The man asked you a question. Where's the hard drive?"

"It's in the walk-in closet," she cried. "In her bedroom."

"You're going to have to be more precise than that," said Fox.

"There's a hidden compartment under the floor in the right-hand corner, way in the back. But you're not going to get much off it—it's damaged."

"Did he ask you what we could get off it?" asked Parris. "Because I don't remember the man asking you that."

"I'm sorry. I'm sorry. I'm sorry."

Fox got up and went back to Kentowski's bedroom, entering the closet. He flicked on the light and went to the back. He then knelt down and slid his hand along the grooves in the planks. When he felt one that was loose, he lifted it, along with two more, all of them roughly three-by-sixteen-inches each. Underneath was a small metal box. He flipped open the lid and saw the hard drive.

Finally.

He turned it to the side and sure enough there was a bullet-sized hole that he could see right through.

Walking out of the closet gave him a side view of the bed in front of him. The night table on the opposite side of it had a photo of a man in a military uniform. Fox walked around the bed to the table and held up the picture frame. He removed the photo from its frame, placed it on the bed, and snapped a picture of it with his Android. Fox then sent it to Dewan as an email attachment, entering: ??? in the subject heading.

He brought the picture with him back into the dining room and placed it before Sparks. "Who's he?"

She studied the picture before looking up at Fox. "That's Jill's brother, Robert."

A red flag went up in Fox's mind. The name combination of Robert and Jill. There was something familiar about that.

"What's his involvement in all of this?" asked Parris.

"You mean," Sparks looked at Parris, over at Fox, then back to Parris, "you don't know?"

He noticed the change in her facial expression, as though she didn't expect Parris to ask her that. "Know what?"

She turned to Fox. "Robert died a little over two years ago."

"Killed in action?" asked Fox.

"That's the official story," she said as she looked down at the table, another tear rolling down her cheek.

"And why do I get the impression that you don't believe that?"

asked Parris.

Sparks took a moment to wipe the tear away. "Jill didn't believe that's what happened. And I don't either."

"Guys?" Dewan's voice came through their earpieces. "The army guy's name is Corporal Jared Small. He did two tours of duty in Iraq and was into his first in Afghanistan at Camp Iron Eagle. I've been listening in to your conversation with Katy. She used to work for EFS, which is the food services division of the army contractor SLR. Here's the good part—she also worked at Camp Iron Eagle in Afghanistan as a food quality inspector at the same time as Corporal Smalls. She was fired around the same time he was killed."

"What did you guys do to Jill?" asked Sparks.

Fox looked at Parris before he took a seat. Meanwhile, she went to the fridge and came back with a twelve-ounce plastic bottle of water, handing it to Sparks. Even in friendly interrogations, one must never give an asset something they could break—such as a glass or a dish. Silverware was also out of the question, as those items could quickly be used to either harm the interrogators or allow an asset the means to commit suicide before they were questioned. The same rule went for pens or pencils. Crayons or magic markers were preferred. She then took a seat opposite Fox and adjacent to Sparks.

"So?" Sparks glanced back and forth between Fox and Parris.

He turned to her. "Jill won't be joining us."

Sparks maintained a blank stare at Fox for a few seconds before looking away. "I see. Did you—"

"No," interrupted Fox. "*We* didn't do anything to her."

"But we believe the people who got to her are the same ones who are after us," said Parris.

"And they'll be after you too," said Fox.

Sparks drank about a quarter of the bottle before putting it down. It was just then that Fox realized why the name combination of Robert and Jill was so familiar. The cyberthief, Kentowski— who also went under the alias of Jill St. John—it was the name of an actress who was married to actor Robert Wagner.

"Oh, you're going to like this one," said Dewan. "SLR's a

subsidiary of Sementem. Coincidence? I think not."

"Are you two still going to kill me?" asked Sparks.

Fox turned to her. "That depends."

"Depends?" Sparks was breathing short and rapid, she was under stress. "But I gave you the hard drive."

"It's useless," said Fox. "How do you expect us to get anything with a bullet hole in it?"

"Jill got something off it."

"What did she get?" asked Parris.

"A chemical formula," Sparks answered. "I can draw it for you."

Fox took a napkin from the holder and slid it over to her, while Parris gave her a magic marker, which she kept handy in her purse. Sparks drew the formula, and when she was done, Parris grabbed the napkin and looked at it.

"That's all I have. I can't tell you anything more," said Sparks.

Parris studied the formula then looked at Fox. "It looks like a complex protein. I can't say anything more about it."

Sparks turned to her. "That's exactly what I told Jill. How'd you know that? Are you a science major?"

"What if I was?" Parris snapped. "You have a problem with that?"

Sparks's eyebrows rose as she gasped. "No, no, no. I—"

"You what?" Parris scowled.

"I...I just didn't think of a hitwoman with your level of intellect. That's all. No offense."

"*Humph!*" Parris placed the napkin on the table, took out her Android, and snapped a photo of it. She then attached it to an email and sent it to Langley in order for it to be cross-referenced with all known chemical compounds in their database. The formula would then be forwarded to the Centers for Disease Control and also to the bio-defense center at Fort Detrick, Maryland. There it would then be cross-referenced and matched with any known chemical or biological diseases or weapons.

Sparks scratched her forehead. "All Jill told me was that she believed that this formula has something to do with the deaths of those thirteen army officers."

Thirteen dead army officers? Fox looked up at Parris and met her eyes. He clearly saw that she was wondering what Sparks was talking about. He turned to Sparks as though he already knew about the thirteen officers. "Is that all you were able to get?"

"I'm afraid so."

He looked her in the eyes. She had to know more. It was obvious that she just didn't know what to tell him. She began to seem uncomfortable, switching from looking at him to Parris and then back to him.

"I told you all that I know about what's on the hard drive," Sparks said. "What more do you want from me?"

"Why don't you start off by telling us why you teamed up with Jill?" asked Parris.

Sparks reached for a napkin, but paused to look at Parris and Fox. "May I?"

Fox nodded once. "Go ahead."

"Thank you," she said, with a hint of apprehension in her voice, before taking the napkin and wiping her face. "Jill was the only person who believed me and wanted to help."

"Help you in what way?" Parris crossed her legs. "How did you two meet?"

Sparks took another few gulps of water and held onto the bottle. "We met in a grocery store parking lot, back home in Huntsville. That's the one in Alabama in case you were wondering. She came to my rescue after my ex-boyfriend, Butch, attacked me. Jill then told me that she knew everything about me, what I've been through."

"What *are* these things that you're referring to?" asked Parris.

Sparks took another sip of the water. "I used to work for a company called SLR, as a food quality control inspector, over in Afghanistan. We were responsible for the well-being of American troops."

"So you'd inspect the food to make sure no one got food poisoning?" Fox thought it best to play ignorant, and ask her a bunch of questions whose answers he already knew. That way he could test her honesty. Parris would catch on quick and follow his lead.

"Yeah, something like that."

"And why aren't you working for them now?" asked Parris.

Sparks breathed out a huge sigh as though she felt she didn't have anything to lose. "I was fired after I was wrongfully accused of not doing my job, the result of which was that thirteen army officers got sick. This was after I had made some drastic changes in the dining hall—especially in the kitchen where food was being prepared. SLR ruined my life. They'll do anything to shut me up."

"Whoa, slow down," said Fox. "Shut you up?"

"Yeah, because I know what's been going on at Camp Iron Eagle."

"You skipped over a few parts," said Parris. "One moment you mention that thirteen officers got sick and, I assume, were the same ones you earlier said had died. Next, you're talking about a cover-up."

Sparks finished off the last of the water. "About two and a half years ago, I applied for the position at EFS. The interview went well and they hired me. I was assigned to work at one of their bases in Afghanistan, where my job was to monitor the quality and safety of food that was served to American troops. I thought of it as my dream job—earning over twenty-five hundred dollars a month, plus room and board. I thought that it was the perfect way to pay off my student loans. Everyone was so nice to me in the beginning."

Fox saw her face go sour.

"When I got there, I was horrified at what I saw," Sparks continued. "I mean, I was annoyed at the way the labor system was set up. You'd think that with so much money being spent to fund the wars in Iraq and Afghanistan, there would be pay equity. For instance, the ones who worked in the dining halls—namely the Pakistanis and the Afghans—they weren't paid anything more than three dollars a day. And they were practically working in sweatshop conditions."

Sparks shook her head. "There were other issues, too. The evening that I started, there was a problem with the electricity. As a result, refrigerators and freezers weren't working. The kitchen area was very dusty, as though no one had cleaned up for weeks.

I wrote all these details in the reports that I gave my supervisor. I also advised kitchen staff about the cleanliness problem and listed the changes that needed to be made."

"So when did the other problems begin?" asked Fox.

"I'm getting to that part," Sparks answered. "Early one morning, I noticed a night-shift worker spreading mayonnaise on hundreds of slices of bread. I was so shocked to see these open bowls sitting on counters, which must have been there for hours. I practically lost my temper. Maybe I was too harsh on him, but mayonnaise must be stored in a cold environment or else it spoils. An entire camp could've fallen seriously ill had they eaten any of those sandwiches."

"And you advised your supervisor about this?" asked Parris.

"Of course. I had to. I made the cook throw away all those sandwiches. I added it to my report, and I met with the person in charge of running the dining facility. I only knew him as Joe, and he wasn't a nice guy. I barely got through explaining to him what I had seen, and he cut me off, started lecturing me on minding my current duties. He told me that I didn't know how to do my job. Then he threatened me with the way he stood over me and literally talked down to me."

"Did you comply with him," asked Parris.

Sparks shook her head. "Of course not. I ignored him and met with the kitchen staff behind his back. I explained food and sanitary protocol, such as washing your hands several times a day, respecting the expiration dates on tomato or barbeque sauce, you know, the works. Soon after, there was a big improvement. I even got along with all of the kitchen staff."

"So what went wrong after?" asked Fox.

"I found out that Joe had friends at EFS—which included my supervisor and other people in the army." She toyed with the empty water bottle. "One evening I was giving a seminar to the kitchen staff on food-borne illnesses such as botulism and E. coli, when the army officer in charge of food services walked in on my seminar and ordered me outside. He started yelling at me for disobeying Joe's orders and made more threats." Her voice got a bit louder, and her tone, more acidic. "I couldn't even continue the seminar I was giving, I was so…so…I just wanted to leave, ask for a transfer to another camp."

"Did you?" Fox asked.

"I didn't even get a chance. The next day, thirteen men and women fell violently ill and were rushed to the infirmary. I tried to find out what was the cause, but I was kept in the dark."

"Who was the doctor in charge?" asked Parris.

"Uh," Sparks's eyes searched the ceiling. "Doctor Grafton. I think that's his name."

"So what happened next?" Fox asked as she paused to take a deep breath and then to swallow.

"The next thing that happened was that they had to be moved to a different medical facility."

"Were you able to find out why?" asked Parris.

"From what I heard, the one at Camp Iron Eagle wasn't equipped to handle what the troops were exposed to." She lifted her water to take a drink and then set it back down, realizing it was empty. "Those troops died when their medevac helicopter was shot down, allegedly by enemy fire."

Parris uncrossed her legs. "You said earlier that you didn't believe that Jill's brother, Robert, was killed in action. Where does he fit into all of this?"

"He somehow found out that there hadn't been *any* insurgent attack on the medevac chopper and that the whole thing had been staged. Through improvised means, he leaked this info to Jill. She then learned that Robert was part of the team that was deployed to hunt down the insurgents. It was reported that the team engaged the enemy in a firefight. As a result, Robert was shot and killed. She believes that the conspirators found out about him and set him up to be killed. I guess that he was hoping that she would find a way to leak it to the press. Now, he's dead."

Parris got up and went to the kitchen.

"It didn't take long before I was fired," Sparks put a hand to her chest. "I was blamed for them getting sick and was sent back home. I complained to SLR, submitting my reports. I gave them everything. If there was a risk of E. Coli bacteria in the food that was being served in the dining facility I monitored, I would've known about it. They never took my complaints seriously."

"Does this *Joe* have a last name, or a title?" asked Fox.

"I only knew him as Joe." She took a deep breath, looking down at her hands, as though she needed the time to collect her thoughts. "So there I was, back home in Huntsville, Alabama, living with my parents, and over my head in debt. I tried to sue EFS and SLR, and even contacted a lawyer. Then my parents were involved in a car accident. Both of them are now in a long-term care facility. They didn't have proper insurance so they've been using up their savings."

Parris returned with three more bottles of water. She handed one to Sparks and slid another across the table to Fox. She then sat down with hers and took a sip while Sparks continued speaking.

"I managed to get a job as a substitute teacher in a local elementary school, but I wasn't making enough. The interest rates on those student loans were killing me. The bank was ready to foreclose on the family home. Even my credit cards were maxed out. I was sued, had a money judgment against me, and the income from my part-time teaching job was seized. It was a nightmare. I knew that I'd never be able to afford a lawyer. Psychologically, I knew that I wasn't even prepared to represent myself."

Parris shifted in her chair. "Did you have any idea what kind of person Jill was beforehand?"

She looked at Parris, and then to Fox. "Well, honestly, my first impression was that she didn't operate legally. Then again, operating legally did nothing for me, did it?"

"You took a big chance trusting her," said Fox.

"She convinced me that people were out to get me. What was I supposed to do? I was financially ruined, and my parents were on their way to being so also. Jill saw to it that my parents' bills were paid and kept the bank off our backs. Call her what you want, but in the end she wanted to avenge her brother's death and also bring SLR to justice. As for me, I just want my life back." Sparks turned to Parris. "Thanks for the water, by the way."

"Don't mention it."

Fox took a sip of his water too, then turned to Sparks. "Jill told me that the hard drive was stolen from Sementem, and that the data on it may be able to send several people to jail. It would save us a lot of time if you could tell us what else she shared with you."

"She told me that she was building a case against SLR, and that Sementem was also involved. She didn't have all the answers but she felt that she was getting close. She brought me over here, not only because I could help her identify any chemical formulas and what they could do, but she also wanted me to work with some of her contacts over here in an independent lab. She believed that SLR, Sementem, possibly the military, might find out what she was up to, and then send hitmen after both of us. She felt that I'd be safest here."

Parris then turned to Sparks. "During the time that you spent with Jill did she mention anything about a man named Umari?"

Sparks made a face as though she was curious to know where that came from. "Umari? As in Faouzi al-Umari, the terrorist who bombed our embassies and the cruise line?"

"Yeah, that one," answered Parris.

Sparks shook her head. "No, not that I can remember. Why?"

Parris got up as she turned to Fox. "May I talk to you for a moment?"

She led Fox to where she was sure Sparks couldn't overhear them—into the back of the master bedroom. Experience had taught them both the dangers of standing too close to a window. Not that a sniper was likely aiming at the unit they were in, but one couldn't be too safe.

"What do you make of all this?" asked Fox.

"Honestly, I don't know."

"At least we have an idea why Alghafari wanted this hard drive."

"And why's that? To recreate another Camp Iron Eagle?"

"That crossed my mind." Fox rubbed above his lip.

"As much as I'd like to believe that," said Parris, "it doesn't tie in to why he'd sell a biological weapon to one of Sementem's competitors. He could've sold it straight to Umari."

"What do we know about his buyer, Helmut Brunner, other than he works for Sementem's competitor? Nothing. How do we know that he's not a spy or that his company isn't a front for something else?"

Parris raised an eyebrow as she turned her head away slightly. "A front for what?"

As Fox looked at her, even though the light from the dining room only partially made one side of her face visible, he knew what she was doing, and he'd be damned if he let her back him into a corner. "A front for…it could be anything."

Parris nodded. "Like Ares?"

Dammit, how could I let her do this? He looked away. "I never said that."

"Fox. Tell me the truth."

He sighed. "All I'm saying is that there are angles that need investigating."

"Yes, I understand that," Parris replied. "But we have to consider the facts. LJ or, Jill St. John—whatever name she calls herself—is a career criminal. She steals company secrets and sells them to competitors. I mean, look around you, this condo was purchased with dirty money. All of a sudden her brother's killed and she develops a conscience to help a young woman who was allegedly set up for failure?"

"What are you saying?"

Parris pointed her thumb toward the kitchen. "Sparks and Jill are two women with personal vendettas. They want it so badly that they're reaching the point that they won't consider any other explanation for what's been going on. As for you, you're allowing yourself to get too connected to Sparks. I'm sorry to tell you this, but you're also looking for something that's probably not there."

"You really believe that? I've analyzed everything both Sparks and LJ have said. Even Dewan was able to back up what Sparks told us."

"I'm not calling her a liar. I'm saying that she is so desperate to get her life back that she's willing to do anything. Especially partnering with someone who could've gotten her killed."

"Did you miss the part about thirteen American troops being killed in Afghanistan due to food poisoning? Not to mention another who was possibly murdered because of what he may have found out."

Parris took his hand. It was her way of comforting him whenever he was worked up. "I don't mean to be a Debbie Downer," she said, "but as I said earlier, the compound Sparks drew resembles a protein."

"Exactly. Proteins can be found in bioweapons."

"They're also an ingredient found in fertilizers, ones that are used on Sementem's GMOs," said Parris. "You're reaching again. Sementem operates a multibillion-dollar-a-year industry and they've practically cornered the international agricultural market. And even though they don't have the best reputation, it wouldn't make sense for them to invest their time in researching bioweapons. I'm sorry to break it to you, but what we've discovered doesn't appear to have anything to do with Umari. Both Alghafari and Brunner are dead. The whole business with the hard drive is an FBI matter, not ours."

Fox knew that she may be partially right. Umari may not have been part of the deal. Then again, once Sementem became aware that their secrets were being sold on the illicit market, they could've alerted the FBI's counterintelligence division. They wouldn't send a hit-squad after Alghafari and Brunner. But if the FBI became involved, and if Brunner was arrested, then he may have revealed what was on the hard drive, which could've eventually led back to what had happened at Camp Iron Eagle. But SLR was involved at Camp Iron Eagle, not Sementem. *Ugh.* These unanswered questions were what bothered him the most.

"I guess we go home now and get debriefed," said Fox.

Just then, Fox heard Parris's Android buzz. She took it and looked at the monitor, then showed the instant message to him. It read: COMPOUND NOT FOUND IN ANY KNOWN BIOLOGICAL OR CHEMICAL WEAPONS.

Fuck.

"Are you convinced now?" she asked. "There's nothing much more for us over here. I'm sorry."

Parris left the bedroom, leaving Fox alone. He put his hands on his hips, sighed, and then joined her and Sparks back in the kitchen.

"So what happens now?" Sparks asked.

"You're coming with us," said Fox. "Start packing. Take only what you need."

"Like, right now?" asked Sparks.

"Now," said Parris.

Sparks got up from the table and went to her bedroom.

Both of their cell phones rang, to which they both tapped their earpieces.

"Agents," came General Downing's voice and both Parris and Fox walked back to the master bedroom.

"Yes, sir," said Fox.

"Dewan tells me that you retrieved the hard drive, but the data's useless."

"Unfortunately," said Fox.

"We're coming home," said Parris. "And we're bringing someone with us. The FBI may be interested in some of the things she has to say."

"You're talking about the Sparks girl? Yeah, Dewan told me all about her too. By the way, Tim Weyland just came around. He's been talking non-stop, gave us all we needed to help pinpoint a location for Umari."

Fox met Parris's eyes. He couldn't believe what he just heard. And from the look on Parris's face, neither could she. "You're joking."

"Son, you know I wouldn't joke about something like this."

"No, sir." Fox said that to satisfy his superior—but he still couldn't believe it.

Parris cleared her throat. "What's the degree of accuracy of the intel, if you don't mind me asking?"

"The SEALs are currently in a suburb of Mogadishu as we speak. I'm over at the White House with Merrick, the president, and the rest of the gang looking at the house the SEALs are watching right now." The general paused and they heard him whispering to someone in the background, then he came back to them. "The SEALs are moving in."

For the next ten minutes, they listened to the general as he gave them short, real-time descriptions of what was going on. Based on what the general told them, the SEALs surprised all of Umari's men as they were asleep.

Over the line they heard a background mixture of gunshots, shouting, and screaming. The heavy gunfire ceased and there were several seconds of silence. Then, from a voice in the background—most likely from the commanding officer in Mogadishu—they heard the four words that would later be the cause of a nationwide celebration: "Target is confirmed dead. I repeat, Faouzi al-Umari has been killed."

"We got him!" yelled the general to the backdrop of cheers. "We got the son-of-a-bitch. Congratulations on your work, you two. Especially you, Doctor Parris."

Parris stared at Fox. She appeared perplexed by the whole situation. "Thank you, sir." Her voice lacked any tone of excitement.

"Both of you, report back over here. That's an order."

"Yes, sir," answered Parris and Fox simultaneously.

Fox began walking toward the dining room when he stopped to turn to Parris. "Good job. Your guy came through." He then continued to the dining room.

Parris didn't respond to him. Fox thought that maybe she didn't know how to react. Fuck, he didn't even know what to make of this. Faouzi al-Umari had been killed. Of course the army would conduct an autopsy on the body to be certain that they got their man, but chances were they had the right person.

Fox sat down at the dining room table and finished off his water. Moments later, Parris sat down opposite him and drank hers. He looked over his shoulder and heard Sparks packing her things. It was over, the mission was accomplished, another major terrorist leader eliminated.

Then why did he still feel that something was missing?

Chapter 19

Toronto Pearson International Airport, Mississauga, Ontario. 6:00 PM, EST, Wednesday.

Parris and Fox hardly spoke to each other during the twenty-hour trip to Toronto. He spent his time watching the in-flight movies while Parris read an Eric Jerome Dickey novel. Sparks was the only talkative one of the three—always pestering Fox while he watched the movies asking questions. "What just happened? Why did he do that? What's her name again?" He got so annoyed with her that he nearly made a scene when he told her to shut up. She apologized and didn't say another word for the rest of the flight.

The meals were okay. Breakfast was better than dinner. Nonetheless, overall, the quality of airline food had been on the decline. When flying domestically throughout the continental US, one could rarely get anything decent beyond pretzels and cashew nuts.

Since the earliest flight available for the three of them was through Canada, they chose the route that took them from Bangkok to Hong Kong to Toronto and, eventually, to Washington. When they got to Pearson they disembarked in order to switch planes. The line-up at customs was long, as expected, but once they got to the agent, they got through quickly since each of them only had one carry-on suitcase.

There was a lot of buzz around that the president was going to be making a special announcement. As Parris, Fox, and Sparks walked through the terminal, things were relatively quiet, with dozens of people gathered around each overhead television, which were normally used to broadcast the arrivals and departures. Now, each monitor had been switched to CNN, where a live broadcast came from the White House press room.

It wasn't a surprise to Fox to see so many watching the news feed. Canadians regularly followed what went on in the United States, unlike the other way around. Usually, when it was something big, it would bump any of their own news.

Sparks came up between them as they walked through the terminal. "What's going on?"

"They got him." Fox kept walking.

"Got who?" asked Sparks.

"Faouzi al-Umari," answered Parris.

Sparks looked back and forth at them. "How'd you know that?"

Fox walked around two ladies who were rushing to get a good spot in front of a monitor. "Next to the OJ Simpson verdict, what else do you think would cause the airport to shut down momentarily."

"Hmmm," said Sparks. "Maybe our president getting assassinated."

"It ain't that," groaned Parris.

"Okay," said Sparks. "May we stop to watch?"

"No," Parris and Fox said simultaneously.

Sparks looked back and forth at Fox and Parris, who kept walking away from the melee as cheers erupted all around them. "Why are you both so grumpy? Ain't this good news?"

"It's swell," said Fox, emotionlessly, as the three walked into the Air Canada Maple Leaf Lounge. The room was empty, with the exception of the three of them and the attendant, who appeared to be more interested in his shift ending. Fox led them to a quieter section that was away from any overhead televisions.

He then sat in one of the lounge seats and took out the new Galaxy Tablet he carried with him. It wasn't OST standard, but it was better than nothing. He had already downloaded the latest agency software from a secure and anonymous website after he had purchased it in Hong Kong. At the same time, he had purchased a few clothing items as well as the carry-on suitcase, considering his last one was most likely sitting in an evidence locker of the Bangkok police department—retrieved from the trunk of his smashed-up rental. All that mattered was that he kept up his appearance in order to get by the customs officials. Through his peripheral vision he saw Sparks sit down—leaving two seats in between them as she watched CNN on the distant overhead television.

Parris yawned as she rested her carry-on beside Fox. "I'm getting something to drink. You two want anything?"

"Just water for me," said Sparks. "Unless they have freshly squeezed orange juice."

Parris turned to her. "I noticed that you didn't order any sodas during the flight."

Sparks crossed her legs. "That's right. The amount of sugar they put in those things could kill you. Maybe not now, but later on."

"Water or freshly squeezed orange juice it is." She then turned to Fox. "How about you?"

Fox got up, holding the tablet. "I'll come with you."

They headed to the bar and Fox looked back at Sparks as she continued watching the White House press conference. He glanced at the overhead television and saw Merrick answering questions from reporters.

Fox then turned to Parris. "How about that. Ms. Ahab's finally caught her whale."

"What did you expect?" said Parris. "This is her moment to shine. She's probably counting all the future votes right now."

Parris turned to the barman. "Three bottled waters, please."

"I'll have a Heineken," said Fox.

While they waited, Parris leaned over and stole a glimpse of what Fox was doing on the tablet. He was accessing citizen profiles. "What are you doing?"

Fox kept his eyes on the tablet. "Just checking up on someone."

"Oh yeah? Who?"

He flipped the leather cover over the screen. "It's nothing

important."

"Seriously, who was it?"

"I said it's nothing. Quit worrying."

Parris sighed as the barman brought over three chilled bottles of water and the beer. Parris paid with her company-issued credit card and then they both turned around to return to their seats. They stopped and stared.

Sparks was gone.

"Did you see where she went?" asked Fox.

"I had my back turned to her the whole time, just like you did."

"Shit!"

They quickly did a scan of the lounge, looking to see if she'd moved, but she was nowhere there.

Fox then handed Parris his tablet. "Stay with the bags." He ran out the lounge and into the crowded terminal. It was a sea of people all around him. Why the hell did Sparks give them the slip? And here, of all places…unless, she had been planning this all along.

Fox tapped his earpiece. "Dewan, I need you to access the CCTVs at Pearson Airport."

"I'm on it," Dewan answered. "What happened?"

"Sparks is missing."

"Hey, bro. I'm not even going to ask how that happened. Give me a moment."

Fox ran out the nearest exit onto the arrivals curb and into the unusually cold, blistery Toronto temperatures. He looked up and down the sidewalk as he rubbed his hands together. God, he must be standing in single digit temperatures there right now. He saw taxis, several passengers being picked up, others that waited on the curb. He then looked above at the monorail terminal. No sign of Sparks. He hurried back inside where he made haste down the terminal. Sparks being kidnapped was unlikely, she would've screamed. Unless the kidnapper had snuck up on her and surreptitiously threatened her with a weapon if she didn't go quietly. Although that probably wouldn't have occurred inside the Air Canada lounge. So, why would she take off on her own?

Fox took the escalator upstairs, bumping a traveler as he

passed, stopping a few feet away from the top. It was pointless to keep searching for Sparks on his own. The airport was just too massive. Besides, Dewan and his crew stood a far better chance at spotting her on the CCTVs, and he could use a moment to catch his breath.

He scanned everyone that walked past him. He spoke into the earpiece. "You see her yet?"

"I have five others helping me, in addition to the facial recognition software we're running," said Dewan. "We're doing the best we can."

"She left her luggage…hang on." Fox thought that he saw her from behind, but when she turned to speak to someone who was walking with her, he saw the woman's face. False alarm. "As I said, she left her luggage behind. So keep that in mind during your search."

"I'm heading to the gate," said Parris through his earpiece. "I can handle the luggage."

Fuck! Parris can't even help me since she has to stay with the bags. Three carry-ons to slow her down.

Ten minutes had gone by, which meant that he and Parris had missed the final boarding for Washington.

"We got her," said Dewan. "She boarded a United Airlines flight to Newark a few minutes ago. You better hurry before they close the gate."

I'm going to wring her neck when I get my hands on her.

Dewan gave him the gate number and he broke out into a sprint. Fox wound up dodging people at every turn—even leaping over a set of luggage at one point. At this stage he couldn't give two fucks about who watched him or what they may have been saying.

As he got close to the gate he noticed very few people were in the waiting area. By the look of things it had just closed. Fox walked beside the jetty entrance, to the window, and saw the de Havilland plane reversing on the tarmac.

"Son-of-a-bitch," stammered Fox, catching the attention of the few onlookers who were seated in the waiting area. Not that he gave a shit. Who knew what Sparks was up to and what trouble she'd get herself into.

"I take it that you missed her," said Dewan.

"How'd you guess?"

Just then, Fox saw Parris rushing toward him with the luggage. She had picked up a luggage cart where she had placed their carry-ons, with his tablet sticking out of her shoulder bag. He walked over to meet her in the hall. She clearly wasn't in a good mood, as she was covered in sweat and breathing heavily.

"I got here as fast as I could," she puffed. "I can't believe we let this happen. How did she get a flight so quickly?"

"I just did some checking," said Dewan. "She booked that flight about twenty-five hours before."

"When we were at the airport in Bangkok." Fox put his hands on his hips, gritted his teeth, and stomped his foot on the ground. "She must have booked it with her cell phone."

"Wait, there's more," said Dewan. "She's got a connecting flight to Albany."

The mention of Albany set off alarms for Fox. "Albany? As in Albany, New York?"

"That's the one," said Dewan. "I'll see to it that we have someone waiting for her in Newark."

"Delay that," said Fox. "When's the next flight to Albany?"

"What?"

"You heard me. I want to know when the next flight to Albany is." Fox saw Parris sigh. A few seconds went by before he got an answer.

"Delta's got a flight. You've got twenty minutes to catch it," Dewan replied.

Fox grabbed his tablet from Parris's shoulder bag and walked away. "Get me on that flight."

He heard Parris rushing to catch up. Any second now she'd try to talk him out of it.

"I think I should run this by Downing first," said Dewan. "You know—"

"Get me on the fucking flight," said Fox through gritted teeth. "I'm bringing her back."

He heard Dewan exhale. "I'll get you on it. Never mind how

much shit I'm going to get in for doing this."

"I'll make it up to you."

"Yeah. Sure you will," said Dewan sarcastically, seconds before Fox's Android buzzed. "I just sent you your e-ticket."

Fox grabbed his phone to check it, then put it away.

"Fox, what aren't you telling me?" came a near breathless Parris, seconds before she caught up. She was now walking alongside him. "You know *why* she's going there, don't you?"

He quickened the pace. "You better keep up if you want to say something."

Parris practically sprinted to keep up, considering that her legs weren't as long as Fox's and thus, covered less ground. "What's so special about Albany? Why is it you can't tell me?"

Fox continued to hurry, as he heard Parris struggling with the luggage. Hopefully she'd give up and let him be. He then heard the squeaking wheels on the luggage cart stop spinning, followed by running. He stopped as Parris darted in front of him, blocking his path.

"Why? Why do you keep doing this to yourself?" A hand went to her forehead. "Lord. Why do you keep doing this to me?"

Fox stopped and exhaled hard. "Our army doctor. Or should I say, *former* army doctor."

"What about him?"

"Back in the lounge you asked me what I was doing with my tablet. I was looking up people who were currently serving over at Camp Iron Eagle. The army doctor Sparks told us about, Doctor Grafton, who oversaw the treatment of the thirteen sick troops, just recently set up a private practice in Upstate New York. Tell me, who goes from being an army doctor for only three years to opening a fully staffed private clinic? And not only that, he did so less than six months after he resigned from the army, with all of his student loans suddenly paid off around the same time."

Parris shook her head. "It's over. Faouzi al-Umari's dead."

"He may be dead, but I don't think it's over," said Fox.

Parris looked up to the ceiling while shaking her head. "Please tell me that you don't plan to pay the doctor a visit with Sparks. Because if you do, you *will* be interfering with the FBI's investigation."

"They haven't started investigating him yet. And they probably won't, considering that there isn't an official investigation against SLR or the army."

Parris rolled her eyes, raised her arm halfway, and then threw it in the direction where Fox had been heading. "Then go. Merrick is just looking for a reason to come after you. If you weren't so damn stubborn, you'd realize that you're just giving her more rope to hang you with. You left me hanging to dry back in Belgium. And now you're doing the same thing to me again."

Fox smirked. "Whatever happened to playing a hunch?"

"You're so fucking hopeless," Parris yelled. She didn't appear to care that people stared at them as they walked by.

Fox stepped back. *This* was a side to her he'd never seen. "Parris. Did I just hear you say the F-word?"

She raised her hands as though in surrender. "I give up. I've always had your back when others didn't. I've lied to Merrick and to others who were out to get you. Even Downing's stuck his head out for you at times. But you think that you're invincible, don't you?"

Fox looked away, unable to bear looking her in the eye.

"Yeah. I thought so." Parris walked around him and back to the luggage cart.

He turned and watched her as she grabbed both hers and Spark's carry-ons from the luggage cart, leaving his there, then she continued to walk away. All this without even looking back. He felt the heat emanating from her, even at this distance. It was the angriest he had seen her in a while. When she got back to Washington to be debriefed, she'd most likely be grilled by Merrick. And if she was still as pissed off as she was now, she'd no doubt throw him under the bus. Fuck it. Let her do what she felt was right. Meanwhile, he had to do what *he* thought was right. Turning around, he grabbed his bag and ran to his gate in a steady jog.

Chapter 20

Diamond Oaks Drive, Magnolia, Texas. 9:47 PM, CST, Wednesday.

Steve Haas exhaled the tobacco smoke, relaxing on his living room sofa as he rested his Cuban in the ashtray. One would've expected that he'd be out and about on his 24-million-dollar, 185-acre private, gated estate that was located over forty miles northwest of Houston. But the truth of the matter was that after having spent a long day at the office, he was like the average person who just wanted to come home and relax. And this was his favorite spot.

Dressed in the silk pajamas his children had bought for him last Christmas, even at the age of sixty-eight he had no plans on retiring. And he'd be damned if he'd let the members of the board push him out either. He turned the page of the Time Magazine he was reading while the television was on for background noise.

Two months before, he'd celebrated his eighteenth year as CEO of SLR, and boy, had he seen the company's share of ups and downs. That's why he'd convinced the members of the board to partner with his friend, Mitchell Stayner of Sementem. Since then, company shares continued to rise as they secured more of the nation's military contracts.

The ringing of his cell phone on the table beside the ashtray was the only thing that could interrupt his reading, next to his wife. Haas picked up the phone with one hand while he grabbed the remote and lowered the TV volume with the other.

"Yes?"

"It's me. I'm at the front gate. We need to talk." Haas recognized Bryan Jeansonne's voice speaking to him through the intercom. He had the front gate system designed so that all calls through the intercom after nine in the evening would automatically be transferred to his mobile.

Haas rolled his eyes. *What in God's name does he want?* "Hold on." He pressed the pound key to open the gate.

A few minutes later, Haas opened the front door to let Jeansonne in. "Jesus, Bryan. It's almost ten o'clock at night."

"I can tell time." Jeansonne scowled as he undid the buttons of his coat. "I didn't want to talk to you over the phone."

Haas turned the latch to lock the door. "What's so important that it can't wait until tomorrow?"

"I can't sleep."

"That's a surprise. Even with all the booze you drink?"

"Quit dicking around. I'm serious," Jeansonne spat. He scratched the back of his neck. "I'm still bothered by the way your friend Stayner handled Collins." Jeansonne paused to look around before he turned back to Haas. "Well, you know what I'm talking about."

Although he didn't appreciate Jeansonne coming to his place whining like a little girl at this hour, he did agree with him. "Why don't we talk about this in my office?" Haas reached out to take Jeansonne's coat. "Allow me."

Jeansonne raised a palm. "It's fine. Besides, I'm a bit cold anyway. I hate winter."

"Suit yourself." Haas led the way to his office, where they were behind closed doors. Jeansonne sat on the couch, while Haas went over to the mini-bar that was built into the cabinet. There were six whiskey glasses, along with some hard liquor.

"You'll have bourbon, I presume," said Haas. What better way to calm down a boozer.

Jeansonne looked at him from where he sat. "Yeah. Sure."

Haas poured one and brought it over. "So, what do you want us to do about this? What's done is done."

Jeansonne took the glass. "It's not so much about what or how it was done. It's *who* Stayner hired to do it."

Haas took a seat behind his desk. "Let me guess. You looked into this guy. What have you found out?"

Jeansonne took a sip. "That's the thing. I couldn't find out anything about this guy. He's just some British-sounding nigger, probably from England."

"For God's sake, Bryan. Must you use the N-word in my house?"

"Sorry." Jeansonne took another sip. "It's just habit. Anyway, if I couldn't find out anything about him, why should we believe that Stayner knows more?"

"For all I know he's probably former British intelligence," said Haas. "You know how these spooks value their privacy."

"I don't care where he's from or who he used to work for." Jeansonne shook the glass to stir his drink. "I don't like him. And I don't trust someone I don't like."

Haas's cell phone rang. He looked at the call display and saw that it was listed as private. He clicked on the phone icon. "Yes?"

"Sorry to call you at this hour, sir."

"That's all right, Don." Haas recognized him as being Don Manning, his source within the FBI. "What is it?"

"You asked me to call you as soon as I got some info about that woman, Katy Sparks," said Manning.

"And?"

"Something strange has happened. She's somehow come into money. The mortgage payments on the family home have resumed—covering all the late payments. Her credit card has also been paid off in full."

"What?" Haas couldn't believe what he heard. "Anything else?"

"Yeah, there's more," continued Manning. "She's supposed to be meeting with two field agents for a debriefing sometime soon."

"A debriefing?" Haas looked at Jeansonne, who leaned forward on the couch as though to listen in on the conversation. "About what?"

"I don't know yet."

"How soon will it take place?"

"I don't know that either." Manning cleared his throat. "All I know is that the Bureau's meeting with her because she has something to say."

Haas closed his eyes. He could swear that his blood pressure just spiked. "I see."

Jeansonne made a beeline over to Haas's desk, where he had both hands on the surface as he leaned over it. "What? What is it?"

Haas spun around in his swivel chair so that his back was to Jeansonne. "Find out where she is and call me back." He then pressed the off icon.

"Hey, level with me here," came Jeansonne's voice behind him. "I heard a bit of what the guy was saying to you over the phone. It's about that Sparks girl."

Haas spun around in his chair and faced Jeansonne now. "Yes it is. And I don't like it one bit." He then relayed what Manning had told him.

"Oh that's just fucking great." Jeansonne downed the rest of his bourbon and clapped the glass on the coaster on Haas's desk. "We need to do something about her. We have to call Stayner."

Haas began dialing Stayner's number. "You ain't getting an argument from me about that." He heard the phone ring once before going to voicemail. When he heard the *beep*, he sighed. "Listen, Mitch, I don't know where you are, or what you're up to. But you need to call me back ASAP. We've got a serious problem." He hung up and tossed the cell phone on his desk.

"We can't wait on him," said Jeansonne. "We need to act now."

"That's exactly what we're going to do." Haas sat forward, resting his forearms on the desk. He pondered the implications of what he was about to do. Sure, it was drastic, but it was either this or have the FBI haul his ass in for questioning. He could afford the best lawyers, but why go through the headache and put the company's stock in danger? He picked up his cell phone.

"Who are you calling?"

"Someone who can clean up this mess." Hass dialed a number and put the phone to his ear. "And when he's done, Katy Sparks will never see the inside of a courtroom."

Chapter 21

Albany International Airport, Albany, New York. 11:23 PM, EST, Wednesday.

Fox sat inside his rented Ford Focus as he waited in the parking lot of the Albany International Airport. Dewan's mobile was on its second ring as Fox rested his elbow on the door's windowsill. At this hour, it was possible that Dewan was home.

"Moshi moshi," Dewan's sleepy voice answered.

Fox guessed it. The guy was sleeping. As to why he answered in Japanese was beyond him.

"What's up?"

"Oh, you again." Fox then heard him fail at stifling a yawn. "I got my ass chewed up tonight because of what I did. The general's pissed at you too."

"He can take a number and get in line," said Fox. "Get up, there's something I need you to check out."

"Yo, man. Didn't you hear what I just said? I got into some serious shit because of what I did for you. And you're not even going to apologize? You're a selfish asshole, you know that?"

Fox closed his eyes as he pondered Dewan's words. Parris had told him off back in Toronto over something similar. He may have used up the last of his favors with her because of it, if not ruining their partnership. Or should he say friendship? What the hell was he thinking? He'd been on missions without her before. He could do it again if need be. Then again, who'd keep him grounded the way she did?

"Look. About earlier," said Fox, "I'm sorry for being such a hard-ass. When I said I'd make it up to you, I meant it. In fact, I'll make it up to you now. What would you like?"

"I don't know if I want anything from you."

Fox clenched his phone. "Come on. Give me a break. I put my ass on the line a lot more times than you can imagine."

"Good for you. I'm going back to bed."

Fox sighed. "What the fuck more do you want?" He paused to calm his voice down. "I already said that I was wrong for yelling at you and getting you in trouble."

"I'm hanging up the phone in three…"

"Come on, man."

"Two…"

"Wizards tickets!"

"One. Hold up. What did you just say?"

"I'll get you Wizards tickets."

"Courtside?"

"Courtside."

"And a chance to meet all the players and get their autographs."

"You're pushing it."

"Uh-oh. I feel a yawn coming on…"

"Fine." Fox shook his head. "I'll hook you up so that you can meet all the players and get their autographs."

"That's what I'm talking about," said Dewan as Fox heard a few noises in the background. "Give me a sec."

The he heard what sounded like a chair being rolled across the floor.

"What you need?"

"I need you to find out where Sparks is now. Don't bother tracking her phone because she'd be carrying a burner. I'd check airport rental car companies first."

"Yeah, yeah. You want me to hack the CCTV archives of the Albany airport, find out which rental car company's desk she visited, then match the time with any cars rented at the same time. I've done this before."

As part of an effort to combat terrorism, the CIA had easy access to the CCTVs of every airport across the United States and its territories. Dewan would be able to easily hack into those from his laptop at home. At this hour, with very little traffic, locating Sparks shouldn't be too difficult.

Only three minutes had gone by before Fox heard the sound on Dewan's end change. He must've activated his Bluetooth.

"I got her," he said. "And to make my job even easier, her car has a GPS—which I just hacked—putting her right outside the home of your army doctor."

"No surprise there," said Fox.

"You mean, no surprise that I got mad skills?"

"Don't flatter yourself," said Fox. "And don't go to sleep yet. I'll be calling you back."

"Yeah, yeah. I know the drill."

Fox tapped his earpiece and drove out of the parking lot onto Albany-Shaker Road as a few snowflakes began to fall on the windshield. When he got to the highway ramp he turned southbound on I-87 where he eventually came to I-90 and headed west.

That silly woman must've known what she was doing would get her into trouble. Then again, she was highly motivated to do what she was about to—whatever it was.

Fox hadn't known how long he'd be on the road, so, while he was in Detroit on layover, he'd grabbed a quick bite. Fast food wasn't the best choice, but that's all that had been available. At least he'd eaten.

Now, he was a little over thirty miles from downtown and he exited the interstate and drove to a new housing development. This community was so new that most of the houses were still being built. Fox looked at some of them as he drove by. They were family style homes, big enough to have at least four bedrooms and hold two cars in the garage. From what he remembered from Grafton's profile, he was single without any children, but it didn't mean that he wasn't living with a girlfriend. Also, since Grafton wasn't on the CIA's terrorist watch list, the information on that file might not be up to date.

He came to Grafton's street, but drove past it to the next one. The fact that there were many vacant lots made it easier for him to see through to the adjacent street. Fox turned down his headlights to remain as inconspicuous as possible while he drove slowly. While he did so, he looked outside the passenger window toward Grafton's house. As expected, he saw Spark's car.

Fox pulled over to the curb, got out, then crossed the two vacant lots. From where he was, he saw Sparks sitting in the front seat—completely oblivious that he was on the sidewalk, approaching her from behind.

Fox shook his head. *Amateur.*

He got to the passenger-side window and bent over, staring at Sparks, who still didn't know that he was there. He knocked on the window, startling her. She jumped up, shrieking, as she turned to him. Fox smiled as he gave her a four-finger wave, then watched as Sparks let her head fall back onto the headrest and closed her eyes, exhaling a puff of vapor. She then turned the key in the ignition to the first setting and rolled down the passenger window.

"I can give you one good reason why your plan isn't going to work," said Fox.

"How did you find me?"

"I'm not new to this," answered Fox. "And I can tell you that you're either going to get yourself arrested, or worse." He reached inside, unlocked the door, and let himself in.

Fox closed the door and turned to her. "Why don't you tell me why you ditched me and my associate?"

She turned on the windshield wiper to brush off the few snowflakes that had fallen on it. After one sweep she turned it off, then stared out her window. "Because I don't know you guys, or what you have planned for me in Washington. Considering that we were heading to the nation's capital, I'm assuming that you work for the government."

"Really? Which agency?"

Sparks looked at him. "Does it matter? You could be FBI, CIA, Homeland, NSA. You could even be the IRS for all I care. Jill didn't trust the American government and told me that I shouldn't either."

"Let's see. We have a career cybercriminal who trades in secrets, money laundering, and identity theft, and you expect her to trust the government?"

Sparks looked away. "It's because of *you* guys not doing your jobs that's caused me to be in this mess."

"Don't blame me for the mess that you're in. Blame SLR. And although you didn't get the justice you were hoping for, it doesn't give you the right to blame the government either. From what you told me and my associate, you didn't even have the chance to bring your case in front of a judge." Fox realized how cramped he was in his seat and slid back his chair to give him more leg room. "But you're right. You don't have any reason to trust me. Nor do I have any to trust you. But I'm curious, what would you have done had I been someone else? As easy as it was for me to sneak up on you, if I was one of the killers you and Jill have been avoiding, you'd be dead."

Sparks still didn't look at Fox, or answer him.

"Nothing much to say, huh," said Fox. "Fine. I'll ask you an easier question. When you see Doctor Grafton, what'll you do then?"

"Just watch him, you know," answered Sparks. "As in *casing* the place."

Fox raised both eyebrows. "Really? What makes you think that he's even home?"

"Well…it's twelve past midnight. He's got to be home."

"Really? Do you see a car in the driveway? Did you think of calling the house phone?"

"If he's away, then so much the better. I'll break into his house and look for clues."

"Is that right? What do know about bypassing an alarm system?"

"Uh, actually I was going to wait for him to come home and…" Sparks grabbed the steering wheel with both hands and rested her forehead on it, then exhaled loudly. "Okay, I don't know what the hell I'm doing. I'm not a burglar."

"No, you *are* a burglar. You're just one who'd wind up on an episode of *America's Dumbest Criminals* if it were still on the air."

Sparks looked at him as she narrowed her eyes, her head still against the steering wheel.

He snatched the key from the ignition.

"What are you doing?" She reached over to take back the keys, but Fox switched them to the other hand, holding them out of her reach.

He got out of the car, turned around holding the door, and bent over to look at her. "If you want answers from the doctor, then you're going to need me to show you how to do it right." He shut the door and left. He was halfway across the street when he heard a car door opening and shutting.

"Wait!"

Fox didn't turn around, but kept walking as he heard her running after him.

"What about my car?"

"Don't worry about it." Fox turned to her. In one swift motion, he snatched her phone from her left pocket, having noticed earlier that she favored that one.

"Give that back." She tried to get it from him, but not before Fox dropped it on the street and stomped on it.

"Is this some kind of payback?" Sparks yelled.

Fox shot her a glance. "Keep your voice down."

She looked down at the mess of plastic and circuitry. "That was a burner phone. All you had to do was ask me to turn it off."

"Yeah right. So you could access the emergency bank fund Jill set up for you? Not a chance." Fox heard her groan loudly. He wasn't surprised that she was pissed off. For all it mattered, he didn't give a shit either. He tapped his earpiece, which called Dewan automatically since it always stored the number of the person that was previously called.

"Moshi moshi," came the familiar, yet annoying, answer.

"I need you to hack into Grafton's home alarm system and tell me its current status."

"It's set to *away*," Dewan answered. "It's been like that since seven yesterday morning."

Holy shit. "That was quick."

"I figured you were probably going to break into his house," said Dewan. "So I hacked into his home alarm system and waited for your call."

Fox led Sparks toward the vacant lot. "Not bad."

She darted her eyes all around before turning to him. "Who are you talking to?"

Fox waved her off. "How about you tell me where he is?"

"According to his cell phone signal, he's...he's...at his home address."

"Didn't you just tell me that his home alarm system is set to *away*?"

"Yeah, I did." Dewan's voice implied he was also confused. Fox waited as he heard him typing. "That's what I said. Hold on, I'm going to try something."

While Fox waited, he and Sparks crossed the vacant lot. He then started the car and unlocked the doors with the automatic car starter, and they both got in.

"I just called his clinic," said Dewan. "The voice mail said that the clinic was closed since yesterday evening and won't reopen until Monday morning."

Fox shook his head. "The son-of-a-bitch went out of town after work and forgot to take his phone. Why do people do that?"

"It's happened to all of us at least once." Fox heard more typing. "Hold on, I'm going to pull up his credit card records."

Fox turned up the heat as his hands were cold. He then heard the typing stop.

"I got something," said Dewan. "He last used his card over at Macy's Department Store at sixteen-fifty-five Boston Road in Springfield, Massachusetts. Just before that he was at Subway."

Fox leaned forward as he instinctively put his finger to his earpiece. "When?"

"Earlier, yesterday afternoon."

"I'm impressed."

"You don't sound like it," Dewan answered. "You're chasing a former military doctor. What's up with that?"

Of course the software Dewan used would've brought up the

entire biography of the person the credit card belonged to.

"Let's just say he's been pretty bad," Fox answered as he entered the address on his tablet's GPS app. Springfield was roughly an hour-and-a-half drive from where he was. "How about hotels? Has he checked into one in that area?"

"Naw. None that I can see."

Great. That means he's staying with someone. Unless he's just passing through town on his way elsewhere.

"Can you hack the GPS on his car?" asked Fox.

"I already thought of that. His car doesn't have one."

"How about gas stations?"

"Way ahead of you. His card was last used at the Hess service station at eighty Saint James Boulevard, still in Springfield. He filled up there Tuesday evening and then bought a few things from the convenience store yesterday evening. Prior to that, he filled up in Albany before he left town."

Which meant that he was likely staying someplace that was in the vicinity of the gas station on Saint James Boulevard. He must've been doing some serious traveling to have used up his gasoline in such a short period.

Fox switched the gear to *drive* and did a U-turn. "Check up on any known relatives, business associates, or friends who may be living in that city, focusing on that neighborhood."

"You'll have to give me some time on that one."

"In the meantime, check up on traffic cams in the vicinity of that gas station around the time that the credit card was used."

"Yeah, yeah. And try to spot the blue Cadillac SUV he drives. Way ahead of you. I told you I got skills."

Fox got to the end of the street and turned. "Out of ten, you just went from a five to a six."

"Whatever."

"Oh, I almost forgot. I need someone to come to get Sparks's rental car."

"Yeah, I got it," grumbled Dewan before he hung up.

Fox tapped his earpiece when he noticed Sparks looking at him.

"Was that Fab?" she asked.

"No."

"Someone higher up than her?"

"No."

"Another government agent?"

"No. And I never told you that I worked for the government."

Sparks adjusted her seatbelt. "A hacker? I heard you talking about checking Grafton's credit card usage and traffic cams."

"Someone like that."

"So are you going to tell me which government agency you work for?"

"I'm on my own." Fox smirked, considering that, technically, he wasn't lying to her when he said that.

"Bullshit."

"Look," said Fox, restraining himself from lashing out. "Can you just let me drive without the interrogation?"

Sparks rolled her eyes and sighed. "Fine."

In less than ten minutes Fox was back on Interstate 90, heading east.

Sparks turned to him. "Since you don't want to talk, do you mind if I turn on the radio?"

"Go ahead." Whatever it took for her to be quiet. She spent the next two minutes trying to find a station she liked. First country music, then a commercial, then more country, then another commercial. She landed on a talk-radio station, but wasn't interested in that either. He then caught a bit of old-school hip hop and, to Fox's surprise, Sparks kept it there as she bopped her head to the beat. Although he was still pissed at her for making him chase her across the state, he was glad that, at least, she had good taste in music.

Before he realized it, he was tapping his fingers on the steering wheel.

"You like this?" she asked.

"*Poison* by Bell Biv DeVoe?" Fox smirked. "My parents used to hate it when I'd play this, back when I was a kid." He glanced at her. "Ironically, the song pretty much describes you."

"Speak for yourself," quipped Sparks. "You ain't much of a gentleman either."

"I'm letting you keep the radio station you like, aren't I?"

"Maybe it's because your mom and pop ain't here to make a fuss about it."

"Can we just…ride peacefully, without you bitching?"

Sparks was silent for a moment before she pushed her seat back, reclined it, and stretched her legs out. "Sure."

Good. Get comfy and go to sleep.

About an hour later they drove past the big blue Welcome to Massachusetts sign. It wasn't long after that they drove across the Connecticut River into Chicopee, which was on the outskirts of Springfield. Fox checked the clock on the dash, which read 2:12 AM. The doctor was most likely getting some shuteye, considering that there hadn't been any more activity on his credit card. Not that Fox was complaining, the amount of traveling was beginning to take its toll on his body. He needed to rest if he wanted to be in peak form—both mentally and physically.

He pulled into the parking lot of the Inn of New England on Burnett Road. He chose this hotel because of its proximity to the junction of the I-90 and the I-291—making it the closest hotel to the Hess gas station where the card was last used. He parked and turned off the engine, then stared at the hotel in front of him. The place had obviously seen better days. The building in front of them looked pretty old and rundown. The hotel's rooftop sign was something straight from the 1970s with only five of the fifteen letters actually working. And judging from the five cars in a parking lot that could easily hold one hundred, he didn't have high expectations once he got inside.

Sparks sat her seat upright and slid it forward, then stared at the hotel for about five seconds before pointing at it. She looked at Fox with a scrunched-up face. "*This* where Grafton's staying?"

"No."

"Then what are we doing here?"

"We're going to get some rest. I'm in the mood for a shower and a good nap, and trust me, you can do with the same."

"What's that supposed to mean?"

"Let me put it this way…if you were going to jump Grafton outside his house, you'd have to do so downwind."

Fox undid his seatbelt. "Now, this is how it's going to happen. We're going to walk inside, arm in arm. I'm going to ask for a room with either a king- or queen-sized bed."

"The hell you are." Sparks crossed her arms, twisting at the waist to look at him. "We ain't sleeping in the same bed."

"If things go south and the police investigate, we're going to need a plausible cover," said Fox.

She pointed to the hotel. "But look at this place. It looks cheap. Did you even bother to check *Tripadvisor-dot-com* before coming here? At least to see if guests have complained about bedbugs?"

Christ. "We're not staying the weekend. It's only for a few hours."

"That's more than enough time for bedbugs to bite you."

"There aren't any damn bedbugs. So quit thinking about them."

Sparks rested her elbow on the windowsill and held her forehead, sighing loudly.

"As I was saying," said Fox, "we need to establish a cover in the event of a contingency. Hotels such as this one are desperate for business, and they'll gladly take cash, which—as Jill would've told you—is untraceable. The receptionist will hopefully think that I'm a cheating husband who doesn't want the transaction showing up on his credit card statement for his wife to see."

"So we don't have to sleep together?"

Fox rolled his eyes. "I'll sleep on the floor if that'll make you feel better. Unless you still believe that there really are bedbugs, in which case, you can sleep on the floor."

Sparks got out of the car, slamming the door behind her. He watched her walk away, then stop to look back at him, both hands on her hips. "Well. We're supposed to be a couple, aren't we?"

He closed his eyes and shook his head, then got out and joined her, locking the door via the button on his key-ring. "On second thought, it's best that you don't say anything. Let me do the talking."

Sparks responded with a *humph* and walked slightly ahead.

Fox didn't mind sleeping on the floor. During his JTF2 training, he had to sleep in the wilderness in northern Canada and also in the Brazilian rainforest—often without a pillow and adequate survival gear. He could handle sleeping on what probably would be a thin carpet and pillow.

When they were close to the entrance, Fox reached ahead and grabbed her arm, pulling her closer to him. "Now's the time, my dear."

"I know that," Sparks grumbled. "You don't have to overdo it."

Fox pulled open the door. "Just smile as though you're excited about what's waiting for you in bed."

"I'll be excited when this charade's over."

"Shut up and get with the program," said Fox through clenched teeth as he grabbed her by the waist and pulled her even closer.

They approached the receptionist's counter, only to see the attendant slouched in a chair behind it with her head hanging low, asleep. She was a pudgy fifty-something woman with unkempt hair, peppered with a few gray strands, wearing thick glasses. Her arms were folded across her stomach, which slowly rose and dropped. All the while, a television was on in front of her.

Fox cleared his throat.

The lady didn't budge.

Fox kicked the bottom of the counter, hard, startling the woman to the point that she had to catch her glasses just as they were about to fall off. She straightened them as she looked up and saw them.

"Oh, hey there." She got up out of her chair. "Sorry about that, I guess I dozed off. It's been a long, busy day."

Whatever. Fox watched her get up with some difficulty. A sign of arthritis in one, if not both, knees, no doubt.

"Good morning and welcome to the Inn of New England. My name's Margery, how can I assist you?" Margery's smile was the nicest part of the hotel so far.

"Hi there," Fox said with a Boston accent. "Man, that was a long drive. You got kings or queens in these rooms?"

"I'm assuming that you want a single room, for one night," said Margery. "Is that correct?"

Fox chuckled. "Wow, you read my mind. How much is that gonna cost?"

"That'll be sixty-five dollars. I'm assuming you're paying cash, right?" Margery nodded.

"There's no getting anything by you, is there."

"Not in this lifetime, handsome," Margery said with a chuckle. "As per hotel policy, you'll have to pay a deposit."

"That won't be a problem." Fox took out his wallet and fished out four twenties for her.

Margery took the bills, licking her index finger before counting them. She put them in the cash register and gave Fox his change. She then picked up a plastic keycard and swiped it through the card scanner, programming the room code into it, then handed it to him. "You're in room one-thirteen, just down the hall. Would you like the *mostly* requested seven-AM wake-up call?"

"You bet," answered Fox as he took the keycard.

"Will do," said Margery. "Will you need anything else?"

"Can we get a receipt?" asked Sparks.

Fox squeezed her waist. "Forget she said that."

"Then enjoy your brief stay." Margery smiled. "And *do* come again—so to speak, that is."

Fox relaxed his grip on Sparks. "We will."

When they were out of Margery's view, Sparks pulled herself away from Fox. After he let them into their room, he turned on the lights and looked at her. "What part of *let me do the talking* didn't you understand?"

"All I did was ask for a receipt."

"It doesn't matter." Fox kicked off his shoes. "Your southern drawl is a dead giveaway that you're not from around here."

"So what? We're in a hotel," said Sparks. "And people who stay in hotels are usually from out of town."

"That's not the point," growled Fox. "If things go sideways and the police get involved, they may check out the hotels. Your accent identifies you, making it easier for the receptionist to remember you if ever she's questioned."

Fox walked away. Maybe it was a bad idea to bring her along. On the plane from Bangkok, she was garrulous. Now she was about to screw things up.

Sparks crossed her arms. "I'm sorry. I'm not the expert. You are."

Fox surveyed the room as he strode over to the curtains and closed them. He picked up a hint of after-shave wafting off them—God knows why they smelled that way. The room itself was about fourteen feet wide, had a twenty-seven-inch television directly in front of the king-sized bed, which, from where Fox stood, appeared to be clean.

Sparks pulled all the sheets from the bed and did a thorough inspection. When she was done she tossed them back.

He looked at her, questioning. "So?"

She appeared disappointed. "The bed's fine."

"Told you so."

Sparks then grabbed a pillow and the comforter, tossing them in the floor space between the bed and the window. "As per our agreement." She then walked to the front door where she kicked off her shoes and hung her jacket on the coat rack.

Fox watched her as she disappeared into the bathroom, shutting herself in. A few minutes went by before he heard the toilet flush, followed by the shower running.

He went to the coat rack where he hung his jacket, then returned to the bed, grabbing the remote from the top of the television on the way. He sat down on the edge, admiring the comfort of it as he sank into the mattress. He flipped through the stations until he landed on a rerun of *The X-Files*. He instantly recognized it as one of his favorite episodes, where Agent Mulder suspected that cockroaches were responsible for several mysterious deaths in a Massachusetts town. Of course, Scully, his partner, always had a scientific explanation for each of the deaths—one that didn't involve the roaches. Those were the days when the show kicked ass.

Ten minutes into the episode, Fox heard the shower stop. A few more minutes ticked by until he heard the hum of a hair dryer. Once that ended, the door opened and Sparks came out, wrapped in a towel, holding her jeans and shirt.

"The hot water ran out." She shrugged. "See. Cheap hotel. Told ya."

He examined her. Her hair was let down and it appeared to be slightly damp. Her breasts were small, but they were busty enough to hold up the towel. She wasn't as thin as LJ was when he'd seen her on the massage table. That aside, she still had one hell of a nice body.

What the hell? He gave his head a good shake. *Focus.* "I'll survive a cold shower," Fox replied while turning off the television. He tossed the remote on the bed as he got up, brushing past Sparks.

No surprise to Fox, the mirror was covered in condensation with steam everywhere. He wiped it off with his hand, only for it to fog up again. The shower rod had rust on it where it was attached to the wall, and a quick glance down showed some around the drain as well. He left the bathroom door open so he could keep an eye out for Sparks through the bathroom mirror, which, thankfully, was beginning to clear. He didn't expect her to run away after she'd agreed to come with him all the way here. Besides, she wanted to get answers out of Doctor Grafton too. She'd never be able to find him without Fox's help. Even if she did take off, he had the car keys in his pants pocket—which he tossed on the toilet with his other clothes, then placed his cell phone and the earpiece on the counter.

He didn't shower for too long. The water barely lukewarm and not lasting as long as he had hoped. He got out just as it turned cold. He dried himself, slipped back into his boxer briefs and muscle shirt, then wandered into the room while he putting his earpiece back in—just in case Dewan called. He'd remove it before he went to sleep.

Sparks was already in bed, under the covers. She eyed him as he hung his pants over the chair in front of the corner table. She wasn't aware that he was in anti-surveillance mode. Although he wasn't looking at her, he could tell that she was watching him.

She yelped. "What the…"

Fox spun around in time to see her in full freak-out mode. "What's the matter?"

"Something bit me." She struggled to get out of bed, her legs tangling in the sheets as she fought her way out. Finally free, she stood on the opposite side of the bed, wearing nothing but her shirt, which hung just low enough to hide her panties.

Fox sighed, his head slanting to the side. "Not the imaginary bedbugs again."

Sparks examined her legs as though she were trying to catch what had allegedly bitten her. "I know what I felt."

He watched her yank off the sheets again, throwing them to the floor, and examining the surface—particularly the area where her legs would've been.

She huffed and stormed away from the bed, straight to the coat rack, grabbing her pants and thrusting them on as she spoke. "We're leaving. I'm not staying here a second longer."

"Don't start this shit again."

"I mean it. I'm leaving."

"Fine, then go. I'll have the bed to myself."

"Typical of you, Rob—or whoever you really are."

Fox tossed the sheets back on the bed and then sat down, the remote in his hand, propping his back against the headboard. He turned the television back on and ran his hand across the mattress. "The bed feels fine to me."

"Bullshit. You're just saying that." She had on her jacket now and both hands at her sides, with clenched fists. "I don't want to stay here."

Fox looked at her, shrugged his shoulders, and gestured to the door. "Then, by all means, go."

He must've been convincing about letting her leave because an *I-can't-believe-you-said-that* expression appeared written all over her face. Then she scowled and crossed her arms. "This is ridiculous. Of all the hotels in town, you had to choose the cheapest, the most low-class, rundown, piece-of-shit building in the vicinity."

"I'm sorry I couldn't accommodate your high-class lifestyle, the one you obtained with your bank accounts being seized, and your family home nearly being repossessed."

"Don't *you* go there. I'll be the first person to admit that I don't come from a wealthy family," Sparks pointed a finger at herself, "but just because my parents had to use most of their retirement savings to put me through college, doesn't mean that I was raised without standards."

"This isn't about standards. It's about us maintaining our cover." Fox got off the bed and stood in front of her. "And I don't know about you, but I'm tired and would like to get some shuteye. But instead, I have to put up with your germ-phobic chicaneries."

"You're a goddamned, selfish, inconsiderate prick," she yelled.

"I'm a what?" Fox chuckled.

"You heard me. You're an egotistical, self-serving, self-indulgent, self-centered asshole."

"Yet, you couldn't do better than Butch."

The slap Fox earned was to his ear, temporarily making all sounds from that side feel as though he were inside a vacuum.

"How dare you."

Fox didn't answer. He didn't even feel angry at the slap, and he could tell that pissed her off. So he went for the trifecta—might as well get a third dig in. "Are you satisfied?"

She went to slap him again with the same hand, but Fox caught it this time. She switched and tried smacking him with the other, but he grabbed that one too. Then, before she could think of kicking him in the shins, or kneeing him in the balls, he had her hands stretched out and he pinned her against the bedroom door with his body.

"Let me go, asshole." She spoke through gnashing teeth as she tried to fight him, her partially muffled cries vibrating against his chest. "I said let me go."

Fox didn't yield. Her protests grew weaker, but she wasn't through struggling—she head-butted his chest, but with limited room, she was unable to snap her head back far enough to deliver a powerful blow. Again she tried, but this time he was expecting it and he flexed his pecs so that her head would strike hard muscle.

She grunted loudly, seeming to lose strength in her third attempt. But this time when she failed to elicit the desired response from him, she buried her face in his chest and began to bite.

The sharpness of her teeth cut into his flesh, but he took the pain and held out longer than she could. And that's when her grunts turned to panting as she relaxed her stance, appearing to be weak from the prolonged struggle. He took a chance and separated himself from her and loosened his grip on her wrists. He felt her hands sliding up his forearms and felt the heat from her open mouth panting against him. Her hands then quickly grabbed the neck of his shirt and pulled his mouth to hers in a hungry kiss, her teeth grabbing hold of his bottom lip and tugging hard.

He forced his hips against her, pinning her against the door, his hands reaching behind to grip her ass and hoist her up. Yes, he was getting hard, and he knew she felt his cock against her. She wrapped her legs around his waist—putting her lower abdomen at the same level as his cock. As a test, Fox backed off a bit, but she followed—calling him back in to her. *Fuck, she wants the same thing I do.* And she teased him by pushing her lower abdomen into him, holding it for several seconds before she relaxed.

Fox came up for air, feeling her warm breath against his face. He then pressed his mouth onto hers, forcing his tongue deep, reacting to the level of passion she displayed as she tangled her hand in his hair, pulling and pushing at the same time. Their tongues wrestled back and forth, his winning as he pushed hers out of the way and captured her top lip between his teeth.

The friction and heavy breathing creating heat between them, Fox unlocked his lips from hers to come up for air. He stepped back from the door—Sparks still firmly attached to his torso—and as he spun around he reached out, grasping onto his jacket which slipped off the hanger into his hand. Gravity took control and he fell on top of her on the bed, his hand now reaching out to prop himself up. He bent his head down, lips and tongue latching onto her neck, sucking hard while his tongue snaked around, searching for the jugular.

Her head snapped back, moaning, as his tongue flitted back and forth, feeling the rapid staccato of her blood pumping through the vein. He pressed harder, and she howled ever louder as he bit down on her shoulder, hard, but not drawing blood.

Consumed with fervor, his hand slid up under her shirt, grabbing her breast, flicking the nipple back and forth with his thumb. She jerked in response to his actions and then let loose a deep guttural moan. He released her then, backing up into a kneeling position, ripping off his shirt and throwing it to the side. But she was quick, matching his desire and surpassing his speed. By the time he looked down, she had removed her shirt, exposing her breasts, and was unzipping the fly of her jeans. Fox backed up off the bed, grabbed the bottom of her jeans by the hem, and with one hard tug they came off, taking her panties halfway down too, yanking her right off the bed with them, and face-first into his hardened cock.

With a grin, Fox held the sides of her head with both hands as she grabbed his ass and pulled him closer, rubbing her face against his dick, making it pop out from the top of his boxer briefs. He thrust his hips forward into her face, back and forth, her open mouth sliding up and down the length of the shaft. She stopped, releasing her grip on his ass, and he was momentarily disappointed, until she reached up and pulled down his briefs.

Freedom.

Then, back to business—he tangled his hands in her hair, holding her there, as the hot wetness of her mouth wrapped around him again, suctioning his strength. Fox flexed his ass out of reflex as Sparks dug her nails in. The pain he would've normally felt was cancelled out by the radiating sensation coming from her mouth. One hand released an ass cheek, only for him to feel two—no three—fingers tickling his balls. His head rolled side to side as disorientation struck, causing his knees to buckle. Before falling forward, Fox spun around, still holding her head and taking her with him, landing on the bed.

With that movement, she climbed on top of him, and another type of warmth met with his groin. It was wet, with a slight bristle of hairs.

Oh, God, this is a rush.

He looked to the side, noticing his jacket hanging off the edge of the bed. He reached for it while Sparks kept rubbing her hot wetness against his cock. Water and sweat were dripping on him as she leaned over, her damp hair hanging down and tickling his neck. He let out a loud moan as his head pressed back into the pillow, causing him to lose sight of the jacket, but he could feel it being pulled closer to him.

"Which pocket?" she huffed.

"Inside...right," Fox breathed and closed his eyes. When he

opened them, Sparks already had the condom out of the wrapper and was rolling it on like a pro.

"You still pissed at me?" The words escaped Fox's mouth, and it took a moment for him to register what he had just said, his focus going to the moist heat sliding down his cock.

"You—" she yelled.

"Are—" She eased down another few inches.

"An absolute a—ahh!" A couple more and she had buried him so deep he hit a wall.

She pulled up, just a bit, then went back down as Fox pumped his hips in sync with her movements, filling her to capacity, hitting the wall again...and again. Sparks then slammed herself down, past her physical limitations as her body gave way to his cock, taking all of him, forcing a scream that seemed to come from just as deep inside of her.

The warmth, the moistness, so soft yet so tight as it yanked his cock, gliding against the protruding lower edge of the head, sending a shock that caused him to thrash about wildly.

"Are you...still...fucking pissed...at me?" Fox yelled.

"Yes, you self-indulgent, selfish—oh, God."

"You know I'm a God"

"Not what I...meant." She struggled to get the words out.

"Then show me. Show me how much I piss you off," Fox taunted, gasping for air.

His arms flat beside him, he forced them down into the bed, grasping handfuls of the sheets as he plunged himself into her, harder with each repetition.

"You wanna know? I hate...you. I hate you. I—" She stopped her train of thought and picked up the pace—harder, faster, deeper. *Fuck.*

Up until that moment, Fox had thought himself in charge, but he wasn't. Not by a long shot. She was controlling him. Disorientation began to stretch its tentacles, surrounding his head, making his vision spin in vortexes. Fox felt as if he was dropping in and out of consciousness as a shock radiated from his groin.

He tightened his death-grip on the bed sheets, his head thrust back into the pillow as he pitched his hips upward so hard that his back formed an arch, lifting his rival off the bed for a brief second as he exploded into her. He collapsed back into the bed, only to thrust his hips up a second time, detonating again inside her before he dropped back down, gasping.

He was out of control. All his frustration and anger rushing to escape as he jerked his hips up a third time. At this point he didn't give a shit how badly he may have been hurting her. His hands lashed out, grabbed her waist tight, preventing her from being bucked off—he had no idea how much his fingers were digging into her. Didn't care. He closed his eyes tightly, opening them in time to see her whip her head behind, her hair breezing back. And another shot of rage pumped into her. This was it—he no longer had control of his own cock. It involuntarily squeezed out every drop of his indignation.

He held the position, feeling the bones in his lower back crack as he arched even higher—hold it, hold it, just hold it. Now breathe. He relaxed, letting his ass fall onto the mattress. He lost strength in his grip and his hands fell limp beside him. The sound of their mutual panting filled the silence around them.

Sparks keeled over onto his chest, using some sort of interior vise-grip to maintain her hold on his cock, which was still rock-solid inside her.

Keep holding that shit in there. Just keep it in. You're going to get to know this dick. You're going to respect this dick. The last thing you'll think of before falling asleep is this dick. Oh, fuck yeah!

She moaned once more, then rolled to the side, finally disengaging herself. Fox was about to turn his head to look at her, but he was unable to do so. All he heard was a long continuous moan. And it was the last thing he recalled before he passed out.

Chapter 22

Inn of New England, Springfield, Massachusetts. 7:00 AM, EST, Thursday.

Fox sprung up at the sound of the loud, jarring noise of the first ring of the bedroom phone. He snatched it off the receiver and heard the recording, telling him that it was a wake-up call. He put it back down, fell on his back, then felt a presence beside him. He looked and saw Sparks lying on her side, facing him. She didn't appear to have been stirred by the ringing phone. He sat back up, letting his face fall into his hands, and sighed.

It was just a fuck. Just a release. She was a beast. He then looked up and smiled. *And it was fucking great.*

The prostitute in Amsterdam came to mind. What was her name again? That emptiness he'd felt the following morning after he'd been with her, he didn't feel it now.

Dammit, focus. It was just a fuck—a basic necessity. Focus.

Fox looked at Sparks, who was clearly out of it. His own doing, no doubt. He got off the bed and went to the bathroom where he pissed, took a shower, and was out. By the time he was dressed, he looked back at Sparks as he went to the front door. She didn't appear as though she'd be going anywhere soon, so he left. He went to the dining room where he picked up a Styrofoam plate and stacked it with muffins and croissants then covered it over with another Styrofoam plate. There was juice, but he noticed that there was also bottled water. So he grabbed two of them and headed back to his room.

Sparks was still asleep when he returned, only she had rolled onto her stomach and was in the center of the bed.

Fox put the plate on the corner table and pulled open the drapes. The room exploded with sunlight. He then went over to the bed where he patted Sparks on the shoulder. "Time to get up."

She groaned and pulled away from him, then went back to sleep.

Fox leaned over, placing his hand on her shoulder, and shook her. She moaned at first, then looked over her shoulder, saw him, then rolled onto her back.

"Good morning," Fox said. "You're a strong sleeper."

She sat up yawning, with a hand covering her mouth. "What time is it?"

"It's half past seven," Fox answered. "I brought us something to eat. And they had bottled water, as you would've asked me to bring I'm sure."

"Didn't you request a wake-up call?"

"It came." Fox took a drink from his bottle. "You were too far off in dreamland to hear it."

She held her head in one hand. "Oh God."

"You'll have plenty of time to recover," Fox said, putting down his bottle and grabbing the remote. He turned on the television, switched stations from the default hotel channel, then raised the volume to help revive her. "Go shower quickly. I want to be out of here in ten minutes, and not a second later."

She was very lackadaisical in her movements, but eventually managed to get herself off the bed to shuffle over to the bathroom.

She was naked and didn't seem to care. When she passed in front of Fox he was certain that she did so on purpose. He turned down the volume as the commercial break ended. ABC news was on, and they were still discussing the killing of Umari. As Fox heard the shower going, the commentators even spoke of Alghafari and his connections to Umari, and to several other incidents.

Sparks was done showering in roughly five minutes and came

out. In precisely nine and a half minutes they had left the room with the muffins and croissants, and were at the receptionist's desk. Margery still wore the same clothes, still looking as though she missed the last ride to the trailer park.

"Good morning," she smiled as Fox handed her the key card. "Your stay was pleasant, I hope."

"It was…great," Fox answered in the same Boston accent he'd used earlier.

Margery looked at Sparks and then back at him and snickered. "I'll bet."

He switched the plate over to the other hand while he took Sparks by the hand. "Take care."

"You too, hon," Margery answered. "And *do* come again."

They were close to the front entrance when Sparks turned to Fox. "If she keeps using the same annoying puns as slogans she'll lose whatever business the hotel's getting right now."

He held the door open for her. "If it works for business, who am I to argue how many annoying puns she uses."

In less than fifteen minutes, they were driving along Saint James Boulevard, approaching the Hess service station. Fox called Dewan, who answered after the first ring.

"What's up?"

Fox slowed down at the traffic light. "You got anything?"

"Nada. I changed the settings on my software program to alert me the moment the credit card was being used."

"Good enough, I'll wait for your call." Fox tapped his earpiece to turn it off as he drove. He saw the service station ahead at the next stop light. The area also had several other small businesses and stores within the same city block, including a CVS Pharmacy that was adjacent to the service station. He drove to the pharmacy's parking lot and parked his car where he had a perfect view of the service station.

Sparks, who had been eating on the way over, turned to Fox. "What do we do now?"

"We wait," he answered. "You'll want to make yourself comfortable because we could be here for a while."

"How long?"

"It could be a few hours."

Sparks didn't say anything. She simply put the plate on the dashboard, reclined her chair, and within minutes was fast asleep.

Yeah, this could be a while, he thought as he turned on the radio. He found some good old BB King, which made him tap his fingers on the steering wheel. He then reversed his chair as far as it would go. If he was going to be here for some time, it was important to not keep his legs locked up in the same position for too long. In about twenty minutes he'd step outside to stretch his legs, and repeat the process twenty minutes later. Not only was that good for him but it would help him from getting bored. There were some clouds rolling over, blocking out the sun. Fox looked at the weather app on his Android, and sure enough there was a forty percent chance of flurries.

He glanced over at Sparks, who was long gone. Fox then looked back toward the service station. *Come on, doc. Where the hell are you?*

Chapter 23

CIA Headquarters, Langley, Virginia. 10:08 AM.

General Paul Downing's office probably had more memorabilia than any other office at Langley. The walls were plastered with pictures of him shaking hands with the president and other world leaders. There were other decorative items such as framed certificates, medals, and practically everything a four-star army general could possibly obtain in terms of accolades. Doctor Nita Parris had been in his office several times. For some reason she was still impressed by what she saw each time she visited—even though there wasn't anything new. She was seated in front of him while he read her report from behind his desk. Although it wasn't a long report—only three pages on what happened in Nijmegen and Bangkok—he took his time. With an elbow on the desk, he held his chin as he flipped the pages.

General Downing let out a long breath as he turned over the last page, sat back in his chair, and looked at her. "That's it?"

Parris clasped her fingers together and rested them on her lap. "That's my report."

"And you really believe that Fox still won't accept this hard drive business as simply a case of corporate espionage."

"He has a right to his theories, and I respect him for that," said Parris. "But I'm looking at the facts, and unfortunately they don't support anything different than what I've reported."

"And this woman, Katy Sparks. What's your impression of her?"

Parris crossed her legs. "If you're referring to her being wrongfully terminated from SLR, I believe her. But as I told Fox, if there was some foul play that occurred at Camp Iron Eagle, it's not for us to investigate."

At that moment the door to Downing's office flung open and Merrick walked right in. No knock, no advance phone call, just her barging in.

"Doctor Parris," she said, smiling. "So good to see you again."

Oh, Lord. Are you kidding me? Merrick, smiling?

Parris saw Downing's lack of reaction. A sign that he wasn't too pleased with Merrick's arrogance, but refused to show it. At least, that's what she thought. Had this been her office and someone decided to barge in the way she did, boy, would she be vexed. And Merrick even acknowledged her as *doctor*, and even before she acknowledged General Downing. That was a surprise.

Merrick turned to Downing. "Hello, Paul."

"Director," the general answered. "I wasn't expecting you to drop in."

"Yes, I know that it's short notice," said Merrick. "But I wanted to see Doctor Parris in person, to congratulate her on her work with Timothy Weyland."

You've got to be kidding me. Parris looked away from her for a moment, then back at Merrick. "Thank you, Director."

"Oh come on, Doctor," said Merrick as she sat on the edge of Downing's desk to face her. "Weyland was able to help the FBI and Homeland interpret the evidence we obtained from Bismarck Securities. Together, we were able to follow the money trail straight to Umari—allowing us to send that greasy son-of-a-bitch to hell where he belongs."

Parris rested her elbow on the arm of the chair as she held her forehead. "Wonderful."

"Hey." Merrick snapped her fingers in front of Parris, much to her annoyance. "You were the one who took out the two men Bismarck hired to kill him."

"One of them was a woman," Parris corrected.

Merrick waved a hand and chuckled. "Same thing. Had you not, as my son would say, busted a cap in their asses, Umari would still be blowing things up."

That's right, she almost forgot. Merrick had a special-needs son who was two years younger than she was. Merrick must have been in a good mood because she rarely spoke of him. Parris couldn't hide her lack of enthusiasm as she looked up at Merrick. "I'm glad I could help."

"And I have some great news for you," Merrick continued. "Your expertise is needed over at the Nairobi station."

"Come again?" said Downing.

Merrick turned to him. "That's right. There's been a few terrorist activities involving al-Shabaab. We need someone over there who can recruit some key assets." Merrick then gestured to Parris. "Considering the fine job she did with Weyland, I couldn't think of a better candidate."

The general then leaned forward. He still didn't lose his temper, although Parris may have done so at this point had she been behind his desk. "With all due respect, why wasn't I informed of this? After all, Doctor Parris reports to me."

"Not anymore," said Merrick as she slid off Downing's desk and stood next to Parris. "Her flight will leave from Andrews at seven AM tomorrow morning."

Merrick patted Parris on the shoulder. "As for Fox, we're going to have to talk about him later on. I know of his trip to Albany and I don't like it one bit."

Parris looked up at Merrick. "To be fair, Fox only went because the asset already knows him. She's more likely go willingly with him than with someone else. That's all."

"Go willingly with him?" asked Merrick rhetorically. "Then maybe you could explain why he's been in touch with Dewan trying to locate a former army physician." She then shook her head. "Such a bright future that kid had. Now Fox had to go lead him astray."

Such a bright future? Parris looked at Downing and then shot a look at Merrick. "You're firing Dewan?"

"That's nothing for you to concern yourself about," Merrick

answered. "Just go home and pack your bags. You have a long flight ahead of you." After she bid her farewells to both Parris and Downing, Merrick left.

Parris closed her eyes and, with her elbows on her knees, she let her head fall into her hands. She then looked up at her superior. "Why do I feel as though I'm being punished?"

Downing closed the file folder that contained Parris's report. "Don't take it personally. It's just the way things are."

"That's it?" Parris said. "Just like that? You're not going to fight this?"

Downing leaned back in his chair. "What's there to fight? Fox took a chance searching for what he thought would've been valuable intel that would help us track a known terrorist and he came up with nothing."

"And as I already mentioned," said Parris, "at the time, I honestly thought we were onto something."

"I thought so too," said Downing. "But it's over, at least as far as the CIA's concerned. We need to focus our energy elsewhere."

Parris swallowed and sighed. "I can honestly say that I agree."

Downing then leaned forward, over his desk, forming his fingers into a steeple, and narrowing his eyes as he looked into hers.

"As I just said," Downing spoke very slowly, as though to make a point, "I *do* mean *elsewhere.*"

He was speaking to her in code. It was now obvious that this was his way of expressing his disapproval with her being transferred so far away. There wasn't any way in hell that he'd approve of Merrick doing what she just did behind his back. All she cared about was her presidential nomination, and she wanted to be sure her political opponents couldn't use any of the recent screw-ups against her. Parris had a good idea what Downing was telling her, but she couldn't acknowledge it in front of him, because she knew that he was trying to keep his hands clean. Who knew, maybe Merrick had Downing's office bugged. The idea wasn't too farfetched,

"Very well, sir," Parris told him before she got up and left.

She arrived at her Georgetown apartment an hour later and

quickly emptied her previous carry-on suitcase and replaced it with other clothes. She then took out her tablet, where she was lucky to be able to purchase a plane ticket for the 1:55 PM flight—being that it was the last one available for the destination she was heading to—then called a cab. She put on her black pantsuit, stacked Blahniks, and threw on a charcoal gray trench coat and waited outside. The DC cab arrived moments later and she got in.

"Where to?" asked the driver.

"National Airport," Parris answered. "US Airways terminal."

Chapter 24

Central Avenue, Jersey City, New Jersey. 12:04 PM, EST, Thursday.

Eight fucking years at that goddamned company with absolutely nothing left to show for it. It was *his* code, it had Kevin Ancheta written all over it for God's sake. Now he was no longer working for them—fired for a false sexual harassment claim. *He* designed the multimillion-dollar code, *he* wrote it. And his employer, or rather, former employer, will make millions from it. *Get a lawyer and sue the shit out of them, we'll back you,* said his former colleagues. That was until it came to questioning them in court, when they all suspiciously developed cases of amnesia.

Fuck 'em.

It had been nearly two months. Someone had to hire him, he had way too much experience. Kevin kept reminding himself of that as he emailed a few more resumes from his station at the Internet café. He didn't have any patience dealing with the landlord, who was waiting for him to give him his rent money.

Kevin sat far back in his chair while covering his face with both hands. He just kept them there, wondering what would happen next. He closed his laptop, removed the aircard, slid it into its carry case and left the café. At least the credit card crooks didn't get all of his money. He still had $180 to his name in his wallet, which he had to make last for another two weeks so that he could eat. It would be nothing but sandwiches and ramen noodles from this point on.

Jesus Christ, he'd been reduced to living like a student all over again. He walked into the corner store, grabbed a pre-wrapped bologna sub and some bottled water, and then went to the cashier where four people were ahead. He wasn't bothered by that because he wasn't in a hurry to go anywhere. He caught a strong whiff of perfume, obviously a brand that was too expensive for someone living in this neighborhood to afford. Kevin couldn't resist. He had to see who was behind him. He turned to face the counter, pretending to look at the cigarettes that were on the other side, when in fact he was staring at the woman through his peripheral vision.

Hold on, is she flirting with me? Kevin finally looked at her, his gaze was met with a smile. Her lips were colored with a luscious red lipstick, and she had dark olive-colored skin and black hair. No way was she from around here. Women like that only came from exotic locations, such as South America or one of those islands. Then again, this was Jersey. All the immigrants were living on this side of the Hudson River for the affordable housing that New York City didn't provide.

He turned away as the line progressed.

"Hello, Kevin."

He turned to her. *What the fuck? She knew my name.* He hesitated as he stared into her eyes. "Do I know you?"

"Of course," she then tilted her head to the other side. "Well, not in person. But we've been chatting for quite a while."

Kevin slid his items in front of the cashier—a black man who had both height and size, with a frown to match. Without looking at him, he rang up the items. "That'll be twelve ninety-seven."

What? "Twelve ninety-seven? That's like thirteen dollars."

"Wow. Aren't you a genius," said the cashier.

"But the flyer said…"

"Did you check the date and time on the flyer?" asked the cashier. "That special ended at noon today."

"Come on, give me a break. That was like, five minutes ago. And I was in line before then. Seriously, cut me some slack."

"Sorry. The price is twelve ninety-seven."

He whipped open his wallet and shoved his hand in it. "I can't believe this."

While he was still looking for a ten-dollar bill, not wanting to break a twenty—knowing full well that he'd spend the money a lot faster—the woman reached past him and slapped a hundred-dollar bill on the counter in front of the cashier.

The clerk looked down at the bill. "Sorry, lady. I know you're trying to be a good Samaritan. But we don't accept any bills over twenty. Store policy."

"And is it store policy to be so cheap so that you have to end a sale at noon on a weekday, knowing full well that most people wouldn't have time to shop since they're on their way to work? Not only are your store policies complete bullshit, but so is your marketing. And the fact that within the last two weeks you've sold precisely twelve packs of cigarettes to the same three different minors, your business must be going through some tough times for you to be breaking the law while denying the gentleman in front of me a measly three-dollar discount for being only five minutes late. And yes, he *was* in the checkout line before noon."

Kevin's jaw dropped as he watched the cashier swallow hard. He appeared as though he was about to have a heart attack. He then looked at the woman, who snatched back her hundred-dollar bill, not taking her eyes off the cashier.

"Come, Kevin."

What the fuck just happened? Kevin watched as the woman headed to the door. She paused to look over her shoulder at him.

"Are you coming?"

He was still at a loss, but by the obvious look of embarrassment, or fear, on the cashier's face, the woman—whoever she was—definitely knew something about him.

Screw it. He turned to her. "I'm coming."

"Wait, guys. Wait," pleaded the cashier. Kevin stopped as he turned to him. The clerk sighed as he looked down, spreading both arms out on the counter as he leaned forward. "You can have the sandwich and the water on the house. I'm...I'm sorry. Please don't call the cops. This store's my life. It's all I have."

Kevin looked at the woman, wanting to say, "Who are you?"

The woman stared at him. "So what's it going to be? I believe he's made a fair offer."

Kevin took the sandwich and the water, walked past the woman, then left.

She was close behind him as he crossed the street. "Aren't you interested in knowing how I knew those things about the shop owner?"

Kevin didn't know what to make of this woman. Sure she was hot, but what did she want with him? Why did she—a complete stranger—help him out like that? They got onto the sidewalk when he turned around to face her, deciding that it was time to get some answers.

"I'm surprised that someone as smart as you, who could write such complex digital codes, which control the foundations of various companies, would be concerned over the cost of a sandwich and water."

Kevin nearly stumbled after hearing that. He turned to the woman and walked back to her. "Who are you? And how *did* you know all those things back there about that guy?" He then shut his eyes tightly as he shook his head. "How did you know what I do for a living?"

Unfazed by his temper, the woman pouted her lips as though to solicit a kiss, then answered, "As I told you before, we've chatted online."

"What, like a dating site?"

"Don't be silly," she chuckled. "You know me as Tap."

Kevin felt the blood drain from his face. "You're Tap?"

Tap smiled.

All this time he'd thought that Tap was a guy, and not even a good-looking one. "Why are you here?"

"I have a proposition for you. One I believe you ought to take seriously, given your current financial difficulties."

"Yeah? And what's that?"

"You designed a mainframe computer with an impressive security code that's going to bring in a lot of money to your former employer."

"You've been spying on me?"

"The people I work with are very interested in you and your work. Besides, we know that you're the real author of this code."

"If you know all of this, then why didn't you do something to help me? In a few weeks I won't even have as much as a pot to piss in."

"The people I work with are very secretive. It wouldn't have been in either of our best interests had we presented ourselves to your aid—at least at that time. But I can be of help to you now."

"What is it you want from me?"

"We're interested in knowing the weaknesses in your code. Since you wrote it, surely you should know if there are any holes in it which could be—how could I say?—exploited."

"And why would I want to do something like that?"

"I just want you to think about it." The woman handed Kevin a business card. "You were robbed. There's no sense in hiding it. If you let me help you, we'll make all of your financial problems go away. Besides, what better way for you to get back at those who've wronged you? Think about it."

Tap placed a hand on Kevin's face—letting him feel how soft her skin was. She then brushed a few strands of hair behind her ear and walked away.

He couldn't believe it. Tap turned out to be some exotic supermodel who'd been spying on him. Now she was offering him a chance to come into money while making those assholes pay. Shit, how could he afford to pass up an offer like this?

Kevin ran after her. "Tap."

She looked over her shoulder before she turned around.

"If this involves fucking some serious shit up for them, then I'm in."

.

Chapter 25

Interstate 94, 30 miles southeast of Eau Claire, Wisconsin. 2:53 PM, CST.

Luis Rodriguez took a quick look at the weather app on his HTC mobile while there weren't any vehicles too close in front. No snow in the forecast for the duration of his ride, just what he wanted to see. He hated winter. The cold, the ice, the snow, the strong crosswinds, all adversaries for a truck driver. Rodriguez didn't have plans on doing this for a living, it was just a matter of taking whatever job he could get.

Rodriguez almost didn't finish high school. He did a bunch of odd jobs such as a cashier at a fast-food joint and sold shoes in a sports store. He was promoted to store manager for two years before he got into an argument with a customer. That ended with him throwing her out of the store—all because she refused to put her shopping bags on the floor so that another customer could use the other half of the bench to try on a pair of shoes. He thought of getting a lawyer and suing the goddamn company for their blatant stupidity in siding with the bitch. However, his lawyer advised against it because the company would simply file appeal after appeal in order to drag out the case as long as they could, thus increasing the amount he'd be handing out in lawyer's fees. In the end he'd end up starving himself before the case was eventually heard.

That was the problem with the people on top. They were so

high up on their horses—counting dollar signs while worrying about the bad word-of-mouth publicity—that they'd sacrifice their own in order to appease one client.

Now he was a truck driver, working for Pepsi. The pay was pretty good. It got boring at times, but the bills were paid, although he was still way behind on his debts. That was the main reason why he took this extra route after one of his colleagues suddenly fell ill. Why the hell had he bet against Seattle in the Super Bowl? That bet lost him over two grand. Now he was stuck picking up as many of these extra shifts as possible if he hoped to break even.

His mobile rang—playing a personalized ringtone to his ex-girlfriend, Wendy. He would've removed her completely from his life had it not been for their son. Had it been up to her, Rodriguez would never have gotten to know his son, Jimmy. Wendy insisted on calling him James, and trying to get Jimmy to accept it as his real name. But Rodriguez knew that that was all about her trying to gain control over their son. For God's sake, the kid was only five years old. Why'd she have to be doing this to him while he was at such a fragile age? In the meantime, Rodriguez wasn't even interested in getting to know anyone else. A strip joint here and there from time to time was as far as he would go. No commitment or pressure to please any woman. If anyone had a problem with that, then fuck them.

After the third ring, he decided to answer it. "Yeah?"

"Hi, Daddy."

Oh my gosh, Jimmy! "Hey there, champ." Rodriguez chuckled. "How you doing?"

"I'm cool. Where are you right now?"

"I'm driving through Wisconsin," Rodriguez answered. "Do you know where that is?"

"Yes, Daddy. That's where the Green Bay Packers were born."

Rodriguez laughed. "I don't know about the entire football team being born over in Green Bay, but you're close enough."

"What about the owners?" asked Jimmy. "You told me that they're Packers too. Wouldn't they all be born there?"

Holy shit. I never thought of it that way. "Yeah, you're right, Son."

"Where are you heading now?"

"I have a very long drive. I'm going all the way to Grand Rapids."

"Where's that?"

"That's in Michigan."

"Hmmm, I don't know where that is."

"That's no problem, Son. When I get back home I'll take out the map and show you."

"Okay. Will you be back home to see me get my orange belt?"

"Aww, come on. You know I ain't going to miss that. I'm your number-one fan." That's when he heard Wendy's voice in the background, telling James to hurry up because she had to use it.

"Mommy says that I have to let you get back to your driving because she has to use the phone."

"That's okay," said Rodriguez. "Promise me that you'll look after yourself."

"I will."

Rodriguez chuckled. "That a boy. Love you, Son."

"I love you too, Daddy. Bye-bye." And he hung up. God he missed that boy already. If only he could bring him on the road with him—at least once a week—just so he could spend more time with him. He'd have to settle with the picture he had of both of them that was taken last Christmas, which he kept behind the overhead visor.

About three hours had passed since he left Minneapolis. It was going to be about a nine-and-a-half- to ten-hour drive. Although it was more convenient stopping at truck stops to eat, he preferred to pack his own lunch from time to time in order to cut his spending. He had packed a few tuna sandwiches along with two soft drinks that he *permanently borrowed* from the bottling plant—the same two which survived when an entire case fell off the forklift. He thought of eating right now. Then the thought came to him that he'd most likely have to take a bathroom break at the rest stop near Mauston—and he remembered it wasn't too clean the last time he was there. It also had a broken toilet and one of the stall doors was even missing. That wasn't a place he was in a hurry to visit again. Yeah, he'd hold off for another hour before eating.

Chapter 26

Springfield, Massachusetts. 2:50 PM, EST, Thursday.

"I got some activity," said Dewan through Fox's earpiece. "But keep in mind that I still haven't seen his car in the traffic cams at the intersections."

Fox pulled his seat forward and started the engine. "Maybe he's driving a rental and he left his own car in the garage back home."

"I spent the last hour checking all the traffic cams around the service station as well as the station's archives from their CCTV. I saw a common vehicle that was present each time the credit card was used. I've narrowed it down to a yellow twenty-twelve Ford Mustang Boss three-oh-two. That's one hell of a rental."

Fox tapped Sparks on the shoulder to wake her. "Where was the card last used?"

"There's a Big Y Supermarket not too far from you. Over two hundred dollars was just put on the card. And I saw the same yellow Mustang driving close by."

Fox saw how anxious Sparks had become. The moment he started the engine, she raised her seat and sat up.

"How long ago was this?" asked Fox.

"About a minute ago."

About time. "Got it. Where's the store located?"

"Ten ninety Saint James."

That's less than three blocks from here.

Sparks put on her seatbelt. "We got something?"

Fox nodded as he drove out of the lot, tearing out onto the street and nearly cutting off a city bus. If Grafton was spending that amount on groceries alone, it would take some time placing those items in the car. He could still intercept him.

Just as he drove into the parking lot of the Big Y plaza he saw the bright yellow muscle car exiting from another location. It turned onto Saint James, heading south, back toward where they came from. Fox made a hard left into the plaza's parking lot and then sped toward the same exit the muscle car took, then followed it.

He was about six cars behind the Mustang. With it being so bright it would be hard to lose. Around ten minutes later, Fox followed the car into a residential neighborhood consisting mostly of single one-story bungalows. The Mustang turned into the driveway of one of those homes, on El Paso Street, near San Miguel.

Fox drove slowly past the house, keeping an eye on the driver. It wasn't Grafton who was standing outside the car. Instead, it was a young African-American woman who was around five feet four, with straight hair. She had way too much *bling* around her neck and ears. On her feet were what appeared to be the latest pair of Jordans, with a polyester tracksuit to match. As for her hair, he wouldn't be surprised to learn that it was a weave.

Fox shook his head. Why didn't this picture look right?

Sparks looked at him. "What's wrong?"

"I'm not sure." He drove for about another twenty feet, until his car was hidden behind a wall of cedars that separated the woman's home from her neighbor's. "Something isn't right."

"Why do you say that?"

"Just from what I'm seeing. The muscle car, the two thousand dollars in purchases at Macy's. Yet this woman's living in a semi-low-income neighborhood?"

"Maybe she's Grafton's girlfriend," Sparks said. "He's probably inside and let her use his credit card."

"I'll go and see." Fox got out and turned to Sparks as he held the door. "Wait here."

He closed the door then walked past the cedars, slowing down when he came to the driveway. The woman was holding two reusable grocery bags in both hands, and she left the car door open, meaning she'd probably be making a second trip.

"Hey there." The woman turned around, but Fox stayed where he was, so as to not spook her. "You look like you could use some help."

The first odd thing that Fox noticed was that she was wearing sunglasses. *Shades on a cloudy day?*

"Oh no, that's okay. I can manage," the woman answered.

Fox stepped forward slowly, making sure she could see his hands. "Are you sure? You have quite a load. Come on. Just let me carry the other bags for you."

"Naw, I'm cool." She closed the door with a bump from her hip, clearly agitated.

He raised both hands, palms out, as though to surrender, then approached her a bit more cautiously, so as not to alarm her. He didn't need her screaming and alerting the whole neighborhood. Her glasses slid down on her nose a bit, and Fox noticed a slight black hue just above the frame, over her right eye. From where he stood, he saw that she had on an unusual amount of makeup as well.

"That's okay. By the way, I'm a friend of Scott. It's strange, because he'd never let a woman carry such heavy items on her own."

"Who?"

"Scott. Scott Grafton, the doctor." Fox slowly lowered his hands. "Aren't you his girlfriend?"

She looked as though she wondered who he was talking about, then her mouth fell open and she froze, staring at Fox, clearly troubled.

Son-of-a-bitch, I knew it. I wasted my time driving all the way over here, only to end up tracking down an identity thief. Fox's open palms went back up. "Hey, you don't have to worry. I'm not a cop. By the way, would you mind taking off your glasses?"

"Yes, I do mind. What do you want?"

"Who did that to you?"

"Who did what?"

"Someone's been using your face as a punching bag. Who do you think you're fooling?"

"That ain't none of your business. Now, can you get off my driveway?"

"Or you'll do what, call the police?" Fox approached her again, slowly dropping his arms as she remained silent. "I didn't think so. I'm looking for the person whose credit card you cloned. So you can relax."

The screen door at the side of the house swung opened and two men—one, a skinny fair-skinned black guy with cornrows, and the other, who was a darker skinned, bulkier type with an Afro—strode out onto the steps. They both wore wife-beaters and had tattoos covering their arms, visible above the U of their vests. Afro towered above Cornrow, and was roughly Fox's height. Neither of them appeared to mind that the temperature was in the low forties, having not bothered putting on jackets.

"Shenice. Who's that you talking to?" asked Cornrow.

"It's okay, Jakeem. He was just leaving." She then turned to Fox, her eyes pleading him to take the hint. "Weren't you?"

Fox kept staring at her, then looked at Jakeem and Afro—who appeared as though they were ready to break him in half. *Forget it. It's not worth the trouble.*

"Yeah, I was just leaving. It's sad that two grown men couldn't take the time to help you carry…" Fox glanced into the back seat and spotted more bags, "all these bags for you." Then he looked over at Jakeem and Afro—it was all about a stare down. The one who backs off first, loses. This woman, Shenice, was most likely trapped in a relationship she didn't want to be in. Jakeem—the likely boyfriend—must've been controlling her.

"Shenice!" yelled Jakeem, startling her.

"Yes, Jakeem."

"Get your ass inside."

"Yes, Jakeem," she said, her voice cracking slightly. By herself, she struggled with the grocery bags up to the side door, squeezing between both men. Jakeem watched her as though he was ready to hit her. Afro kept an eye on Fox the whole time, as Jakeem let go of the screen door, holding his arms out to the side. "You got a problem?"

Fox raised his hands, as though in retreat. "I'm cool."

Jakeem pointed to the street. "Then you best get your ass off my driveway."

Fox backed away, facing them. They didn't take their eyes off him until he disappeared behind the cedars. That's when he heard some yelling. It was Jakeem screaming at Shenice. He got back in his car while Sparks stared at him.

"What happened," she asked.

Fox didn't answer, but instead shook his head as he held onto the steering wheel and exhaled. What was the point? They most likely wouldn't be able to help him find Doctor Grafton. But Shenice would likely get another shiner, or worse.

"You okay?" Sparks asked. "What happened back there?"

Fuck that shit! "Stay here." He got out and slammed the door, then marched back up to the house, clenching his fists as he walked up the driveway. The yelling coming from inside got even louder as he approached. He yanked open the screen door, then pushed open the actual door behind it—which wasn't locked.

Fox found himself in the kitchen where the stench of cigarettes hit him the moment he walked inside. To his right he saw the sink piled high with dirty dishes. A half-eaten lasagna sat on the stove in a Pyrex dish—barely covered with aluminum foil. Even worse was the filthy ashtray on the kitchen table. The room could've used with a few sprays of industrial-strength air freshener too, as the smell of used cooking oil and cigarettes was overwhelming.

More yelling came from behind the wall that was adjacent, to his left. He walked toward the opening and got a good look at the living room. That's where he saw a shitload of illegal equipment commonly used by identity thieves. He passed through the opening in the divider wall and looked to his right down the hall. Fox saw Afro, whose back was to him, as he took up the width of the hall. He partially saw Jakeem, standing in front, and Shenice must've been facing Jakeem.

"What the fuck did you tell him?"

"I didn't say nothing to him," she answered with tears in her voice. "I'm telling you the truth."

"Bitch, are you lying to me?"

Fox heard what sounded like a punch, followed by the sound of someone falling to the floor as Shenice's cries got louder. Jakeem then bent over and dragged her into a room. "Huh? What did I tell you about lying to me? You want the cops to be poking around here?" He then exited the room, slamming the door on his way out.

"She was telling you the truth," said Fox.

Both Afro and Jakeem turned, obviously freaked out to see him.

"Nice stuff you've got in the living room. I'm sure all the luxury items you've purchased are sitting somewhere in a storage unit, ready to be sold. Am I right?"

"The fuck?" Jakeem squeezed past Afro. "You think you can just walk up in my crib?"

That's when Fox felt the cold metal of a gun barrel press against his temple. Damn, a third thug in hiding. Fox was betting he wouldn't shoot him, not without Jakeem's orders.

"You were just asked a question," said the gunman. From the sound of his voice, he had to be a teenager. "Answer it."

Jakeem and Afro then walked toward Fox, forcing him into the open area where the kitchen connected with the living room. The place was a bit cramped, what with all of the equipment, but it was doubtful that all four of them lived there.

"So what's it going to be?" asked Jakeem. His face was so close that Fox could smell the strong stench of tobacco on his breath. "You ain't got much to say now, do you?"

Fox turned his head slightly, toward the man with the gun, seeing him better through his peripheral vision. He'd guessed right, the punk couldn't have been a day over seventeen. He wasn't as burly as Afro, or as muscular as Jakeem, which is probably why he felt more comfortable with the gun. It hurt Fox to see youngsters being led astray by older punks.

Fox turned to Jakeem. "What's there to say to someone who needs to beat a woman into buying his toilet paper?" A small chuckle escaped him. "She's probably better at wiping your ass than you are."

Fox was savagely cuffed in the stomach by Jakeem, forcing him to double over and drop down on one knee.

Jakeem rubbed his fist. "So you want to be a smartass, huh?"

Fox coughed. "No. Actually I wanted to be down here. It puts me at—how should I put it?—a better dick-punching height."

Fox snatched the gunman's hand, bending it outward, which forced the teenager to shift positions in order to prevent his wrist from being broken. Simultaneously, with his other hand, Fox fired a hammer-strike blow to Jakeem's balls, dropping him to the floor. Wrestling for control over the gun, Fox managed to aim at Afro's leg and then he squeezed the trigger. The bullet caught him in the left shin. As big a man as he was, he came crashing down onto the kitchen table, smashing it in two as he clutched his leg, screaming obscenities.

As Fox got up, another gunshot went off into the ceiling before he head-butted the teenager—smashing the cartilage in his nose and causing blood to splatter. Fox pulled the gun out of his hand as the kid went down screaming, clutching his face with both hands.

As Fox looked around him, Afro was still bawling, while clutching his leg. The gunman was on his knees, crying like a sissy, while holding his nose as though it was about to fall off. Then there was Jakeem, clutching his groin in a fetal position, while yelling obscenities.

"Shut up." Fox pointed the Ruger SP101 .357 Magnum at Jakeem while keeping an eye on the others.

They took a few seconds to pipe down before Fox turned to Jakeem. With the tip of his shoe, Fox flipped him onto his back. "Don't worry, you only have about five more minutes of pain left. But it'll be about two to three days before you'll be able to piss straight. So you'll want to sit in the meantime, while using the john."

Fox heard a door open in the hallway. When he looked up, he saw Shenice holding onto the wall for support with one hand, while she held her jaw with the other. Her face was wet below both eyes. What did he see there? Was it distress? Awe? Gratitude? He couldn't tell. How did she ever wind up with a creep like

Jakeem to begin with? Low self-esteem maybe, combined with his influence over her to make her feel loved—when in fact all he saw in her was a decoration and a caretaker.

Fox relaxed as he stared into her eyes. "If you have a girlfriend or family you can stay with, go now." He looked down at the boyfriend. "Jakeem's never going to lay another hand on you again." Fox pointed the gun at Jakeem's head as he pursed his lips and shook his head, as a tear slid down his cheek. "Will you?" Fox kept the gun pointed at him, wanting his last words to sink in.

The pleas for Fox not to kill him were in Jakeem's eyes, which he then shut tight.

Fox lowered the .357 and looked at Shenice. "You're welcome." Then he turned around and left.

As he walked down the steps onto the driveway, to his surprise and anger, he saw Sparks come out from hiding behind the muscle car. She was obviously using it as a shield when she heard the gunshots.

Fox shook his head, tucking the .357 away in his waist holster as he walked toward her. "I told you to stay in the car."

She didn't answer immediately as she appeared to be breathing quickly. "I…I had to be sure that you were all right."

"I'm fine, as you can see," he said, taking her by the arm and making her walk quickly with him. He opened the car door for her and slammed it shut after she got in. He then hurried to his side, got in, and sped off.

A half hour later they were heading westbound on the I-90 toward Albany. Sparks didn't say a word for the length of the drive. Her head was leaned against her window, and she stared outside, blankly. While driving, Fox heard a special news bulletin on the radio where police responded to shots being fired in a house on El Paso and Merida Streets. When they got there they not only found three men who were badly wounded. But they were in a home which had a credit card embosser, 500 blank credit cards with magnetic strips, a card skimmer, a card graphic printer, a program to import credit card information onto them, numerous credit cards in other people's names, along with a list of names of people with their dates of birth and Social Security numbers.

Also among the items were over $100,000 worth of credit card receipts. Related to the story, a woman, Shenice Stansberry, had turned herself in.

She could've made a run for it, even gotten away perhaps. Maybe she did at first, until she realized that she didn't have anyone else to turn to.

Fox called Dewan, who answered after the first ring. "I was just about to call you."

"Really?"

"Yeah, I was going over Doctor Grafton's credit statements and noticed an anomaly. You need to get out of Springfield because I think that he was a victim of identity theft."

Fox slowed down as there was traffic buildup. "I know. I just took them out."

"What?"

"I'll tell you about it later. Anything else?"

Dewan appeared to fumble for his words. "Yeah. The credit card was just used at two-oh-one North Main Street in Northville, New York. He used it to purchase some wine, pasta sauce, coffee, eggs, bacon, OJ. He then went to two twelve North Main Street to buy some condoms. It's somewhere not too far from Sacandaga Lake."

"You mean *Great* Sacandaga Lake."

"Yeah, whatever."

"Check to see if Grafton owns any property or timeshares in that area." There was silence as Fox heard keyboard tapping on the other end.

"He's got a cabin up there. I'm sending you the address."

"Good. Keep me updated."

"Like I've got a choice."

He hung up and Fox checked his tablet, seeing the email from Dewan. He used the Google Maps app to get the directions. It also gave him a driving time of roughly three and a half hours. He'd try to do it in less.

Chapter 27

Indianapolis, Indiana. 3:40 PM, EST.

The flight from Washington was an hour and fifty minutes long. During her cab ride to the airport, Parris used her tablet to learn as much as she could about the area surrounding the Turbo service station on State Route 37, where its receipt originated. It still bothered her that Radovan "The Electrician" Babić could be in Bloomington and there weren't any deaths—either natural or accidental—around the time that the receipt was printed. Other than Indiana University, there was a Coca-Cola distribution center, and a few companies that involved transport and software, but it was mostly farming community.

When Parris got to Indianapolis, she took a cab to the southwest corner of town where she went to an army surplus store—owned by a former marine—that was listed in the CIA's database. These stores were run by retired marines and spooks, who occasionally did business with current ones. The fifty-something, balding, tattooed store owner could've passed for a biker. He didn't ask Parris any questions when she presented him a small list of items she'd need. He led her to the basement, which was accessed through the back of the store—an area that was off limits to regular clientele. Once she got what she came for, she handed him an envelope filled with cash and asked him to throw in the SUV that was parked out back.

Several minutes later, she was cruising down SR-37 with

her wares in the back. She tapped her earpiece and called out Dewan's name for the voice-dialer feature. She had to clear the air with him. At least let him know that she was his friend and that she'd stand by him all the way. Instead of him answering, she got a recorded message that the number she had just called was disconnected. She tapped her earpiece as her heart sank.

She did it. The bitch actually fired him. Parris slammed her hand on the steering wheel. *Dammit, Ridley.* His selfishness finally claimed its first victim. And to think that she'd foolishly defended him in front of Merrick. Why did she continue doing this? Why? That was it. She needed to get away from Fox. She had to get as far away from him as possible. Perhaps Nairobi was the solution. She was done defending him and his rogue behavior. Finished. She'd look into this one last thing in Bloomington, then be back in DC on time for her flight from Andrews.

The clock on the dashboard indicated that it was 5:20 PM when she got to Bloomington, and a few minutes after that when she saw the illuminated sign that read *Turbo* in the distance. The service station was large, with three rows of two gas pumps in each. Parris drove around the pumps and parked in front of the store. She walked in and flashed her newly purchased fake FBI badge for the attendant—a heavyset, bearded man. He wore a jacket with a mini service-station motif on the left side. He also wore an IU Hoosiers baseball cap, obviously showing that he was a fan, as well as probably covering up a bald spot.

"Good evening. I'm Special Agent Erica Hinkson with the Federal Bureau of Investigation." Parris put away her badge. "Are you the owner?"

The attendant smiled. "You're speaking to him. The name's Dirk."

"It's nice to meet you, Dirk. I'm going to need a moment of your time," said Parris.

Dirk appeared to be a bit nervous when he nodded. "Uh, sure. What can I do you for, ma'am?"

Parris took out her tablet from inside her trench coat and showed him the picture of Babić. "The Bureau has reason to believe that this man has been inside your store. Do you recognize him?"

The attendant took the tablet and scratched his beard. "He looks familiar. Then again, we have so many people coming in and out. It's hard to always place a face." Just then Parris heard the door chime and saw Dirk's attention shift. Parris looked over her shoulder and saw a plump woman, who was around the same height and build as Dirk. She wore the same Hoosier cap and the same jacket—she looked like the female version of Dirk.

The woman stared at them as she approached. "What's going on?"

"Hey, Joey." Dirk then nodded to Parris. "FBI."

Parris turned to Joey—a name that she assumed was short for Joanne—and smiled as she flashed her badge. "Special Agent Erica Hinkson. You must be Dirk's sister."

Joey deadpanned. "I'm his wife."

Shit. Parris's smile dropped. "I'm sorry, I just…"

It was pointless. Parris could see the word *FAIL* floating above her. She showed the woman the tablet and cleared her throat. "I was just showing your husband a picture of someone the Bureau needs to talk to."

Joey circled around to the back of the counter beside her husband. "Oh yeah? Who?"

Dirk then pointed to the picture on the tablet. "This guy. Have you seen him?"

Joey took the tablet. Not even a second passed before Parris saw a reaction on her face. "Yeah, I've seen him. It's been a while though. He'd come here driving the same company truck." She handed the tablet back to Parris. "Is he in some kind of trouble?"

Dirk looked at her. "Duh. He must be if the Feds are looking for him."

Joey rolled her eyes. "We don't know that for sure."

"What else would it be?" Dirk fired back. "If Federal agents or the mafia was looking for you, I'd think you were in trouble."

"And why the Sam Hill would the Feds or the mafia be looking for me?"

"Where would you like me to start?"

"Sorry, I don't mean to interrupt." Parris raised her hands to calm them both down. She then turned to Joey. "You said that the man in the photograph was driving a company truck. Do you remember which company it is?"

Parris heard the door chime again. She glanced over her shoulder and saw another customer walk in and wave a hand at them. "How's it going, Dirk. Hey, Joey."

It was always hard getting the attention of small business owners who watched over the cash register. There was always a chance someone would walk in and distract them, making it difficult for them to focus on anything they were asked.

"Hey, John," both Dirk and Joey replied simultaneously as the customer went to the refrigerated section at the back.

Dirk then turned back to Parris. "Now, what were we just talking about?"

"The name of the company," Joey reminded him.

"That's right," Dirk said waving a finger. They then looked at each other as they bounced names off one another until Dirk turned to Parris. "Micecorp. Yeah, I think that's the one."

Joey rolled her eyes. "He means *Maiz-A-Corp.*"

"How do I get there?" Parris jumped in as to be sure they didn't start arguing again.

"Just drive back up north on the thirty-seven for about three miles, then make a left," said Dirk. "Nothing but cornfields on both sides for the next ten miles. But you'll know you're there when you see the silos to your left."

Typical directions from someone who was raised in a rural area. She'd end up using her GPS anyway. "Thanks. As for the man I'm looking for, do you know if he lived around here?"

"Sorry," said Dirk. "That I don't know."

"That's no problem," Parris smiled as she shook her head. "When he'd come here, was there anything in particular that he'd buy?"

"Just gas," said Joey. "He'd swing by every week. Occasionally he'd buy a cup of coffee. But that's it, he never talked to us. I found that odd, because we were always the one's who'd initiate a conversation with him. But he wasn't the chatty type."

"You know what?" said Dirk as he pointed to the back where John had just picked up two cases of beer. "This here gentleman lives around here. His name's John Kerpius. He owns a farm not too far away. He may have seen the man you're looking for."

Parris turned to Kerpius as he put both cases on the floor between them.

"I heard my name being called," said Kerpius. "What's going on?"

"Hello, Mister Kerpius." Parris flashed her badge. "I'm Special Agent Erica Hinkson with the Federal Bureau of Investiga—"

"I ain't the one bootlegging movies off the web, if you're asking," said Kerpius, his voice slightly high in pitch while he shook his head and waved his hands in defense.

"You can relax, sir. I'm not here for that." She smiled as she handed him the tablet. "The Bureau needs this man's help. Have you seen him?"

Kerpius took it and nodded. "Sure did. I saw him with the Maiz-A-Corp people on my farm once. We don't talk though. But those guys pay me good money to use my land. Can't complain about that."

"Are you gainfully employed elsewhere?" asked Parris.

"No, ma'am." Kerpius chuckled as he tapped his chest. "I'm retired. I grew up on a farm and have been working on it, since I was eighteen, with my pops. I took it over when he passed away. When some reps from Maiz-A-Corp showed up on my doorstep with a lot of money, offering to rent the land, I couldn't refuse. That's why I could afford to retire early. Nowadays I spend most of my time helping Mary with her church activities."

"Mary?"

"That's my wife."

"I see." Parris nodded. "I have to be honest with you, I haven't met too many farmers. What do you mostly grow?"

"I specialized in corn and soy. Been doing so for years," Kerpius answered.

"Sounds like a lot of work, having to wake up early before dawn and then finishing late at night."

"That's how it used to be," said Kerpius. "A big part of me still misses it. You know as the saying goes, old habits die hard."

"Yeah, I know what you mean," said Parris. "You've probably

been buying the same corn and soy seeds from the same vendor for years, huh?"

That's when Kerpius's smile dropped as he frowned. "Yeah, you can say so."

Parris raised an eyebrow. "Oh? You don't sound too happy about that."

"It's those Sementem assholes, excuse my French. Once you start buying their seeds then you're stuck buying from them forever."

Sementem. Them again. "Why's that? Can't you just switch suppliers?"

"I wish it were that simple," said Kerpius. "Their GMOs, don't get me wrong, they do one hell of a job keeping my crop yield safe from pests and weeds. But they're just too damn expensive. The problem is if I switch seeds, I have to worry about cross-contamination from a neighbor's field, who's using Sementem's patented seed. Sementem's taken over the Midwest—practically the entire country come to think of it. And in order to make our lives even more miserable, Sementem sends their *Seed Police* to anonymously show up and search everyone's fields. Never mind that I have *No Trespassing* signs all over my property. That's never stopped them. If they were to find a single plant that originated from one of their seeds on my property, then they'd sue me for patent infringement."

"So in order to avoid that problem, you just continue to purchase their seed," said Parris.

"And just pray that I have a great yield." Kerpius rested his elbow on the counter. "They keep raising the prices of their seed each year. So if my yield falls short, then I don't make a profit. And don't bother asking me about saving unused seeds for the next season, they're genetically created to go bad if they're not used by a certain time after they've been sold."

Parris brushed a strand of hair that fell over her eye. "Wow. I never thought that farming had such as ugly side to it."

Kerpius shrugged his shoulders. "It don't have to be that way. It just is."

Now that she'd hit a nerve with him—which triggered a

rambling rant—she got the confirmation that his corn was also from Sementem, all without even asking him.

Parris then looked at all three of them. "Throughout all of this, have any of you noticed anything suspicious about this man when you saw him, or the people he was with?"

"Aside from his lack of being sociable, no," said Dirk.

"I mean, he'd sometimes say 'Hello' or 'Thanks.' You know, that sort of thing," said Joey. "Come to think of it…you asked us if he lived around here."

Parris nodded. "Yes, I did."

Joey rested her elbow on the counter. "I can't tell you if he lived around here. But from his accent, he sure wasn't *from* around here. I can tell you that."

Good, one of them was starting to remember more about Babić.

Kerpius turned to Dirk and Joey. "You guys are lucky because I didn't even get that much out of him." He then turned to Parris. "As I said, they come over and do their work in my cornfields, pay me good money to lease my land, and that's that. I don't ask no questions as long as they keep paying."

Parris handed a business card to Kerpius and one to Joey. She felt that she got as much as she could out of all three of them at the moment. "Thanks for your help. If you remember anything else—especially if there was something out of the ordinary—please call."

Kerpius took the card. "I sure will. You have a pleasant evening, ma'am."

Parris thanked Dirk and Joey and headed back to her SUV. Once inside, she thought of calling Downing. She picked up her cell and began dialing, but when she got to the fourth digit she stopped and turned off the call feature.

What's the point? Merrick is probably monitoring every call that Downing receives. She knew that Dewan had been in contact with Fox. It won't take her long to find out that I'm over here, especially if I call.

The hard knocking on her driver's side window startled Parris to the point she nearly dropped her phone. It was Kerpius, and he was waving an innocent little wave. Parris turned on the SUV and lowered the window.

"Sorry. Didn't mean to scare you, ma'am. I'm just glad I caught you before you left."

Parris smiled as she sighed with relief. "Yes, Mister Kerpius. Was there something else you wanted to add?"

"There is, it's because you asked if there was anything out of the ordinary with those Maiz-A-Corp people." Kerpius then rested his hand on the roof of the SUV. "I don't know if this can help you much, but a few weeks before harvest, there were crop dusting planes flying over my cornfields."

"Really? And why's that unusual?"

Kerpius chuckled. "Because any kind of dusting or spraying is done early on in the season." He then took his hand off the roof and began gesturing with his hands. "Take for instance, when you're growing corn, or any crop, you incorporate your pre-emergent herbicide into the soil *before* planting, which lasts up to four to six months. There's no need to be spraying herbicide later on, especially so late in the season as those Maiz-A-Corp people were doing."

"What if there were other insects? Ones that were not affected by the GMO corn?" asked Parris.

"Ha! If that were to happen, then you'd crop dust your fields a lot sooner, no later than July first. I remember several years ago I had to do so because of some pesky spider mites. Sprayed on one application near the end of June and that took care of the problem until harvest."

"Is it possible that there were weeds unaffected by the pre-emergent herbicide?" Kerpius already had Parris's attention when he'd mentioned the late-season crop dusting, but she wanted to be sure she explored every angle.

Kerpius crossed his arms and rubbed his chin. "Yeah, that's possible. But even if a few weeds managed to grow, you'd just need to spray some *Weed-Over* herbicide once or twice to kill 'em off." Kerpius went back to speaking with his hands. "Since those plants—the corn plants that is—are GMOs, they'll keep on growing. But still, that would be done earlier in the season. It won't make much of a difference a few weeks before harvest. If you ask me, they're just wasting money hiring those crop dusters." Parris recognized *Weed-Over* as Sementem's patented herbicide that was specially designed to be used around their own patented GMO crops without harming them directly. It was a clever marketing ploy used by Sementem. The most potent herbicide on the market would kill any crop except Sementem's own GMOs— forcing people to invest exclusively in Sementem's brand.

Parris looked away from Kerpius for a brief moment as she started thinking. It appeared that the more that she explored the assassin's reasons for being here, the more questions presented themselves. Whether she'd eventually connect everything was another issue. She turned back to Kerpius. "How friendly are you with the other farmers around here?"

"I know many, we've been friends for years. A lot of us go to the same church. But not all of them are retired like me, so not all of them are leasing land to Maiz-A-Corp."

"That's fine. Would you do me a favor?"

Kerpius's face lit up when she asked him that, as if he was elated at the idea of assisting the FBI with an investigation. "Sure."

"First, I need you to contact your friends who lease land to Maiz-A-Corp and ask them if they had their cornfields crop dusted around the same time as yours. Secondly, those who aren't with Maiz-A-Corp, please find out from them if there were any anomalies which would've required them to spray their fields during the season."

"I'd be more than happy to do that for you, ma'am."

"One more thing," said Parris. "I'm going to need to pass by your farm and collect soil samples from the areas that were sprayed last month, if you don't mind."

"Sure, pass by anytime. I only live ten miles away." Kerpius took out his cell phone and Parris's business card. "I'm sending you my address. When do you plan on stopping by?"

"Probably sometime tomorrow."

Kerpius put away his phone and her card. "Just stop on by whenever you're ready. You're always welcome to come in for a drink. Or if you'd like to stay for dinner, both Mary and I would be happy to have you over."

Parris smiled. "I may take you up on that dinner invite. I'm not a huge fan of eating out."

Kerpius stepped back from the SUV. "Then you don't have any excuse not to come by." He laughed a short laugh, which then dropped as he approached her window, looking around him before reducing his voice to a whisper. "By the way. Is there anything I need to be worried about? You know, you wanting to collect soil samples and also searching for that man you showed me on that flat computer thingy of yours."

"I wouldn't worry if I were you. But since this is a federal investigation, I'd appreciate you not telling anyone about our conversation, since that could hinder the Bureau's efforts. But I won't need to have you sign any legal documents to that effect now, will I?"

Kerpius backed away waving both palms in front of him. "No, ma'am. I'll do anything to help you guys out. You can count on me."

"I know I can." Parris winked at him as she raised her window and started up her SUV.

She was about to open the GPS app on her tablet when her phone rang. When she looked at the call display, she saw that it was a blocked number. She hit the call-answer icon. "Hello."

"Moshi moshi."

Parris paused. She didn't know whether to be happy or not. "Dewan?"

"Yeah, it's me."

"Listen, before you continue," Parris interrupted, "I just want to say how sorry I am for what happened to you. It's really not fair. You're the best tech support the CIA's ever had. Merrick was crazy to fire you."

"But that's just what I wanted to tell you," Dewan continued. "I'm down, but I'm not necessarily out."

"What are you talking about?"

"I'll cut to the chase. Two guys showed up at my workstation late this afternoon and escorted me to a room. There, they took away my security clearance, my phone, the whole works. They then told me that I'm no longer working for the agency. So I head home, and just as I get out of my car and I'm about to go inside my apartment building, I got jumped. A bag was thrown over my head and I was injected with something. The next thing I know, I wake up in some house, God knows where. I have a computer workstation, just like the one at work. Some scary-looking dude in a mask hands me a phone and the general's on the other end."

"What?"

"Freaky, huh? Anyway, he tells me that my kidnapping was staged in order to throw Merrick off because she had my apartment bugged."

Parris couldn't believe it. Downing had thrown himself under the bus to buy her, Dewan, and Fox some time. He was committing career suicide, especially if Merrick found out what he was up to.

"Then we don't have much time," Parris said. "Now that you're back, I need you to check up on something."

"Shoot," Dewan answered.

"I need you to find out everything you can about Maiz-A-Corp. They're located in Bloomington, Indiana."

"That's it?"

"For now."

"Give me a few minutes and I'll call you back." Dewan then hung up.

She opened the GPS app on her tablet and entered: Maiz-A-Corp, Bloomington, Indiana. The app came up with an address and gave her the directions. She was brought back up the same way Dirk had told her to go. She was then driving on a lonely road surrounded by dried-up leftovers of harvested corn plants when her phone rang.

She tapped her earpiece. "Hello?"

"I have the info." It was Dewan.

"Go ahead."

"Okay. Maiz-A-Corp specializes in farming on existing properties, in other words they pay rent to farmers in order to use their land. They've been in business for over fifteen years. The company suffered huge losses up until four years ago, when things turned around. They operate throughout the entire Midwest, specializing in maize. What's so special about this place?"

Parris slowed down once she saw the grain silos to her left. "Our *electrician* was here."

"Doing what?"

"I'm not sure." She stopped as she stared across the road at the buildings. It was dark, but there were a few lights attached outside the main building, which was only one level and about the size of a tennis court. "All I know is that he was seen driving a company truck around the area, which means he was associated with Maiz-A-Corp. Anything else?"

"There's a lot. I can send it to you," said Dewan. "Are you casing the place?"

"Doing what I can." Parris tapped her fingers on the steering wheel. "Send me everything."

"For sure."

"You're a sweetheart, Dewan. We'll talk later, and welcome back." Parris then remembered something. "Are you still there?"

"Yeah, what's up?"

"Have you heard from Fox?"

"I spoke to him earlier. He's with Katy."

"Is he back in DC yet?"

"Nope. Why?"

"It's nothing serious," Parris said. "I'll call you if there's anything else."

"I'll be here."

Parris hung up and did a U-Turn, heading back down the road to SR-37. On the way she drove by a sign indicating that sweet corn was for sale. She didn't think anything of it at first, but something at the back of her mind told her that she should buy some—not for eating, but for a testing comparison to the soil samples she'd collect later on. She looked at the clock on the dashboard. It was only 6:40 PM. They should still be open for business. She slowed down, did another U-Turn, and drove back to the farm. She bought five ears of corn. Since the owner appeared to be at least in his early seventies, she asked him if, by any chance, he did any business with Maiz-A-Corp. It turned out that he did.

Parris was back on the road a few minutes later, and drove to the southwest corner of Bloomington where she made a quick stop to the Wal-Mart. There, she bought a few glass dishes with covers from the kitchen section, along with a small spade from the gardening section. She then headed to the north end of town, to the Hampton Inn on North Walnut Street. It was an area where she was surrounded by a Denny's, a Steak-And-Shake, McDonald's, and a liquor store, as expected, called Bloomington Liquors. No university town would be complete without a few of those.

She checked in, asking for a room on the ground floor, on the same side as the parking lot where her SUV was parked. After settling in to her room she ordered a pepperoni pizza and then took a hot shower. The water pouring down her body was so relaxing that she stayed under it for a good ten minutes. When she was done, she came out dressed in nothing but a towel.

She grabbed her tablet on the way to the bed and read up on what Dewan had sent her. She wasn't planning on staying the night—the information she was about to review was too sensitive for her to read in a public place such as a coffee shop or a restaurant.

When the pizza arrived, she slipped her trench coat over her towel and made a fast transaction, tipping the delivery man generously. Parris then ate it while she reviewed everything Dewan had sent her. So far, she had read up on Maiz-A-Corp's blueprints to the building, their business contacts, and even the alarm company that they were with—including the password needed to deactivate the alarm.

Her phone rang and she picked it up, seeing that it was Kerpius. "Yes, Mister Kerpius."

"Hello, Agent Hinkson. I have those names you wanted."

"That was quick."

"You know me," Kerpius continued. "Never leave something important to the next day when you can take care of it now."

Parris picked up the pen and notepad that were on the table, courtesy of the hotel. "All right. I'm listening." She wrote down the names and addresses of each person Kerpius named. She made sure to separate the ones who dealt with Maiz-A-Corp from the ones who didn't but who still used Sementem's GMO corn seeds. Once she got those names, she thanked Kerpius and hung up.

She checked out the list of Maiz-A-Corp's business contacts and was not surprised to see that they dealt exclusively with Sementem for their GMO corn and their own brand of herbicide.

Enough with Maiz-A-Corp, Parris moved on to revising the list of farms that Maiz-A-Corp paid rent to. The company had several offices all over the Midwest which were in cash-rent deals with several dozen farmers in many states, but primarily in Indiana, Tennessee, Illinois, and Wisconsin.

After having read everything, she decided that breaking into Maiz-A-Corp's offices may not be necessary. She'd only need to get the soil samples, then be able to ship them same-day delivery to Langley. Hell, the IU campus was within driving distance, and she could use one of those labs and do the testing on her own. She'd have to improvise on getting inside, but it could be done.

Fox, once again, was on her mind. She was leaving for Nairobi tomorrow morning and he most likely didn't even know yet. And as much as she was still angry with him, she couldn't just take off without at least saying good-bye. Not after all they'd been through.

Screw it. Just get it over with. She dialed Fox's number and the phone rang once before she heard the beep of the voicemail. She tapped the off icon and put down her phone. She'd try again later.

Parris grabbed her suitcase, threw it on top of the bed, and opened it. Within minutes she'd changed into a black jogging suit and running shoes. She then shoved the bowls and spade into the knapsack, threw it on her back, and replaced the other clothes into her suitcase and was out the door.

Chapter 28

Great Sacandaga Lake, New York. 7:53 PM, EST, Thursday.

Fox's patience was tested several times as he encountered a few traffic snags on the interstate. About four spots, between Springfield and Albany, traffic slowed to a crawl as there were several instances of black ice. Not surprisingly, a few bad drivers found themselves in the ditch. As a Canadian, Fox could only roll his eyes at the fact that so many Americans didn't understand the concept of slowing down when road conditions were poor. Fortunately, his rented car had on snow tires, which was rare, but it didn't mean that he'd be driving like a bat out of hell. Fortunately, the salt trucks were out, but the entire drive took nearly four and a half hours—an hour longer than it would've normally taken

The doctor's cabin was isolated from the road, tucked away in the bush. When Fox and Sparks arrived, he turned into a driveway that had various dips and turns. He didn't drive all the way, but pulled over to the side when he had traveled about three-quarters of the way in. He turned off the vehicle—the last thing they needed, after having come all this way, was for the car's headlights and engine to betray their presence.

Fox checked the dashboard clock and then looked at Sparks, who was wide awake. She surely didn't want to miss this moment.

"How are we going to do this?" she asked.

Fox opened the glove compartment and took out a small

flashlight he had purchased on their way there, pocketed it, and got out. "There is no *we. You* are going to stay in the car. And I mean it."

"How are you going to make him talk?" Sparks asked as Fox got out.

He turned around, bending toward her while holding the door. "You let me worry about that." He then shut the door and walked up the rest of the driveway.

Although it was pitch-black, and he was surrounded by tall pines and birch trees on either side of the driveway, there was a porch light he could see between the trees. The average person would've needed a flashlight to help them, but this type of hike was nothing new to Fox. His JTF2 training required that he survive in the wilderness on his own. He often slept on the rocks in northern Manitoba with ravenous mosquitos. There was nothing much to munch on but a few fruit snacks, and a small amount of water. Sometimes it was in the dead of winter, where Canadian temperatures could dip as low as minus 60 Fahrenheit up in the northern parts of the country. He'd also been placed in another extreme environment, where he'd had to survive a few weeks in the Brazilian rainforest. This was all without the use of any special equipment. But now, Fox kept things simple and stuck to the dirt driveway. At least there he had less of a chance of tripping over a rock or a tree root and injuring himself.

He wouldn't have time to case the cabin, which was relatively small. At most there was only one bedroom, a kitchen, and a living room. The ideal place for a weekend getaway for two, designed mainly as a place to crash—not necessarily for luxury—where most activities would be spent outdoors. Grafton's car was parked out front, confirming that he was there. With the exception of the porch light, it was completely dark inside.

Fox took his Android and changed his phone settings to not accept any calls. In this mode, the phone wouldn't even ring or vibrate if someone tried to reach him. Instead, all calls would automatically go straight to voicemail while keeping a record of who called. Fox then moved to the window that was farthest from the porch light and peeked inside. He didn't see anyone, yet he heard a faint knocking sound. He came around the front, twisted the doorknob which, to his surprise and content, opened the door. *Doesn't anyone lock their doors anymore? First he forgets the phone, and now he forgets to lock his front door. How careless can one be?* The knocking sounds were a lot louder from inside, and appeared to be coming from behind the wall, possibly in another room. Fox didn't have to worry about closing the door too silently, since the noises drowned out any clicking sound the door would make as it latched shut. He took out the flashlight and turned it on, waving the beam from one side of the room to the other. He saw the kitchen area, with a dining room table on one side. On the other was a couch, facing the wall, where there was a fireplace.

Fox heard some grunting noises along with the knocking. He turned back in that direction and shone his flashlight onto a closed door, and grinned.

Sweet.

He turned off the flashlight and crept over to the bedroom, carefully opening the door. He peeked around it and saw a moving silhouette in front of the window. He still heard the grunting which was obviously from a man, likely Grafton. Even better, Grafton's back was to him. It wasn't too often that he had the opportunity to catch a live sex show, but he wouldn't be around long enough to watch—if it was even something worth watching.

"Can…your…husband work your ass like I do?" grunted Grafton.

"Uh…uh no," a woman answered, unenthusiastically.

What the fuck? She's cheating on her husband? And with an underperformer. No way.

"Are you about to come yet?" panted the doctor.

"Oh yeah. I'm almost there," said the woman, who sounded more bored than anything. "By the way, are you almost done?"

Damn, this was worse than bad porn. Fox took out his Android and tapped on the camera app. He then changed its settings to night-vision video and began recording. Fox casually filmed them from behind, then circled around in front where he captured their faces. Through the smartphone's screen, Fox saw that Grafton had his eyes closed tightly as though he was trying to force himself to ejaculate. The woman he was banging, on the other hand, had her forehead in the pillow. She looked up once and Fox saw her face. She appeared more frustrated than excited, as though her expression said *I'm cheating on my husband in the middle of nowhere for this?* Fox was surprised that she hadn't noticed him when he was standing a few feet away.

Oh, for God's sake. Time to end this bad show. "Smile."

The girlfriend gasped and her head shot up, followed by a scream.

"Yeah, I knew you were feeling it, baby," yelled Grafton. "If you can just scream my name, it'll be even better."

"Shut up, you idiot. We're being robbed," she screamed as she jumped back, knocking Grafton off balance and onto the floor.

Ouch, ass attacked!

"What?" Grafton scrambled onto his feet, hollering when he saw Fox—who would've been a silhouetted figure from where he was. His hands shot up. "Oh my God! Don't hurt us, please. Just...just take what you want."

"Shut up, both of you." Fox did his best raspy-voiced-Christian-Bale-as-Batman impersonation as he put away his phone. He then took out the flashlight and shone it in their faces. He circled to the front of the bed, putting himself between them and the doorway, grabbed a pair of plasticuffs from his jacket pocket, and tossed them to the doctor's feet. He then shone the flashlight on them.

"Bind her," said Fox.

The doctor looked down at the plasticuffs, then toward Fox. "Bind her? As...as in BDSM?"

Fox stomped his foot hard on the floor, startling both of them. "Do it."

Grafton snatched the cuffs and stumbled over to his girlfriend. A minute later he had both her hands tied behind her back.

"Lock her up in the closet."

There was still some whimpering, but Grafton hurried with her, over to the closet, checking over her shoulder at Fox on the way. Once she was in, the doctor closed the door. He then turned to Fox, who had to squint as the flashlight shone in his eyes.

"Turn around, down on your knees, hands behind your head," he said.

The doctor obeyed.

"I'm holding a gun and it's aimed right at the back of your skull. If you make any sudden moves, or do or say anything I don't like, then I'm pulling the trigger. Is that understood?"

The doctor nodded repeatedly. "Yes. I understand. Just don't shoot me."

He only needed to believe that a gun was pointed at him. He'd be so scared he'd confess anything. Fox then took out his phone and turned on the app for voice record.

"Doctor Scott Grafton, you worked at Camp Iron Eagle in Afghanistan, as the head army surgeon. You oversaw an incident a little over two years ago, where thirteen soldiers died. What did they die from?"

"I…I can't remember that."

"Thirteen soldiers, Doctor. Thirteen," Fox yelled. "Good men and women who served their country honestly and with integrity. I'll ask you one last time. What killed them?"

"I'm not sure what they died from. It…it appeared to be an allergic reaction," the doctor's voice began to get scratchy. A clear indication that he was scared out of his wits. Fox wouldn't be surprised if he began to piss all over himself soon.

"The official medical report was that they died from an E. coli infection. Why'd you falsify the diagnosis?"

"I didn't have a choice. They made do it."

"Who?" said Fox loudly, making the doctor shake.

"The orders came from General Jeansonne," Grafton answered. "I mean, they came from up top."

"You're a doctor and you swore the Hippocratic Oath," said Fox. "Yet you betray the trust of your patients? Give me one good reason why I don't execute you now? You peace of shit!"

"I'm a patriot. And the general told me that it was a matter of national security that the deaths of those soldiers be declared as an E. coli infection."

"Yet, you think that they died from an allergic reaction. Correct?"

The doctor nodded. That wasn't a good sign, Fox needed to re-establish that he was the one in control.

"I asked you a question. You *will* answer me with yes or no."

"Yes," the doctor cried while nodding. "Yes, it was an allergic reaction."

"How did you know for sure?"

"We did autopsies. The lining of their stomach cavities were in terrible shape. They were all porous. I mean, God, I'm talking about dozens of holes. I thought at first that they had been exposed to some new chemical weapon, but that theory was ruled out."

"What brought on the allergic reactions?"

"I'm...I'm not sure."

"Then tell me what you *are* sure about."

"I...I believe that it may have been something they ate." Grafton swallowed. "There was a food inspector, or quality control expert—whatever you want to call her—that was snooping around. The head of the dining hall couldn't stand her, and General Jeansonne thought that she was becoming a nuisance. Jesus, she was only doing her job. They set things up to make her get the blame."

"They what?"

"She was set up. It was all a cover-up by the army. She had a nickname. Sparky, I think. She saw all the problems and potential health hazards in the dining halls and in the kitchens. And she cleaned things up. I mean, *really* cleaned things up."

"You're admitting that Sparky was framed for the deaths of those thirteen soldiers?"

The doctor swallowed. "Yes. Yes she was."

"Why'd you leave the army?"

"I couldn't take it anymore. I had to get out of there. I just had to."

"I thought you were a patriot."

"I am...but I...I didn't want to lie anymore."

"Bullshit!" Fox came up close to the doctor and pressed the edge of the smartphone against the back of his neck. He'll think it's a gun.

"Please...please don't shoot me."

Getting back control again. "As soon as you left, your outstanding school loans were paid off, you bought a new house, and opened up a private clinic. Someone paid you to keep quiet. Who?"

"I don't know for sure. My guess is that General Jeansonne had something to do with it. When I got back here, I received a parcel that was full of cash, with a note telling me to forget the whole thing and move on with my life."

"Have you heard from them since?"

"No. Never heard from them again. I've told you everything I know, I swear."

"Oh I believe you, Doctor." Fox stopped his phone from recording the conversation. "I also believe that you're not going to tell anyone about our little chat."

Fox walked back to the closet and pulled open the door without turning his back on Grafton. The woman, although secure, had managed to roll over onto her side. Fox held the phone above her, making sure that the volume was on maximum, and played back the video for both of them to hear for a few seconds and then stopped it.

"You're not going to tell anyone about me, you understand?" Fox then looked down at the woman. "Because if I find out that either of you squealed, I'll see to it that your husband gets this video." The woman didn't reply. There were only short breaths, indicating how scared she was. "One more thing," Fox watched as she tried to turn her head toward him, "you need to find yourself a better lover. Grafton may know human anatomy. But when it comes to satisfying you, you and I both know he was way off."

Fox put away his phone, turned on the flashlight, aiming it at the doctor as he passed him, and even into his face as he backed away from him. "As for you, Doctor. I wouldn't leave the state." He then left.

Very soon Fox was back outside and running to his car. He got in and saw how anxious Sparks appeared.

"How'd it go?" she asked.

Fox sighed and shook his head. "He's no God."

"Huh?"

Fox played back the recording for her as he started up the engine. "Just listen for yourself."

He reversed down the driveway and onto the street while he listened to Grafton's embarrassing moment.

"Oh...my...God!" Sparks looked away from the phone to Fox. "You're kidding."

"Trust me. It was much worse watching it in person. You should be glad I insisted you wait in the car." Fox switched the gear to *drive*, then sped off.

Three minutes later, when the recording ended, Sparks was shaking her head. "Unbelievable. That son-of-a-bitch was paid off. What do we do next, send this to the FBI? Because they'll have no choice but to go after SLR and those men in the army."

Fox took back his phone and pulled over onto the shoulder of the road. "Not so fast." He then sent the audio and video recording to Downing as an email attachment. "The FBI can't use this because SLR's lawyers will claim that Grafton was forced to talk under duress. It also doesn't prove that the army and SLR staged an insurgent attack on the helicopters the victims were being transported in."

Sparks waved a hand in frustration. "Then what was the point of all of this? This was a complete waste of time."

Fox drove back on the road. "Not really. I know people who'll know what to do with this information."

While he had his phone, Fox changed the settings back to receive calls. Seconds after he had done so, his phone buzzed. He glanced at it and saw it was a missed call from Parris. "And speak of the devil."

Fox called her back and she answered after the first ring. "Fab, I saw that you called."

"I did," Parris replied. "I take it that you're with Sparks."

"Yeah, she's with me." Fox put the phone on speaker and glanced briefly at Sparks. "Say hello to Fab."

Sparks leaned closer to the phone. "Hello."

He then turned off the speaker, transferring the call back to his earpiece. "As you heard, she's fine. Had to make a few detours, but we're on our way to DC. How was the debriefing, by the way?"

"Nothing too exciting, you know how it is," Parris replied. "But that's not why I called."

"What happened?"

"I'm currently in a cornfield near Bloomington, Indiana."

That caught Fox off guard. "At this hour? It's almost a quarter to nine. What are you doing there?"

"Following up on the service station receipt."

The Electrician, that's right. Fox smiled. "So, you decided to play a hunch, eh?"

"In a way, yes."

"And what did you find?"

"The service station owner and his wife both recognized the picture of our killer. I later learned that he's associated with a farming company called Maiz-A-Corp."

"What do they do?"

"They lease agricultural land from farmers. They're very active throughout the Midwest," she answered. "I just finished collecting soil samples from one of those farms, for analysis."

"What are you hoping to find?"

"A connection," Parris answered. "I found out that a few weeks before harvest, Maiz-A-Corp had all their cornfields sprayed via crop dusters."

"So late in the season? I thought all that gets done early on."

"It does, and did, according to their records. Whatever herbicides they applied in the beginning of the season, should last through to the end of October—which is around harvest. I'm hoping that traces of whatever they sprayed will still show up in the soil or some of the leaves, even in minute quantities."

"Our mystery compound perhaps?"

"I'm betting on it."

Fox took his phone and sent her the audio file. "I'm sending you something."

"What is it?"

"My little chat with Doctor Grafton."

"I'm not going to ask how you made him talk."

"It wasn't that hard. Once I let him know who was in control, he sang like a bird."

"What did he say?"

"He corroborated Katy's version of what happened at Camp Iron Eagle. That she was set up. He also said that he was under pressure to attribute the deaths of the soldiers to E. coli, when, in fact, he believed that they died from a severe allergic reaction."

"What? What were they allergic to?"

"He believes that it was something they ate."

"That's odd. Did they have any prior food allergies?"

"I…don't know. I didn't think of asking him that."

"Fox, aren't these meals screened or vetted for certain soldiers who may have food allergies? Because even if they were, I can see one slip up, but thirteen?"

"Or they may not have had prior food allergies," said Fox. "Isn't it possible that some foreign substance within the meals they were served caused the allergic reaction without them necessarily having a prior food allergy?"

"But why *those* thirteen?" said Parris. "There are hundreds that ate at the same place."

She had a point. Why did those specific soldiers die? He switched on the speakerphone feature then turned to Sparks. "What was that part again about you catching a staff member making those sandwiches one night?"

"You mean when I caught him with hundreds of sandwiches that were left out in the open in a non-chilled environment?" Sparks asked.

Fox nodded. "Yeah, that one."

"I made him throw them out because of the mayonnaise that had been spread on the sandwiches. They were sitting out of the fridge for hours," said Sparks. "Why?"

Fox brought her up to speed on what Parris had found out, leaving out the details of her debriefing. "Isn't it possible that not all of the sandwiches were thrown out? If those remaining sandwiches somehow went bad, maybe—I don't know—due to bad meat, couldn't that account for those deaths?"

"Impossible," said Sparks. "I made him throw everything out. That went for the sandwiches, the meat, the exposed condiments, everything."

"So you made him start all over from scratch?" asked Parris.

"Exactly."

The pickup truck Fox had been following unexpectedly slowed down, causing him to slam on the breaks. "Shit. What the fuck?"

"I know you weren't talking to me," said Parris sarcastically.

"No, just some truck driver ahead of me." Fox drove around him. "Anyhow, just listen to the recording I sent you. Maybe there's something on it you'll catch that we weren't able to." He then heard Parris suck her teeth.

"Damn," said Parris.

"What's wrong?"

"State Trooper, I'm being pulled over," Parris answered with a sigh. "I'll call you back."

"Sure thing," said Fox before he tapped his earpiece. He wasn't worried about her, she'd handled more dangerous people on her own. A State Trooper was nothing.

Sparks adjusted her seatbelt. "Fab sounds as though she knows her stuff."

"That's why I love working with her." Fox saw the road sign indicating that they were ten miles away from I-90. About ten minutes later, he turned onto the ramp leading onto it, when his phone rang. It was Parris's ringtone.

Fox tapped his earpiece with a smile. "How much was your speeding ticket?" Rather than hear an answer, he heard heavy breathing that was loud enough that his grin vanished. "Are you okay?"

"I'm…I'm fine for now," Parris answered, pausing between words as though she was catching her breath. "I'm getting the hell out of here."

Fox glanced over at Sparks, who was staring back at him. She obviously sensed that something was wrong by the tone of his voice. "What happened?"

"I must've rattled some cages down here," said Parris as her breathing became more under control. "Because the men who just pulled me over weren't State Troopers."

Chapter 29

Bloomington, Indiana. (Several Minutes Earlier), Thursday.

Parris had stepped out of her SUV and then slid on a pair of gloves after feeling the cold nip at her fingers. Gone were the five- to seven-feet-tall cornstalks that would've been on both sides of the road over a month ago. As she had grabbed her knapsack from the passenger seat before closing the door, all she'd seen was a mess of dried-up husks and leaves. From what Kerpius had told her earlier, the sweet corn plot—which was sprayed weeks before it had been harvested—would've been growing to her right. The field corn was on the opposite side of the road.

She'd unzipped the bag and had taken out her flashlight, noticing her breath in puffs of vapor once she'd turned it on. She had been grateful that it wasn't windy because that would've been murder. Had Fox been with her at that moment he would've lectured her on how Canada was a hundred times worse and how many Canadians would still be outside in their shorts and t-shirts. Yeah right. It had been over eight years since she'd moved to the USA from Barbados, and even during that time she still couldn't get used to the cold, probably never would. Who was she kidding? She didn't want to. She hadn't planned on spending more than a half hour filling the five containers with soil and any dried up leaves from what remained of the plants.

It had been so quiet outside that Parris had heard the dried leaves crunching under her shoes as she'd walked into the field. When she'd made it about twenty yards in from the road, she took out her spade and one of the Pyrex 2-cup round storage dishes and had begun to fill it. When she'd finished, she'd slapped the blue lid on it, labeled it, then dropped it in the bag before heading across the road and doing the same thing,

Twelve minutes after that she was back in her SUV, where she'd felt anxious to start up the engine, just for the heat. After she'd removed her gloves and rubbed her hands in front of the vents, she'd made a U-turn and had driven off. That's when her phone had rung. Fox had been returning her earlier call to him.

A part of her had still felt mad at him, but she'd been happy to hear his voice. And the longer she'd listened to him, the more she'd felt an ache in the pit of her stomach that she'd have to break the news to him. But he then spoke of Grafton and what he'd found out from him, which had intrigued her.

As they'd talked, she'd noticed a set of headlights appearing in the distance, and the closer they got, a distinct set of red-and-blue flashers had appeared above them. The car had slowed down and crossed over the center line at a slight angle in order to block her path.

She'd had no idea why she'd be getting pulled over by a State Trooper, but she had to let Fox go. She would call him back after.

She hung up and peered in the rearview mirror.

Why'd this guy have to show up now? It's not as though he could stop me for speeding.

She got out of her car, badge in hand, and walked toward the trooper—stopping slightly ahead of the hood of her SUV. It was from there that Parris saw that there was a second officer in the passenger seat, which she found odd. Normally, state police didn't travel in pairs unless one was in training. But why would there be a training session at this hour?

The officers got out together, without shutting off their vehicle. They had the appearance of being state troopers, both of them were taller than she, and built as though they were participants in an Iron Man competition.

Parris raised her badge. "Good evening, Officers. My name

is Special Agent Erica Hinkson with the Federal Bureau of Investigation."

"Agent Hinkson."

Parris was startled by how loud and authoritative the driver spoke.

"Do you mind telling us what business the Bureau has in these parts?"

"It's an ongoing federal investigation, I'm not at liberty to disclose the details," Parris answered calmly. "But if you call Lieutenant Durnil, he'll confirm everything." *There's no way I'm letting these guys talk me down.*

"May I see your badge?" asked the second officer.

"Certainly." Parris held it out for him to see. "May I know your names, Officers?" *Always answer by asking them a question. Show them who's boss.*

"We received a report that someone was seen wandering through the corn patch," said the first trooper as he approached her. The other did the same, but moved to a flanking position five feet away from him, while lowering both hands to his sides. *What happened to either of them calling it in to verify who she was? Come to think of it, why hadn't they identified themselves?*

"Officers, I just asked if you could identify yourselves," she asked again.

"Hold on a bit, Agent Hinkson," said the first trooper, still speaking loudly. "You still haven't answered our question. What business does the Bureau have over here?"

"And I'll tell you again that I'm not at liberty to say, and to check with Lieutenant Jeff Durnil. You *do* know who he is, don't you?"

"Of course we do," he snapped. *That confirmed it. If these men were State Troopers, then she was the First Lady. The only Durnil who worked for the ISP in these parts was* Curt *Durnil—a* Sargent. The second officer closed in and stopped a few feet away from her. His hands were close to his gun. *He was definitely the one that would shoot her.*

The officer reached out to take her badge. When she went to hand it over, she flicked her wrist and an ASP tactical baton—

duct-taped to her forearm—extended from inside the sleeve of her jacket into the palm of her hand. She swung once, and the phony officer felt twenty-six inches of cold steel strike his jaw—sending blood and teeth from his mouth and onto the concrete. From that proximity, the second officer barely had enough time to pull his weapon from its holster. Parris whipped out her opposite arm and a second concealed ASP tactical baton extended. The first blow was to the man's elbow—fracturing the olecranon.

His first reaction was to grab the spot where he felt a tremendous amount of pain—leaving him defenseless. He was about to drop an F-bomb, but didn't finish the word before Parris swung both sticks, slamming them against each of his temples. The combined force of both steel rods against this particular area of the skull would leave him with an epidural hematoma. The man's body twisted and dropped. Even if an ambulance were to come and get him, he'd most likely die on his way to the hospital.

The first man was on all fours. The blow she'd given him would've left him momentarily disoriented—only to wear off about now. She ran up to him and did an underarm swing, striking him in the shoulder and flipping him onto his back. Like a dagger, she plunged the baton down onto his exposed neck, stopping just short of his larynx. "What's Maiz-A-Corp been spraying on the corn?"

He choked and spat out more blood, along with another tooth. He'd choke on his own blood if he didn't keep swallowing.

Parris applied a bit more pressure on his larynx. "I said, what's Maiz-A-Corp been spraying on the corn?" This time she spoke with the same authoritative voice he had used on her. She knew that she hadn't seen him slip anything into his mouth, unlike The Electrician.

"I don't know anything about the corn," the man said as he coughed some more. "We were just sent here to kill you. I swear that's all I know."

"Who sent you to kill me?"

The man coughed while shaking his head rapidly. His breathing intensified as he squeezed his eyes tightly. "We only know him as Mister Lucas."

Parris applied a bit more pressure on his neck. "Where do I find him?"

"He…" The man grunted as he blew blood from his nostrils and coughed some more—wheezing to catch his breath. "He finds you."

Those last three words didn't sit too well with Parris, who then slammed the ASP into him—crushing the imposter's larynx. He kicked and thrashed on the ground for about half a minute before he stopped—lying motionless on the road and staring at the stars. Parris turned to his partner, who was still on his stomach with his head to the side.

She dropped down on one knee and slammed both batons straight down into the concrete, reducing them from twenty-six inches of pernicious steel to a harmless nine-inch rubber handle. The ringing of a mobile phone echoed above the sound of the cruiser's engine. She looked down at the driver as the phone rang a second time. She knelt down, removed it from his belt clip, and answered it. She didn't say anything in order to let the other party speak first.

For roughly five seconds there was silence, then, "Hello, Doctor Parris."

She hated these robotic altered voices, they always gave her chills.

"It *is* Doctor Nita Parris I'm speaking with, is it not?"

"Mister Lucas," she answered.

"I've heard so much about you, and of your colleague Ridley Fox," said Lucas. "We would've met in Düsseldorf except that I had some business to finalize with Alghafari."

"Then let's meet now." Parris looked down at both bodies. "Just give me a time and a place."

"Aren't you rather cocky this evening? You ought to be careful with what you request."

"Don't overestimate yourself," Parris replied. "The two thugs you sent after me made that mistake."

She then stood and checked both directions of the road. She didn't see anyone, but it was possible that Lucas may be attempting to triangulate her location. "I'd like to stay and chat a bit longer, but I've gotta keep moving. I'm sure you understand."

"Don't give yourself too much credit," said Lucas. "Anybody can be gotten to." He then hung up.

Parris wiped the phone with her sleeve to remove any fingerprints. She then quickly removed the battery, the SIM card, wiped them off, then dropped them all on the road and stomped on them—leaving a mess of broken glass, plastic, and motherboard pieces. She then hurried back to her SUV, fired up the engine, and took off, driving around the imposters and their vehicle. Parris then called Fox. Mister Lucas—or whoever he was—wouldn't have sent two men to kill her unless she was close to uncovering something.

Fox answered after the first ring. "How much was your speeding ticket?"

Parris checked the rearview mirrors—both inside and outside—breathing heavily as she was still perturbed. So far it appeared that no one was coming after her.

"Are you okay?"

"I'm…I'm fine for now," Parris answered as she focused back on the road. "I'm getting the hell out of here."

"What happened?"

"I must've rattled some cages down here. Because the men who just pulled me over weren't State Troopers."

There was a brief pause on the other end. "Are you hurt?"

Parris slowed down as she came to the end of the road and turned onto the next street, ignoring the stop sign. "I'm fine. I just spoke to the guy who sent them to kill me, someone by the name of Mister Lucas."

"What did he tell you?"

"He knew about us being in Düsseldorf, and basically confessed that he took out Alghafari." Parris's heart kicked up a notch as she saw a pair of headlights ahead, closing in fast. The car zoomed by. When she checked her rearview mirror, she saw that it kept driving. "He knows who we are."

"Are you seeing a pattern now?" asked Fox. "The hard drive, Alghafari. You were right, it wasn't about Umari."

"No it wasn't." Parris glanced at her knapsack. "Whatever's

going on, it goes beyond corporate espionage or even the military cover-up Sparks spoke of. This is something much bigger. And I have a feeling that it's already started."

Chapter 30

Eastbound I-80/I-94, Gary, Indiana. 8:45 PM, CST/9:45 PM, EST.

The pain pierced Luis Rodriguez deep in the stomach like dozens of tiny blades. For the past twenty minutes he'd felt unsure whether he was going to shit his drawers or vomit all over the steering wheel. Fuck, he'd probably end up doing both if he couldn't get to the truck stop soon. He saw the Burr Street exit sign ahead. There was a truck stop a block away from the interstate. He accelerated to the exit, and less than three minutes later, he parked his truck in the vast parking lot fit to hold a few dozen trucks. The place was packed, with trucks lined up from one end of the lot to the next. And, as luck would have it, there weren't any parking spaces that were close to the restaurant.

He climbed down from his truck, slamming the door behind him, then hurried to the restaurant. When he got there, he yanked open the glass door—not caring if someone was behind him—and rushed straight to the men's room. Thank God there was an empty stall waiting for him. He didn't waste a moment pulling down his pants and drawers and getting onto the bowl, letting nature take its course. Ten minutes later his stomach was still burning.

Fucking stomach ache. Why now?

He looked at his watch and cursed at the fact that this pit stop was about to put him behind schedule. Another three minutes passed and he was almost certain that he was done. He must've blown over ten feet of toilet paper to wipe himself. He stood and pulled up his pants when vertigo struck him. He threw out a hand against the stall for support, resting his forehead on his other arm. He was burning up. Rodriguez would definitely have to call this one in and tell his boss to get someone else to take over the shipment. There was no way he'd be getting better anytime soon. Fuck, he may have to check into a hospital. He lifted his head off his arm, noticing the wetness that was left on it.

He turned around to flush and almost screamed at what he saw. What mostly came out of him was his own blood. *What the fuck's happening to me?*

An ambulance. He had to call one right away. He reached for his mobile on his belt clip. Dammit, he'd left it in the truck.

He stumbled out of the men's room, sweat pouring down his face and accumulating on his hands. The bathroom door felt five times heavier right now than when he'd entered. He turned to his left and saw the payphone ahead of him. More blades punctured him from inside and he stopped to grab his stomach with one hand while holding onto the wall for support with the other. Gritting his teeth and closing his eyes, he forced himself to walk—step by painful step.

Rodriguez was almost within reach of the phone when a man, who looked like another trucker, came out of nowhere and snatched it.

"Please," he begged, "let me…I need to use that." Rodriguez reached out and tried to grasp the man's shoulder.

The man turned to him. "Whoa. Back off! What the hell's your problem?" He shoved Rodriguez slightly, but it felt as though he had been hit by a forty-pound medicine ball. He fell to the floor, and when he tried to sit up, he barely had enough strength to do so.

The trucker spoke to him. "Hey, buddy. You all right?" The man hung up the phone and rushed over to him.

Rodriguez looked away, toward the dining room. He saw a young boy who was about Jimmy's age, standing a few feet away and staring at him. The child's face bleached as he continued to stare for a few more seconds, then all of a sudden he ran away screaming.

This definitely caught the attention of everyone in the dining area, as Rodriguez began coughing.

"Hold tight. I'm calling an ambulance." It was the trucker again.

The blood he spat up caused other screams to erupt as he heard others yelling.

"Someone call nine-one-one."

"We need a medic. Is there a doctor or nurse in here?"

Rodriguez looked at all the faces that stared back at him. "Jimmy. My son. I have to see my son." He fell on his back. Seconds later he was staring up at several faces as people began to crowd around him.

"Give him room."

He began to choke on what tasted like blood. He felt someone help him sit up as he spat out more of it all over himself. That's when he saw the same little boy in the crowd of people. Those eyes, those frightened eyes.

"Someone tell my son, Jimmy," he coughed some more as his voice faded. "Please tell him that his daddy loves him."

The last thing Luis Rodriguez saw was the scared, innocent stare of the little boy.

Chapter 31

Manhattan Avenue, Jersey City, New Jersey. 9:50 PM, Thursday.

Tap and Ancheta were in a tongue-struggle as they stumbled into his bedroom. She tore at his shirt, trying to get him to take it off. He did the rest and tossed his t-shirt to the floor just as Tap pulled off hers and threw it to the side, exposing her black silk bra. With both hands she shoved Ancheta in the chest, making him fall onto his bed. She climbed on top of him and squatted on his groin, moving her hips around in circles. She closed her eyes and only heard their heavy panting as Ancheta's hands were all over her ass. He was getting hot, and she rubbed her head with both hands as she closed her eyes and swayed.

Yes. She could feel the hardness of his cock under her, just wanting to burst out of his pants. She could do this for the next few minutes and maybe make him come without taking off the rest of her clothes. But that would be cruel.

Her phone rang. Although the sound was faint, she still recognized the ringtone. She had left it in her coat pocket. She stopped gyrating and sighed, looking up at the ceiling.

"What?" said Ancheta as the phone rang again. "Don't. They'll leave you a message."

Tap climbed off him. "I'm sorry. But I have to get that."

"You can't be serious."

She ran out of the room. "I'll only be a minute, I promise."

She walked over to the coat closet, yanked open the door, and grabbed her phone from her coat pocket. "Yeah?"

"It's done." It was Lucas. "Give Ancheta our regards." He then hung up.

Tap looked over her shoulder, knowing that Ancheta may be listening. "Oh, that's wonderful. I'm sure he'll be happy to hear this." She put the phone back in her coat pocket, then walked over to the couch in the living room where she had left her purse. She unzipped it and took out an HK USP45 and a suppressor. She screwed the suppressor onto the threaded barrel and walked back to the bedroom.

When she got there, Ancheta was still lying on the bed, the way she had left him. Only this time he was dressed down to his boxers. He noticed the .45 in her hand and jumped up in a seated position.

"What's going on?"

She aimed for his forehead and squeezed the trigger. End of story.

The desperate little shit thought that he actually stood a chance with her. She preferred men who played rough, not like this scrawny little nerd, who was nothing more than the perfect catch for her honey trap. She snatched her shirt off the floor and put it on while she headed back to the living room. Had she not been in such a hurry she would've jumped into the shower just to wash Ancheta off of her. The mission was simple: meet Ancheta, gain his trust, and let him think that he was getting paid by a hot computer hacker he'd been chatting with for the past several months, in order to gain access to his creation. The sex was optional.

What Ancheta didn't know was that Tap's real name was Erela Ganz—a name she went by when she used to work for the Mossad—until she and her older sister, Dafna, were recruited into The Arms of Ares, who helped them fake their deaths and gave them new identities. She didn't miss being called Erela, but she did miss her sister. The last she'd heard of her was that she was killed during a failed op in Montreal a few years back. She didn't know by whom, but, nevertheless, as things went in this business, she knew that she'd cross paths with them eventually.

Ganz collected the spent shell casing, removed the suppressor from the .45 and put them all in her purse. Once she had on her coat and shoes, she was out the door.

Chapter 32

Bloomington, Indiana. 9:52 PM, Thursday.

In addition to the extendable batons, some of the items that Parris had purchased from the ex-marine back in Indianapolis were three different license plates. She felt slightly guilty that, of all the places that she could choose to steal another SUV, she chose a church parking lot. The twenty-four-hour Wal-Mart had several vehicles to choose from, but they also most likely had CCTV cameras all over. Which was why the Baptist church she was currently at was a smarter choice. She didn't know what would be going on at this hour on a Thursday night, but she heard Gospel singing, with a very powerful lead female vocal coming from inside, so she figured that it must be a choir practice.

It took less than three minutes for her to switch the license plates, bypass the cheap alarm system, and then drive off. This plan may not be perfect, but it would buy her some more time— from being pulled over by The Indiana State Police, or any more goons Mister Lucas might send after her.

From the church, she drove out of town to the farm of Kerpius's friend, Jack Snyder, who was one of the names on the list he'd given her. He was one of the farmers who didn't do business with Maiz-A-Corp, but still used Sementem's GMO corn. Parris was interested in knowing if his soil samples would yield different results from Kerpius's.

Once she had collected soil samples from Snyder's field,

Parris drove south on I-65 across the Ohio River into Louisville, Kentucky. She looked at the dashboard clock and saw that it was thirteen minutes to two o'clock in the morning. There were many independent testing labs across the Midwest, but she'd needed to get out of Indiana. The first place Mister Lucas's men would be searching for her would be any laboratory that specialized in food testing. Her dilemma would be to find one that was within a two-hour drive, so as to not spend too much time on the road, but be far enough from Bloomington to make it difficult for Lucas's men to find her.

She was on the phone with Downing during her ride and had shared everything with him. He agreed to set up things for her at Morton Laboratories, which specialized in metallurgical, non-metallurgical, environmental, petrochemical, and even food and microbiological testing. There, Parris could test her samples.

It occurred to her that she still had not yet listened to the recording of Grafton that Fox had sent her earlier. So she played it, listening through her earpiece. For the first few minutes there wasn't anything that was any different from what Fox had told her. However, he'd forgotten to mention the part about the porous stomach lining that Grafton claimed to have observed during the autopsies.

Porous stomach lining? Why does that ring a bell? Parris paused the recording and slowed down when she thought she saw a Kentucky Highway Patrol cruiser parked on the shoulder up ahead. When she got closer, she saw that the officer had pulled over someone. The part about the porous stomach lining came back to her. She knew that she'd heard of, or read about, it someplace but couldn't remember where.

Parris un-paused the recording and listened to the rest of it. After having spent the last few minutes driving through the city's industrial park, she saw the building used by Morton Laboratories. She parked her SUV outside, carried her bag with the soil samples, and walked to the building.

Doctor David Crickmore, who ran the facility, met her at the door. Crickmore had a full white beard and wore an old plaid blazer without a tie. As Parris approached the door, he extended a hand. "You must be Special Agent Erica Hinkson."

She nearly did a double-take after hearing the man's British accent. Not what she had expected to hear in these parts. "Doctor Crickmore, thanks for assisting the Bureau at this hour."

"Sure," he answered with a smile. "I don't get such requests regularly." He then looked at her the way a concerned father might look at his daughter, as though he knew she was hiding something from him. "Are you all right? If you don't mind me saying, you look as though you…I don't know, took a tumble."

Parris waved her hand. "I'm fine. Will you show me your lab?"

"Of course." Crickmore locked the door behind her and gestured down the hall. "Right this way."

The laboratory was fully equipped with everything that Parris needed. She put the knapsack on the counter, along with the plastic bag containing the five ears of corn she had purchased earlier.

"May I ask what I'm supposed to do with these?"

Parris slid the corn over to him. "I need you to run an antibody test on the corn."

"Sure," said Crickmore. "That won't be too difficult. Any specific antibody?"

"Just the one that's most abundant," answered Parris as she removed the Pyrex dishes with the soil samples from her knapsack.

Within minutes, Parris had on a lab coat and had synthesized a sample of the known compound using the various elements that were already at her disposal in the lab. Once that was done, she had a solid sample of the compound, which she then placed in the mass spectrometer and activated it. It didn't take too long before she got a reading, which was in the form of an *x versus y* graph—where the x-axis represented the atomic mass units of the elements. The y-axis, on the other hand, measured how many ions of a given mass were detected, or its relative intensity, that were displayed on the computer she used. This reading would serve as a comparative sample. She would then do a mass-spec reading of the soil sample taken from Kerpius's farm and another from Snyder's.

What was known so far was that Maiz-A-Corp did a late-season crop dusting on Kerpius's farm, as well as all their other clients—according to the info Dewan sent her. However, Snyder, who wasn't associated with Maiz-A-Corp, didn't. If Kerpius's sample contained traces of the mystery compound and Snyder's didn't, it would prove that Maiz-A-Corp used a different variant of the same fertilizer than Snyder did—and most likely all other non-Maiz-A-Corp farm owners who used Sementem's GMOs.

Parris didn't expect Crickmore to find any residue of the compound on the ears of corn. It most likely would've been washed off while the corn was being prepared for shipment or for direct sale. Most of it would've likely been absorbed by the plant itself. Corn, like any organism, have a number of self-defense mechanisms in order to protect themselves from any harmful foreign substance. Plants do so by chemically modifying hostile compounds in order to detoxify them. This would be expressed in an increase in the number of antibodies in the plant, which is what Doctor Crickmore was looking for.

Parris's phone buzzed. When she looked at the call display, she saw that it was Downing. She excused herself from Crickmore and walked to a corner of the laboratory where she tapped her earpiece.

"Yes, sir."

"I'm sending you something," Downing answered. "I just got word that the CDC was notified of an incident in Gary, Indiana."

"What happened?"

"A truck driver dropped dead in a restaurant," Downing answered. "Witnesses say he was seen entering the men's room and collapsed when he came out. I want you to go there and take a look."

"Has the cause of death been determined?"

"No one knows what killed him. He was just seen coughing up blood before he died."

"I wouldn't mind doing so," Parris looked over her shoulder at Crickmore, "but I have my hands full here at the lab."

"Tell Doctor Crickmore that he'll have to finish up on his own," said Downing. "You're the only agent with the qualifications, and you are closest to Gary, so I need you there. I'm hoping that you'll spot something that the others won't."

She looked at the clock on her phone, it was almost ten minutes to three o'clock AM. "With all due respect, sir, I think I'm close to uncovering somethi—"

"Listen to me," Downing's voice sounded more desperate than authoritative. "An autopsy was ordered by the coroner's office due to the unusual way the man died. The victim's stomach was full of holes. Like he had one huge ulcer. Sound familiar?"

Parris felt a pinch deep in her chest. *Doctor Grafton's confession. The porous stomach lining.* "I'm heading there now."

Chapter 33

Spade Financial Group, 2121 K Street, Washington, DC. 5:00 AM, EST, Friday.

F ox was happy to be off his feet. The roughly eight-hour drive from Great Sacandaga Lake was non-stop, except for gas and a brief stop in Schenectady where he and Sparks grabbed a quick bite. The road conditions contributed to the drive being nearly two hours longer, as black ice once again slowed traffic down, especially as they got close to New York City.

The Spade Financial Group, which was established in 1971, offered several financial products from short-term savings plans to 401Ks. They also specialized in personal and group disability, medical, critical illness, and life insurance policies. What 99.9% of the world's population didn't know was that Spade was also a front for the Central Intelligence Agency. Furthermore, some of Spade's offices around the world also served as field offices. There was a lot of opposition over the choice of hiding CIA offices within a well-known company. Proponents over the choice simply stated that the best place to hide a spy agency was in plain sight.

Sparks was currently in the conference room with the two FBI agents who were liaisons to the CIA. Another agent from Langley sat in on the meeting in the event that Sparks forgot to mention something to Parris and Fox. The debriefing was expected to last for at least an hour. They weren't in the actual Spade offices on the top floor of the seven-story building, but on the floor below.

Although the CIA agreed to share some of their intelligence with the FBI, they were kept in the dark about their connection to Spade.

His conversation with the general was much shorter than Sparks's debriefing, and he used the extra time to lie down on the couch in the office and catch up on some much needed sleep. He had asked the FBI agents, Chase and Stills, to knock on the door as a courtesy. That way he'd know that they were about to take Sparks to one of their safe-houses. With everything she knew, they may just end up being able to build a case against SLR and Sementem. But Fox was still skeptical about how successful they'd be at making any arrests. These guys were snakes. They'd slide in, unnoticed, and do their damage, then slither out before someone could trap them. And, as far as snakes went, they'd go as far as coiling up together to protect themselves and leave one out of the loop to take the fall.

Fox didn't know how long he'd been asleep, but when he heard the knock on the door, he stared at the ceiling briefly, wondering how he was going to handle having to tell Sparks good-bye. There was a second knock and Fox got off the couch. He answered the door, but instead of seeing the agents, it was Sparks. She had a half smile as she stared back at him, but her eyes clearly showed her sadness. Agents Stills and Chase were several feet away, near the glass-door entrance to the hallway.

Sparks lowered her head, cleared her throat, then looked at Fox. "Hi."

"Hey there, yourself," Fox answered. "You're all set?"

She shrugged her shoulders. "I guess. The FBI believe that it's best that I remain in a safe-house for the time being."

"I'd have to agree with them." Fox nodded to the two agents, who did the same in return. "How'd they treat you? Not too rough with the good-cop/bad-cop routine, I hope."

"They were nice to me," Sparks chuckled. "They brought donuts and coffee, but I didn't have any."

"That's no surprise," said Fox. "FBI agents tend to have an affinity toward donuts, just like regular cops. As long as they're cops around, you'll never hear of the donut industry needing a government bailout."

Sparks chuckled a bit louder as Fox smiled back at her. But it didn't last, as her smile died down quickly. "So, I guess this is it." She attempted to force a smile. "We won't be seeing each other again, will we?"

Fox tilted his head to the side. "Perhaps. You never know. If not in person, then maybe on TV when you testify against SLR. This could be the case of the century."

"Oh stop it," said Sparks. "You trying to get my hopes up?"

"There's nothing wrong with thinking positively, is there?"

"No." She looked away briefly and then back at him. "I guess not."

"Hold on." He went back inside the office to grab his windbreaker that was tossed on the arm of the couch. Sparks stepped aside as Fox exited, closing the door behind him. "I'll walk with you downstairs."

Bad move. Why are you allowing yourself to get attached to her? You've already slept with her. It ain't happening anymore. It just can't.

Fox and Sparks joined the two agents at the elevator. A few minutes later they walked outside onto K Street, where the agents had parked their car. Since they'd arrived around a quarter past six in the morning, they didn't have any difficulty finding a spot in front of the building.

Agent Chase walked around the front of the black Crown Victoria, while Stills waited outside the back passenger door for Sparks. She held onto Fox's hand and turned around to hug him, forcing herself hard against his groin as she buried her head in his chest. He got careless and let his hands slide toward her lower back before he stopped. She lifted her head from his chest and stared into his eyes as he stared back into hers. She went up onto her toes as she brought her lips closer to his. He lowered his head, then pecked her on the lips quickly before withdrawing.

"You're a brave woman, Katherine Sparks," said Fox. "You'll be fine."

Appearing slightly dejected that he didn't give her a *real* farewell kiss, she turned her head to the side. She then wiped below her eye, nodding. "I understand."

Fox felt the pressure lighten around his groin area as she pulled away. He could tell that she didn't want to let him go, but still took the initiative to turn away. He watched Sparks walk to the car as Stills opened the door for her. She was about to get in when she suddenly turned around.

"May I at least know your name?" she asked. "Your *real* name?"

He smirked. *What the hell? It won't make a difference at this point.* "I'm Ridley Fox."

The smile reappeared, and this time it didn't seem forced. "Thanks…Ridley." She then got inside and Stills closed the door behind her. The tinted windows made it impossible for Fox to see her, but he knew she was staring at him. He remained where he was as he watched the Crown Vic drive westbound on the elevated portion of K Street, then take the loop on the 22nd Street overpass, and head back east on K Street.

***

The bus stand on K Street at the corner of 22nd was a good spot to wait. It may have been over an hour and twenty minutes, but that was short compared to some other jobs The Motorcyclist had done. Once his employer told him where and when the FBI would be meeting to pick up the target, all he had to do was sit and wait for them to get in the car and drive. He would've preferred taking her when she showed up, but one look at the man she was with told him that he'd be better off waiting.

The Motorcyclist had two items with him, a knapsack filled with C4 explosives and an HK P2000SK. He watched the Crown Victoria drive past him—taking the loop for the 22nd Street overpass, above the lower section of K Street—then head east. He hurried to his motorcycle that was parked right outside the bus zone, fired it up, and was in pursuit.

Chapter 34

Sparks wiped away another tear and swore that there wouldn't be any more. She didn't want to show this side of her in front of Ridley, but she couldn't help it. Why that was, she still didn't know. She didn't have problems crying in front of Butch whenever he'd yelled at her. But Ridley—who was tougher, smarter, and, not to mention, had a warrior's cock she would've ridden all night had he not worn her out so quickly. *Ugh.* What had he done to her? He could've hit her at any time for having abandoned him and Fab back in Toronto. But he didn't. He could've turned her over to the FBI once he had caught up with her in Albany. But he didn't. Instead he volunteered his time to help her. Now, as a result, the FBI was listening to her.

"You doing all right back there?" asked Agent Stills from the front passenger seat.

"I'm fine," Sparks answered.

"Just let us know if you need anything," said Agent Chase, who slowed down as the traffic ahead did the same.

Once the cars ahead drove off, Chase did too. Sparks admired how K Street was designed—with two express lanes separated by a median from the service lane.

"Is this your first time in Washington?" asked Stills.

"Yes it is," Sparks answered, pausing when she heard Chase coughing. "Aside from my latest trip to Thailand and from working in Afghanistan, I never spent much time outside of Alabama."

"How do you like it so far?" Stills asked.

"I haven't seen much," she answered, "but so far, I like what I see."

"It's a nice little town," said Stills. "Way different from Huntsville, I'm sure."

Chase caught her attention as he began coughing again. "It's way different than Huntsville."

Stills looked at his partner. "You all right?" He reached into his pocket and handed Chase a tissue. "Here, take this."

Sparks leaned to the side, hoping to get a better view of Chase through the center rearview mirror. "Maybe we should get him some water."

"I'm fine," he said as he stopped coughing. "I'm fine."

"You sure?" asked Stills. "You don't look too good."

"I'd have to agree," said Sparks, noticing that Chase was sweating. "That cough doesn't sound like your typical dry cough."

"I think you better let me dr—" Stills was cut off when Chase hurled a mass of bloodied vomit all over the steering wheel, his side of the dashboard, and a bit on the windshield.

"Son-of-a-bitch!" yelled Stills.

Sparks gasped. What the hell was she seeing? The car suddenly jerked forward and rammed into the taxi cab in front. Sparks flew forward but was caught by her seatbelt as it dug into her chest, but it didn't stop her head from whipping forward, then snapping back into the seat.

***

The Motorcyclist stayed three cars behind as he followed the Crown Victoria in the slow lane. He'd wait until they were stopped by the next traffic light, then he would speed up alongside, throw the bag on top of the roof, and *boom*, job done. He heard what sounded like two cars colliding up front, followed by the simultaneous screeching of several tires. He too had to jam on his brakes. He looked around the car in front of him, trying to see ahead. The traffic wasn't moving, maybe both lanes were blocked. A few moments later he saw two cars drive by in the service lane—motorists who were obviously too impatient. He peeked in between the lanes of traffic and saw a driver exiting his car and walking to the back as though to check the damage.

What do you know, the Crown Vic was involved in the accident.

At that moment, he saw one of the FBI agents get out from the passenger side to talk to the pissed-off cab driver. This job was getting easier by the minute.

***

Sparks saw stars as she tried to focus on what was happening around her. The first thing she saw was Chase unbuckling his seatbelt and fumbling for the door handle. He held onto his stomach as though it were about to fall out. *That's right. He had just vomited and had lost control of the car.*

She undid her seatbelt, grabbed the headrest of Stills' seat, and leaned forward. "We need to call an ambulance."

Stills looked behind. "You hurt back there?"

She shook her head. "Not for me, I'm fine. I'm talking about your partner."

Stills had his cell phone to his ear as he got out of the car. Sparks looked ahead just as the cab driver in front of them yelled and waved his arms, pointing to the damage incurred to the rear of his car. Stills flashed his badge to the driver and he quickly calmed down. Agent Chase was still moaning and it didn't appear that he was going to get any better.

Sparks slid over behind Agent Chase and let herself out. She was about to open the driver's door to assist him when she heard Agent Stills.

"Get back in the car. I'll handle this."

She looked above the roof at him. "But he needs help."

Stills lowered his phone. "The ambulance is on the way." Just then, his phone rang and Stills brought it up to his ear.

"What? Who is this? You're telling me to what?"

Sparks saw him looking away, toward the service lane, and she turned too, when she heard the sound of a roaring motorcycle speeding toward him.

"Get down," yelled Stills.

Although she heard him, it didn't register.

"Goddammit, Sparks, get your ass down!"

She looked at him, bewildered, as he drew his gun. There was a *bang*, startling her. When she looked back to the front of the car, she saw the cab driver drop to the ground. Sparks heard screaming in the background, then Agent Stills fired off a shot and the motorcyclist returned fire—striking Stills in the shoulder. He flew into the trunk of the taxi.

Reality caught up with her as she ducked between the Crown Victoria and another car beside it. There was more gunfire—coming from the direction of Stills and from the motorcyclist—but Sparks stayed low, with a severe case of the shakes. She glimpsed at the cars behind them. Doors were swinging open and people were running away. There was a brief pause in the motorcycle's engine before she heard an object hit the other side of the Crown Victoria, then the motorcycle sped away.

"Bomb!" Stills screamed.

Her first reaction was to run like a bat out of hell, which is what she did. She couldn't help but look over her shoulder where she briefly saw Stills shuffling away from the passenger side of their car, holding what appeared to be a bag.

The fiery plume instantly consumed him, right before she felt a scorching wave blow over her. She briefly felt herself airborne, until her right shoulder struck a metallic surface and she slid across the concrete. She didn't know why. It took her a few moments before she realized that she was crawling on her hands and knees. All she heard was an intense ringing. Using the side of a minivan, she helped herself onto her feet. She didn't let go of it as she stumbled forward, only to catch herself on another vehicle. *My...my balance. My God, I can't stand, everything's spinning.*

She then noticed that the car she held onto had its windows shattered. The bomb. Yes, it was a bomb. The motorcyclist, he'd just tried to blow her up. The cars. They were closing in on her, she had to get free of them. She slid between an SUV and a car, and stepped over the double lines that separated eastbound and westbound K Street. Totally exhausted and disoriented, she fell back against the side of the hood of the SUV. Losing all strength in her legs, she slid down onto the street with her back against the front tire.

She deeply inhaled the cool morning air. Air, it was the best thing that she had around her at the moment. Her head got heavy and dropped, and as she looked down she saw the blood on her jeans. It was then that she realized that the palms of her hands were wet. She turned them over to look, only to realize that she had bits of glass embedded in them. But she didn't feel any pain, she had just come from crawling on them...palms down. The shock wave, it would've shattered the windows of every car within a certain radius, she remembered. An adrenaline surge, it was the only explanation why she didn't feel any pain.

Her hearing began to return as the ringing began to wane. The motorcycle. She heard its engine again. Her heartbeat increased its pace as she looked around, searching for it. It wasn't there, yet she could hear the engine. There was a roar then, as she looked east in the direction of the explosion, she saw a flaming overturned car that took up both lanes on the westbound side of the street. It was then the cyclist appeared. He drove through a small space between the burning vehicle and the median that separated the express lane from the service lane.

No, this can't be happening. Sparks watched as the entire street around the assassin began to close in around him as he sped up and screeched to a stop a few feet in front of her.

Sparks shook her head violently as she watched him look down at her. It was as though he wanted to absorb the moment.

"No. Please, don't hurt me."

Her words didn't appear to have any influence over him. All she saw was her reflection in his tinted visor as he took out a gun and pointed it at her.

Tears streamed from her eyes, wildly, as she closed them tightly and screamed.

What happened next was something she couldn't explain. She heard screeching tires and the crunching of metal that came almost simultaneously as she felt a huge draft, as though a high-speed object flew past her in close proximity. Startled, she opened her eyes and stopped breathing momentarily as something above caught her attention. Sparks looked up and saw a body flipping in the air with a motorcycle. It was as though everything moved in slow motion. She heard the crashing sound of metal against concrete while she distinctly counted the remaining four flips the cyclist made before he hit the ground—bouncing once off the concrete about two feet in the air before crashing on his back.

Sparks caught the pungent whiff of burned rubber before she turned to the sound of a slamming car door to her right. It was the same car she had been in for the past several hours since she'd left Albany. It was now sideways on the street with curving skid marks leading up to it and a burning vehicle in the background. The warrior who stood in front of the car with his gun was none other than Ridley Fox.

He had the coldest look that Sparks had ever seen. It was as though several years of accumulated rage had emerged—turning him into a whole different person. When she'd first met him in Bangkok, she'd been scared of him. Seeing that look in his eyes now made her almost wet herself. He walked past her and the mangled motorcycle as though she wasn't there. It was the person who'd nearly killed her who Ridley was focused on. She looked at the assassin and saw that he was still fidgeting. He was lucky that he could do that much after the way he was sideswiped.

Ridley's back was to her as she watched him stop by the cyclist's waist, and point his weapon toward the killer's helmet. Sparks looked away with closed eyes, seconds before two loud gunshots rattled her. The shock didn't last long, as she opened her eyes and turned in time to see the motorcyclist's legs spasm for a few moments before they came to rest.

Ridley then looked around him as though he was scanning the area. He walked back toward her while holstering his sidearm. He knelt down in front of her and put a hand on her left cheek as she stared into his eyes. The coldness that she'd seen moments before was gone.

"You're safe with me."

Never had four words ever brought her so much assurance. She should've felt relieved, but instead, she felt a tightness in her throat that led to an eruption of tears. She didn't hold back, not this time. She felt Ridley's hands under her legs and lower back before she was lifted and carried. She buried her head in his tight chest, not wanting to see anything around her. The warmth of him against the side of her face, the beat of his heart, and the grip of those powerful hands. *Ugh.* That was all she wanted to feel and hear.

She heard a door being opened and then felt herself being lowered. She opened her eyes to see Ridley placing her into the back seat of his car. He then closed the door and got in up front. Moments later they were driving, just as she heard sirens.

Chapter 35

CIA Headquarters, Langley, Virginia. 8:07 AM.

It had been a while since General Downing had pulled an all-nighter since he'd been in charge of the National Clandestine Service. Even if he wanted to go to sleep, he knew that it would be impossible. What, with Parris in Indiana, having survived an attack by two hitmen dressed up as state police a few hours ago, and then having to set up an extraction for Fox and that Sparks woman after someone tried to blow her up. Now he was on the phone with Fox, gathering the latest details of what happened.

"As I said," Fox spoke through the speakerphone. "I noticed the tango while he sat in the bus stand. Had he gotten on the bus, I wouldn't have thought anything of it. He obviously didn't think that I was watching him the whole time."

Downing adjusted himself in his chair. "How is Ms. Sparks now?"

"She's a fighter," Fox answered. "She was shaken up at first, but she's talking now. Have you heard anything from Parris?"

Downing shook his head. "Nothing yet. She should've arrived in Gary by now."

The double doors to his office burst open with such force it blew some of the papers on his desk. As expected, it was Merrick. Downing sighed as he said to Fox, "I'm going to have to go."

"Stay on the line, Fox," ordered Merrick as she dragged a chair over to the general's desk. "I got here as soon as I could."

Downing knew that Merrick just came back from the White House where she would've been in an early morning meeting with the president and the secretary of defense.

Downing gestured to the spot where she sat. "By all means, come on in and sit wherever you please."

Merrick appeared to ignore his sarcasm as she leaned closer to his phone, apparently not aware that it was sensitive enough to pick up voices from as far as ten feet away.

"What the hell happened this morning?"

"A hit was put on our asset," answered Fox.

"You mean the young woman the FBI wanted to question," said Merrick.

"She's also our asset, which is why she's under our protection now," said Downing.

Merrick was taken aback slightly as Downing watched a sarcastic grin appear. "Under *our* protection. Under whose orders?"

"Under mine," said Downing.

Merrick raised an eyebrow. "What?"

"Based on what Fox told me, I have reason to believe that there's a mole," said Downing.

"A mole," Merrick answered. "From within the CIA?"

"We're not sure yet," Downing answered. "The leak could've originated from us or it could've originated within the FBI. As of now I'm more willing to believe the latter."

"Whoever ordered the hit knew when and where to wait for us," said Fox.

Merrick looked at the phone. "How do you know you weren't followed?"

"Because I would've spotted them," said Fox. Downing heard in his tone that he was doing his best not to blow up at her for that insult.

"What about the two FBI agents who were escorting her?" asked Merrick.

"Fox called us as soon as he saw something was off," cut in Downing. "We connected him to Agent Stills so that he could warn him."

"It was too late," said Fox. "But they managed to buy Sparks some time before I got there."

"The building's inner and outer surveillance CCTV videos are being reviewed as we speak," said Downing. "The only ones that knew about that meeting were Fox, Parris, our FBI liaison, and the two FBI agents—Chase and Stills."

"So you think. Because one of you guys fucked up, didn't you?" Merrick then turned to Downing. "Speaking of Parris, I got a call from Andrews about an hour ago. She hasn't shown up for her flight at oh-seven-hundred hours as she was supposed to. Why do I get the feeling that you had something to do with that?"

Downing met Merrick's stare with his own. "*Doctor* Parris wanted to tie up a few loose ends."

"Like what? Please don't tell me that this is about your so-called precious hard drive?"

Downing leaned in closer, on his desk. "As a matter of fact, yes."

Merrick placed an elbow on the edge of the desk and held her head. "Oh for Christ's sake. You put her up to this, didn't you? You went behind my back—"

"Doctor Parris has found some valuable intel which could explain why Alghafari was so interested in selling the hard drive in the first place."

"—and coerced an operative to disobey a direct order from me."

"I didn't coerce her to disobey anyone," yelled Downing. "She was doing her job."

Merrick stood and slammed both hands on Downing's desk. "She has no job to do out there. Faouzi al-Umari is dead. Alghafari's dead. Brunner's dead. We're not responsible for bringing their killers to justice. That's for the FBI and for BPOL over in Germany. So I don't want to hear anything more about this stupid hard drive."

"That *stupid* hard drive, as you call it, may just explain why a trucker in the Midwest died under similar circumstances as thirteen good men and women did over in Afghanistan nearly two years ago."

"What are you talking about?"

"I didn't think you'd know about that because you're too busy kissing ass in the White House, trying to secure endorsements for the presidency."

Merrick gave Downing a once-over, from his feet to his head, appearing stunned. "How dare you."

"I'll say it in layman's terms," yelled Downing. "You're an ass-kissing, pencil-pushing bitch who's been more focused on getting into the White House while ignoring important clues that could very well be precursors to a major attack on American soil." There, he got it out of his system. How long had it been that he'd been wanting to say that? Too damn long.

Staring at her, he saw a darkness that grew in her face as though she were an unattended pressure cooker that was ready to blow. She lifted her hands off his desk, brushed off her pantsuit, and straightened it, maintaining eye contact.

"You *will* remember this moment," she said calmly. "I can name five, no, actually six people who are better qualified to do your job."

Downing pointed to his wall of fame, where his pictures hung. "I didn't earn stars playing Ping-Pong." He then narrowed his eyes as he used the desk to help him stand, glaring into Merrick's eyes. "So if you're looking for a fight, then you'll have to bring better ammo and grow a *real* set of balls."

There were two knocks on the door and Downing's secretary, Marie Vasel, entered. "I'm sorry but this can't wait."

Merrick turned to her. "I don't care. Who do you think you are, barging in here?"

"It's your son," Vasel said louder as she looked at Merrick. "He's just been admitted to Georgetown. They're saying he has a serious stomach ailment."

Chapter 36

Georgetown University Hospital, Georgetown (Washington, DC).

General Downing wasn't able to keep up with Merrick after they exited the elevator on their way to the ER. As much as he tried to, Downing's artificial leg and cane slowed him down. Merrick, on the other hand, ran ahead, shoving past everyone who got in her way and not even caring whom she knocked over. Downing was behind her by about a half-minute when he arrived near the emergency room. He was on time to see a woman in scrubs, whom he assumed to be the head surgeon, talking to Merrick. Downing stopped where he was as he watched the events unravel. He saw the surgeons' lips move and noticed the despair in her eyes. He didn't need to hear what she said—it obviously wasn't good news.

Merrick cupped her mouth with both hands, slowly turned, then collapsed on one knee as the surgeon went to catch her.

Downing had known Merrick personally for the past four years, but had only been acquainted with her when she'd served on the US Select Senate Committee on Intelligence ten years before. While she was head of the CIA, she'd always been a hard-ass. And, as much as they didn't see eye to eye on many things, they still managed to get things done. There had been successes, but there had also been failures. Not once during any dark period had he seen Merrick shed a tear, more or less break down and cry the way she did at that moment. It was only now that he was reminded that she was a mother and also a single parent. Downing never knew who the father was. He wasn't sure if Merrick even knew.

The general couldn't imagine the pain of losing a child, but it was the first time that he commiserated with Merrick. And as he thought back to the argument they'd just had in his office back in Langley, it burned him that she had to come here on such a horrible note.

He walked toward her just as the surgeon helped Merrick onto her feet. When she saw him, she turned away. Downing dropped his cane and grabbed her, spinning her around and pulling her into his embrace. It took a while but she eventually returned the hug. It was obvious that she didn't want him to see her like this, but this wasn't a choice he would let her make. She was still a human being.

Chapter 37

2510 Burr Street, Gary, Indiana. 7:12 AM, CST.

P arris rolled down her window and flashed her FBI badge for the Gary PD officer as she approached the taped-off area. The officer was convinced of who she was and let her pass. The truck stop not only consisted of a gas station, but at least three different restaurants. What was usually a place where travelers could fuel up and have a meal was now a sea of red-and-blue flashers from at least a dozen local and state police cruisers. Dressed, once again, in her black pantsuit, charcoal gray trench coat, and low stacked heels, she parked the SUV and headed toward the restaurant where the deceased had collapsed. Blocking the entrance were two Gary PD officers who, after taking one look at Parris, eyed her in a way that made her feel that they were more interested in getting her phone number than tending to their current duties.

They both smiled and straightened their caps as Parris flashed her badge and held it open a bit longer than usual—wanting them to take the time to respect the three capital letters on it.

"Good morning, Officers. My name is Special Agent Erica Hinkson from the Federal Bureau of Investigation. I'd like to speak to whoever's in charge."

"That would be Detective Harris," said the officer with the name 'Wright' pinned on him. He then gestured toward a set of trucks where Parris saw a tough-looking forty-something African-

American woman walking toward them. "That's her right there."

Parris thanked them and went to meet the detective. She flashed her badge and introduced herself by her alias.

Harris tilted her head after being shown the badge. "The Bureau, huh? Why would the Feds be interested in this incident?"

"We've received word that a victim by the name of Luis Rodriguez died under strange circumstances," said Parris.

"*Strange* is an understatement. More like downright bizarre," said Harris. "I've seen some horrendous stuff over the years. I mean, just last January we arrested a mother and the child molester who paid her to have sex with her four-month old daughter. That's the kind of shit I'm used to dealing with."

Harris looked towards the diner and pointed. "As for this? I don't know what to say."

Parris looked back toward the restaurant, noticing that it was crowded. "This is a crime scene. Why are those people still in there?"

"CDC's orders. They want to be absolutely sure that Rodriguez didn't die from some contagion," said Harris. "They've been there all night. That's why I've got officers watching all the exits. We had to get a Port-O-Potty placed outside the back entrance since the restaurant's bathrooms are off limits."

"I was told that he had internal hemorrhaging," said Parris. "Any idea what caused it?"

"I didn't get any answers yet, so I can't tell you." Just then, they saw a soft drink delivery truck held up at the entrance. Harris shook her head. "Excuse me for a second."

Parris watched Harris march off in the direction of the truck, whose driver appeared to be arguing with the same police officer who'd allowed Parris to pass.

"What the hell's going on?" Harris yelled. "Can't you see the police tape? I don't care if you park on the freeway. You're not getting in. So get your truck out of here."

Harris walked back to Parris, shaking her head while pointing her thumb behind her towards the reversing truck. "Do you believe that fool?" She then put her hands back in her pockets. "Now, where were we?"

"I was about to ask you if you found anything in Rodriguez's truck that he may have been eating."

"Yeah, we found an empty sandwich bag and two soda bottles. One of them's empty," said detective Harris as she pointed toward the victim's truck. "We believe that he ate a chopped egg sandwich, based on the crumbs that were found in the bag."

Parris saw the company logo plastered on its trailer. He delivered soft drinks for a living.

"If you ask me," said Harris, "if his sandwich was responsible for what happened to him, I'm going to have to vet my grocery list from now on."

Parris heard the ringing of her earpiece. She turned to Harris. "Excuse me a moment." She walked away, to a more isolated area of the parking lot. "Yes?"

"Doctor Parris, it's David Crickmore."

Please tell me that you have something. "Yes, Doctor."

"I want to update you on my findings," said Crickmore. "Is this a good time?"

"Sure, go ahead."

"You were testing four soil samples. Two of them were labeled Kerpius-FC and Kerpius-SC and the other two, Snyder-FC and Snyder-SC," said Crickmore. The FC were the initials for field corn while the SC stood for sweet corn. "The Kerpius-SC sample tested positive for your chemical compound, whereas none of it was found in the Kerpius-FC, nor both Snyder samples. As for the corn you provided, there was a high presence of a certain type of antibody. One I'm not familiar with. However, all soil samples *did* yield similar substances that are typically found in crop fertilizer. What's significant is that there was a higher concentration of fertilizer in the Kerpius-SC sample than the others."

"Thanks again, Doctor," said Parris. "I need you to send me your results. I'm going to text you my email address."

"Certainly. Is there anything else I can do for you?"

"No, that'll be all for now. I think the Bureau can handle things from this end. Thanks again for your help."

Parris texted him her email address. Nothing made a damn bit of sense. Why would Maiz-A-Corp knowingly spray a toxic fertilizer on any of their crops near the end of the season? Kerpius already mentioned that it was a waste of money for them to do so. Furthermore, they only sprayed the sweet corn and not the field corn. Why?

Parris walked back and found Detective Harris speaking to an Indiana State Police Officer.

"Special Agent Hinkson," said Harris. "This is Lieutenant Jeff Payne." Parris and Payne shook hands.

"Pleased to meet you," said Payne. "So what are your thoughts about all this?"

Parris looked at Rodriguez's truck. "I'm not sure yet. What was the deceased's itinerary?"

"He was on his way to Grand Rapids, according to his boss," answered Payne. "He was supposed to have delivered his shipment to the company's distribution center for eleven o'clock last night."

"Okay, thanks." Parris handed each of them her card. "If there's anything else, just let me know."

They said their good-byes and Parris walked back to her vehicle. When she got in she let her head fall back into the headrest. She grabbed her tablet and saw the email from Doctor Crickmore. She took a few minutes to thoroughly read his analysis and the notes that he took. The results didn't surprise her and she forwarded the email to Downing—who'd make sure it got to the right people.

Parris sighed. She'd traveled so far, and yet nothing gained. All she wanted now was a quick snack. She saw the convenience store that was a part of the gas station, and outside the cordoned-off area. She drove across the lot and parked her vehicle next to the building.

She got out, wondering what she could have. A sandwich came to mind, along with some juice—either orange or cranberry would do. She went inside the store and walked straight to the refrigerated section, where the beverages were stored behind glass doors. She pulled the door open and grabbed an orange juice bottle from inside. She saw bottled water beside them, behind another door.

Oh, what the hell.

She grabbed one of them. After all, that's what Sparks would've taken. Just then, Parris spotted the soft drinks behind another door and smirked, recalling why Sparks never drank them. What was it that she said? 'The amount of sugar that they put in those things… can…kill…"

Her lips parted as she looked up from the shelf.

The smirk disappeared from her face as several alarms went off in her head. The plastic juice and water bottles fell from her hand, bouncing on the floor and rolling away. The world around her appeared to move in slow motion as both hands shot up to her head. She felt the coldness on the tips of her fingers from having held onto the bottles. As she released her head, she distinctly heard the tune from the lottery terminal play a few moments before the clerk told her customer in a generic voice, "Sorry, no winner." Her outstretched arm led her to the adjacent wall where the soft drinks were being stored behind a glass door. She yanked open the door and grabbed the first canned drink within reach and looked at the ingredients.

There it was.

She let the can drop and grabbed another on a higher shelf and checked the ingredients.

There it was again.

She dropped that can also and grabbed another—this time an energy beverage.

Shit. She saw it again.

She backed away, looking all over the store.

The mayonnaise. Where's the mayonnaise? She stumbled down the hall, grazing a bearded man in a checkered black-and-red coat as she shot by him. She circled around the end of the aisle, ignoring the African-American college-age female clerk who had raised a finger to her as though she was about to ask her a question. *Where was it?* She checked the shelves on both sides of the aisle.

Mayonnaise. There it is. Parris grabbed the bottle and ran her finger down the list of ingredients until she saw it.

Holy shit. It was there too. It's been staring right at me all along and I never saw it. She realized that she was breathing very hard, as though she had run a 200-yard dash. She put the mayonnaise jar back on the shelf and held onto her forehead with one hand while holding onto the shelf for support.

"Excuse me, ma'am?"

Parris heard the cashier's voice, but it didn't register.

"Hey! You there. The sista in the Hillary Clinton suit and the fancy shoes," said the cashier loudly. This time, she caught Parris's full attention. She turned to the clerk, still breathing hard.

"Yeah, you." The cashier leaned over the counter and stared right at Parris. "Did you forget to take your meds this morning? I'm about to call the po-po, 'cause you beginning to scare me."

Parris scanned around her and saw that everyone was staring at her. She then looked back at the cashier before she walked over, taking out her badge. "I'm sorry about that."

The clerk's head rolled back on her neck as she saw the badge. "FBI?" She then looked up at Parris and pointed. "You's the po-po?"

Parris turned around, raising her badge high above her. "Listen up, everyone. My name is Special Agent Erica Hinkson of the Federal Bureau of Investigation. As of now this store is closed. So I'm going to ask that you return your goods to the shelves immediately and avoid shopping for groceries from anywhere else for the rest of the day. This also goes for eating out from any restaurant until further notice."

"Uh, ma'am," said the man in the red-and-black checkered coat. "I haven't had any breakfast yet."

Parris threw a pointed finger in his direction as she took two steps toward him, narrowing her eyes. "You'll just have to wait. Now put your sandwich and drink back on the shelf and leave the store." Parris did a once-over of the store, glancing at everyone who stood where they were, staring back at her, dumbfounded. "That means now!"

The loud, threatening tone of her voice sent everyone scurrying for the exit. Some not even taking the time to replace what they were about to buy back on the shelves. Instead, they dropped them on the floor and ran.

"Uh, Agent Hinkson," said the cashier before Parris turned to her. "What about the food that's already at home. Can we eat that?"

"As I said, do not eat anything. All you should drink is water. Sometime today there will be a special news bulletin advising you on what's safe to eat, if anything." Parris watched the door as the last shopper exited before turning back to the clerk. "I'm leaving, but the state police will be coming here to take over. As of now, the only thing your customers can purchase is gas. Is that clear?"

"Uh, what about lottery tickets?"

Parris shook her head. "That's fine. Just don't let anyone walk out of here with either food or drinks."

The clerk nodded rapidly, her eyes wide open. "Yes, ma'am."

Parris rushed back out to her SUV while she called Downing. His secretary, Marie Vasel, answered.

"Nita, darling. How are you?" That Jamaican accent of hers was the only one of its kind in the agency.

"Not well, put me through to General Downing. It's urgent."

"Hold on, love."

Parris had just entered her vehicle and slammed the door as the general picked up. "What did you find out?"

"We have to alert the CDC, every health agency in country, and put out a nationwide alert," she said as she reversed out of her parking spot. "The Unites States is currently under attack. And I think I've figured out how it's happening."

Chapter 38

CIA Safe-house, Virginia (Classified Location).

Fox observed the taciturn waters of the Chesapeake Bay as he leaned on the porch banister. He was on the second floor of a secluded three-bedroom country cottage. There wasn't any sign of civilization for miles. The only noises were normal woodland sounds. In the summer the bay would be packed with sailboats, floating by in the distance. At this time of year he may still see a navy vessel.

The grounds surrounding the cottage had every kind of electronic surveillance and anti-trespassing device imaginable, including a German shepherd named Roosevelt. If anyone were to be able to get within thirty yards of the house without being detected, there was a chance that the CIA would recruit them. Even if anyone managed to beat the surveillance and thought of shooting through the windows with a sniper rifle, the one-and-a quarter-inch polycarbonate bullet-resistant windows would present a challenge. And if the sniper were to think of attacking at night, they'd also have to also contend with the blinds being closed.

In addition, the house had live-in operatives who anyone would've assumed were just the average elderly couple spending their retirement years living in the country. Although they may not appear to present a danger to anyone, the so-called retired couple that a few people knew as Dennis and Glenda, were well versed in handling any kind of firearm. They both came from the previous generation of spies who first cut their teeth in the business when they worked at the Moscow Station during the 1980s. Their house had a total of three sawed-off shotguns, four Glocks, and several thousand rounds of ammunition at their disposal.

Fox wasn't surprised that Downing had to hang up suddenly. Although he was glad to hear Downing put Merrick in her place— considering that he was about to do the same—he felt the tiny hairs rise on the back of his neck when he overheard Ms. Vasel mention something about Merrick's son being hospitalized due to some stomach ailment. He didn't have all the details, as it had been over an hour since. He did, however, recall Sparks tell him that agent Chase threw up blood before he crashed the car. Could it have been something he had eaten? If so, then what? Fox had made a few calls to find out as much as he could about Agent Chase. From what he was able to learn, he never had any prior food allergies. Finding out what caused him to get ill would be next to impossible since most of his body had been consumed in the blast.

The incident—labeled as The K Street Bombing by the press— was currently the main topic on every news station across the country. So far, no one was able to identify the man who'd side-swiped a motorcyclist with the rear end of his car before getting out and shooting him, execution style, only to take off with the woman said motorcyclist was about to kill. Two witnesses claimed that they tried to film the mystery man with their cell phone cameras, but the camera feature malfunctioned. Once the man was gone, oddly, their camera app began working again. This prompted all sorts of conspiracy theories from the mystery man being a secret agent, to the crazy idea that the woman was rescued because she was on some kind of *Irrelevant List*, as seen on the TV show, *Person of Interest*.

That was all Fox heard as he drove to the extraction point, where he abandoned the car with Sparks to switch to a van. They were then accompanied by two CIA agents, who brought them to the safe-house.

Fox turned to the sound of the screen door sliding open to his

side. It was Sparks, dressed in a sweater. Her hair was all tousled
and she was still a bit pale.

He turned back toward the bay. "You shouldn't be out here,
Katy."

She joined him. "I don't like being cooped up."

"Oh, come on. You have ample room in there. And you have
an endless supply of reading material and TV to watch. It should
keep you occupied until this is all over."

"But when?" she asked. "How much longer? Someone nearly
killed me this morning. Jill warned me that SLR would be after
me."

Fox turned to her and held her by the shoulders. "If it was SLR,
they failed."

"What do you mean, if? If SLR didn't put the hit on me, then
who did?"

"It's under investigation." He walked with her back inside.
"Don't worry, we'll find out who it was."

Just as he had stepped inside, Fox's phone rang. He went back
outside, closing the inner door, not bothering with the screen door.
He then tapped his earpiece. "Yes."

"Comrade Fox." It was Maksim Antanov.

"I wasn't expecting to hear from you."

"Then today's your lucky day, yes?"

There was a pause, it was as though Antanov had been cut off.

"Are you there?" asked Fox.

"Yes, I am." Another pause. "My apologies."

"What's with all the breaks?" asked Fox. "I hope you're not
tracing this call because you'll find that'll be very difficult."

"I'm not trying to trace your phone's location," said Antanov.
"And I don't feel comfortable calling you because I don't know
who may be listening. Even though I'm talking to you with
satellite phone."

Antanov spooked? That isn't normal. "What's going on?"

"I spoke to a friend of a friend, who also has acquaintance
who has another friend. And I found out something more about
Alghafari that I think you'll want to share with your colleagues."

"What makes you think we're interested in Alghafari? He's

dead."

"Come on. I know that Alghafari was doing business with Faouzi al-Umari—who your CIA colleagues were after," said Antanov. "And I'm willing to bet that you were involved in that shootout in Düsseldorf where the scientist Helmut Brunner was killed."

"Tell me what you found out about Alghafari."

"For starters, he had stopped doing business with Umari, or any of his associates, for at least the past eighteen months."

"What? Why?"

"I'll get to that in a second, yes?" answered Antanov. "Alghafari wanted to form new relationships and was thus in contact with other people. The man you know as Brunner was a scientist working for Schwarzwald Industries, which is based out of Berlin."

"Let me guess, Alghafari's moved into industrial espionage."

"I never said that," Antanov corrected. "All I said was that Brunner was a scientist at Schwarzwald. However, my friend who has another friend who knows an acquaintance…well, you get the picture, told me that Brunner's an Iranian spy."

"What?"

"Just bear with me for a minute," Antanov pleaded. "From what I was able to learn, Brunner, through Alghafari, had found a way to sneak a bioweapon into Israel that was guaranteed to have the potential to wipe out her entire population. The notes to make this bioweapon were supposed to have been obtained in Düsseldorf, which as it turned out, was the night he was killed. Significantly, Alghafari suffered the same fate."

Son-of-a-bitch. I knew that it wasn't industrial espionage. "Were you able to find out what this weapon is?"

"Unfortunately, no."

Time to try another angle. "Does the name Lucas mean anything to you?"

"Uh…no. But I can ask around," answered Antanov. "Why?"

"Just a name that's been floating around lately. Do you know anything about the people who killed Alghafari and Brunner?"

"The organization that disposed of them is the reason why I'm in hiding. That's because I'm sure they have ways of finding out that I've been talking to you," said Antanov. "I'm only taking my chances telling you this because you'll have a better chance at stopping them. The most I can do is hold them off, yes?"

Fox gritted his teeth as he turned around to face the other way. "Who are they?"

"A group that we're both well acquainted with." Antanov didn't say anything else. It was as though he was afraid to say the name, but Fox knew of only one organization that both he and the Russian mob-boss-turned-asset were well acquainted with.

"Ares." The name spilled out of his mouth as Fox turned back toward the bay. That sounded plausible, they were mostly made up of ex-spies from the former Soviet Union and other countries. They traded in weapons and intelligence. They were the only ones bold and powerful enough to take out Alghafari. But that would mean they were the ones who were after the hard drive. Additionally, they went as far as killing everyone who came in contact with it. *Mister Lucas, The Electrician. Were they Ares operatives? Sementem, Maiz-A-Corp, were those both fronts for Ares? Could the bioweapon Antanov spoke of already be here in the US?*

"Fox," said Antanov. "Are you there?"

He ran a hand through his hair. "Yeah, I'm here. Just lost in my thoughts."

"Now you understand why I'm in hiding," said Antanov. "I wish I didn't find out about what I know now. I feel like I...I have target on back of my head."

"As long as your source, or sources, aren't compromised, you should be safe."

"There's more," said Antanov. "And after this, you have to promise me that you won't try to contact me until this is over."

"You have my word."

"The reason why Alghafari hasn't been doing business with Umari is because it is rumored that he was very ill and had died."

The fuck? "What are you talking about?"

"I mean it," said Antanov. "The man your countrymen went to kill over in Mogadishu has been dead long before."

"Then who was running the group?"

"I don't know who it was. All I know is that when he took over, Ares was more interested in working with him. And if what my sources say is accurate, then that person's already in your country."

Which could mean that whatever weapon Alghafari was planning to help Iran smuggle into Israel could already be here. "Please tell me that you have a photo of this guy you could send me."

"Nyet."

Shit. Fox sighed as he paced back and forth across the porch. *Did Lucas take over from Umari? He confessed to putting the hit on both Alghafari and Brunner, not to mention that he tried to take out Parris last night.*

"Comrade…are you still listening?"

"Yeah, I'm here."

"Okay, I thought I lost you. Listen, I don't have anything more to share. I must go. *Do svidaniya,* comrade."

Fox heard a click and the line disconnected. He then headed inside, where he went downstairs, and walked to the dining room, where he saw Sparks setting the table. Glenda was bringing over the omelets to add to the bacon and sausages that were already on the table. Meanwhile Dennis buttered the toast.

Glenda turned to him. "So are you staying for brunch?"

"I'd like to but I need to head back to DC," Fox answered.

"You sure?" said Glenda as she made room for the plate on the table. "I understand you haven't eaten anything since four AM."

"You ought to stay, son," said Dennis from the kitchen counter. "You don't have to eat much, but you still need your strength."

Maybe a quick bite won't hurt. Besides, who knew when he'd get his next meal. Fox took off his jacket and hung it on the back of the chair, opposite where Sparks sat.

Dennis brought over the toast. "Good call, son."

Fox held up his phone. "Excuse me for a moment. I just have to make one more call first. Then I'll join you." He was about to call Downing when his phone rang. He looked at it and saw that it was, in fact, Downing's name on the call display. Fox tapped his earpiece. "Yeah."

"Are you still at the safe-house?" There was panic in his voice.

"Yeah, what's wrong?"

"Have you all eaten yet?"

"We were just about to sit down and—"

"Tell everyone to stop eating, don't even drink the orange juice. That's an order," said Downing. "Parris just figured out that the nation's food supply has been poisoned."

Chapter 39

Westbound I-80/I-94, west of Gary, Indiana.

Parris was pushing around thirty over the speed limit as she sped westbound in the fast lane of I-80/I-94 toward Chicago. She knew that she'd never make the 9:30 AM flight out of O'Hare to DC, considering that it was rush-hour. But she didn't want to miss the next flight at 11:40. Speaking via her earpiece, she was on a three-way call with Fox and Downing. "How many losses so far?"

"We're fine," said Fox. "No one ate anything."

"Merrick's fine, but in her present state she can't run things," said Downing. He had already explained what had happened to her son. "Eight more men and women at Langley, including the Deputy Director, have been rushed to the hospital. Our FBI liaison team took a few casualties too."

Oh Lord, thought Parris as she swung into the second lane from the median to overtake a slowpoke who had no business driving in the fast lane. Four lanes of traffic and this guy had to pick this one. "So who's in charge?"

"I've taken over as DCI," said Downing. "The president just confirmed my temporary status and a nationwide press release has been issued by all state health departments to warn the public."

"Congratulations," said Parris.

"Ditto," said Fox.

"No need to congratulate me, it's only temporary," said

Downing. "With regards to everything that's been going on, both of you are to report directly to me. The last thing I need is the inspector general sticking her nose into this and going all legal about it. Just get back to DC, ASAP."

That's when she heard Downing disconnect, leaving just her and Fox.

"What the hell's going on?" asked Fox. It was understandable that he wouldn't be in the know, since he wouldn't have read the full report she sent to Downing.

"I discovered evidence of major food tampering, possibly at the genetic level," said Parris.

"So the chemical formula from the hard drive was a toxin after all."

"No it wasn't." Parris slowed down to allow the person ahead of her to move to the next lane before she overtook them. "I have reason to believe that it's an enzyme, a catalyst in other words—a compound that may have led to the changing of the genetic structure of the corn that it was sprayed on, making it toxic for humans. But it wouldn't be consumed in the reaction."

"You don't sound like you're entirely sure."

"Genetic testing on Sementem's GMOs could only confirm my theory, but that would take about two to three weeks. I've just made an educated guess."

"Based on what?"

"Are you familiar with how GMOs work?"

"A bit, but not in detail," said Fox. "I know that GMOs are designed to control insects. Don't ask me about the science."

"Okay." Parris slowed down since there was a bit of congestion. "To begin, there are certain bacteria that exist that are harmful to insects. One of them, Bacillus Thuringiensis—or Bt for short—is one such bacterium that produces protein toxins which are fatal to insects. A given strain of Bt can produce several different toxins which kill different insects. What's important to know is that the genes that encode the information to make the toxin can be transferred from the bacterium to a plant in order for it to produce the toxin on its own. That way, farmers don't have to go through the arduous task of spraying insecticides on their crops."

"In other words, that's how the Bt crop is made," said Fox.

"Correct," Parris nodded. "The toxins are stable within the gut of an insect. In fact, it's the digestive enzymes that serve to *activate* the toxin by removing the ends of the protein. And once this happens, the toxins bind to specific molecules on the surface of the gut and create pores in the cells, killing the insect eventually."

"Similar to the porous stomach lining we've seen in the victims," said Fox.

Parris honked as someone from the lane to her right tried to cut in front of her. "Exactly. That was the specific detail you shared with me from your interrogation of Doctor Grafton that allowed me to connect the dots. Without that, I don't know how I would've figured it out."

"But how can the chemical formula change the genetic structure of the corn? Has Sementem produced some kind of mutant Bt Corn?" asked Fox.

"I wouldn't think so. Are you familiar with GMO-resistant pests?"

"Yeah," said Fox. "Insects who've evolved to the point that insecticides or GMOs don't harm them."

The traffic came to a dead stop and Parris punched the steering wheel. "Shit."

"You okay there?"

"It's this damn traffic." Parris contemplated whether or not she should drive on the shoulder. Why not? If someone got in her way, she'd flash her FBI badge at them. That's when she saw what appeared to be smoke up ahead, someone's vehicle was on fire. Just what she needed.

"Where was I?" she asked.

"You were talking about insects that are immune to GMOs," Fox answered.

"Right," she said, recalling what she was about to tell him. "Over the past few years, GMO-producing companies like Sementem hit a roadblock. The overuse of the same GMOs greatly reduced the populations of insects that are affected by them. On the other hand, it led to the propagation of insects that are immune to them. The same problem occurred with weeds, because superweeds began to emerge. As a result, GMO companies had to find which Bt toxins would kill these strains of insects. In the case of Sementem, they also had to adapt their own herbicide so that it would control the superweeds without harming their own GMO crops. They were the only company that got around that roadblock, while other companies failed, which allowed Sementem to have a monopoly over the bio-agricultural industry worldwide."

Parris heard sirens getting louder from behind. When she looked in her rearview mirror, she saw that cars were beginning to move over away from the center median. She was able to distinguish the sirens as belonging to a fire truck. In fact, she felt that there was more than one.

"But if Maiz-A-Corp's been spraying a toxic chemical on the corn, how would it have gone undetected by the FDA and other government agencies?" asked Fox.

"As I said earlier, the chemical compound is a catalyst," answered Parris. "I gathered soil samples from two different farmers—one that's a Maiz-A-Corp client and another who isn't. The soil sample of the Maiz-A-Corp client showed traces of our mystery compound whereas the other didn't. Think about that for a moment. Why would there be two different variants of same brand name fertilizer used on two identical Sementem cornfields?"

Parris noticed that the car behind her was moving slightly to the side as the sirens got louder. "Hold on for a sec." There wasn't any point in speaking since her voice would be drowned out by the sirens coming from the trucks, which she now saw in her outer rearview mirror. In fact, there was an ambulance that was ahead of the two trucks. And it led the way as they all were about to pass by on her left. She couldn't sit here, not in this moment of national crisis. She had a little under two hours to make it to O'Hare or else she'd be stuck waiting for the two o'clock flight—if it didn't get cancelled due to what she predicted would be an impending state of nationwide panic that could shut down the entire nation. The second fire truck was about to pass her, she didn't even see its taillights before her mind was made up.

Fuck it.

She spun her steering wheel hard to the left and stomped on the accelerator, jumping onto the shoulder where she tailed the fire trucks. She had driven for almost three-quarters of a mile, unimpeded, behind the screaming vehicles before they came to the accident scene. Parris remained on the shoulder lane, pushing her luck that she'd be able to beat the jam. She then saw the cause of the congestion, a hatchback was on its roof while two more cars and a minivan had spun out on their sides. All of them took up the three lanes from the median, leaving the far right lane open, which forced the traffic into a bottleneck. As soon as the fire truck in front moved to the side, Parris gunned the accelerator and flew by before any of the highway patrolmen could notice her—as she would've been shielded by the trucks.

She moved back over one lane to the right, as everything ahead of her was clear. "To answer your question, this would be an efficient way of staying under the Department of Agriculture's radar. They test crops regularly, but the chances of them detecting anything unusual is highly unlikely because they wouldn't know what they're looking for."

"Like looking for a needle in a haystack when, in fact, you should be looking for a piece of thread."

"Precisely," Parris answered. "Remember when I told you about Maiz-A-Corp spraying the herbicide a second time so late in the season?"

"Yeah. The farmer you questioned told you that it was a waste of time and money."

"Not unless you were trying to maximize your damage," said Parris. "Here's how I think things happened. Maiz-A-Corp would apply their pre-emergent herbicide at the beginning of the crop season—the variant without the mystery compound. We'll call it Herbicide-A. This herbicide will control the weeds without affecting the actual corn, which will maintain its own defense against insects. Once there's a satisfactory yield, Maiz-A-Corp applies the second variant—Herbicide-B—which contains the mystery compound."

"In other words, Herbicide-B mutates the corn," said Fox.

Parris was quickly approaching the exit to the I-294/I-80 split. She stayed in the far left lane, which would keep her on I-294, which bypassed Chicago and would take her to the airport. "It's not like that. Plants, as well as animals, have their own internal self-defense methods that help to detoxify harmful substances from their systems. If a plant is sprayed with a toxic substance, it reacts by producing enzymes that acetylate the compound and inactivate it."

"Sorry to stop you but you'll have to speak in layman's terms," said Fox.

"Acetylating the compound is simply a process where an enzyme adds an acetyl chemical group to a compound. In this case, think of the plant unleashing numerous *specific* enzymes that outnumber Herbicide-B's toxin by ten to one. However, only *one* enzyme is needed to acetylate Herbicide-B's toxin to render it inactive. Are you following me so far?"

"So far so good," said Fox.

"Now, we have all these remaining enzymes floating around with no Herbicide-B toxins left to inactivate. What happens next? They inadvertently detect Sementem's Bt toxin—the one that's naturally produced by their GMO corn that protects it against insects. *Those* enzymes mistake it for a threat to the plant and thus acetylate it. As a result, *those* enzymes inactivate Sementem's Bt toxin—rendering it harmless to insects. However, in doing so, the enzymes modified the same Bt toxin to become toxic to humans. Thus when it's consumed by us, the toxins bind to the guts— making pores as it does with insects—killing us. Do you *now* understand how they sabotaged the corn?"

"Perfectly."

"I mean, I hate to say it, but their plan was brilliant." Parris approached the toll booth. She hadn't thought that the I-Pass the marine provided with the vehicle would come in handy, but driving through and being billed automatically was definitely a lot more convenient than waiting in line to pay. "The Bt Corn would pass the normal tests. When sprayed with the compound, the plant absorbs it and transiently produces an enzyme that detoxifies the compound but also modifies the Bt toxin, making it toxic to humans. Once the compound has been detoxified, the plant itself will appear normal in most scientific tests, except that the Bt toxin remains modified."

"Hence, why there are so many deaths," said Fox. "Corn derivatives can be found in the most common foods."

Parris then heard Fox ask Sparks what kind of donuts she and the FBI agents had during her debriefing. Sparks answered that there was a mix.

"Ask her if any of them were jelly-filled," asked Parris. She listened to Fox ask the question.

"She said yes, because she remembers Chase asking her if she wanted the last one," said Fox. "She didn't eat any. So he ate it."

"And I'll bet you that he ate all of the jelly-filled donuts," said Parris.

"But some of the donuts were cream filled," said Fox. "Isn't there high-fructose corn syrup in those donuts also?"

"Yes. However I suspect the reason why Agent Stills wasn't affected is because those creams are made by heating them. Any toxin is likely to be inactivated at temperatures over a hundred and eighty Fahrenheit. So any food or drink item that's processed with any corn derivative at high temperatures would be safer to consume."

Parris switched lanes to overtake another person who refused to move over to let her pass. "But that doesn't go for everything else, like soft drinks, sports drinks, salad dressing—"

"And mayonnaise," said Fox.

"You got it."

"This could explain what happened at Camp Iron Eagle," said Fox. "The mayonnaise wasn't spoiled. It was toxic. Sementem had to have known what happened."

"And since SLR's a subsidiary of Sementem, they had every reason to help in covering up the incident."

"With a little help from the army. Brigadier General Jeansonne to be precise," said Fox. "Which is why they went as far as faking an insurgent attack. They needed to destroy the bodies."

"Don't forget that they killed Kentowski's brother, Corporal Small, and made Sparks take the fall. Next thing you know,

Brigadier General Jeansonne retires from the army and winds up as the CFO of SLR. Sounds like a reward for helping them with the cover-up."

Parris heard Fox sigh. "Right. Ironically, when Sparks ordered the disposal of those sandwiches, she inadvertently wound up saving hundreds of lives."

"Precisely."

"But what I don't understand is that since Sementem knew that their GMOs were dangerous, why would they take a chance on producing the same strain that killed our troops?" asked Fox.

"Because they've lost billions in the last twelve months," said Parris. "Many European countries have banned GMOs. And since Sementem controlled most of the market, they also stood to lose the most. Secondly, their GMOs are the most effective against resistant pests. Researching an alternative and safer GMO would be costly. My guess is that since they knew that the chance of someone discovering a fatal flaw in their GMO was roughly one in a million, they decided to keep their GMO the way it was. After all, they're cashing in on it, right?"

"The almighty dollar," said Fox.

Parris switched off the heat inside her vehicle, as it was beginning to get too hot. "But what bothers me is that I can't help but believe that Maiz-A-Corp is a front for another organization. Sementem wouldn't sabotage their own GMOs."

"How about it being a front for an organization called Ares?"

Oh Lord. Things were going so well until he had to bring that name up. "Why do you keep assuming that they're involved?"

"Since I got a tip from our friendly Russian mobster nearly a half hour ago," Fox answered.

"Antanov called you?"

"He's scared shitless." Fox then told Parris about Brunner's connections to Iran and about Umari's connection to Ares.

"If what Antanov told you is true, it would mean that Brunner was planning to duplicate in Israel what's happening now over here. Do you think Mister Lucas took over Umari's organization?"

"Possibly," answered Fox. "It's hard to tell at this point. We don't have a picture, a voice signature, we have nothing on this guy. I can't help but feel that there's something else that we're missing."

"Like what?"

"Ares doesn't attack nations. They manipulate situations that eventually cause countries to go to war. And they do so behind the scenes by trading in weapons or intelligence."

"So you think they'll try to frame a country for this attack?" asked Parris.

"I wouldn't bet against that," Fox answered.

***

When Parris and Fox ended their call, Fox walked over to the living room where the others were fixated on the television—watching the latest developments on ABC News. So far, every ER in this time zone was filled to capacity. The west coast, so far, had not faced the brunt of the attack.

Sparks turned to Fox as he stood next to them. "So what's going to happen?"

"I have to go," he answered.

"Does that mean we have to throw all this food out?" asked Dennis.

"What you're serving should be fine," answered Fox as he turned to Glenda. He then walked to the table, grabbed his jacket from the back of the chair and put it on. "Just be sure the food has been cooked at temperatures over two hundred degrees Fahrenheit. But you should stay away from every cold beverage, except for water. You'll be hearing from Langley soon about this."

Dennis took Fox's plate to the counter, shoved the omelet and bacon between two slices of toast then put it in the oven for a few minutes. When it was done, he took it out and put the meal into a sandwich bag. Dennis then walked over to Fox and handed it to him. "If the people responsible for this attack are stateside, then you're going to need your strength if you're going to put these assholes six feet under."

"One more thing," said Sparks as she ran to the fridge and came back with a six-pack of water bottles, handing them to him. "Go get 'em."

Ambushing him, she grabbed the front of his jacket with both hands and pulled herself up to his lips, forcing her tongue in deep. His tongue didn't have time to fight back. She wanted to be in control this time, and Fox didn't argue as he put his arms around her, holding her tight. When she had run out of fuel, Fox pulled away just as he felt himself getting hard—not something he wanted to share with Dennis and Glenda in the same room.

There weren't any more words he could say to her. He didn't want to say another good-bye—that french kiss was enough. He pulled gently out of her embrace, walked to the front door, and left.

Moments later, he sped away on the two-lane state highway through the woods when his phone rang. He tapped the earpiece. "Yes."

"My contact came through with new information." It was Antanov.

"I thought you said you wanted to cease all contact for now," said Fox.

"I know what I said. But you have to see this."

"What is it?"

"My contact sent me a sketch, which I'm now sending to you. They believe that this is the person who has taken over from Umari. Or should I say, is masquerading as him. I have to go. I hope this helps." Antanov then hung up.

Fox slowed down and pulled over onto the shoulder. He grabbed his tablet and saw the email from Antanov. He then opened the email attachment.

Antanov, this better be something good...oh, fuck me!

Fox felt a dryness hit him deep in his throat. He swallowed hard as he tried to absorb what he looked at. "You've got to be shitting me! How the? No way. No fucking way!"

He stomped on the gas and called Parris. She answered after the first ring.

"What's going on?"

"I've got some real shitty news," said Fox. "And if you're still driving, you better pull over."

Chapter 40

FBI Safe-house, Silver Spring, Maryland.

F BI Agent Sam Wilmore parked the brown delivery truck between the safe-house driveway and the leafless birch tree adjacent to it. When he looked out the passenger window to his right, he saw the suburban two-story, three-bedroom home where he was to make his delivery. There was nothing unusual about a UPS van driving through this neighborhood at ten o'clock in the morning. As far as the neighbors were concerned—those who were currently at home—someone was just receiving a parcel. No big deal. Wilmore grabbed the ten-by-fourteen-inch box that contained a few books for the person the agency was protecting. He wouldn't mind living in a house as nice as this one, but his wife was satisfied with the apartment they had in Prince George's County, despite the rising crime rate.

The only thing Wilmore knew about the asset was that his last name was Weyland. Other than that, he didn't know anything about him, or why he was under FBI protection. But being in a safe-house, where there weren't any communication devices such as a cell phone, iPad, or laptop, the asset must be agitated. The assets in these safe-houses at least had a television—the best that tax dollars could buy—where they could watch anything they wanted. But this guy didn't watch too much TV, he mostly read books, and that was all Wilmore had been delivering so far.

A few days ago the asset had asked for all twelve books written by Joseph Finder—which he had finished in less than five days. Now he was asking for all the books written by some guy named Barry Eisler. He was picky, saying that he wanted paperbacks and not an e-Reader. Not that the FBI objected, since e-Readers were electronic devices that could be traced like a cell phone. The agency's policy with regards to books was so strict that even the agents posing as a middle-aged couple weren't permitted to borrow books from the library at the risk that their library card, once scanned, could compromise the location of the safe-house. All forms of entertainment—including books—had to be approved by the agency.

Wilmore strode up the walkway, passing the blue Chevy Malibu that was parked in the driveway, and rang the doorbell twice. He saw no sign of someone coming to the door. Normally when he rang, someone would say something like "Just a moment" or "Be right there." He rang again, twice, rapidly. A few moments went by and there still wasn't an answer. This was odd, because he was expected. He'd heard the doorbell from outside, so it wasn't broken.

Wilmore knocked hard. "Hello? Is anyone there?"

He waited a few moments but there wasn't a response, so he took out his mobile and called his supervisor. The call was answered after the first ring. "UPS has made contact but customers aren't responding to sign for their package. Waiting for instructions."

A few seconds passed before there was a reply. "Acknowledged. Proceed into the house."

The operative banged on the front door three times, then pressed down on the handle. Surprisingly, the door was left unlocked.

"Mark? Carol? It's Tyler, the UPS man."

Once he closed the door behind him, Wilmore quietly placed the parcel on the floor and took out his Glock .22, which was concealed in a hip holster.

"Mark. Carol. Anyone?"

"Hi, Tyler." It was Weyland's voice coming from behind the closed door to the powder room, which was just adjacent, to his right. "Come on in. Mark and Carol are out in the back yard."

Wilmore shook his head and holstered his sidearm. He picked

up the parcel and walked to the living room where he heard Weyland. "You had me worried for a minute."

"Sorry about that." Weyland left the powder room, wiping the lenses of his glasses with a handkerchief before putting them back on. "I'm sure you can appreciate why I couldn't answer you in a timely fashion."

"Yeah, it's okay," said Wilmore as he handed Weyland the parcel. Looking at this guy, he felt that he would fit right in among the cast of the *Big Bang Theory*—if ever they were to add a new character. What the hell did a geek like this do to piss off the people who wanted him dead?

Weyland's face lit up like a child getting the Christmas present they'd always wanted. He took the box and hugged it as he danced with it. "Yes, I've been wanting to read these for such a long time." He then stopped hopping around and turned to Wilmore. "Thank you."

"You're welcome." Wilmore walked past Weyland. *Weirdo. Probably hasn't been laid in like, forever.* "I just want to have a word with Mark and Carol." He walked through the kitchen where he could access the back yard.

As he grabbed the handle to the back door, something caught his attention in the living room, adjacent to where he was. There was red splatter on the carpet. His instinct guided him to the living room, where he gasped at seeing the bloody mess on the floor. His brain barely had a chance to register what he saw in front of him before he felt the thin, sharp steel slice the back of his neck. He slapped his hand to where he felt the sting of the blade and spun around. Immediately, Wilmore received two cross-diagonal slashes across his face before he felt the object shoved into his stomach. The attacks were so fast that his brain lagged in registering what was happening to him.

Wilmore came to, seconds later, and found himself lying on his back grimacing from the pain. He forced his head up slightly and was horrified to see what looked like a chef's knife protruding from his stomach. It was then that he saw Mark and Carol beside him. Their faces were so severely slashed that they were barely recognizable.

The asset then squatted on top of his thighs with both knees to his sides. The only difference was that this wasn't the nerd from before. The grin, the look in his eyes, the hair which had suddenly become a wild mess. No, this was a monster in a nerd's body.

"Weyland?" Wilmore wheezed. Talking had never been this difficult for him.

Weyland wagged his finger and shook his head. "No, no, nooo."

That's when he pulled out the blade—its sharp edge slicing the inner wound making him scream in agony. "Timothy Weyland's gone."

The voice. What the hell's happened to his voice? It had become throatier, huskier.

"My name's Faouzi al-Umari," he said as he slid up over his waist and leaned over—his face so close to Wilmore's that a drop of saliva fell from his mouth onto his cheek. "But you can call me Al."

Chapter 41

O'Hare International Airport, Chicago, Illinois.

"Stupid, stupid, stupid."
       That's all Parris kept repeating to herself as she hastily walked down the terminal to her gate—dragging her carry-on by its handle. Fox had the foresight to advise her to pull over onto the shoulder, because she certainly would've lost control of her car once she saw Timothy Weyland's sketch.

Both left and right, restaurants were either closed or were currently closing. Owners or managers were pulling their accordion doors shut, as their patrons received refunds and left. As she walked by a Starbucks she saw some idiot arguing with an employee because he didn't get his latté. The full details of the food scare were being left out of the news, so as to minimize a panic. The last thing the country needed to know was that they were under attack. The only other news she recalled hearing of before the state health department advisory was of a bombing on K Street in Washington—which was quickly bumped off by what was going on now.

So far, her flight had not been cancelled, but others had been delayed—no doubt, due to airline crew members falling ill—and it took everything not to just drop her handbag on the floor and scream. Timothy Weyland—or whoever he really was—had not only played the CIA and the FBI. He had played her. Never mind the agency analysts who'd determined that Weyland was the best choice for a recruit. She, Doctor Nita Parris, was the one who'd met him at the George Washington University Bookstore. *She* recruited him as a mole within Bismarck Securities. *She* trusted him and the intel he gave. And after all the time she'd spent getting to know him, all Parris saw was a huge nerd who spent too much time reading that he couldn't even be distracted by a porn magazine had it been slipped in his bag. Everything about him had been a lie. One big fucking lie.

This was by far the biggest failure in intelligence in the CIA's history. Or maybe it would be safe to surmise that this was the biggest failure in intelligence ever. Even though the death toll was slowly tapering off, it had still easily surpassed the 3000 mark that was set on 9/11. Parris didn't care to find out how many people had died this morning, and she didn't want to know. All she wanted was to get her hands on Weyland.

She heard the phone ringing through her earpiece, and tapped it to answer. "Yes?"

"*Hello,* Doctor Parris."

Parris tightened her grip on the carry-on's handle. She felt her blood heat up as she stopped where she was. That voice. It was a bit throatier than she remembered it, but there was no denying who it was. "You've got some nerve calling."

"Aw, are you mad at me?" said Weyland.

Parris's first instinct was to check her surroundings. She had a creepy sensation that she was being watched. "Putting a hit on yourself as part of your ruse to frame Bismarck? Had I known it then I would've shot you myself."

"Come on, Doctor. You don't mean that."

"How about we meet at the Hooper-Adams Hotel so you can find out?"

"Uh, I think I'll pass," said Weyland. "Come to think of it. Maybe I went a bit overboard, you know, with the whole double-hitman thing."

Oh, get on with it already. "What do you want?"

"I just had to make sure that you weren't among the thousands with a tummy ache this morning. And also to let you know that it's nothing personal."

"I'm alive and well. Too bad for you that I figured out how you and Ares tampered with the corn. There would've been way more fatalities."

"Bravo! You figured it out." Weyland began to chuckle. "I always saw you as a brilliant scientist. Why don't you come work for me?"

"You're funny."

"No, seriously. I think it'd be fun for us to work together, instead of against each another." Weyland sighed. "But since you're not game, I won't hold it against you. The truth is, I like you. Which is why I'd appreciate if you'd stay out of my way. This isn't your fight."

"What's that supposed to mean?"

Weyland chuckled. "You'll find out later this afternoon." And he was gone.

Parris tapped her earpiece and called Downing. Vasel answered and put her through.

"Yes, Doctor Parris," said Downing. "Where are you?"

"I was about to board my plane, until Weyland called me. There's going to be another attack."

Chapter 42

National Counterterrorism Center, McLean, Virginia.

The rigorous security protocol Fox went through at the front gate was standard for every employee and visitor to the National Counterterrorism Center, or NCTC. Exceptions weren't even made for someone as high up as General Downing. Fox knew the procedure far too well: shut up, show your ID, and the guard takes ten to fifteen seconds to sign you in. While that process went on, there was a second guard with a bomb/chemical-sniffing German shepherd who inspected the vehicle. The dog didn't find anything, and turned its head away from the car. The first guard gave Fox back his ID. He put it away and drove off.

Then he parked his car and walked into the lobby of the six-story structure that was also known to the employees as Liberty Crossing. Although it wasn't obvious from the outside how much of a fortress the NCTC really was, inside, surrounding its homely furniture and carpeting, it had blast-resistant walls and bullet-proof windows. Once Fox passed the lobby and walked into the heart of the NCTC—the Op-Center—he was in an environment lifted right out of an episode of *24*. Surrounding him were dozens of computer workstations with ergonomic keyboards and wraparound monitors. Manning each station were analysts from the CIA, the FBI, and the NSA. The day's top threats were displayed on wall-mounted display screens. In this case, it was the amount of collateral damage that resulted from the number of food poisonings across the country. The top news-makers being the number of traffic-related accidents coming from contaminated drivers. The number of food-borne illnesses was more severe in the eastern-most states, pushing all hospitals to capacities never before seen. Adding to the mess was the recent call to ground all commercial flights.

In the midst of the cacophony that made up the Op-Center, he heard a familiar voice in its usual sarcastic tone. "Hey, Canadian."

Fox turned to see Dewan walking toward him. "Hey, nerd. Glad to see you've made it."

"Yeah, 'cause I know you'd miss me if I hadn't," quipped Dewan.

"Just keep boiling your Similac until this is over and you'll be fine."

"Yeah, and you do the same with your Metamucil. By the way, you heard about Merrick?"

"Yeah. I was on speakerphone with her and Downing when we got the news."

"There's more." Dewan checked over both shoulders, as though to be sure no one was eavesdropping. "I heard that she's no longer seeking the POTUS nomination."

"Seriously?"

Dewan gave a quick nod. "For real. That's what I…*overheard.*"

This kid's incorrigible. "Or listened in on, that's what you're really trying to say."

Dewan shook his head. "Now, I never said *that* exactly."

"You've got to break that bad habit."

"Sure. When you stop banging the assets in cheap hotels."

The fuck! Fox shot him a look.

Dewan smiled as he nodded. "So, you think you're a God?" He then began to clap his hands imitating Eddie Murphy. "Hercules, Hercules, Hercules!"

The earpiece. The damn thing must have automatically called Dewan when Sparks slapped him the first time.

Dewan patted him on the shoulder. "Don't worry. Your secret's safe with me."

Fox pulled his shoulder from under Dewan's hand and looked

into the Op-Center. "What's become of Weyland?"

Dewan shook his head. "He's pulled another disappearing act. The UPS truck he stole was found abandoned, just off of New Hampshire Avenue near the Beltway. He could be anywhere at this point."

Fox looked back at Dewan. "We can start by finding out who Timothy Weyland *really* is. Then we'll have a better chance at predicting his next move."

Dewan scratched behind his ear. "I've already started. Downing asked me to look into every known living associate of Faouzi al-Umari."

"And?"

"Nothing yet."

"Keep looking."

"Yeah, I better get back to that." Dewan then bumped fists with Fox. "I'll talk to you soon." He then went back to his workstation.

Fox glanced over at one end of the center where there was a conference room. Separated by a floor-to-ceiling soundproof glass wall, he saw Downing in a meeting with the directors of the FBI, the DHS, and the NSA. He walked up to it and waited outside. Downing eventually saw him, excused himself, and left the room to join him.

Downing waved an arm to the wall-mounted displays. "You see this mess, son? The whole country's gone to shit."

Fox looked at the displays. "I'm seeing it. Did Parris make it out okay?"

Downing turned away from the displays. "I arranged for a helicopter to fly her from O'Hare over to Grissom AFB in Indiana since all other flights are grounded. She should be wheels-up by now."

He and Downing walked away from the conference room. "How's she taking this?"

"Not too well."

Fox shook his head. "I wouldn't either. The Select Senate Committee on Intelligence will surely try to hang this on her."

"You don't have to tell me that." Downing pointed a finger at him. "And I'm going to see to it that it doesn't happen."

Fox glanced back to the conference room. "What are the other directors talking about?"

"For starters, the attorney general's considering dropping all charges against Bismarck Securities in exchange for their cooperation. It appears that Weyland—or whatever his real name is—planted a whole set of red herrings. He wanted us to find him."

"You mean, he wanted us to *extract* him," said Fox.

"That's another way to put it."

"And we took the bait." Fox looked into the Op-Center. "What was he doing, *precisely*, at Bismarck? I know his job was to hack companies. But which ones?"

"That's what we're looking into right now. Bismarck's tight-lipped about revealing their clients, also trying to avoid any legal blowback for letting Weyland slip under their radar."

"Speaking of legal," said Fox, "what's the situation with Sementem, SLR, and the officers over at Camp Iron Eagle?"

"The FBI expects to get a warrant before the end of the afternoon. We can expect them to raid their offices by the end of the evening. Of course they'll all be hiding behind their lawyers."

Fox rubbed his forehead. "No surprise there."

Downing wagged a finger. "And that doctor you spooked in Upstate New York? He's come forward to the FBI, with his lawyer."

Fox smirked. "So he's going to talk."

"His lawyer's looking to make a deal." Downing looked over Fox's shoulder and Fox turned around to see Dewan running toward them.

"What's going on, son?" asked Downing.

"You told me to keep an eye on Sementem's activities. Their CEO, Mitchell Stayner, just left in the middle of a conference in New York City. He's on his way to his home in the Hamptons."

Downing nodded. "Good. Now go back and check on the others he works with."

"Way ahead of you, sir." Dewan smiled. "SLR's CEO, Steve Haas, as well as the members of the board from both companies, are currently flying to Long Island right now on their private jets."

Downing looked at Fox while giving thumbs-up to Dewan.

"You see that? The kid's read my mind." He turned back to Dewan. "Go see to it that the jet is waiting at Andrews to take Fox and Parris to Long Island."

"Right away, sir." Dewan nodded and returned to his workstation.

Downing then turned to Fox. "I want you and Parris to head up to The Hamptons to see what those guys are up to. Mind you," he raised a hand and tapped his chin, thinking, "Stayner's company has a lot of skeletons in their grand walk-in closets, so his home's likely to be equipped with the latest in anti-surveillance equipment."

Fox smiled. "Have you ever known that to stop me?"

Downing returned the smile. "Never."

Chapter 43

Near Brooksvale Recreational Park, Brooksvale Avenue, Hamden, Connecticut.

Ed Ray remembered when he'd counted down the months that were left ahead of him before he'd drive his last school bus. He was in his forty-first year of driving elementary-school-aged children, and every year for the past five of those years, he'd been telling his family and colleagues that it would be his last. Then, a month after his retirement, he'd show up wanting his job back because he couldn't stand the sight of seeing a school bus almost every day and not be the one who was driving it. After throwing three retirement parties for him, his colleagues finally gave up.

Ray had thought that retirement would be great, that he'd be able to spend more time with his wife, take his grandchildren out to the park, the whole works. But the reality was that his daughter had divorced her husband, leaving her raising two daughters and a $120,000 balance on the mortgage. The lawyer's fees were even worse, and to add fuel to the fire, she had another $20,000 in credit card debt to pay off.

So, it wasn't *only* that he enjoyed driving the kids around, but the job was the only way he could bring in enough cash to help his daughter while she looked for another job. This was why he didn't hesitate grabbing any extra hours he could get, which included driving these kids to and from Brooksvale Park. He enjoyed taking the kids on their fieldtrips. This one consisted of visiting the nature wildlife garden and also the barnyard animals. In addition to being the driver, he gladly accepted being the chaperone who accompanied their teacher, Doris, who sat behind him. At seventy-one, Ed imagined that she must be the oldest teacher at Wallingford Elementary.

Behind him was the typical rowdiness he had come to expect from kids this age, but they weren't so noisy as to distract him from driving. It had been at least fifteen years since he'd had to stop the bus, get up, and tell the children to pipe down.

The site of a woman in a beige fur coat, lying on her side, in the middle of the road made him hit the brakes. There was a mixture of screams and laughter from the kids as they all lurched forward.

"What is it?" cried Doris as she peered over Ed's shoulder from behind him.

That's when Ed saw a sports car in the ditch. It most likely belonged to the woman in the road. He grabbed his cell phone and was about to dial 9-1-1 when he noticed that he wasn't getting a signal. He looked over his shoulder at Doris. "Do you have your phone on you?"

"Yes." Doris grabbed it. "I'm calling nine-one-one."

Ed pulled the lever to open the door and then got up.

"My phone's not working," said Doris. "I can't get a signal."

"Me neither." Ed rushed down the steps, his arthritis in the knees acting up. "Keep trying." He attempted a sluggish jog toward the woman. "Miss? You all right?"

She had her back to him as she lay on her side. When he got beside her, he got down on one knee and put a hand on her shoulder, hoping that she wasn't seriously injured. At least there wasn't any blood around her, which to him, was a good sign.

The woman's head turned toward Ed so quickly that it startled him, and his hands reflexively shot up, with open palms. She pointed an object at him, and before it registered in his mind that it was a riffle, he felt the instant agony as tiny objects pierced his chest—accompanied by staccato noises—throwing him onto the concrete.

He was at a total loss as to what had just happened. The last thing he saw as his sight began to get blurry, was a man in a fur coat and blond wig. But it was the maniacally twisted Cheshire-cat grin that got to him the most, when the madman turned the gun toward his face and fired.

***

Umari took the man's phone and removed the SIM card and battery before crushing it under the heel of his boot. He was then joined by three others who stepped out from behind the car in the ditch. Classic blond-woman-lying-in-the-road prank, it never failed. Even this old geezer couldn't resist being the good Samaritan. Surely he and the others on the bus would've called 9-1-1, only to have their calls blocked by the portable cell phone jammers Umari and three of the four henchmen had.

He turned to the sounds of screaming coming from the bus—a beautiful chorus that ranged from altos to sopranos. One henchman dragged the driver's body into the bush, while two others—one carrying a small sports bag—ran to the bus. A Hummer overtook it from behind and screeched to a stop on the other side of the road, a few feet past Umari. He watched the old lady and a few of the brats pulling on the lever to keep his men from boarding, but all it took was pointing their HK416s at them, and, as expected, they all went scrambling to their seats.

Seconds later his men were inside. One of them got behind the wheel, while the other removed a circular object, about twice the size of a smoke detector, from his bag. He then held it up to the ceiling where the magnets latched it in place. The first henchman returned to the Hummer after hiding the driver's body, followed by Umari, who climbed into the back. He gave the order and they were off, followed by the school bus.

In under eight minutes they arrived at the picnic area of the park, turning off Brooksvale Avenue into the parking area. Umari got out without his HK416—still dressed in drag—after both the Hummer and the bus parked diagonally across the lot. As he walked around the bus from the front, one of his men forced the teacher off the bus at gunpoint, while the other kept watch over the children.

"Doris." Umari smiled as he pointed a finger at her. "Doris Shanks, the grade-five teacher at Wallingford Elementary." He got a kick out of seeing the surprised look on her face at the mention of her name. Hacking the school board's servers had been a cinch. He knew enough, from how many children would be on the bus, to Ed the driver, right down to approximately when the bus would be arriving at his "accident" scene.

"Please," Doris begged as the tears ran down her face. "They're just children. They don't deserve this."

"Now, now, Doris." Umari put an arm around her and walked with her toward the Hummer. "They're safe, for now. I just need to borrow them for a few hours." He then reached into the purse he carried, took out a tissue, and dabbed her cheeks with it. "Let's wipe those tears, shall we? You want to look your very best when the police arrive."

Another tear rolled down her cheek. "Why are you doing this? What do you want?"

Umari wiped the tear away, then unzipped a pocket of Doris's windbreaker, put the wet tissue inside, and zipped it shut. He then gestured toward the bus. "Tonight, I'm going to make these kids very famous. Oh, and I'm going to need your phone."

Umari removed the phone from her other pocket. "Thank you." He took the phone from its leather carrying case, pulled it apart, then dropped everything to the ground, stomping on the pieces. Then, placing a hand on one of her shoulders, he motioned with the other to the inside of the bus—more specifically, to the circular object that was stuck to the ceiling.

"That, my dear, contains white phosphorus—a very incendiary chemical weapon once it's exposed to oxygen. If any of those kids try to get off the bus," Umari pointed to three black objects that his men were placing throughout the inside of the bus, including both doors, "the motion sensors will trigger the dispenser and barbeque the little brats alive. I'm sure the kids would believe it more if it came from you, than from me. Don't you think?"

Doris didn't answer.

"I think so. Now, you'll have to excuse me. I'm just going to say a quick hello to them, right before we turn all those devices on." He pinched her chubby cheek and wiggled it before boarding the bus.

Umari was greeted by a delightful chorus of screams as he stood up front. *Was this fear again?* He imagined so, but Goddammit his ears were beginning to hurt. Imitating them, he hollered louder than they—shaking his head while flailing both hands. It was only a few seconds later when he realized that he was the only one still bawling. He stopped, caught his breath, and scrutinized his catch of nine- to ten-year-olds. He watched them as they all cringed in their seats—some even crying. It was then that something stung at his nose. It was the very strong smell of urine.

Good.

"Hello, boys and girls." Umari brushed away some of the wig's hairs that were distracting him. "My name's Al, and today we're going to play a game I used to play when I was younger than all of you. It's called Duck-Duck-Goose. Except we're going to change the rules just a teeny weeny bit, to be more suited for kids your age. Whoever is Goose, gets to go to a very special place."

There were two children to a seat on either side of the aisle. Umari walked slowly, placing his hand on the head of the child that was closest to him—ignoring the one that sat next to the window.

"Duck." It was a boy in a wheelchair. Too much trouble to wheel him out, so he switched to the other side of the aisle.

"Duck." It was a girl with pigtails. *Ugh.* He couldn't stand pigtails. She didn't even acknowledge him. He alternated back to the other side as he walked to the next row.

"Duck." *The only Asian kid on the bus. Hmm, pass.*

He placed his hand on the head of a skinny African-American girl with cornrows. She reminded him of a young Nita Parris. She was staring ahead and began shaking even more when he touched her, tears rolling down her cheeks. She looked like a good catch—wait. There was someone else, adjacent and sitting three rows behind. He was so obese that he had a seat to himself.

Without looking at the girl he was beside, Umari removed his hand. "Duck." Then, bypassing the other rows, he went straight to the overweight kid, placing his hand gently on his head.

"Goose."

The child looked at Umari as he knelt down at his side. "Hello, little man. You're our winner today." Umari gave a sigh—a mixture of relief and euphoria. "And *you* look scrumptious!"

Chapter 44

The Hamptons, New York. Early Friday afternoon.

The phone call Mitchell Stayner had received over an hour ago was the one he hoped that he'd never get. If there was anything worse than the news he'd received, it was learning of these events during his speech in front of the Business Social Responsibility Conference.

Where was Lucas, and why wasn't he answering his phone? He'd hired him specifically to prevent this nightmare from happening. All this time he'd been convincing himself that everything would be taken care of. And now people all over the country were dying. More were soon to come, unless they figured out what the hell they'd been eating or drinking. And if ever this was traced back to his company, he, among others, were going to be in a shitload of trouble. This was no longer about covering up the deaths of thirteen expendable soldiers. This was an entire nation. God forbid this epidemic hit other countries around the world.

Now, his chauffeur drove the black Bentley up to the front gate, which opened at the touch of a button from inside the car. Once inside, Stayner was driven the rest of the way to his waterfront mansion.

Being the CEO of a multinational company had its perks, more than enough to allow Stayner to be able to afford the thirty-million-dollar, eight-bedroom, ten-bathroom mansion, with its own jetty into the Long Island Sound.

He was dropped off by the walkway leading to the front door. As soon as he got inside he heard shouting coming from the conference room. It was hard to conceal the fact that he'd arrived, as the rest of the board members, as well as Haas and Jeansonne, were facing the door as soon as he opened it.

Stayner unbuttoned his jacket, but didn't bother to look at anyone. "My apologies for being late, ladies and gentlemen. I was in the middle of a speech."

"Well, whoopty-fucking-do," said Jeansonne. "While you were pretending to be hero of the year, the rest of us have been waiting for you—munching on nothing but crackers and cheese."

"You assured us that this would be buried," yelled Haas. "Now this could bury us."

The shouting and arguments erupted all around him. He raised his open palms to calm everyone down. "People, people, people. Sementem's lawyers are fully aware of what's going on. We've been through rough patches before, nothing that we weren't able to fix. I don't see why this will be any different."

Jeansonne downed the rest of his brandy. "For Christ's sake, Mitch. We're not talking about your company dumping PCBs on some town of niggers in Alabama twenty years ago. We're talking about poisoning the entire country. How are we going to cover that up?"

"We'll find a way out, just as we did before," said Stayner. Despite the others, he was able to cover up his anger and worries with the veil of calmness. "We'll stick to our usual story of plausible denial. It'll be hard for anyone to pin this on us, so long as they don't know what they're looking for."

"Plausible denial?" Haas turned around, headed in the opposite direction, and then turned back. "How long do you think that'll hold up?"

"Long enough for Katy Sparks to be properly dealt with. Oh, speaking of which, you may want to let me know next time you're planning a hit on someone."

Haas's lips thinned out as though he were grinding his teeth, and redness appeared in his cheeks.

"Yeah," said Stayner. "I know you were responsible for that bungled hit on K Street. You want to explain that?"

Stayner waited for Haas to answer. But Jeansonne jumped in instead.

"Goddammit, Steve." Jeansonne nearly spilled his drink as he turned to his colleague. "You said that she'd be taken care of."

"She was, dammit," yelled Haas. "The man I hired came highly recommended."

Stayner slammed a fist on the conference table—silencing the entire room. "Stop it, both of you."

It was the first time in a while that he had lost his cool, and everyone in the room realized it. He stared at them—men and women he'd known for years. He knew all their secrets, and they knew some of his. They wouldn't dare sell him out. As quickly as they could knock him off his pedestal, he could just as easily reach out and pull them all down with him.

"I wouldn't worry so much about her," said Stayner as he became calm once again. He then chuckled. "Besides, who's going to believe her? She lost all of her credibility when she was fired."

"You want to take that chance?" asked Haas. "SLR has multimillion-dollar contracts with the United States Army—our biggest client. If news of what really happened to those thirteen soldiers gets out, we'll lose those contracts."

"Fuck the contracts," said Jeansonne as he poured himself another glass. "We could end up spending the next twenty years in jail."

Stayner turned to Jeansonne. "Let's not jump the gun here. Besides, if you and your army mates ever wind up in prison, it'll be for those kickbacks you received from mid-east countries who were supplying you with paint and other stuff."

Jeansonne narrowed his eyes. "Is that a threat?"

"I'm stating a fact."

"That sounded like a threat to me."

"As well to me," said Haas. "And may I remind you that your hands are just as dirty in this affair as the rest of ours."

Jeansonne sighed and looked at his empty glass. "I'm going to need something stronger."

The crowd erupted in angry protest again as Stayner stood in the middle of the room, surrounded by all of them. These people weren't the whining bastards who had nothing better to do than protest his company's GMOs, the new labelling laws, and anything they could throw at his company. Those ones he could handle. However, the quarrelers who surrounded him had more clout, and it only spelled trouble for him if he were to lose control of them.

The noise settled and Stayner noticed that heads were turning toward the doorway.

Gunshots.

The crowd silenced as Stayner turned to the entrance to the conference room. The doors opened and Lucas walked in—dressed in black, as usual, but without the silver tie. But this time he wore, what appeared to be, black army clothes. He was flanked by four others who were dressed the same way.

Stayner pointed past Lucas as he was approached. "What's going on out there? Why was there shooting?"

"Just a little catharsis."

"What?" Stayner lowered his arm. "You didn't shoot the guards, did you?"

Lucas walked past Stayner, staring at everyone. "Also your chauffeurs."

There were whispers throughout the room as all eyes focused on Lucas and Stayner.

Stayner turned to Lucas, whose back was to him. "I was beginning to wonder what the hell I was paying you for."

Lucas turned around to face him. "You paid me to ensure that your company's dirty secrets didn't fall into the wrong hands. Which I've done."

"I'm not so convinced of that." Stayner pointed toward one of the floor-to-ceiling windows that overlooked the Long Island Sound. "People are dying out there. Poisoned off *my* seed. And you tell me that you've done what I paid you to do?"

Lucas put an index finger to his lips. "Shhh. I can appreciate why you're frustrated." He turned to everyone else. "As well as the rest of you. But you must all understand that you could've never expected to cover this up."

"What?" Jeansonne turned to Stayner. "Where the hell did you find this nut-job?"

"You've got some nerve," Stayner said to Lucas. "I don't know who you really are. But don't think for a second that I don't have the means to find out. So you might as well tell me what you want."

Lucas smirked as though he was surprised by the question. "Want? I already have what I came for. In fact, I came to bid you farewell. But before I go, there's someone who's been wanting to meet you. Umari, won't you join us?" One of the men who'd come in with Lucas walked up behind him. He removed his cap, better displaying his intense stare.

Stayner studied him. Those eyes. That stare. There was something about him. He didn't know what but felt as though he should. He couldn't recall seeing him among Lucas's crew before. He looked back at Lucas, who raised an eyebrow.

"What's the matter?" asked Lucas. "Not to sound cliché, but you appear as though you've seen a ghost."

"Oh, he has." said Umari as he circled Stayner. "I'm sure that he hasn't lost a bit of sleep since that day in Paris almost eight years ago, when I was kidnapped and then held hostage. Sound familiar?"

Paris? What the hell does he know about what happened in Paris?

"Come on," said Umari. "Don't pretend that you've forgotten. My captors demanded a ransom payment—one that you never paid. Meanwhile, I laid in a tiny cell in the dry desert heat. I couldn't even get a glass of water because they wanted to keep me weak. I thought of taking my own life. But the man who you know as Faouzi al-Umari wouldn't allow it."

Umari now stood in front of Stayner—face to face.

That stare. And yes, those eyes. It couldn't be.

Stayner shook his head and began backing away. "No. No. This isn't happening. You weren't supposed to come back. You're supposed to be dead."

"Sorry to disappoint you," said Umari. "Nice to see you again, *Dad.*"

Chapter 45

Dropped jaws, gasps, and shrieks erupted all over the room as Lucas's men drew their HK416s. Hands raised high as the group of twenty or so men and women were forced into a corner.

"What the hell is this goddamn mess?" slurred Jeansonne. "Dammit, Mitch. I told you this Brit nigger was bad news."

Lucas raised an eyebrow, turned to Jeansonne, raising his Beretta M9A1, then fired. There were several shrieks coming from the corner as the top left edge of Jeansonne's head was blown off.

Lucas put a finger to his lips. "Shhh."

Jeansonne remained standing as he stared back at Lucas, not having processed what had just happened. Maintaining the stare, his hand reached up and felt the moist surface of his brain. The former general's lower lip hung low and then he fell backward, like a plank, onto the floor.

"You keep some interesting company." Umari stared at the men and women in the corner.

"Son, please," Stayner choked up.

"Son?" Umari laughed. "You finally acknowledge me as family. Even after you left me to die."

"I did everything that I could to get you back."

"Now, you know that's complete and utter bullshit," yelled Umari. "You and I both know that you manufactured my kidnapping."

Stayner's eyes shot wide open as he shook his head. "No. That's not true."

"Your fat-assed, non-musical, embarrassment of a son—whom you constantly yelled at for showing more interest in computers than in his violin—brought you so much embarrassment that you couldn't care less what happened to him. Tell the truth, *Pops.*" Umari waved his arm at the others. "Tell them."

Stayner shook his head again. "That isn't true. Your mother and I loved you just as much as…as…" He looked downward, to the side. It was as though he couldn't say the name.

"As much as whom? My baby brother, Phil?"

Stayner looked at him, his eyebrows narrowed.

Yeah. Got you there, didn't I? "Is that why you and Mom were at his bedside in the hospital every day? You and I both know that I never got a quarter of that amount of attention. He was your saving grace. I wasn't. He always did what pleased you, whereas I was the independent one—the rebellious one. And when Phil died, you just couldn't stand the idea that I was all that was left to carry on your legacy."

He watched as Stayner swallow hard.

"Son…"

"Stop calling me *son*," Umari hissed. He then looked over at his father's colleagues. "Tell them the truth about me."

Stayner's breathing got heavier. It was as though he was about to choke.

"Would you rather I tell them?" Umari pointed to himself.

"You're a bastard!"

Umari inhaled deeply and then exhaled. Relief.

"You're not my real son. You're just some freak of nature I ended up raising because your mother was a fucking whore, cheating on me with my head of security, resulting in…in you." Stayner puffed. "There. Are you happy?"

Umari smiled. He got the man to spill his most well-kept secret, and in front of his colleagues. Or should he say his subjects? The king had shown his true colors—he was, in fact, a tyrant. "How did it feel, leaving me to die? I know Mom didn't take your attempted filicide very well. You know, not many people get up and walk after they've thrown themselves from a balcony, twenty stories above the concrete."

Stayner closed his eyes at the mention of that incident.

"Oh come on. Don't pretend as though that was painful for you. My kidnapping was your way of getting even with Mom. You couldn't care less that I was imprisoned in a tiny cell in the middle of the desert that stunk of piss and shit. You couldn't care less that I was literally starved to the point that any normal human being would've killed and eaten their cellmate."

Umari turned to the others. "As you can see, I never put the weight back on." He then turned back to Stayner. "Faouzi al-Umari knew that he'd never get a dime out of you. So he thought of the next best thing. And that was to turn me—or should I say brainwash me—into being one of his followers, then send me back here to wreak havoc. Instead, I wreaked havoc within his own cell and turned his own men against him instead. Pretty neat, huh? All it took was a single laptop and some Wi-Fi. After all, I had years of practice." He pointed at Stayner. "You just never bothered to take the time to notice. What do you think of my 'stupid computers' now?"

He heard Lucas step forward as he turned to him.

"But I noticed," said Lucas. "And a fine mess he made of his captor when I paid them a visit."

"I've had an appreciation for knives ever since." Umari brandished a Bowie knife and rushed Stayner, grabbing him by the collar and forcing him backward into the conference table, while panicked cries came from some of the board members. "But I have a better idea. I'm going to perform an experiment, one which is closely associated with what you do—filling people's stomachs."

Stayner shook his head as his eyes began to get wet. "Don't... don't make me drink it. I can, I mean, we..."

"No, no, no, no, *noooo*," Umari said calmly, feeling the heat of Stayner's breath all over his face. "I'm not going to make you eat or drink anything. I'm going to help you give the public what it wants. Would you like to know a secret?"

Stayner didn't answer.

"No? Well I'm going to tell you anyway." Umari nodded, once, toward Lucas. "My friend Lucas and I had originally made a bet.

Take this knife, for instance. As you would've probably guessed, it's extremely sharp. I was going to cut you open—just slice you right down the middle—and pull out your intestines. Our wager was how many times I could wrap them around you."

Umari looked away briefly, to the huddled crowd in the corner. "But I had second thoughts about that because, really, there are better ways to make you suffer. Killing you wouldn't be as much fun, so I had a better idea. I figured the best way to punish you would be to take away what matters most to you. No, I'm not going to hack into the company's bank accounts and drain them." Umari shook his head. "Money doesn't mean much to me. But I am going to let you live long enough so that you can watch as your greatest creation destroys this country—the one that abandoned me—from the inside out."

Stayner managed to force out a few words in between short breaths. "All those people. Tens of thousands—dead or dying. Because of you. Isn't that punishment enough?"

Umari then laughed as he lowered the hand with the knife, to place it on his chest, while he still pinned his father with the other. "You think that *I* poisoned all those people? I didn't do that." He nodded his head toward Lucas. "It wasn't him either."

Umari then turned to everyone huddled in the corner, gesturing wildly toward them with the Bowie knife. "You guys did this. You knew that your GMOs were dangerous. You knew this ever since you learned that you accidentally manufactured a fertilizer that would alter the genetic structure of your seeds, making them toxic to humans instead of insects. But you still used the same GMO. Never mind that the Camp Iron Eagle incident should've been a wake-up call to you." He paused as he saw the look of surprise on his father's face. Obviously he hadn't expected him to know about that incident. "Did you actually think that you could keep *all* of your dirty little secrets hidden?"

Stayner was still standing in the same spot, hunched back over the table using his hands for support.

"Now, what was I saying?" Umari glanced away briefly. "Oh yes. I was just talking about your GMOs. You knew they were too dangerous to be sold. The only dilemma was that it was bringing in billions in profits to Sementem. Your solution? Modify the fertilizer, which made your GMOs toxic, by removing a chemical compound that Lucas and his organization like to refer to as *The Demeter Code*—and case closed. You were so arrogant, so conceited, and so full of yourselves that you never considered that even one person out of seven billion could figure it out? Guess what? *I* was that one person."

Umari watched Stayner close his eyes tightly and clench his teeth.

"We could all assume that if ever the truth came out, you'd find a way to get out of it without ever spending a day in prison—you're all too big to fail and too fucking important to jail. So you see, it's not really fair for you to blame this epidemic on me, or my friends. This is *your* seed that caused all of this. All I did was show everyone what they were feeding on."

Umari then backed away from Stayner and turned to Lucas. "I'm done."

"Smashing!" Lucas gave a hand signal. Two of the henchmen shouldered their rifles and went to the door, then returned, carrying a duffle bag. They placed it on the table beside Stayner and backed away.

"What's in the bag?" asked Stayner.

Lucas unzipped it and pulled the bag down around a muffler-sized canister. "Just a little farewell present."

On the keypad at the center of the canister, he punched in a combination. A red digital display lit up to forty seconds and began to countdown.

"In less than thirty-eight seconds, sarin gas will be released into this room." Lucas reached into the bag, took out a gas mask and tossed it to Stayner.

Umari turned to him as he caught it. "And you're going to watch all your friends—or should I say *colleagues*—die, as they try to fight you to get your gas mask. I'm sure they're all wishing that you hadn't installed reinforced glass when you built this house."

Lucas's henchmen backed toward the door, keeping their HK416s aimed at the crowd. Then, Umari and Lucas left the room, watching as Stayner fumbled with the mask. They were the last to exit, just as they saw the others rushing Stayner. It would be every man for himself. Just as they closed the double doors, there was a loud pop that came from the canister and the sarin gas was released.

The yells and screams Umari heard behind the doors brought a wave of euphoria over him. The man who'd never loved him, who'd left him to die in a foreign desert, was finally getting his comeuppance. About ten seconds later, the room was silent.

Lights out.

He turned to Lucas. "Final phase?"

Lucas raised an eyebrow. "Indeed."

They left the mansion, joined the others inside the Hummer that was parked out front, and were gone.

Chapter 46

27 miles east of Shirley, Long Island, New York.

Fox shared a trail mix with Parris on their way from Long Island MacArthur Airport. From what they'd heard on the radio, the number of food poisonings across the nation appeared to have plateaued. Yet, overseas, certain areas of the Middle East had erupted in celebration. Although many leaders in those regions were quick to condemn those who'd rejoiced in the deaths of thousands of Americans in a single day, it didn't stop many news pundits from taking to the airwaves. Several were quick to point fingers and claim that this was a foreign invasion and that America should retaliate with military force.

That's when Parris turned the radio off. Fox couldn't blame her. Up until now, no official statement had come from the White House over the matter. A hot topic such as this one would never stay airtight. A leak was bound to happen soon and the truth about Sementem would come out. But if it was learned that the company was exploited by a sociopath who knew of the true dangers of a seed they refused to take off the market, then the shit would go flying into the fan.

Fox was feeling hungry, and a New York Sirloin would hit the spot at the moment, but it wasn't in the cards for him right now. Such a big meal would make him drowsy, and he needed to be fully alert if he and Parris were going to take these assholes down, once and for all.

Despite the fact that this operation was a joint task force, the FBI wanted to run the show. Fuck that. He, Parris, Downing, and Dewan had been on this for the past several days. The death toll would've been ten times worse had Parris not found out the origin of the attack. While the FBI would be following procedures, going through "proper" legal channels, Weyland and company would be making their getaway. Worse yet, Stayner and his colleagues would be getting rid of any incriminating evidence.

Fox slowly drove past the entrance to Stayner's mansion. The first red flag—the gate had been left open.

"Does that look normal to you?" Parris had obviously noticed the same thing.

Fox shook his head as he stopped and then reversed. "Definitely not." He turned in and proceeded up the driveway. Farther in, they saw several cars parked on the side, in the visitor's area.

Parris unbuckled her seatbelt. "Stop the car."

Fox did as requested, and she got out. He leaned toward the passenger window and watched Parris head over to the parked cars. Then he noticed someone sitting behind the wheel of one of them. She went to that car, leaned toward the driver for a few seconds, then opened the door. The driver fell out, and she immediately drew her sidearm. Fox was about to get out when he saw her running back to him.

She closed the door as she got in and turned to him. "The drivers—they're all dead."

Fox looked toward the mansion. "How much you want to bet that the others didn't fare much better?" He continued up the driveway until they came to the house. No surprise, even the front door was left open. They both had their sidearms drawn and went in.

The bodies of the three guards were the first thing that they saw.

Fox tapped his earpiece. "There's been a shootout. So far Stayner's security and the guest chauffeurs are confirmed dead."

"How many?" came Downing's voice.

Fox took a quick look at the bodies on the floor. "Three dead so far in the house."

"I'm guessing about twelve more in the parking area," said Parris who also had her earpiece turned on.

"House is quiet," Fox said to Downing. "Looks like you were right, sending us out here."

"I want more eyes in there," said the general.

"Right." Fox and Parris put on a pair of glasses—similar to Google Glass, but slightly more advanced. These sent a live video feed straight to NCTC. Fox turned his on, and Parris did the same, giving Downing, Dewan, and a team of analysts everything in real time as they saw it.

"My God," said Downing.

Parris moved on ahead of Fox. He was about to follow her when he glanced at the second sentry. There was something peculiar about him. He appeared to have put up a fight, and it looked as if there was a partial boot print on his face. Even though he had two bullet wounds to the chest, his assailant still went as far as stomping on his face. However, it was his left eye which stood out. It was swollen and also surrounded by the boot print. Fox hadn't noticed that with the previous victim.

"What are you looking at?" asked Downing.

"His eye," said Fox. "Did you notice?"

There was a moment of silence before Downing answered. "It looks irritated. Maybe an infection brewing."

"Likely from something that came off the boot of whoever attacked him." Fox stood as he kept staring. "Parris, come take a look at this."

He heard her approach as he took his smartphone and tapped the app that activated the phone's electron microscope. "I'm sending you guys some pictures."

Holstering his Glock, he took out a handkerchief and wrapped it around the index and middle finger of his left hand. He then used the same fingers to pull up the dead guy's eyelid while snapping a dozen highly magnified pictures of his eyeball. Fox didn't know what the sentry had been exposed to, but he didn't need to take any chances getting any of it on his hands.

"Fox." Parris was stooped beside a third sentry. "This one's still alive."

He put away his phone, picked up his sidearm, and joined her. The sentry had caught a bullet to the abdomen, and the fact that he was still breathing was pure luck. Most victims with the same wound wouldn't have lasted this long, yet this one appeared to have somehow managed to crawl in from outside, indicated by the trail of smeared blood leading up to where he was.

"Can you speak?" Parris asked the sentry.

The man's eyes flickered as they rolled toward Fox and then back to Parris. "They're…they're all dead inside."

"Who did this?" asked Fox.

The sentry clearly struggled with his breathing, coughing and sputtering. "They're all dead…gassed…except for Stayner. He ran out wearing a mask."

Parris and Fox looked simultaneously toward the conference room. The doors had been left open, likely by Stayner when he'd escaped. If they'd been gassed to death, then traces of whatever gas killed them may have been aired out through the front door.

Fox looked back at the guard who stared, eyes wide, as though he was trying to communicate something through them.

"Do you know where they went? Any idea?"

The man coughed some more.

"His son…he said he was going to make Stayner pay."

Parris looked at Fox, appearing taken aback, as was he. He then noticed the sentry drifting off. *Oh shit! This ain't the time for you to be dying.* "Did he say anything about another attack?"

He didn't get an answer, and Fox knew not to expect one either. *Fuck!* "Did you guys get all that?"

"We got it," answered Downing. "Get out of there."

Parris and Fox removed their glasses as they left the house and headed back to their car. He couldn't help but notice how well maintained the lawn was. There were plants and other flowers around, but none near the walkway, and none of them appeared to have been disturbed. It was reasonable to assume that whoever left the boot print on the guard's face had the mud caked on their boot from another location.

"Look at this," said Parris.

Fox turned to her. She stood on the edge of the driveway,

staring down at the lawn, at a set of tire tracks. He immediately recognized the pattern—he had seen those several times, back in his JTF2 days.

"We've got ourselves some Hummer tracks," Fox said. "That's the vehicle they rode in."

"Searching for a Hummer," said Dewan as Fox leaned closer to the dirt and activated the Electron Microscope App, snapping a few more pictures of the soil. "I'm sending a few more soil-sample pics for comparison with the soil on the guard's face."

"We've just finished analyzing the first set you sent us," said the general. "There's a lot of bacteria that got into his eye. The closest match we have is that it appears to resemble one called *Shewanella Oneidensis*, I don't know if I pronounced that correctly."

Parris grabbed Fox's arm. "Yes, you did. But are you sure?"

The general cleared his throat. "As I said, that's the closest match we found."

"If it's that, then it would mean that the assailant could've been walking through an EPA-restricted area." Parris and Fox got back inside their car. "And he must have been there not too long before he showed up here."

Fox drove off, turning to Parris. "You mean, like a dumping site?"

"Not entirely. Shewanella's a bacterium that's used to metabolize metals and also clean up toxic spills. It's a process called bioremediation. There are other types of soil bacteria that perform similar functions, and they do this by breaking down metals. They then produce oxygen, or other harmless gases, as byproducts."

Fox pushed down harder on the accelerator, speeding down the driveway. "So chances are, whoever was here would've been around an area where there may have been a toxic spill within the last few months."

"I'm on it," said Dewan.

Parris took out her tablet.

"What's on your mind?" asked Fox.

She began tapping at the screen. "I'll tell you in a bit."

They reached the end of the driveway and Fox turned left onto the street, when they heard Downing. "There isn't any sign of soil bacteria in the last pictures you sent, Fox. Shewanella or otherwise."

"I'm not surprised." There wasn't anything wrong with being certain. A few minutes went by and Fox took the onramp onto the Sunrise Highway toward New York City. It was at that point that both his and Parris's smartphones buzzed.

"I just sent you something," said Dewan.

Parris opened the message on her tablet.

"What is it?" Fox asked her.

She tapped the screen. "It's a map of the country with red dots scattered throughout various areas."

"These are all the known sites where the EPA and local state authorities have scheduled cleanups within the last twelve months," said Dewan.

"We can eliminate Ohio and Indiana. Whoever was at Stayner's home must have come from somewhere closer." She paused as though she were examining the map. "I'm guessing Connecticut."

"Why there?" asked Downing.

"I was just checking something else a few minutes ago," said Parris. "Earlier this year a Connecticut-based company had been charged with illegally dumping and burying petroleum-contaminated wastes throughout the state. The concentration of S. Oneidensis found in our sample could indicate a recent cleanup."

"Connecticut's just a helicopter ride away." Fox accelerated in the fast lane. "How many sites?"

"They've only listed one, and it's on the company's actual property."

"It's funny that you mention Connecticut," said Dewan, "because earlier today, a bus full of children went missing near Brooksvale Park, and that's in Hamden, Connecticut. Where's this company located?"

Parris looked up from her tablet. "Just east of Hartford."

"What are the probabilities of Umari being able to move a busload of children, unnoticed, over a great distance?" asked Dewan.

Fox turned on the windshield wipers as it began to snow. "Not too high. Even if he were to switch buses, he wouldn't be able to move them too far without someone spotting them and calling the police."

"Which rules out leaving them at, or around, the company," said Parris.

"Is it possible that they were dumping elsewhere?" asked Fox.

"I'll ask the FBI liaison to question the company's CEO," said Downing. "Make a deal with him to give up other locations he may have illegally dumped."

"That ain't going to happen," said Dewan. "He died less than an hour ago."

Fox sighed. "Let me guess, food poisoning?"

"His last meal, according to the coroner, was a hamburger with mustard, ketchup, and mayonnaise," said Dewan.

Parris closed the cover on her tablet. "He couldn't have been the only one in the know. There's got to be other senior company members."

"True," said Dewan, "but they ain't going to be saying much either. Want to know what they ate?"

"Dammit," stammered Downing.

How Dewan managed to multitask the way he did was beyond Fox's comprehension.

"Oh, this just in, guys," said Dewan. "We don't have to worry about the school bus anymore. I've been following the police bulletin boards. They've just located it."

Chapter 47

Shady Grove Metro Station, Derwood, Maryland.

*D*eviate from your route and we'll kill your family. We'll be watching you.

Those words were stapled in Dwight Benjamin's mind as he boarded the DC metro, heading downtown. Nearly an hour earlier, he was on his way to his car, having left early due to the food scare that had gripped the entire nation. Thirty of his colleagues had already been rushed to the hospital earlier that day. When the president had addressed the nation two hours before, all Benjamin could think of was to head home. His wife, Melinda, had already called him to say that she had picked up the kids from school and would meet him at home. Up until that point, he'd thought that his family was safe.

Why should he have expected someone to ambush him with a gun while heading to his car in the company parking lot? The next thing he knew, a van screeched to a stop behind them, and he was forced to get in. They made him wear a vest—one similar to the ones suicide bombers wore—and a smartphone was placed in front of him. All he was allowed to see was a video where Melinda parked her minivan in the driveway of their home, with their kids, Jeff and Adam, jumping out and racing to the front door. It was all that was needed to convince him that a sniper was ready to take them out. They never told him why he and his family were being targeted. Benjamin begged them to know what he had done wrong, only to be threatened with a gun to his face and told to shut up.

The friendly announcement over the PA system that the Metro was about to depart did nothing to comfort him. The doors closed a few seconds later, followed by the Metro accelerating. Benjamin was to remain inside and not unzip his coat. There were only six people with him in the same Metro car—people who, by all counts, would likely never survive what was about to happen.

What Benjamin didn't know was that he wasn't the only victim. At this moment, three other Sementem employees boarded trains at the terminuses of the DC Metro's blue, orange, and green lines—wearing similar vests concealed with windbreakers—all heading downtown. In Philadelphia, New York City, and Boston, other Sementem employees had also boarded subways. All of them wondering what they did to deserve this.

Chapter 48

Somewhere in Connecticut.

"Helloooooooo, Xavier," chanted Umari as he entered what was once a doctor's office, holding a water and soda bottle in each hand. "How are you getting along with Franjo?"

Xavier looked up at the ex-marine, from the table where he had been made to sit. He looked back at Umari without answering.

"Come on." Umari put the bottles in front of the boy, pulled up a chair, and sat beside him. "I know Franjo looks like a scary man, but once you get to know him, you'll see that he's like a very big teddy bear." Umari chuckled as he turned to Franjo, who stood at the doorway, expressionless. He then ruffled Xavier's hair and put an arm around his shoulder.

"It's okay," said Umari. "I'll make sure that Franjo doesn't hurt you."

Xavier turned to Umari. "Why am I here? I want to go home."

"I know you do." Umari patted the boy on the head. "But don't you want to get away from Mommy and Daddy for a while?" Umari looked at the empty plate. "I see you ate the grilled cheese and bacon sandwich we prepared for you. Did you like it?"

Xavier turned away from him. "I'm thirsty."

"Of course you are." Umari gestured to the two bottles. "Which is why I brought you these. But before you choose, I'm going to explain to you the rules."

"What rules?"

Umari grinned. "Nothing too difficult to understand. Once you learn them, we're both going to have a lot of fun."

Chapter 49

DC Metro, Between Dupont Circle and Farragut North Stations.

All Dwight Benjamin wanted was a tall glass of water. The Metro cart gathered more people with each stop—all the seats were taken now, leaving others to stand. He felt himself getting sweaty. The vest was uncomfortably warm against him. The man he shared the two-seater with read from a book. He didn't care to check what he was reading, nor did Benjamin care to look up at anyone else. He just didn't want to see the people that he knew were most likely going to die because of him.

The Metro slowed down, which piqued Benjamin's curiosity because he hadn't heard the announcement over the PA system that they'd soon be arriving at Farragut North Station. The train suddenly stopped abruptly, jerking Benjamin forward so that he caught himself on the seat in front of him. He gasped as he thought the sudden jolt would trigger the detonator. When the train stopped, he heard at least one curse word shouted from within the crowd, and caught a whiff of burned rubber—obviously from the wheels.

For over a minute, the Metro remained idle. It was the first time that Benjamin looked up, but no one appeared to be too agitated. After all, unscheduled stops were common every once in a while.

"Ladies and Gentlemen," came an eerie man's voice over the PA system. "This is Faouzi al-Umari, and as you now can hear, I'm alive and well. I'd like to apologize in advance for this unscheduled stop, but I thought that I'd inform all of you that your service will be interrupted…indefinitely."

"Oh God. It's happening," Benjamin cried just as there was chatter and whispers.

"That's right," said the voice. "You're being held hostage. If you're all here this evening, riding the metro in Washington, DC, or the subways in New York City, Philadelphia, or Boston, then congratulations, you've survived my previous attack that scared all of you into going on a nationwide diet."

The previous chatter morphed into panicked cries. Benjamin let his head fall against the back of his chair and closed his eyes.

"Now, if you're wondering what's happening, I've handpicked certain passengers who'll play a vital role in the last phase of my operation. Underneath their jackets, they're wearing suicide vests. But instead of the explosive vests you're all used to hearing about, these ones will dispense white phosphorous. And trust me, it's *very* lethal." Benjamin couldn't hold back the tears as he heard Umari list the trains with the Sementem employees by naming their current locations, including his.

"By the way," the voice continued. "I should warn you in advance that I have complete control of the entire infrastructure of your subway systems. That means I control the trains, the ventilation system, and the closed-circuit TVs. I even disabled the chemical weapon detectors and every security system that's supposed to protect you from people like myself. If anyone attempts to force open the doors or smash a window in order to escape, it'll trigger the nearest vest and you'll all be cooked alive."

"Oh my God," cried Benjamin as his head sunk into his hands, knowing that several eyeballs were on him. Just the mention of white phosphorous jolted him.

"And one more thing," said Umari. "I'm sure the Feds are going to be showing up and using cell phone jammers to prevent a remote detonation. I'd strongly advise against that."

Benjamin heard Umari sigh. "I'm sure you all regret that a wireless network was installed in the subway in the first place. Anyhow, you must be all asking yourselves why I am doing this," continued Umari. "It's all part of an experiment. With me is my friend—a ten-year-old named, Xavier. He hasn't had anything to drink in the last few hours, so he's very thirsty right now. In front of him is the choice of a soft drink or water. If he chooses the soft drink, the vests will be turned off and all of you get to walk away. However, you should know that Xavier's classmates—who are being held prisoner—will perish, as will Xavier. However, if Xavier chooses the water, he'll not only save himself but also his classmates. Unfortunately, the rest of you don't get to live."

Benjamin heard mixed emotions around him. Most were obviously scared. The rest appeared to be in denial as to whether this was really happening.

"You're probably all wondering the same thing: 'How do I know if I'm on the car with the person with the chemically weaponized vest?' It's simple. Just look for the passenger who's wearing a red jacket with the word Sementem."

That did it. They'll know it's me. They're going to kill me. Benjamin saw everyone looking around.

"By the way," the voice continued. "For those of you who aren't on the metro or subway car with the Sementem employee, you're not in any danger. So *now* would be a good time for you to run for your lives."

Chapter 50

Wallingford, Connecticut.

Fox stood with Parris, across the street from the entrance of an old drive-in theater that had not been active since the mid-1980s. Downing had gotten a helicopter to bring them from the Hamptons over to this location, where they would be joined by members of the Special Activities Division—a unit of the CIA that was similar to the SEALs. Dewan filled them in on what was happening with the DC Metro and the other subways—including their connection to Kevin Ancheta—who wrote the code for the mainframe computer system for those city subway systems. Unfortunately, he was found dead in his apartment. As for the situation in DC, Philadelphia, New York City, and Boston, the National Guard was assisting with crowd control as thousands fled the metros and subways. So far there were dozens of trampling-related injuries and three confirmed deaths. With the hospitals being unable to accommodate any more patients, it only made the situation worse.

Of course, the press was having a field day with this event, as this day was also its busiest. Brooksvale Park had become a media circus too, with dozens of reporters camped out in the parking lot where the school bus was located, with TV station helicopters hovering overhead. It was frustrating for the FBI to keep them all at bay, and from getting too close as the Hostage Rescue Team worked diligently on site to figure out how to get the children off the bus.

Fox was currently with Parris, looking at Google Maps on her tablet. They had opened a map of Connecticut, where they believed illegal dumping had taken place. One particular spot of interest was the Sandy Grove Sanatorium. It was very active during the 1960s and closed its doors in 1978. Today, it was an old, decaying, abandoned building located next to the Connecticut River, just south of Newington.

During its glory days, it held up to one hundred and thirty-two patients in its two-story structure that could fit in a football field. Weyland and Lucas had made a wise choice, considering that the place was shrouded by the surrounding woods, making it very difficult for satellites to spot anyone who may have been coming and going from the place. However, one of the NSA's satellites—which was equipped with ground-penetrating radar was able to pick up traces of the spill on the grounds where there wasn't any tree cover. The GPR technology, although in its infant stages, still had a 70% accuracy reading.

Upon learning this intel, Downing had a drone fly briefly over the sanatorium, where analysts were able to determine with a 98% certainty that the place was currently being occupied.

All of them agreed that Lucas and Weyland would've also chosen this location due to it being restricted to the public. Landmines were highly unlikely, considering that if anyone were to venture off in the area and set one off, the blast would most likely attract unwanted attention, exposing their hideout. At most, they'd use the latest state-of-the-art detection equipment, which would be set up in various spots, but they'd also have to use several generators to power that equipment.

Parris and Fox both turned to the sound of an approaching van that drove around the front of their vehicle and stopped beside it, facing the opposite way. The side door opened and Wim stepped out, accompanied by an unknown. Jim, who was driving, came out and joined them. All three wore full body armor from head to toe, with the exception of their masks.

Fox gave the unknown a once-over. Standing at around five feet four, he appeared to be more a tennis player than someone in the CIA's Special Activities Division. "What's *Chicken Little* doing here?"

Wim turned to Fox. "This young man, whom you refer to as Chicken Little, is Corporal Sean Greenberg, one of the division's top snipers."

Fox smirked as he rubbed his finger over his left eyebrow. "What's your military experience, Corporal?"

Greenberg took a step forward, as though he was addressing his superior. "I served four tours of duty in Afghanistan and six in Iraq, sir."

"Really?" Fox wasn't too impressed. "What's your top performance?"

"My best performance was taking out three Taliban machine gunners from a distance of one-point-fifty-one miles, sir."

Holy shit. That's among the top five in the world. "Not bad, Corporal. At ease, and you don't need to address me as *sir*."

"As you wish." He answered with the same tone as before, knowing his rank. Downing sure knew how to pick them.

"How about you two get dressed," said Wim as he gestured to the van, which would've contained Fox's and Parris's body armor.

The team, with the exception of Greenberg, would be armed with Heckler & Koch MP5SD3s, which were also noise-suppressed and chambered in 9mm with a 700-round-per-minute rate of fire. Along with these, they'd all be equipped with fragmentation grenades, flashbangs, and an MK23 .45-caliber ACP with a modified KAC suppressor and tritium laser aiming module, or LAM, with four selector modes: visible laser only, visible laser/flashlight, infrared laser only, and infrared laser/illuminator. The body armor they wore were designed with the latest in surveillance/detection technology, with night-vision and thermal detection built in to the eye sockets of the face plate.

Greenberg was equipped with an M40 Sniper Rifle which used 7.62x51mm NATO rounds. On any good day, these rounds were powerful enough to blast through a brick wall, taking out anyone who thought that they could use it as a shield. A single shot from that rifle was powerful enough to blow off the top half of a person's body.

Half an hour later, Fox, Parris, and Greenberg were on the road that ran behind the sanatorium, separated by close to 150 yards of wooded area. Demeere and Gessner were dropped off earlier, en route, by the Connecticut River. It was from there they would attack the sanatorium.

Within seconds of having parked, Fox was outside, next to the wire fence that surrounded the perimeter, wielding a pair of heavy-gauge wire cutters. Moments later, they all passed through the opening he'd made. They fanned out in the dense woods, which were only partially lit by the full moon, each donning their night-vision goggles as they went. Greenberg left Parris and Fox to climb a tree—one which gave him a clear line of fire to any spot in the building. Any hostiles would, if provoked, be attacking from behind the walls and not from outside. It would be up to Fox or Parris to let him know via earpiece when and where to fire.

Parris and Fox were less than eighty yards away from the building, where they each turned on the thermal imaging feature of their NVGs, and lay flat on their stomachs to observe all activity before them. Unlike popular belief, thermal imaging cameras, or goggles, cannot see people through walls. What they do detect is the heat signature that radiates from an object or person. For instance, in this case, it was unlikely that the entire sanatorium would've been heated—due to it being abandoned. However there would be a room, or a few rooms, where Weyland and Lucas would be congregated with their henchmen. The equipment they'd be using would also be generating heat. Their combined body heat would also give off a signature which would be picked up by thermal imaging. This would, in turn, give Fox, Parris, and the others a general idea which area of the building to strike.

In this case, there was a heat signature detected on the second floor, in the east wing of the sanatorium, which, from Fox and Parris's point of view, was to the left of the center of the building. According to their blueprints, that put them where the administrative offices once were. It only made sense because those were the most spacious rooms in the building.

Demeere and Gessner would be approaching the building from the other side. They would, with the aid of a grappling hook, climb to the roof and walk to the spot above the heat signature—which would most likely be where the hostage was being kept. They would then apply plastic explosive in the form of a ring near to that area. Once Fox and Parris were in position, a signal would be given and they would blow a hole through the roof, throw the flashbangs inside, secure the hostage and Weyland's computer, and insert a malware-containing flash drive to be uploaded in it. As a result, the NCTC would then have access to the entire network being used by Ares and upload one of the NSA's own nasty worms which would lock them out and prevent them from detonating any of the bomb vests or the device inside the school bus. This would buy the HRT time to evacuate the hostages.

The team was on radio silence, as it must be assumed that the hostiles would've been equipped with frequency and GSM/UMTS detectors—designed to alert them of any unwanted guests.

Penetrating a building had a few issues when it came to hostage rescue. The bad guys knew to expect the good guys to come crashing through the doors—a few of which weren't boarded up like the windows were. That's why some of them would most likely be booby-trapped with explosives, if there weren't already sentries guarding those entry points.

Looking up to the roof, Fox and Parris spotted two white silhouettes running over to the center of the building. Demeere and Gessner were in place. He and Parris got up to run to the far left of the building, to the basement entrance. At the door, Fox switched his goggles from NVG mode to regular, pulled out a flexi-cam from his left-thigh cargo pocket and linked it to his goggles. Since they were on the side of the building, Greenberg wouldn't be able to provide any cover. Parris checked their flanks with her suppressed MK23, while Fox slipped the snake-like lens beneath the door. If it was wired, then he'd know. If there were armed sentries nearby, he'd spot them. Through his goggles he scanned the threshold, the hinges, the striker plate, and then the door knob. He scanned the interior, which consisted of a rusted metal staircase and an entryway to the hall straight ahead. All clear. He withdrew the cam and went to work on the lock. Once he heard the click, Fox gently pulled it open.

Parris entered first with her MK23 at the ready, low, with Fox behind her. She peeked out into the hallway and saw no one, turned to Fox and gave him the all-clear hand signal. That confirmed it. The party was going to happen on the second floor. And that's where they headed.

Chapter 51

U mari walked up to Xavier from in front and leaned forward with his hands spread wide on the table. "Clock's ticking, young man. I know that you're dying to have a little sip from either glass." Umari watched as the kid teared up, shaking his head.

Aww, the little shit is crying again. Umari smiled as he backed away. "Come on, don't start crying now. I hope you're not thinking that we're responsible for this. This has only lasted this long because you won't choose which glass to drink from. You're just going to end up allowing everyone to die. All your friends, and all those people in the subways will never see their families again."

Umari walked around the table and knelt beside him, putting an arm around his shoulders as he gestured to the two glasses. "I don't want you to make me hurt everyone. I want to be able to save one of the two groups. But I need your help."

Xavier rubbed the back of his hand across his eyes. "Why don't you just let them all go if you want to save them? Why do you hate them so much?"

"I don't hate them. Truth is, I don't even know any of those people. But there's one person on each of those occupied subway and metro cars who's done some very bad things that have hurt a lot of people. The police won't even throw them in jail. That's why they keep on doing very bad things that continue to hurt everyone—even your friends on the school bus. And these bad people have friends that aren't on the subway with them, who,

I'm sure, are watching everything on the news right now. They need to be taught a lesson."

"What lesson?" Xavier asked. "What did they do wrong?"

"They've been hiding very dangerous substances in the food we eat, and making themselves very rich from it. A lot of people have gotten very, very sick and died as a result. So, you need to send them a message that they can't get away with what they've done. Do you understand now?"

"No, I don't."

"I wouldn't expect you to. You're still young. That's why I've made things so easy for you." Umari turned to the two glasses. "All you need to do is choose a drink. Water or soda, which would you prefer?" He stood and checked his watch.

"You have precisely eighteen minutes and forty-two seconds to decide." Umari left and walked into the adjoining room where Lucas sat with his legs stretched out on the splintered desk.

Lucas turned to him. "Would you prefer that I persuade him? I'm beginning to lose my patience."

"But this is what makes it so much fun." Umari clasped his hands together. "We have four major cities in a state of panic and every city in America with a subway system has closed them down. Hospitals nationwide are filled to capacity, people are afraid to eat, the list goes on. All of this is going on while the whole world watches. The fates of the subway hostages—as well as the lives of those school children—will be decided by one child."

"I still don't know why you didn't include Baltimore," said Lucas. "They've got a subway system too."

Umari scrunched up his face. "Baltimore's got nothing else going for them except the Ravens—whom I'm a fan of, I might add. So we should give that city a break."

Lucas rolled his eyes and stood. "I need some air. I don't know how you can stand the stench of this place."

After Lucas left, Umari went back into the other room where the two glasses still remained untouched in front of Xavier.

He smiled as he tapped his watch. "Tick-tock, little man."

Chapter 52

L ucas kicked a pebble across the floor as he left the office. He'd be happy to end this right now—unleash the white phosphorus in the subways and on the school bus, then throw Xavier from the second-floor window. More casualties brought more fear and anger. And that lead to more irrational thinking. And once SLR and Sementem were out of the picture, Ares could move on to the next phase. But he just wanted to leave this place. Not that it gave him the creeps—because it didn't. But the longer they all remained here, the more likely that they'd be discovered. And that wasn't a comforting thought.

A creaking sound. Lucas definitely heard it coming from somewhere above. He looked up at the ceiling where he heard a longer creaking. Something, or someone, was on the roof. Shit. They were about to be ambushed.

***

Parris stood behind Fox as he used the flexi-cam to check into the hall as they stood by the entrance to the second floor. He saw a man with an AK-47 slung across his chest, walking toward them. He looked at Parris—she was ready to be given the signal. He looked back through the flexi-cam and waited for the sentry. He was ten feet…eight feet…six feet. Fox gave Parris a nod and she pivoted into the hall with her suppressed MP5 and put a round through the sentry's left cheek at point blank. As he fell, Fox pivoted out in the hall on time and caught him. Parris stepped out of the way and covered the hallway as Fox dragged the sentry into the stairwell. If the shot had attracted any attention, they'd know soon enough. No one was seen coming around the corner up ahead.

Parris led the way as she and Fox crept forward, running slowly until they came to the corner. Parris switched off her NVGs and peeked around the bend as she saw lights up ahead. She also saw a tall black man, about fifty yards away, heading in the opposite direction. Sure she could take the shot, but it would only alert the others—compromising the operation. She checked her watch. One more minute before the roof would be blown.

**

Lucas paged his henchman, who was in the north wing. No answer. The creaking sound above got louder as he heard what also sounded like cracking and snapping. There was a loud crash as dust and smoke blew out from the doorway to the main office.

**

What the fuck just happened? Parris saw the same expression on Fox's face as she turned to him. There were still forty seconds before Demeere and Gessner were to blow the roof, but what she heard wasn't the bang of an explosion, but more of a crash— as though something heavy had fallen from above. Shit, please don't let it be that the roof caved in underneath them. But it didn't matter now. Both she and Fox each grabbed a flashbang, then in unison, tossed them down the hall just as the first set of gunfire erupted. Their MP5s up, and two explosions of light bounced off the walls and the ceiling. They then switched on their radio communication.

"Demeere, Gessner, do you copy?" yelled Fox.

No answer.

"Hold still," came a voice, followed by an explosion of debris behind them as Fox and Parris turned to see a tango go down. It was Greenberg's voice, and he had just taken out a sentry who had snuck up on them from behind.

"Status update, people," came Downing's voice.

Fox swung back around toward the lit part of the hallway. "We've engaged the hostiles."

"Reinforcements are already on their way," said Downing.

***

Lucas saw two people in the distance, just as one of his men was taken out. Most likely by a sniper. He dashed into one of the patient rooms, only to see the wall that separated it from the office was mostly damaged from the ceiling that had caved in, as a plume of dust and debris clouded his vision. He could partially see through the cloud that two men, dressed in what appeared to be body armor, were amongst the debris, scrambling to get up. He dashed through the opening, climbing over some of the debris behind one of them, and wrapped his arm around his neck in a chokehold—pulling him back into the room. Lucas watched as he attempted to reach for his MK23, but Lucas tightened his hold around his neck. With a quick jerk, there was a satisfying snap, and the man's body went limp. That's when he heard two objects bouncing on the floor in the hall.

Not good.

He snatched the man's MK23, and rolled away on the ground, closing his eyes and covering his ears, just as he heard a loud bang.

Lucas opened his eyes and quickly got back onto his feet, feeling his heart pounding as it kicked into overdrive. He didn't know how many of them there were, but so far he had counted two in the hall, and the two who fell through the ceiling. Adding the sniper made it a total of five, minus the one he had just disposed of. If there were more, then they would've seen them by now. It was going to be a do or die combat.

***

Son-of-a-fucking-bitch! His satellite phone was broken. Umari held both the broken antenna and the cracked body of the phone, looking down at it. And he had just reset the timers on the bomb vests two minutes ago—meaning that in eighteen minutes, everyone on the subways and the children in the school bus would die. Just as his experiment was getting to be fun, these two assholes had to fall through the ceiling. They never thought that a building this old wouldn't have had the proper maintenance it should've had since it was condemned two decades ago.

Franjo helped him up as he coughed out the dust he had inhaled. "Where's Xavier?"

"Right where you left him." Franjo pushed him out of the way as he whipped out his sidearm and fired two rounds.

Umari turned to see one of the two men fall back. It didn't appear to have done much harm to him since he was wearing body armor. Umari coughed some more, then got up to go check on Xavier, who he saw hiding under the table, shaking and in a fetal position. He flipped the table over, knocking over both glasses with it.

"You stupid little shit," Umari yelled as he grabbed Xavier's arm and pulled him. "You just couldn't be a good boy and pick a glass. Now everyone's going to die because of you. Everyone." He yanked the boy by his shirt collar, but he was too heavy.

Damn obese little fuck. He searched for his laptop. There it was, on the floor. How it got there, he didn't know. And right now, he didn't care. He couldn't let the SEALs, or whomever they were, get it.

Franjo ran up to the threshold. "Sir, we have to go."

Umari grabbed the laptop, closed it, and stood, while turning to Xavier. "I wish we could hang out a bit longer. But it just wasn't meant to be." He turned and joined Franjo as he heard gunfire being exchanged in the hall. The stairs were on the opposite side of the office entrance, he'd have to wait on Lucas and Franjo to help get him across. He'd just tucked his laptop securely under his arm when he felt something. He looked at what he had touched and saw that it was a flash drive. Funny, that wasn't his, and he never inserted any at any time that evening.

No, it can't be.

He kneeled, placing the laptop on the floor, and opened it. Fortunately the screen was still in screensaver mode and it didn't ask him to enter his password again, because that would've been a longer wait. He only looked at the screen for a few seconds before he threw the laptop against the wall, breaking it in two.

Chapter 53

National Counterterrorism Center, McLean, Virginia.

"I'm in," Dewan screamed as his fingers raced over the keyboard. He couldn't believe it, but they came through and got the malware on Weyland's computer. His counterpart from the NSA, with whom he shared the table, uploaded one of their worms into their network. Three minutes later she looked up from her computer.

"The worm's in place."

Downing grabbed Dewan's shoulder and peered over it.

"Do we have control of the subways?" Downing asked.

"Even better," answered Dewan. "I even have access to the devices inside the school bus. I've just deactivated the motion sensors. The kids can get out safely."

Downing turned to his FBI counterpart. "You getting this?"

"Damn right I am." She had her phone to her ear. "I'm contacting the HRT now."

Downing turned back to Dewan. "How long have we got before the timers run out?"

Dewan stared at the digital clock on his computer. "Less than fifteen minutes."

"What's your ETA on shutting down those vests?"

Dewan typed furiously. "I'm still working on it. I lost touch with Weyland's laptop, but I managed to copy most of the files that were on it. I'm reading the programming code right now. He may have been able to trigger the phones through his laptop also."

"Wouldn't that mean that Ares would be able to do so from wherever they are?" asked Downing.

"I think they would've done so already, once they realized that they were locked out of the subway's mainframes." Dewan continued typing. "I'm guessing that only Weyland had control of the vests and the school bus, while they controlled the subways."

"I don't care what it takes," said Downing. "I want those vests neutralized."

Chapter 54

DC Metro, Between Dupont Circle and Farragut North Stations.

"**Y**ou got on the Metro, knowing that this was going to happen, you son-of-a-bitch. Why didn't you warn us?"

"Why didn't you just…just throw yourself off a bridge?"

"We're all going to die down here because of you."

The shouts continued all around Benjamin, and his face and clothes were completely soaked with his own sweat. He kept his eyes to the floor, unable to look at anyone.

"All right, everyone. Just lay off him," yelled the woman from the seat in front of his. She was a heavyset African-American, well into her fifties, who looked like she'd stopped more than her share of fights in her day. "You heard the nut-job on the speaker, this man you're about to lynch isn't the only one. So just cut it out, your bitching isn't going to get us out of here any faster."

Benjamin looked up as he saw the crowd shifting. A man pushed his way through, knocking another passenger into the side of the bench in front of Benjamin in order to get just shy of an arm's length from him. "You think we're getting out of here alive, lady? Wake up." The man then pointed at him. "This asshole's on a suicide mission. They all are."

"We're still alive. So perhaps Umari doesn't plan on killing us," the big woman argued.

"Goddammit, lady." The same man tried to push his way

through, but others held him back. "These terrorists aren't going to stop until our country's wiped off the map. I'm surprised someone your size didn't choke to death earlier today."

That didn't sit well with some of the other women, who simultaneously railed on him for that comment. Amidst the shouting, Benjamin couldn't hear who was saying what.

Why me? Why did I have to be the one? was all he kept saying to himself. He was just a regular guy who worked from nine to five, sometimes later. Now everyone on this metro car was going to die as a result of something he had absolutely nothing to do with. The car began to rock back and forth as shoving ensued. Benjamin climbed up onto his seat, using the window and ceiling for support.

"Enough, all of you," he screamed. The shouting died down progressively. "Dammit, will you all pipe down? You're not helping." The shouting fell into whispers.

"Did you ever stop to think how I got this vest put on me? Let me tell you what happened." He looked left and then right, at the dozens of angry faces. "I was ambushed in the parking lot and shoved into a van at gunpoint. They forced this vest on me—saying that if I tampered with it, it'll go off. They threatened to kill my family if I didn't obey. What was I supposed to do?" Benjamin wiped a tear from his eye. "What the hell would you have done if you were shown a video from the point of view of a sniper, just as he was about to shoot your wife and kids? Because that's what I was forced to watch."

The atmosphere appeared to change. Even the man who looked as though he was about to beat him up had calmed down a bit.

Banging on the back door startled everyone. Benjamin looked to the back.

"It's the FBI," someone yelled. "They're trying to get in."

A few moments went by before the door opened.

"Listen up, everyone," roared a commanding tone from the door to the back of the car. "I'm Special Agent in Charge Jeremy Konrath of the FBI's Hostage Rescue Team. The good news is that we've taken back the DC Metro. You're safe for now."

There were multiple cries of "Praise Jesus" and "Thank you,

God," that erupted, but Agent Konrath seized control. "Listen up because we only have one shot at this. You are to exit in an orderly fashion through the door which you're closest to. It's vital that you do not push or shove because any excessive vibrations to the train may set off the vest."

Benjamin climbed down from his seat as he watched the crowd slowly dissipate. He reached out to the woman who had defended him and grabbed her shoulder, catching her attention. "I don't know your name, but thanks."

A few tears streamed from her eyes as she placed a hand on top of his. "Don't you worry. The good Lord was looking down on all of us today. You're going to be fine."

Benjamin was behind her as he was about to follow her outside onto the tracks. There were two men wearing green Hazmat suits standing below him, as he expected them to assist him. Instead, they raised their palms to stop him.

"Sorry, sir, but you can't leave yet," one of them said.

"What?" Benjamin watched as all the passengers were escorted away. "I can't stay here."

"You're going to have to remain behind until we can figure out how to disarm the vest," said the other one, who was a woman. "Please back up, sir."

That did it. He'd never see his family again. He then saw a tall, intimidating man with a lot of size to him approach through the door at the back of the cart after the last passenger disembarked. He held one of those rifles that looked like the ones the riot police carried. He must've been in charge.

"Are you Dwight Benjamin?" By the sound of his voice, he knew that it was agent Konrath.

Benjamin swallowed as he nodded rapidly. "Can you just get this damn thing off of me?"

The two agents in the Hazmat suits climbed aboard as Benjamin took a seat.

"I know this isn't easy for you," said Konrath. "But trust me, at this very moment my colleagues in the other metros—as well as the subways in Philly, New York, and in Boston—are doing the same thing to help your colleagues."

"Can you get this damn vest off of me or not?" Benjamin's yell died out into a sob.

Konrath gestured to the two agents in the spacesuits. "You're in the company of Agents Daniels and McGlade. They have a lot of experience with bombs."

Benjamin shook his head. "But this isn't a bomb."

The Hazmat agent in front and to his left knelt down and reached out to him. "We know that. We're going to have to unzip your jacket." It was the female agent. "I'm Agent Daniels, by the way."

Benjamin didn't stop her as she pulled down the zipper. She then helped him to take off the jacket.

"It's just as he said," said Daniels. "Good ol' fashion cell phone trigger."

Benjamin looked at both agents. "Can't you guys just cut the power to the phone or use your machines to scramble the phone signals?"

"As your hostage taker said earlier, not such a great idea," McGlade answered as he pointed to the clock on the vest. "The vest is backed up with a timer. Cutting the power supply will detonate the phone."

"The guys who make these vests aren't stupid," said Daniels. "So they wouldn't design a detonator which could be neutralized by cutting off the power. They always design one where the *active* timer *prevents* the vest from exploding."

McGlade then drew a circle with his finger over the vest. "Had you ripped out any of the wires then you and all the passengers would've been playing harps by now."

"And you've got less than thirteen minutes left," said Konrath as he stood between Daniels and McGlade, patting both of them on their shoulders. "He's all yours guys."

Konrath then hightailed off through the back door.

Benjamin let his head drop back. He stared at the ceiling and closed his eyes as tightly as possible.

Thirteen minutes before I die.

Chapter 55

National Counterterrorism Center, McLean, Virginia. 5 minutes to detonation.

The NCTC had a direct line to every FBI agent responsible for the disarmament of the vests. Dewan and the rest of his team had spent the last ten minutes reading through the data that was hacked off Weyland's laptop.

"I got something," yelled Dewan.

Downing walked over. "Can you shut off the vests?"

"I think I've found the programming code for them."

Downing leaned over his shoulder as he was joined by his counterparts. "Do you think, or are you sure?"

A drop of sweat rolled off his cheek and fell onto the desk. "I think I'm sure."

There was silence in the entire center as Dewan felt all eyes were on him, he could even feel the body heat coming from those who stood around him—namely Downing. Not all was lost when his computer had lost touch with Weyland's, as the code he looked at was very familiar. From what he read, the vests could either be detonated, or killed, with a phone call.

Dewan grabbed his headset. "Attention, bomb squads. My name's Dewan Douglas at the NCTC. I have a number for you to dial in order to defuse the vests."

Downing grabbed a headset for himself. "This is General Paul Downing of the CIA. We're going to play it safe, so we're going to only try one. If it works, then we'll use it on the rest."

"General Downing, this is SAC Konrath over at Farragut station. You're going to have to tell me who's going first."

Downing adjusted his headset. "Can you confirm that the area surrounding where you're at is secure?"

"Yes, sir."

"Then we'll start with your agents."

Dewan looked up at Downing. He saw in the general's face that he didn't feel comfortable with the call.

Downing turned to Dewan. "It's all yours, son."

Right, three minutes left. "Am I speaking to the agents by North Farragut?"

"This is Agent Daniels and I'm with Agent McGlade," came a reply.

"Okay, here's the number."

***

"We got ourselves a number," said Agent Daniels.

Benjamin looked at her, thinking that he'd pass out at any moment. It was a wonder that he hadn't yet shit himself. He couldn't remember the last time he'd ever set foot in a church, but he swore that if he lived through this then he'd be in church every Sunday—he'd even clear his schedule to attend Bible study. He swore he'd be a changed man.

He saw Agent Daniels reach forward and press the keypad, taking her time with each number. After the sixth, she paused as though she were unsure.

"Mister Douglas, will you please repeat those numbers again?"

Oh for Christ's sake. Don't tell me you dialed the wrong one.

"That's correct, I've dialed those numbers so far...got it." Daniels then pressed the remaining four digits on the keypad.

Benjamin closed his eyes tight, scrunching up his face, as he waited for the vest to explode in a puff of smoke.

It didn't happen.

Instead, the vest stopped humming, the beeping of the timer stopped, and the vibrations diminished until they ceased. "Did it work?"

"The vest has been defused," said Daniels. "I repeat, the vest has been defused."

Chapter 56

Parris saw the muzzle flash up ahead just as she dashed through the doorway on her side, while Fox did the same on the opposite side. She heard the bullets chewing up the wall she stood behind for cover.

"Fox, speak to me."

"I'm good," he replied through her earpiece, to her relief. "Greenberg, you copy?"

"I'm still here," he answered. "No more tangos spotted below you."

"What about the one shooting at us?" asked Fox.

"Can't spot him," Greenberg replied.

Parris peeked around the threshold just as the gunfire ceased. That's when she heard footsteps scurrying down the stairs, which were located across from the main office. Weyland and his backup were making a run for it, no doubt.

There was a muzzle flash a split second before she heard staccato gunfire, and she pulled her head back inside. The body armor and face mask would protect her, but a high-caliber gun would still be powerful enough to knock her down, if not knock her out. There was another round of gunfire—it wasn't from down the hall but from across from her. Fox was returning fire. She looked to see him signaling her that the coast was clear.

With her MP5 raised, and its butt against her right shoulder, she advanced with Fox to her side. When they came to the office, Parris made a sweep, while Fox did the same for the stairwell. She saw Demeere on the floor among debris, with a section of the wall behind him that was missing. She glanced up and saw the gaping hole in the ceiling from where he fell. Gessner was nowhere to be seen as she advanced into the adjoining office. Instead, she saw a boy curled up in the corner. He was shaking, clearly in shock, but thankfully alive.

"I've secured the hostage," Parris said. "Hostage is alive."

"Roger that," came Downing's voice.

Parris swung the MP5 around her shoulder as she knelt down in front of the boy. She lifted her face plate so as not to frighten the child any more than he was already.

The kid shook his head in tremors. "I'm sorry. I'm sorry."

Parris put a hand on his upper back. "It's okay. We're the good guys. And we're going to get you out of here."

"The man tossed a flash drive over to me after he fell through the ceiling," the kid then swallowed as he fought the tears. "I put it in Al's laptop when he wasn't looking."

Is he serious? "You did what?"

"I inserted the flash drive into Al's laptop," the boy said as he started crying. "I thought that's what the soldier wanted me to do."

"It's okay." Parris wiped the tears off his face. "You did the right thing. But we can't stay here, it's not safe. Can you stand up?"

The boy nodded.

"Good. Then let's go." She grabbed his coat off the floor and helped him into it. "Fox, is the hall clear?"

"I'm good," he answered. "I'm going after Lucas and Weyland."

She took the boy by the hand and they hurried to the hall. "What's your name?"

The boy wiped his cheek. "Xavier."

"That's a nice name. I'm Nita," she answered as she grabbed her MK23 then flipped back down her face plate. "Don't let go of my hand."

"Agent Parris," came Greenberg's voice. "No more tangos spotted on my end. Do you require any assistance?"

"Meet me downstairs. I'll hand over the hostage."

"Heading there now."

Parris rushed with Xavier toward the stairwell from which she came and eventually came upon the first dead body.

She looked down at Xavier. "Close your eyes." When she checked, she saw that he had obeyed.

The blast Parris heard, immediately made her pull Xavier against her as she hunched over him to shield him from any flying debris. The youngster clutched her tight as he screamed.

"We have to hurry," Parris said as she released him and took his hand. "Just keep your eyes closed."

They came to the stairs where she saw the other body. Parris continued holding Xavier's hand as she led him around it—telling him to mind his step—before they walked down.

"Fox. Are you there?" No response, communication must be down. *Please be alright.*

She made another sweep of the bottom of the stairs as they descended. "You can open your eyes now."

Parris pointed the MK23 to the floor, keeping her trigger finger ready for any surprises. From the look of things, the tangos had fled. She pushed open the emergency exit door, swinging her MK23 toward the man who approached her.

When she saw that it was only Greenberg, she lowered her weapon.

"Take Xavier." Parris handed the boy to Greenberg, and he freely went to him.

Greenberg took Xavier's hand. "Where are you going?" he asked Parris.

"I'm going to help Fox."

Chapter 57

F ox had turned on his NVGs then placed the butt of his MP5 against his left shoulder as he'd scanned the hall. Parris had just gone into the office and he'd heard her speaking with someone who turned out to be the hostage.

She'd secured the boy and confirmed he was alive, and Downing had acknowledged. That's when Fox told her he was going after Lucas and Weyland and he'd turned to see Parris and the kid running in the opposite direction, knowing they'd be fine.

He had seen Weyland and another person rush across the hall and down the stairs. But the black guy was still on this floor. He had to have been the one who'd shot at him and Parris earlier. He checked his flanks as he was in front of two rooms. Clear. He pivoted to the left where he spotted a body lying on the floor. The person wore the same body armor as he—by his build it looked like Gessner. Fox swept the room before entering and knelt down. He flipped the body over to lift the mask, hoping to be able to get a better feeling for a pulse on his neck. A small object rolled out of the victim's hand as he did so.

Shit!

Fox dove for the door, sliding across the floor just as the force of the explosion hurled him through the hall and into the wall. Had it not been for the headgear that protected his ears, he would've been suffering from an extreme case of intense ringing. The body armor absorbed most of the impact from the wall, but he still felt a little pain in his upper back where he got the brunt of the blast.

Fox didn't even have a chance to process everything in its entirety when he suddenly heard three gunshots, followed by powerful impacts to his back.

Fox cried out as he fell face-first back to the floor. Those shots were definitely from up close or else he wouldn't be feeling so much pain. He was suddenly grabbed by the neck and pulled backward, then dragged across the floor.

"I can't believe that you fell for that one." The voice was British and baritone. Fox had lost both his MK23 and MP5. He was then thrown, hitting the floor, and rolling to a stop. He still felt the piercing pain in his back as he struggled to turn over as quickly as he could—but he was sluggish. He turned and saw the man's silhouette. There was a bit of light that shone on him from one side, he was dark skinned, wore his hair in short locks, and was close to being Fox's height. But the moment was brief, as the man charged him with a flying kick to his gut—a heavy blow that winded Fox as he rolled over across the tiles.

The headgear was ripped off of him, then Fox was pulled up and thrown headfirst into a closed door, which burst open on impact. Between the pain in his back and forehead, Fox managed to focus enough to hear the man charging him from behind. He rolled out of the way, the man's foot barely missing him as it came stomping down. Fox then threw his elbow, connecting with his opponent's ankle.

The man grunted and stumbled to the side. Fox used the moment to get up, but was barely standing before two strong arms wrapped around his waist from in front, lifted him, and carried him backward with such speed that it took him a half a second before his brain registered that he had been bashed into another wall. Debris and dust rained down, showing the dilapidated and worn integrity of the building's structure. Fortunately for Fox, the armor absorbed some of the impact. He returned the attack by cupping both fists and slamming them down on his adversary's upper back, while he was still arched over, followed by a knee to his chest, and a shove, sending his opponent back a few feet.

No effect. *What the fuck is this guy on?*

Instead, the man smiled. "Ridley Fox. I've longed to make

your acquaintance. It disappoints me that it'll have to be brief."

"Lucas, right?" Fox moved away from the wall, raising both fists, and Lucas responded with a two-finger salute before he raised his own.

Fox moved his fists in circles—he was ready. "You won't be happy making my acquaintance."

"Perhaps," Lucas answered. "But in the meantime, let's play." He then danced around, kicking both feet as though he were mimicking Muhammad Ali.

Fox looked at Lucas's build and thought back to his fighting moves. He must have been on an elite military squad at some point. And, although he looked younger than Fox, he fought as though he'd been doing so all his life. But he was, at most, an inch taller.

Fox threw the first set of punches, not landing any blows as Lucas either dodged or blocked them. Fox couldn't keep this up, or else he'd end up tiring himself out, to which point Lucas would finish him off easily. Lucas responded, not only by punching, but by kicking. Fox blocked them, but damn did he feel those blows. Being quick, Lucas snuck in a kick to Fox's stomach which knocked him back. He followed through with another, but Fox caught it. Almost instantaneously Lucas did a side somersault, lashing out his opposite leg and connecting with Fox's jaw so powerfully that he felt it dislocate.

A swirl of colors flashed before him, seconds before he crashed onto the cracked tiles. He was then flipped onto his back and opened his eyes in time to see Lucas drop one knee onto his chest, putting enough pressure on him that he couldn't get up. The knuckles that bashed his dislocated jaw sent a jarring pain, as Fox's head was knocked to one side—only to be bashed again to the other.

He wanted to scream, but he held it in—fighting the pain which radiated from the jaw and extended just below his nose. The metallic taste of blood was in his throat and he coughed it out.

Lucas didn't seem to be bothered that Fox's blood covered his hands, as he grabbed his hair, pulled hard and lifted his head up off the floor. "I'm surprised. Frankly, I'm very disappointed." Lucas's warm breath was the only thing which kept Fox conscious at the moment. "I was expecting a lot more from you."

Fox grabbed his wrist with both hands to pry his hand off him, but he didn't have the strength to do so. The blast, the repeated slamming against the wall, and the constant beating had left him broken. He knew that he wouldn't win this fight. Not in hand-to-hand combat. Without either of his guns, he was at a loss.

"It's a shame I only learned of you after you disposed of my Russian colleagues," Lucas continued as he twisted Fox's hair in his grip. "But as you can see, I'm not like the others. I'm quicker, more agile, and a lot stronger than you, or anyone else you'll ever meet. The Special Air Service saw me as a freak of nature. The Arms of Ares sees me as an anomaly. No matter what the others think, I'll always be the best there is."

Fox coughed up some blood and tried to mumble something, but it came out barely audible.

"What's that?" asked Lucas.

He swallowed and forced the words the best he could. "You're right. I can't beat you, at least not in the way you anticipated."

Fox held Lucas's hand in place with one hand while he reached for the last remaining fragmentation grenade on him, pulled the pin, and used the last ounce of strength he had in his arm to toss it. The gesture surprised Lucas, who looked away toward the bouncing grenade. During that precious moment, Fox shot an inward blow to Lucas's wrist—making him lose the grip on his hair—then wrapped his arms around him while burying his face in Lucas's chest. Fox then spun around with him, putting Lucas in between him and where the grenade bounced—using him as a shield.

Fox swore that he'd heard the grenade fall through a hole in the floor, as the bouncing became faint. Only a split second later there was an explosion from underneath them as the floor rumbled, followed by a blast of heat which erupted from below as both men were propelled briefly upward.

Fox lost his grip on Lucas as they both fell into the darkness and the smoke.

Chapter 58

Parris stopped running as she came around to the front of the sanatorium. A full moon shone bright above. Although it was a decent source of light, it wasn't enough. She flipped down her face mask and turned on the thermal imaging. Using the zoom feature on her lens, she scanned the front yard, which stretched all the way to the Connecticut River. The front entrance would've been more easily accessible for Weyland. Had he gone through the back to where the Hummer was parked, Greenberg would've spotted him. The only place for Weyland to go was toward the river. Knowing him, he must've had a contingency plan to escape.

Something moved in the distance, about fifty yards out. It was faint, but it was definitely someone running away.

"Tango spotted running toward the river," said Parris into her earpiece, switching her NVG from thermal back to regular night-vision. She then ran toward the river, but, although the body armor did wonders to protect and incorporated the latest in surveillance tech, the extra weight coming from it—along with the weapons— slowed her down.

Parris came to the barbed-wire fence. She stood within an arm's length from it and searched up and down its distance. She then checked the ground. It was all mud—hardened from the frosty weather, and with barely a blade of grass. No footprints. Weyland would have to cut through the fence with a pair of wire cutters in order to get through. And it was doubtful that he had any on him—unless as part of the contingency plan he'd already had an opening cut out in advance. She switched back to thermal and looked to the right, and then to the left again. A white figure was moving in the distance, about seventy to eighty yards away, appearing to climb through the fence.

No way in hell you're getting away. Parris bolted to the spot, and, sure enough, she saw that the fence had been cut. She climbed through the hole and ran north along the river. She saw the target ahead of her as she closed in on him. He wasn't going to try swimming across the river. It was too wide and would be way too cold for anyone to survive in these temperatures.

She was about forty to fifty yards behind him when she switched to regular night-vision mode. Sure enough, it was Weyland. Parris grabbed her MK23, turned on the laser, pointed it at the ground by his feet, and fired two rounds.

"Give it up, Weyland," Parris yelled. "The Feds are on their way. And they won't hesitate to shoot you on sight."

Weyland ignored her and kept running, which left her no choice but to fire another round. Dirt shot up in the air, a foot ahead of him, where the bullet impacted. It appeared to work, as he stopped abruptly, raising both hands above his head. Parris heard what she thought was laughter coming from him as he bowed his head.

"You did it, Doctor Parris," he yelled as he turned around to face her, slowly raising his head. "You finally caught me. So, what happens now?"

"Shut up and turn around," she yelled as she walked in his direction while she kept the MK23 on him. He would've noticed the green dot shining on his chest by now and know that she was serious about blowing him away if she needed to.

Weyland nodded and then turned around with a smile. Without lowering her weapon, Parris grabbed a pair of Flex-Cuffs from her back pocket.

A bullet struck her just below her left shoulder, lifting her off her feet briefly as the MK23 flew from her hands—seconds before she landed on the dirt and gravel. She felt an intense burning at the spot where she was struck as she tried to stifle her cries. She felt for the spot where she was hit. There wasn't any breach of the

Kevlar, but damn was she in agony. She tried to get up by using her legs, but she only ended up pushing herself backward on the soil. A set of footsteps approached her and soon after she saw Weyland and the sentry that must have shot her.

Dammit. The sentry. I overlooked the one who helped Weyland escape.

The only thing Parris heard was the river flowing several feet behind them. While the sentry kept his HK416 pointed at her, Weyland knelt on top of her, his knees on either side, and grabbed the MK23. He then pulled off her face plate and tossed it to the side. "Looks like I have the upper hand now. You just couldn't listen, Doctor. I told you to stay out of my way, and now, I'm going to have to kill you." Weyland sighed as he slowly shook his head.

"Are you going to kill me as Timothy Weyland?" Parris grunted. "Or will you do it as Faouzi al-Umari. Or how about I call you by your birth name, Cari Kenneth Stayner?"

Weyland's lips parted as his eyes widened. "What did you just call me?"

His real name. He couldn't stand to be called by it. "Cari Kenneth Stayner. That's who you really are. The son who wanted revenge on his father for abandoning him, that he went so far as to sabotage his company's product."

"Timothy Weyland and Cari Kenneth Stayner are both dead. My name is Faouzi al-Umari," he said as he was about to point the MK23 at her head. "But you can call me…"

Parris snaked her arm on the inside of Stayner's wrist and deflected the angle he pointed the sidearm. She then grabbed his collar, pulled him downward as she swung her head upward, head-butting him in the nose, as she simultaneously pulled the MK23 out of his grip.

He shrieked as he fell off of her, in the direction of the sentry, holding his nose while Paris rolled over, away from them. With Stayner being so close, the sentry couldn't risk shooting her without harming his leader. He was too late to aim his HK416 at Parris before she swung her MK23 toward his head and squeezed the trigger. The bullet entered through his chin, shattering the bone and taking a chunk out of the back of his head as it exited. He fell to the ground beside Stayner, who went to grab his rifle, which had fallen a few feet away.

Parris tightened the grip on her weapon with both hands and aimed it at Stayner. "Don't. You'll never make it."

He raised his hands, as though in surrender, as he stood. A stream of red poured over his mouth and chin, which he didn't even bother to wipe away. He had to have been in agony, but he just didn't show it. Her adversary remained where he was for a few seconds before he started giggling and rushed for the rifle.

Parris squeezed the trigger and a bullet struck him in the left shoulder—knocking him backward as he stumbled into the river. Parris then stood, holding the MK23 with one hand. Fuck detaining this sociopath, she already gave him a chance and he didn't take it. The first shot didn't appear to do much to him, as he still mocked her with that stupid grin.

She squeezed the trigger again, hitting him in his center of mass. Stayner stumbled backward, splashing into the river. His smile disappeared momentarily as he was knee-deep in the water, struggling to regain his balance. He then stumbled forward, toward her.

Parris didn't have any thoughts going through her mind at the time. It was nothing more than a reaction that caused her to squeeze the trigger. The third shot struck him in the heart, causing him to spin around and land face-first in the river. She felt her feet sink into the mud on the embankment as she splashed her way into the river, stopping as the water came just above the ankles of her boots. She watched as Stayner's body floated away with outstretched arms, spinning slowly as it was carried downstream.

She no longer felt any pain from the gunshot, which made her wonder if she'd ever been shot. The impact would definitely be visible on her skin.

The crack of the explosion behind her startled her into spinning around with her sidearm drawn, just in time to see the concrete and rubble blowing out from the side of the sanatorium, followed by the section above it collapsing.

Her heart rate kicked up a notch as her breathing intensified. "Ridley!"

Chapter 59

"Ridley," Parris shouted through her earpiece as she climbed back through the open hole of the fence. *Come on, answer me, dammit!* "Greenberg. Do you copy?"

"Affirmative," Greenberg answered.

"Xavier, is he—"

"He's safe and secure. All tangos were eliminated."

"Where's Fox?"

"I haven't heard from him, Demeere, or Gessner."

"We've lost Demeere and Gessner." Parris found a new burst of energy as she sprinted across the front lawn of the sanatorium. "Fox, do you copy? Please answer." Still nothing. *Maybe he lost his earpiece. Yeah, that's why he's not answering.*

"Fox?" She was in the area close to where the blast had occurred. The heat emanating from the rubble in front of her warmed up her face slightly after having the cold bite into it from running. She climbed onto the pile—looking everywhere for her partner. She was now inside the building, and when she looked up she saw a part of a room on the second floor—what had remained after its floor collapsed.

"Any sign of Fox?" asked Downing. It was the first time that she heard from him for the past several minutes.

Left, right, and in back, then ahead again. "I'm still searching," Parris answered. She continued looking around her. Left, right, front, back.

She heard some rubble shifting to the side and Parris turned in the direction of the sound. She saw what appeared to be a leg. She climbed over the rubble. "I think I found him."

She got on her knees and began clawing away at the rubble, scattering several bricks at a time, until the leg was free. It was definitely the same issued outfit that she wore. And the boot size was definitely Fox's.

"Fox," she cried out in relief. "Hang on. I'm going to get you out of there."

The adrenaline must've still had its effect because she was clearing away rubble very quickly.

When she saw his face, she gasped at the two black eyes, and several bruises on his cheeks and forehead—even his jaw looked crooked. She kicked up a notch and cleared the rubble off his chest. His body lay within a slight depression in the rubble. She didn't drag him out, at the risk of further injuring him. She leaned closer to his face and waited. She felt warm air on her cheek—he was breathing. *Thank God.*

"He's still breathing. Call the medics."

"They're already on their way," answered Downing.

"Tell them to hurry," she cried as she wiped away a tear.

"Their ETA's three minutes," said Downing. "You two hang tight."

She sat down behind him, gently lifting him so that she could rest Fox's head in her lap. "Can you hear me?"

There wasn't any answer.

"Come on, please say something."

She saw his left eye open. There was a moment of searching, but he finally saw her. Parris swallowed as another tear rolled down her cheek. She smiled and chuckled as she grabbed his hand. "You're going to hang on until the medics get here, Warrant Officer," Parris said and then swallowed. "And when they get here, you're going to hang on some more. That's an order."

Fox coughed twice as his grip tightened on her hand. His lips then moved.

"What is it?" Parris lowered her head closer to his.

"You lost. You lost…the bet. I told you that I'd wind up in your arms." He coughed some more.

She sat up to look at him. He was grinning. A tear escaped her left eye and dropped onto his chest as she began giggling. "You're incorrigible, you know that?"

Fox began chuckling with her as she playfully slapped him in the chest.

"Ow, ow, ow," Fox cried out with a grimace. "That hurt."

"Oh please, I took a bullet several minutes ago. Don't tell me a little girly slap penetrated your Kevlar."

"I don't think you know your own strength," Fox answered.

There was a deep guttural roar several feet behind them, startling them. About fifteen feet away, the black man she had seen earlier was throwing bricks and debris to the side, as he dug himself out from under the rubble.

Lucas. It had to be him. At least that's what her instinct told her.

He slowly got up and stood, and she saw him from the side as he appeared to catch his breath. He stumbled a bit as he tried to keep his balance. When he did, he slowly turned his head toward her. Blood covered most of his face and hands, and half of his chest was exposed, his clothes mostly in tatters, singed from the blast. But what grabbed Parris were his eyes. There wasn't any surprise or relief. Only pure, cold anger. They narrowed and his eyebrows curved downward—giving the impression that he'd lost his humanity and become a wild beast who was ready to bear fangs and claws. He didn't need to verbally threaten her, the look he gave her was enough.

Parris slid from under Fox, scrambled to her feet, and grabbed her MK23, holding it with both hands as she pointed it at Lucas. She didn't know how he'd managed to survive the blast, or the fall, without body armor. As for how he managed to even be standing—while Fox lay on the ground badly injured—raised even more questions. Whatever reasons there were, hopefully the sight of her sidearm would deter him from taking any form of hostile action.

Lucas took a step forward with his right leg, followed by a grimace. He began to compensate by shifting his weight onto his other leg, as he limped forward, breathing heavily, frustration in his eyes. It was as though he couldn't accept being beaten.

"Stand down, Lucas," yelled Parris as he struggled with another step forward. "You don't have any more hostages—neither in the subways nor on the school bus. They *all* got out alive."

Lucas dragged another step forward.

"Your men are all dead. Timothy Weyland, a.k.a. Faouzi al-Umari, a.k.a. Cari Kenneth Stayner, is dead," yelled Parris as she shook her head. "And I *will* end you too, right now, so help me, God."

Lucas was now about five feet away from her when she saw a change in his facial expression. He then stumbled and fell to his knees, managing to catch the ground with his hands. She watched as his triceps bulged as he pushed himself back up onto his knees, breathing very loudly as he raised his head to her. Parris didn't take any chances, keeping her weapon on him.

In the distance she heard propellers, getting progressively louder by the second. Lucas looked up, as though he was searching for the helicopter, even though he would've been looking up at what was left of the building above him. He then looked back at her for a few moments, his head rolled backward and he fell onto his side, tumbling down the heap of rubble until he lay on his back at the bottom.

Parris lowered her sidearm and stared down at Lucas. He was still alive, but was barely conscious.

A few moments passed and a Bell Medevac Helicopter hovered overhead, shining a wide searchlight beam over the sanatorium. The light stopped moving when it shone down on Parris, Fox, and Lucas through the exposed side of the building, which had collapsed. Above the sound of the propellers, Parris heard the faint sound of sirens, growing louder. The press wouldn't be far behind. In less than half an hour, this spot would be the most talked about area in the country.

Chapter 60

Mumbai, India. Four days later.

It's all gone to hell.

He couldn't glance at a single newspaper, turn on a television, or log onto the Internet without seeing something about him or his company. Where the fuck did it all go wrong? Never had he screwed the pooch so badly in his life—trusting Lucas, who was actually working with Cari all along. All that mattered was that the son-of-a-bitch was recovered from the Connecticut River. As far as he was concerned, he'd had it coming. Both him and his whore of a mother. He picked up the small bottle of scotch and went to down it when he realized that it was empty.

Fuck it. He threw it against the wall, smashing it into shards.

A few knocks to his bedroom door—it was not what he needed at this moment.

"What?" he yelled.

"Your car's arrived, sir."

"I'll...I'll be right down." At least he could still command some respect in some parts of the world. His suitcase wasn't even unpacked, since he'd only been there for two nights without having left his suite. Circumstances forced him to constantly be on the move until his lawyers could come up with a strategy. They, as well as anyone, would never be able to reach him, due to his burner phone. But he could reach his lawyers whenever he wanted to.

It took him around ten minutes before he was checked out, and was at the front entrance where his car waited for him. Just as he opened the door, he felt a pair of hands grab him and what felt like a needle puncture his neck.

"Jesus, what the fuck," he cried out as he struggled to see his attacker, but to no avail as his head felt heavy. He would've fallen had it not been for someone catching him and then pushing him into the back seat of the BMW. He felt someone shoving his legs to the side as they appeared to make room for themselves in the back seat. After he heard the side door slam and felt them moving forward, he saw blackness.

He woke up, not knowing how long he'd been out for. As of now, he was seated upright, feeling that his jaw was hurting for being perched up against the window for God knew how long. His head was still heavy and he felt a headache coming on. When he looked to his right, he saw a white woman—mid-fifties to early sixties—with her legs crossed. But boy, did she have a scowl.

"Hello, Mitchell."

He straightened up as his eyes went wide. "Who are you and how do you know my name?"

The woman sighed as she shook her head. "They always said that you were an arrogant dick, and now I can see for myself that you really are. How long did you think you could hide when your face is on the front page of every goddamned newspaper you can find?"

Suddenly it clicked, there was something familiar about this woman, he knew her, or at least he thought that he knew her. He was sure that she was...of course, that was it. "You're that CIA Director woman."

"CIA Director woman?" said Merrick. "I'm the Director of Central Intelligence, and yes, I'm a woman."

Stayner turned away with a chuckle as he shook his head. "So that's how it is. The CIA's out to bring me in, and you want to take all the credit so that you can boost your chances of winning the Presidency. Dream on, bitch, no one's going to vote for you."

Merrick raised an eyebrow. "I didn't come here to bring you

back to the US to face justice. I just wanted to show you something, since it's not likely that I'll have another chance to do so."

"Yeah, like what?"

Merrick reached into her jacket pocket and took out a photograph. She then held it out for him to take.

"That's my son, Jake. I invested a lot of time raising him on my own after his father abandoned him. He died from a fatal allergic reaction. I did everything for my son, and now he's gone."

Stayner took the photograph. "Hey, I'm very sorry for your loss. But what happened last week, my company's not responsible for that."

"Just like they weren't responsible for the deaths of twelve of our troops—no, let me correct that number, *thirteen* of our troops—at Camp Iron Eagle?"

Fuck. Camp Iron Eagle. That name keeps coming up again and again. "Look, my company's currently investigating—"

"Bull-fucking-shit," Merrick yelled. "Of all the trifling excuses you can come up with, you still have the audacity to deny any responsibility for your actions. You don't even remember who I am."

"I already told you that I recognized you as the CIA Director."

"That's it? You don't remember anything else about me? You really don't?" Merrick sighed as she let her head fall back in the seat.

"What the hell do you want, lady?"

"Don't you fucking raise your voice at me," Merrick spat. "I have a squad, armed to the teeth, standing outside this vehicle. I just have to say the word."

She couldn't have been joking, and Stayner raised his palms in retreat. "Am I supposed to know you?"

"Take a look at the picture," Merrick answered.

"I already saw it. And as I said, I'm sorry for your loss. Let me make it up to you, just give me a chance."

"There's nothing you can do to make up for the damage that you've done. Whether it's the damage you've done now, or the damage to the young girl you got drunk and then impregnated thirty years ago."

"What?"

"South Padre Island, Spring Break. You were a freshman, who later transferred to the London School of Business. Sound familiar?"

He began to think. Yeah, he did remember going to South Padre, but that was so long ago. He couldn't even remember what happened, considering that he and his friends were always drunk. He remembered being locked up for a DWI before his father intervened and used his influence to get him out. As for impregnating someone, he must have had sex with at least four different girls that week. How far a reach did the CIA actually have?

Stayner turned to Merrick. "Since you know more about what happened in my personal life thirty years ago than I do, maybe you'd like to tell me more about the girl I *allegedly* impregnated."

"Not allegedly." Merrick produced a manila envelope and handed it to him.

Stayner took it and pulled out what appeared to be DNA results. "What's this?"

"What the fuck do you think it is?"

Stayner looked over the sheet of paper that contained pictures. He then read what was written on it, and it nearly made him choke. "How the hell did you get my DNA?"

Merrick smiled. "Remember Heidi? She serviced you in your hotel suite while you were in New York. That condom you used? A perfect way to collect DNA."

"How dare you?" he hissed.

"There's no limit to how far I'll go to get what I need." Merrick straightened her jacket. "Did you notice anything else on those documents? You obviously didn't read the best part."

Stayner looked over the sheet another time. It took him about twenty seconds before he saw it, then shot a glance at Merrick.

"Surprise, surprise. *I'm* that girl you impregnated thirty years ago."

Holy shit, this can't be. No fucking way. He looked away from Merrick as he dropped the document.

"And guess what? Mitchell Stayner, you *are* the father of Jake

Merrick—*our* son."

Stayner's head dropped into his hands as he heard Merrick opening her passenger door.

"You're also an accomplice to your own son's murder. Forget about me taking you into custody, and making you face a long and expensive trial at the expense of the American tax payer. I believe in swift justice, which is what you'll get over here." She then slammed the door.

Stayner opened his door and got out, running after Merrick. It was then he saw the two guards who flanked her. "Wait. Please, you can't leave me here." He then looked around. They were walking up a hill, somewhere in the mountains. "Where the hell are we anyway?"

Merrick, with her guards, turned to him. "Karnataka. Does that name ring a bell? No, maybe not. It's one of many areas where Sementem's responsible for ruining the lives of several hard-working farmers when the Bt cotton seeds failed to produce a profitable yield. Your company bankrupted many farmers in this area with its *not-so*-ethical practices. Others committed suicide, being unable to provide for their families. Of course, you would never have read about those stories because you just don't give a shit."

She walked back to him. "You never gave a shit about me, your ex-wife, your children—you don't give a shit about anything, except yourself. It's all about you, Stayner. You selfish, greedy, prick." She then turned from him and walked with her security detail to the top of the hill where her car was parked.

"Dammit," he yelled. "What do you want from me?" It was at that moment that he noticed one of Merrick's guards speaking on a cell phone briefly before putting it away.

"I don't want anything from you." Merrick gestured to the top of the hill, where, what appeared to be, a posse of several dozen people suddenly appeared. They all had something in their hands, from shovels to pitchforks.

"On the other hand," Merrick continued. "The farmers of Karnataka do have a score to settle with you." She then walked away with her guards.

"You can't do this to me," Stayner screamed.

Merrick ignored him and kept walking away.

"I'm the CEO of Sementem. I've been responsible for everything you eat. Many countries would still be in famine if it weren't for me."

Merrick refused to stop, refused to look at him. She and her guards were less than ten yards away from her car when the farmers began to walk down the hill. Formalities aside, these guys weren't here to talk. He ran back down the dirt road to the BMW, nearly stumbling on the way. He scrambled into the driver's seat, slammed the door, and pushed the starter button. Nothing happened. He pressed it again, several times, as hard as he could, but the engine wouldn't catch.

"Oh come on," he yelled as he kept hitting the button. He glanced into the rearview mirror—the mob was closing in. How else was he going to start the goddamned car? Oh hell, who was he kidding? He hadn't driven a car in over ten years. He didn't know anything about the mechanics of it. The car was being pushed from behind now. He looked to the side—he was surrounded.

"What are you doing?" he yelled. "What are you people doing?"

The car was still being pushed forward. He banged on the driver's door window. One of the men looked at him with a scrunched up face. It didn't take a genius to figure out that he was pissed. Stayner saw a similar expression on the faces of the others around him. But where were they taking him? A few moments later, he saw the answer ahead of him—the edge of a cliff was fast approaching.

"Stop it!" He banged on the window and yelled. "Do you know what you're doing? You can't do this." He continued to scream as he stomped on the brake, but all he felt was a loose pedal. Fucking Merrick had the brakes disabled as well as the starter.

"I've got money. I can pay all of you. You'll never have to work a day in your lives again." They kept pushing. "Are you listening to me?"

They suddenly let go of the car and it continued to roll, on its own, down the slope. Stayner looked behind and saw everyone lined up. When he looked back in front, he screamed. The door. Yes, he'd make a jump for it before he went over the cliff. The door handle broke off in his hand.

"Motherfuck!"

Stayner screamed as he held onto the steering wheel as though it would provide him with any protection. The car had gathered sufficient speed that when it went off the edge, it flew for several yards before it nosedived. With the car in freefall, at ever-increasing speeds, Stayner passed out before the BMW smashed on the rocks below.

Chapter 61

Thurgood Marshall Federal Courthouse, New York City. Four months later.

Sparks could hardly breathe as she was mobbed on all sides by reporters who shoved their digital recorders and microphones at her. It had been like this ever since she'd left the courtroom. They still mobbed her as she passed between two of the four-story Corinthian columns and down the majestic granite steps to the Cadillac Escalade that waited for her. Below the clear blue skies, and the welcoming mild spring temperature, lay a part of the city which had its secrets. However, one of the best kept secrets in the nation had finally been exposed that morning in the building she just left.

Sparks's bodyguard, Jeff Meek—a former CIA operative and Ridley Fox's personal choice—had warned her of what lay ahead had she chosen to come to the courthouse. However, she insisted on being there to witness her former army colleagues from Camp Iron Eagle—including Joe, and other employees of SLR who were officially charged with conspiracy to murder for covering up the deaths of fourteen army officers. Also present were other employees from Sementem, who'd had full knowledge of the dangers of their GMO, long before the attack on America, and federal prosecutors hammered them with various crimes.

Ironically, the prosecution's most powerful piece of evidence were files that were recovered on Cari Kenneth Stayner's laptop.

Sparks would never forget the look on Joe's face after he saw her while he was being led away in shackles. She didn't need to gloat, she just wanted for him to see her. Now he could sit in his jail cell knowing that she would not be silenced and that she had won.

Even worse for Sementem and SLR, Sparks heard on the news that a class-action lawsuit was being filed against Sementem, on behalf of every food and beverage company who collectively lost billions in revenue due to them having to recall most of their corn-based food products. Other class-action lawsuits were expected to follow. Additionally, with Mitchell Stayner's alleged suicide, the company's stock continued to plummet faster than lead balloons. As for SLR, it was just announced that the United States Army would be dropping their contract. Furthermore, all government agencies wouldn't be doing business with them. Other companies and organizations were expected to follow suit.

Just before she'd arrived to the courthouse, Sparks had gotten off the phone with both her parents. They were back at home—albeit with the help of a nurse. Her mother had the least-severe injuries and was expected to recover faster than her father. Sparks couldn't care less who recuperated quicker, she was just glad that they were both home and on their way to recovery. And since Jill St. John—whose real name was Amy Small, as Sparks had recently learned—had covered her tracks so well, there was no way to know for sure who covered all her parent's medical expenses, as well as the other debts.

Sparks's lawyer, who had been hired to represent her through anonymous means, told her that he was convinced he could get her a sizably handsome settlement from SLR, Sementem, and the United States Army for what they put her through. The evidence against them was way too solid for them to be able to deny her previous allegations, which would nullify the previous settlement agreement she'd signed with SLR. Even better for her was she had since received several job offers from food and beverage companies across the country. They desperately needed a quality control expert and were guaranteeing her a job with a starting salary of around $45,000, with full health benefits and a 401K. She had to admit that the offer was attractive, and that she could continue doing what she liked.

Meek managed to keep the reporters at bay as she neared the bottom of the stairs. He then leaned to her ear. "You ought to look across the street."

She did, and couldn't help but smile when she saw Ridley Fox and Fab—who she had recently learned was actually Doctor Nita Parris. Although he was on crutches with a leg in a cast, it didn't surprise her that Ridley refused to stay somewhere in a bed. Both he and Nita were dressed for the weather—Nita even wore a fancy pair of stacked boots. Whether they were Gucci or Louis Vuitton, she couldn't tell.

"Thank you," she mouthed, her hand wiping away a tear as she smiled. They both nodded once in response.

Sparks then escaped the vultures as she climbed into the Escalade. Meek closed her door as she slid over to the opposite side to look across the street. She caught one last glimpse of Ridley and Nita before the reporters crowded in front of her window. She looked away just as Meek got into the front passenger seat and turned to her.

"You okay back there?"

Sparks reflected briefly on that question just as the driver pulled away from the curb. "I feel great."

And for the first time in months, she actually did.

The End

Acknowledgements

Once again, I've written a book that was very complex in its subject matter. Prior to writing it, I sought assistance from several professionals who were able to help me understand and interpret material that was present throughout the story. Without their help, I never would've been able to write this story as detailed as it is. There are so many of you I'd like to thank for all your support. However there are those I must give special mention to.

I'd like to begin by thanking Simeon Sanchez, who has a degree in Intelligence and Security. Your knowledge of the CIA—as well as how the intelligence community works inside and outside the United States—helped me overcome several roadblocks in the plot.

I'd also like to thank Sargent Curt Durnil of the Indiana State Police in Bloomington, Indiana. Thanks to you, Doctor Nita Parris was able to identify two phony Indiana State Troopers and save her life. I know police work is very demanding and time consuming. I'm really grateful that you spared several minutes for an interview.

Up until now, I've never held a gun, let alone used one. I contacted an acquaintance of mine, Marc "Animal" MacYoung of www.nononsenseselfdefense.com for help. He referred me to his friend, Jeff Meek of www.carryoncolorado.com. I found Jeff to be very enthusiastic on sharing with me everything he knew about firearms. Furthermore, I appreciated his help in beta-reading every scene in the book that involved shootouts, as well as recommending the right sidearms that Parris and Fox would use, not to mention Mister Lucas and the other villains.

I'd also like to thank Doctor Neil Crickmore of Sussex University in the United Kingdom. The bioweapon known as *The Demeter Code* would never have existed had it not been for Doctor Crickmore taking the time to correspond with me, over several emails, which spanned from September 2012 to March 2013. I've read several articles about the science, but only Doctor Crickmore was able to clearly interpret how genetically modified organisms and the Bacillus thuringiensis work.

Many of you don't know this, but there's a large financial investment by authors with regards to publishing a novel on their own. In early 2013 I started a crowdfunding campaign on IndieGoGo.com to help me cover some of the costs. I'd like to thank everyone who contributed to my campaign. Keeping my promise to those who contributed a certain amount, I'd like to extend a special thanks to Andre Chevalier, Nancy Green, Michelle Bertol, and Beverly Morris.

To my great friend, Jacob Morneau de la Chevrotière. I cannot express how grateful I am for everything you've done. You've helped me redesign my website, promote all my novels, and you've introduced me to wonderful people who've make a difference in my career—including your lawyer, Lionel. You've invested so much more in me than a friend could ask for. I'm so honored to have you for a friend.

I'd also like to thank my friend, Minna Savolainen, who, in addition to designing and creating those beautiful promotional posters and flyers, has helped me edit my website and also promote me and my books in Finland where she lives.

To my fellow "Rainiacs," I love you all for believing in, and supporting, me from the moment I joined your group. Thanks to Karen Wade, Scott MacKenzie, Doctor John Jones, Tory LaPrath, Amy Pabalan, Kimi Little, Cat Neko Kotyonok, Kat Hana, Mel Siebel, Diane Baker, Julee Robinson, Jim Gessner, Rayna Ramzey, Mags Jenkins, Paula Lanier, Todd Rockhold, and Martha Willis for helping me choose my personal logo as well as others that were used in my promotional campaign. I'd also like to thank the talented Radu Georgescu for designing my logo.

Among you I'd like to especially mention Wim Demeere, who beta-read every martial arts scene in *Demeter*, in order to verify that every combat scene was as realistic as possible.

It's important to mention my buddy, Doctor John Jones, for beta reading the story. When we finally meet, I owe you an ice cream.

Thank you to Tom Friddle and his friend, Jim Snyder for their time and assistance in sharing their knowledge on growing and harvesting corn. The information they shared was very crucial to writing the chapters which took place in Bloomington, Indiana. Furthermore, it helped me to choose the right time of year for the story to take place.

Thanks to Pam Goodliffe, whose scientific expertise helped me bridge several spots in *Demeter*. I must also commend you for suggesting that I use Elemental Phosphorus in the story. After having researched its several uses, it made a lot of sense that Mr. Lucas and company used it.

I'd also like to extend a special thanks to Pam Goodliffe, Paula Lanier, Lisa Martinez, and Dale Corbin for beta-reading the sex scene. I never wrote one before. To be honest, I didn't anticipate writing one in this story either. However, it just happened.

By the same token, I'd like to especially thank New York Times Bestselling Author, Eric Jerome Dickey—who's a master at writing sex scenes. I never expected him to take time off from his very busy schedule to beta-read my sex scene and also respond to me within a couple of hours. Not only did he approve of it, he even made a few suggestions to make it better.

I also want to thank bestselling author, JA Konrath, who continues to offer help to indie authors everywhere.

For introducing me to the literary market in Barbados and on getting me my first television interview, I'd like to thank Erica Hinkson of Book Source in Barbados.

As part of my promotion, I recorded the first three chapters of *Demeter* and broke them up into seven parts. To add some flavor to the readings, I teamed up with Jeremy Vajko, who provided the music score for each episode. Once again, I'm grateful for his help.

No novel could be considered up to publication standards without professional editing, formatting, and cover design. That's where my team of professionals come into play. I'd like to once again thank my content editor, Victory Crayne, Lisa Martinez my copy editor, Carol Webb my book cover designer, and Signe Nichols my ebook and print formatter.

One would expect it to be easy to gain a following in one's own home town, but it wasn't that simple. Fortunately I had a lot of help from Monty Weekes and his wife Gail Brathwaite, for hosting and helping me plan my book-launch party at their salon. Furthermore, an extra thanks for introducing me to the Montreal media.

Last but not least, I'd like to thank my family, Stanley, Cynthia, Randy, and Deidre Brooks for their continued support.

References

1. Danger of Biological Warfare made worse by Genetically Modified Foods http://www.topsecretwriters.com/2012/01/danger-biological-warfare-genetically-modified-foods/

2. Monsanto's Bt corn — breeding superbugs & harming human health, by Anne Sewell http://digitaljournal.com/article/326208

3. Hackers Linked to China's Army Seen From EU to D.C., By Michael Riley and Dune Lawrence http://www.bloomberg.com/news/2012-07-26/china-hackers-hit-eu-point-man-and-d-c-with-byzantine-candor.html

4. China is biggest cyberthreat says congressional report, by Natasha Lennard http://www.salon.com/2012/11/08/china_is_biggest_cyberthreat_says_congressional_report/

5. Chinese Military Group linked to Hacks of More than 100 companies, by Kim Zetter http://www.wired.com/threatlevel/2013/02/chinese-army-linked-to-hacks/

6. Following the Hackers' Trail by CHLOE WHITEAKER http://go.bloomberg.com/multimedia/following-hackers-trail/

7. Unsanitary Acts, by Jim Height http://www.northcoastjournal.com/010804/cover0108.html

8. Seeking Address: Why Cyber Attacks Are So Difficult to Trace Back to Hackers by Larry Greenemeier, http://www.scientificamerican.com/article.cfm?id=tracking-cyber-hackers&page=2

9. Viewpoint: How hackers are caught out by law enforcers By Prof Alan Woodward, http://www.bbc.co.uk/news/technology-17302656

10. Vulnerability Lets Hackers Control Building Locks, Electricity, Elevators and More, by Kim Zetter http://www.wired.com/threatlevel/2013/02/tridium-niagara-zero-day/

11. Matthew Keys Case Shows Rogue Employees Can Be Just As Dangerous As Hackers by Gerry Smith http://www.huffingtonpost.com/2013/03/19/matthew-keys-rogue-employee-hackers_n_2903021.html

12. The Trafficker: The decades-long battle to catch an international arms broker, by Patrick Radden Keefe.

13. My Life With A War Addict, by Clare Longrigg http://www.telegraph.co.uk/news/1473612/My-life-with-a-war-addict.html

14. Cell Phone Bombs, by Christa Miller http://www.officer.com/article/10250461/cell-phone-bombs

15. Damned Connecticut, by Ray Bendicci http://www.damnedct.com/cedarcrest-hospital-newington/

16. Cybercriminals Today Mirror Legitimate Business Processes http://www.fortinet.com/sites/default/files/whitepapers/Cybercrime_Report.pdf

17. Mobile Mass Spectrometry http://www.epa.gov/esd/factsheets/mms.pdf

18. Buried Secrets: Nearby Ohio company accused of burying and dumping petroleum waste; area impact uncertain, by Rachel Morgan and Patrick O'Shea http://www.timesonline.com/news/local_news/buried-secrets-nearby-ohio-company-accused-of-burying-and-dumping/article_12d279ed-d247-5135-807c-e8a3ac00946f.html

19. Common Soil Bacteria can Clean up Nuclear Waste http://www.ens-newswire.com/ens/mar2009/2009-03-17-092.asp

20. Ohio Fracking CEO Pleads Not Guilty in Federal Toxic Waste-Dumping Case, by Mike Ludwig, Truthout http://truthout.org/news/item/14577-ohio-fracking-ceo-pleads-not-guilty-in-federal-toxic-waste-dumping-case

21. Crime of Parents Killing their Kids is not so Uncommon,

by Larry Oakes http://www.startribune.com/local/162485846. html?refer=y

22. Spotting Illegal Toxic Waste from Space, by Jaymi Heimbuch http://www.treehugger.com/clean-technology/ spotting-illegal-toxic-waste-from-space.html

23. Red Light District Amsterdam http://www.amsterdam. info/red-light-district/

24. Amsterdam Red Light District Overview 2013 with Mariska Majoor http://www.youtube.com/watch?v=IJ9SFqu2Q Xk&list=SP1B06D0959634C739

25. http://www.tripadvisor.ca/Hotel_Review-g188590-d232492-Reviews-De_L_Europe_Amsterdam-Amsterdam_ North_Holland_Province.html

26. Longest Sniper Shot Broken by ITS Crew http://www. itstactical.com/shooting/longest-sniper-shot-record-broken/

27. Ten Terrible Cases of Kidnapping and Abuse http:// listverse.com/2008/08/28/10-terrible-cases-of-kidnapping-and-abuse/

28. To Catch an Identity Thief, by Anita Bartholomew http:// www.rd.com/home/catching-identity-thieves-true-stories/

29. How Corn Syrup is Made http://www.madehow.com/ Volume-4/Corn-Syrup.html

30. PCR to Detect Genetically Modified Organisms Field Trip http://www.btci.org/k12/bft/GMOpcr/GMOpcr_background. html

31. Infection-fighting antibodies made in plants as effective as costlier conventional version By Michael C. Purdy http://news. wustl.edu/news/Pages/20188.aspx

32. How Mass Spectrometry Works, by William Harris http:// science.howstuffworks.com/mass-spectrometry1.htm and http:// science.howstuffworks.com/mass-spectrometry3.htm

33. Here are 16 Everyday Foods that Contain Corn http:// www.businessinsider.com/everyday-foods-contain-corn-prices-soar-2012-7#mayonnaise-14

34. Corn—Iowa State University Center For Crops Utilization Research. http://www.ncga.com/uploads/useruploads/ cornusesposter.pdf

35. How Peanut Butter Is Made. http://www.youtube.com/watch?v=6H_M6yw32M0

36. Monsanto Hid Decades of Pollution – PCBs Drenched Ala Town but No One Was Told, by Michael Grunwald http://www.commondreams.org/headlines02/0101-02.htm

37. Around the World; Monsanto Worker Held in Industrial Espionage (Associated Press) http://www.nytimes.com/1983/01/10/us/around-the-nation-monsanto-worker-held-in-industrial-espionage.html

38. Dangers of High Fructose Corn Syrup including List of Products http://worldevolved.blogspot.ca/2009/06/what-are-dangers-of-high-fructose-corn.html

39. Old Detergent Factory in Düsseldorf, Germany http://www.28dayslater.co.uk/forums/european-international-sites/53615-old-detergent-factory-d%FCsseldorf-germany-august-2010-a.html

40. How Satellite Phones Work by Nathan Chandler http://electronics.howstuffworks.com/gadgets/travel/satellite-phone3.htm

41. Even in the Desert with a Satellite Phone, You're Getting Hacked, by Lara Heintz http://motherboard.vice.com/blog/satellite-telephony-is-unsafe

42. Billionaire Heir Helly Nahmad's Art Gallery Raided By Feds In Russian Mob Gambling Sweep, by Richard Behar http://www.forbes.com/sites/richardbehar/2013/04/16/billionaire-helly-nahmads-nyc-art-gallery-raided-by-feds-in-russian-mob-gambling-sweep/

43. Halliburton in Iraq Kickback Flap. http://www.cbsnews.com/news/halliburton-in-iraq-kickback-flap/

44. BangkokVanguards|Blog http://bangkokvanguards.wordpress.com/our-city/bangkok-haunted/

45. Credit Card suspects go on a $100K shopping spree, by Craig Cassidy http://www.modbee.com/2013/02/14/2579480/sonora-modesto-police-crack-credit.html

46. Weather in Thailand. http://www.travelfish.org/weather/thailand

47. Suvarnabhumi Airport, New Bangkok Airport Guide.

http://www.bangkokairportonline.com/node/54

48. White Phosphorous Can Be Safely Handled And Transported With New Technique, Researchers Say, Science Daily. http://www.sciencedaily.com/releases/2009/06/090625141452.htm

49. KRRS Threatens Action Against Monsanto, The Hindu, October 21, 2013, http://www.thehindu.com/news/national/karnataka/krrs-threatens-action-against-monsanto/article5254628.ece

50. Wireless Network To Be Built In Montreal's Subway. http://www.ctvnews.ca/sci-tech/wireless-network-to-be-built-in-montreal-s-subway-1.1470796

51. Gary Man Gets Life Sentence in Infant Sex Case. http://abc7chicago.com/news/man-gets-life-sentence-in-infant-sex-case-/62930/

52. CIA Spy Valerie Plame Says 'Homeland' Has 'Jumped The Shark This Season.'

http://www.thewrap.com/cia-spy-valerie-plame-homeland-jumped-shark-season